THE
MAMMOTH
CHEESE

ALSO BY SHERI HOLMAN

A Stolen Tongue
The Dress Lodger

THE
MAMMOTH
CHEESE

a novel

Sheri Holman

Atlantic Monthly Press
New York

Published simultaneously in Canada
Printed in the United States of America

FIRST EDITION

Libarary of Congress Cataloging-in-Publication Data

Holman, Sheri.
The mammoth cheese : a novel / Sheri Holman.
p. cm
ISBN 0-87113-900-6
1. Historical reenactments—Fiction.   2. Presidents—Election—Fiction.   3. Mothers and daughters—Fiction.   4. Women dairy farmers—Fiction.   5. Rural families—Fiction.   6. Multiple birth—Fiction.   7. Cheesemakers—Fiction.   8. Cheesemaking—Fiction.   9. Virginia—Fiction.   I. Title.

PS3558.O35596M36 2003
813'.54—dc21   2003041796

Atlantic Monthly Press
841 Broadway
New York, NY 10003

03   04   05   06   07   10   9   8   7   6   5   4   3   2   1

To my daughter, Elizabeth Hanover Redmond, who allowed me to see it from the other side

PROLOGUE

Like a dog unaware it was about to be put down, Manda Frank's cottage sat in the long shade of her new house. There was nothing wrong with the old place, from what the governor could see. It was built narrow in the shotgun style of the 1920s, with an asphalt roof and a mange of wavy gray asbestos shingles. Cinder blocks propped up its front porch, but at least it had a porch, which was more than his grandparents had had in the end; and the Depression glass windows, running floor to ceiling, let in as much light as an eastern exposure could. It had been big enough for Manda and Jake and their daughter Rose, with a shed to store the dogs' food and a two-acre run out back to start them on rabbits. Still, thought the governor, it was sure to go.

"Over here, sir."

Governor Brooke's press secretary, Sandy Jameson, led him away from the done-for shack and over to the new house on the same lot, a half-finished two-story colonial, pink and naked with exposed insulation. Construction had started the week after the news was announced, but Manda had gone into labor at thirty-two weeks, and even with men working around the clock, the place was still a mess of tenpenny nails and half-hung Tyvek, with scraps of stamped lumber littering the yard and rolls of roofing paper leaned up against the west wall of the old place. Sandy was directing him toward a man sweating in his too-tight button-down oxford shirt. His face was red from the heat and he looked ready for a beer. But then, weren't they all? It had to be ninety-five degrees outside.

"Right this way, Governor," said the man, whom Sandy informed him was Francis Marvel, the contractor on the house. "We've got great things planned with the donations we received."

Adams Brooke paused, waiting as he'd been taught for the cameras to catch up. Because of the special circumstances, there was easily five times the number of normal reporters today, most of whom, their not being assigned to the political beat, he had never met. As they walked toward the house, Francis Marvel unrolled a blueprint. Here was where he intended to put an entertainment center with surround-sound viewing, and there a Jacuzzi for the exhausted parents; right here would be double refrigerators and double ovens for all of Manda's extra cooking. You'll have to use your imagination, Francis Marvel was saying. He had laid out the rooms large and spacious with vaulted ceilings and intercoms and mood lighting and stain-resistant carpet, but it was clear from the tension in his jaw, he was beyond upset that they had gone ahead and delivered Manda's children before most of the Sheetrock was even in place.

Adams Brooke was about to step in behind the contractor when he felt the sudden draft of camera lights shifting away from him. Their suffocating heat had been the hardest thing to get used to on the campaign trail, but now, without them, the governor felt oddly chilled. He turned to see what had unseated him and discovered all of the fish-eyed lenses and trolling red lights trained on a small girl in the front yard. Summer-tanned and gangly, she looked to be about five years old, and, he could tell, was perfectly miserable in a dress. Her fizzy, erupting curls had been matted down with gel and barrettes by her grandmother, who stood behind her, beaming for the cameras in her fieriest red slacks suit.

Are you jealous? Can you love them? Are you worried about sharing your mommy and daddy? The reporters asked the little girl so many questions, which her Mamaw ordered her to answer politely, but Rose (the older daughter, Sandy whispered) didn't really know what to say. To her the babies were just a blur of cameras and light and tiny bald heads. Beside him, Brooke could hear the contractor describing futuristic bunk beds that would fold into the wall like those you see in European train cars, but he had stopped listening. The poor little girl in the yard was barely able to answer one question before another was fired at her.

"Excuse me, please," he said to Francis, leaving the contractor in the doorway. He walked back to the crowd of reporters and gestured for them to let him through. The governor squatted so that he could look into her eyes. They were the golden-brown of autumn corn.

"Miss Rose," he said amiably. "There has been all this talk of babies, but I'm curious what you think we should know about *you*."

The little girl stood shyly with her hands behind her back, leaning into her grandmother's legs.

"Answer the governor, sweetie," urged her grandmother. "He's come all the way from Washington."

Rose Frank took the measure of Governor Brooke, to the delight of those filming, and then, after a thoughtful second, reached into the front pocket of her sundress and held out a small swatch of purple and sky blue carpet. "This goes in my room," she said. "I got to pick it out myself."

"Well, why don't you show me where it will go," suggested the governor gently, and reaching out, took her hand. With all the cameras trailing, Rose led him through the shell of a two-car garage covered by a blue tarpaulin, past the new donated car seats, navy blue and flocked with yellow ducklings, stacked next to a wall of donated disposable diapers. Rose Frank led the governor and reporters into the new house, through the raw, half-built hallway and up the stairs to a room that looked down over the red clay driveway and that was to be hers alone. The babies, all eleven of them, had to share three rooms, she told him in explanation of everything she felt, but she got one all to herself.

"Excuse me, Governor," said Sandy, glancing nervously at his watch. "But if we're going to get by the hospital and still make the university fund-raiser tonight, we need to get going."

"Thank you, Sandy," replied the governor. "Miss Rose, it has been a pleasure to meet you."

Rose ducked shyly as the cameras turned to follow Adams Brooke out of the house and into the chauffeured black Buick waiting out front. The secret service and white news trucks caravaned down the driveway and onto the dirt road that ran past the Franks'. Almost immediately, the rough road gentrified to pavement, and Adams Brooke rolled down his window. Having grown up without air-conditioning, he had never gotten used to the stale dead flatness of it. His press secretary elbowed him in time for the governor to spot a woman at the end of her driveway, wildly waving a *Brooke for President* poster. Behind her stretched a rolling farm, dotted with dairy cows. Jerseys, he correctly identified, just like those his grandparents kept. That seemed like a good omen, and he was looking for good omens anywhere he could find them with the election being so close. He gave the woman a hearty thumbs-up as they sped by. "Remember—Family Matters!" he called.

"So tell me about the Franks," said the governor, settling back against the black leather seat. His secretary consulted his notes.

"They're young," he said. "Twenty-three. He collects recycling—paper, tin; she raises hunting dogs. They've beaten the record by three. From what the locals have told me, they had their daughter in high school, then five years went by with nothing. The husband wanted a son. Watch out, though—there's talk of revoking her fertility doctor's medical license."

Adams Brooke scowled. "It's an American's God-given right to have as many children as she likes. I can't support a woman's right to choose if I don't support her right to choose this."

Sandy Jameson nodded slowly, as he did whenever he disagreed with the governor, and turned his attention to the landscape passing outside. Being a Chicago kid, he was fascinated by the imperialist aspirations of Southern kudzu and marveled at the way it grew through the canopy of trees along the route, dropping down to smother an abandoned car or to claim for itself the entirety of a broken-down pole barn.

A few miles out, winding Snakehill Road straightened into School Street, and the convoy slowed toward town. *Now Entering Three Chimneys, Virginia,* they read. *Population 781.* The sign stood just before a spire of red bricks set back from the road, the oldest of the town's eponymous chimneys, and all that remained of an eighteenth-century way station between Staunton and Richmond. Technically, it belonged to St. Barnabas Episcopal Church, but sentimentally, it was the property of the church's pastor, Leland Vaughn, who with his wife and grown son inhabited the rectory next door. Just past the simple Colonial-era church, Three Chimneys began in earnest, and Adams Brooke was treated to as charming a small town as he'd encountered on his long and arduous campaign. Twenty-four great spreading oaks, donated in 1896 by the First Baptist Ladies Horticultural Society, and representing each president of the United States—excluding Abraham Lincoln—had been planted as a colonnade at the corners of School and each intersecting block for the length of the town. Wrapped in white lights like snow princesses, these trees greeted Baby Jesus each December; girt with wide yellow ribbons, they fretted over hostages and mourned missing veterans. Now that the entire country—the entire world, for that matter—was trained on Three Chimneys, the oaks wore pink and blue sashes for the Frank Eleven, with rattles hung from their boughs like polystyrene icicles.

More satellite vans crowded the two-lane street, parked with their wheels on the sidewalk so that traffic might flow. As the governor's car inched through town, he recognized all the familiar hallmarks of a small Southern hamlet. Snow White Tea Room, with its greasy windows and patched screened door. Mercer's Hardware. Tinton's Grocery, where neighbors were still allowed to buy on credit. A white clapboard Community Center sat off the town square, beside its accompanying marble obelisk War Memorial, carved with the names of the glorious Confederate dead. Adams Brooke had grown up in a town nearly identical to this one in eastern North Carolina. That town now had four super stores five miles in any direction, and chain businesses had long ago uprooted the locals. It cheered him to see holdouts like Three Chimneys, and it was for towns exactly like this that he vowed to take back the White House.

"Marvin, if I might trouble you." He leaned forward and entreated his driver to pull over. Sandy looked anxiously at his watch, but knew better than to rush the governor at moments like this. His employer was not a religious man, but he did believe in destiny—at least of the manifest sort. If he could take one person at a time, in one small town at a time, he could eventually take the entire nation.

Governor Brooke stepped out of his sedan and walked to the green, where the town entrepreneurs were hawking T-shirts to raise money for the babies' college funds. Before she became the most famous mother in America, few of her neighbors even knew Manda Frank by sight. If they knew anything about her, it was that she had once pulled her hunting rifle on a teacher who gave her a bad grade. (The gun wasn't loaded, the charges were magnanimously dropped, and the arrest never appeared on her permanent record.) Beyond this, Manda Frank, with her long, dark hair and hard, boyish features, was a mystery. She might be spotted, in the early spring and late fall, wandering the woods in her bright orange vest, following her dogs with a brace of fresh-skinned rabbit slung over her shoulder. Manda was perhaps the last person in Three Chimneys anyone expected to become famous, and certainly not after the fashion in which she did.

Now her neighbors thrilled as Governor Brooke bought a T-shirt and pulled it over his long-sleeved pinstriped shirt. The T-shirt sported silk-screened portraits of Manda's eleven babies, and below were written the words: "Three Chimneys' Small Miracles."

"Who is the gifted artist responsible for this?" asked the governor. A trim woman with hair like powdered sugar reluctantly stepped forward to take credit. She was introduced as Mrs. Leland Vaughn, wife of the local Episcopal priest.

"This is some town you have here," he said.

"We try to give help where it's needed," answered Mrs. Vaughn.

Adams Brooke smiled at the kindly woman and bought two cups of pink lemonade to benefit the Frank Fund. He took them back to Sandy and his chauffeur. It was awfully hot to be driving with no air-conditioning.

"Okay," he said, climbing in. "Let's go to the hospital."

At first, she was hidden from him by Mylar balloons and the jungle of flowers that crowded her small, private room. The sprays—roses and gardenias and birds-of-paradise—were magnificent, practically every florist in Charlottesville, and even a few as far away as Richmond, having been cleaned out. The governor's eyes landed on a card attached to one especially opulent bouquet: the prime minister of England. On the muted television that nodded beatifically from a corner of her room, he noticed the featured story was about her and the children. "Welcome Frank Eleven," read the caption.

Downstairs, in the University of Virginia Hospital parking lot, he had fought his way through a sea of well-wishers and curiosity-seekers and a handful of protestors, picketing the irresponsible use of fertility drugs. Three Chimneys Elementary's fourth-grade class had arrived by school bus to serenade the Franks on their recorders, but not allowed onto the maternity floor, they settled for entertaining those below with "Go Tell Aunt Rhody" and "Ode to Joy." The media was even thicker here than back in her hometown, and much of it attached itself to Governor Brooke as he made his way upstairs. The cameramen, too, were barred from her room, though when the floor nurse wasn't looking, one managed to wedge his lens inside.

When he finally saw her, Manda Frank lay enormous and pale against her white cotton sheets. She was probably not an unattractive woman under normal circumstances, he guessed, but now she was horribly bloated from the pregnancy and green from a bad reaction to anesthesia. Her long, Indian black hair fell limply on either side of her heavy face, and her eyes were closed behind glasses pearled with thumbprints no one had thought to wipe away for her. Governor Brooke longed to reach out and clean them on his shirttail, but he knew that would strike them all as too familiar.

"So where are you hiding them?" he asked jovially. "Where are you hiding Three Chimneys' newest Democrats?"

The two men sitting on either side of her rushed over to pump the governor's hand.

"I can't tell you how honored we are that you would come all this way," Jake Frank, the babies' father, stammered. He was as skinny as his wife was large, with a prominent Adam's apple and a scant brown mustache.

"And you must be Reverend Vaughn." Brooke turned to a silver-haired older man wearing a cleric's collar. "I understand we have you to thank for these little ones. You bucked the doctors when they said it couldn't be done."

"*Pastor* Vaughn, please. It's friendlier," said the priest, whom Adams Brooke placed at about sixty-five. "You don't play eeny-meeny-miney-moe with your family's future," he continued. "It was in God's hands."

"Is she sleeping?" asked the governor.

"In and out."

"Don't wake her," said the governor. "She looks like she's had a rough go."

Manda Frank had been on mandatory bed rest for over six months, spending the last few weeks almost upside down to ease her overworked heart, and taking her food intravenously so that the babies would have more room. The terbutaline pump they stuck in her leg to forestall premature labor made her heart race and her skin crawl with fire ants; the magnesium they alternated with it kept her dizzy and nauseated and her jaw so slack she couldn't even spit out her toothpaste. Her contractions had started around week twenty anyway, as many as twelve an hour, even with the pump. Manda's uterus went about its appointed duties, working away like an inmate with a pickax, with only the medicine and her sheer will holding the babies inside. At twenty-two weeks, they sewed up her cervix. When finally the babies were so crowded the stitches started to snap, the doctors gave her a shot of Celestone to help develop their lungs, said a prayer, and delivered them the next morning. When she woke, a nurse was handing her a blurry Polaroid of her eleven children, their eyes and mouths taped as for a kidnapping, their chests and arms growing tubes like eyes on a potato.

"Where are the little ones?" asked the governor. "They are all doing well?"

"So far, so good," said Pastor Vaughn. "They're in the NICU. We can take you down there, if you'd like."

"I can't believe I'm standing next to the man who might be the next president of the United States," gushed Jake. "Pastor Vaughn, will you take our picture?"

All the time the men were talking, through all the white teeth and pop of flashbulbs, Manda Frank had a slow itch building inside her head. It was an image not of the eleven red new potatoes laying immobilized in the NICU. Nor that of her husband saying, We're naming the eldest after you, Governor: Adams Frank. Jake Junior, he's number two. Nor the loud guffawing when the bedside phone rang again a few minutes later and Pastor Vaughn answered it, stammering, Yes, oh thank you yes, Mr. President, she's doing quite well, and the governor reaching over and taking the phone good-naturedly from her minister's hand, saying, I'm sorry, you're too late, Mr. President, I'm right here with her. And if you lose by eleven votes (winking at Jake), we'll know who to thank! No, the image she had in her head was of old brown and black Turbo, the first hunting dog she ever raised, when she was fourteen, who got pregnant three weeks after Manda bought her. She waited and waited for that dog to lay down those puppies; she brought her extra food, massaged her swollen belly, rubbed liniment on her hard red nipples. But the puppies never came. Finally months past when she should have been due, Manda took the dog to the vet. The doctor examined her closely, took blood, tested the milk leaking from the distended teats, and shook his head. I don't know what to tell you, Manda. This dog's no more pregnant than you or I.

"Did you remember to feed the dogs?" Manda looked up abruptly, speaking for the first time since the visit had began. The whole room turned to stare at her. But why? she wondered. It was a perfectly reasonable question. If the dogs weren't fed, they'd tear each other up. Her husband sat down worriedly and took her hand, Adams Brooke broke off the fine speech he was extemporizing on the American family and the Franks' exalted place in it. Everyone from the lurking cameraman to the nurse who came to take her blood pressure to Pastor Vaughn looked embarrassed at Manda's question, and the governor took the ensuing silence as his cue to leave.

I

THE ELECTION

"Politics [is] a subject I never loved and now hate."

—Thomas Jefferson to John Adams, 1796

CHAPTER ONE

It was a long walk to the end of the driveway. Margaret Prickett saw the sun glint off Mr. Kelly's U.S. Post Office truck, nearly airborne from the pink and blue balloons tied to his side-view mirrors in cheerful disregard of government regulation. He loved kids, probably because he had none of his own, and kids loved him. When her daughter Polly was a little girl, she used to leave wax paper cups of Pepsi inside the mailbox, the red flag raised so that he wouldn't drive past thirsty. And though by the time he opened the little black oven the cola was flat and fatty with melted wax, in gratitude he would always leave her a rubber band. It was a splendid economy.

Mr. Kelly got out of his truck only when there was something to sign for, yet to Margaret's eyes, that morning he stepped out seemingly empty-handed. Two days ago, she had ordered some flour from King Arthur's, but that couldn't be here so soon, could it? She waved to him, a big hearty arm-sweep, as if to say, Great to see you. Got something good? He waved back, an unenthusiastic little shake from the wrist which could only mean, Registered letter.

Sure enough, she spotted it on his clipboard, the little square of serious pale green. She stopped about fifty yards away from him, suddenly overwhelmed by the mid-afternoon heat of the day. She felt drowsy from the narcotic tangle of honeysuckle and wild morning glories that overgrew the fence beside the gravel driveway, and nearly deafened by the lawn mower whir of dog-day cicadas. Maybe she could just turn around and calmly walk back to the cheese house. Lock herself in and make August deal with Mr. Kelly. Maybe she could just stand here until he disappeared like the mirage he looked to be in the heat, a postal spectre no more valid than a canceled stamp.

Margaret saw his eyes go from the letter to the house behind her, and some primal protective instinct took over. She pulled herself together and made herself be polite.

"Just give me your John Hancock right here," Mr. Kelly said, trying not to look at Margaret directly when she reached him. As the mailman, he probably knew more town secrets than the expatriate shrink, Andrew Friedman. "Been to see Manda yet?"

"Can't get through the crowds," Margaret answered, happy to have something else to talk about. "We'll take some food over when she gets home. Polly's dying to see the babies."

"You can't imagine the mountain of letters she's been getting," he said, taking back his pen and tearing off the little green indictment. Couldn't say it got lost in the mail. Couldn't claim to have never seen it. "And stuffed animals out the ying-yang. Even a full-sized purple gorilla like you'd win at the fair."

"Amazing," replied Margaret, taking the letter.

"Well, give my best to the young one." He tipped his hat as he climbed back into the truck. "Tell her things are mighty parched out on the trail without her."

"Will do." Margaret smiled and watched him pull away. She turned back to her hundred acres, imagining the entire parcel yellow and blighted, the barn incinerated, the house blasted to its foundation by the bad news she would release when she opened this envelope. The entire history of Prickett Farm seemed to stand between Margaret and breaking the seal. She slowly started back up the driveway.

Like the Vaughns, the Pricketts, too, could claim one of the town's three chimneys. Margaret walked past the tower of bricks that sat up the hill by the path that led through the woods to the Franks' new house. Though a perfectly good shade tree grew not fifteen yards farther on, for as long as anyone could remember, the Pricketts' herd of buttery Jerseys had grazed their way across a rolling pasture of Potomac orchard grass to this chimney for their midday nap. The history of the cows' partiality could be read by all who had the eyes to see: the much-hoofed grass from barn to stream, the long detour from stream to woods (avoiding the horrible spot in the middle of the meadow where years before Tiberia's Queen had dropped a putrid calf, sending the whole herd leaping and bellowing about); the down-hill path back to the barn, hard-packed and nearly bald from hungry rushing. But afternoons always found the herd sidled up to the ruined chimney as it cast its long sundial shadow upon them and counted off the hours till evening milking. An old farming adage says that Holsteins will look for the filthiest place to lie down, while Jerseys search out the cleanest, and in some collective cow memory, these girls must have sensed the echo of solid oak floors and imported rugs beneath their shaggy bellies; for back in the old planter days, when the county still sent a delegate to the House of Burgesses in Williamsburg, the cows' chimney had been attached to one of the wealthiest homesteads in Orange. It had heated Mr. and Mrs. Mandeville Prickett, their son, three daughters, and any number of hour-old infants that had been vainly warmed before they were on their way to the graveyard out front. It went on to thaw a second generation of red-cheeked Prickett children, plus the nieces and nephews, the half-frozen out-of-town guests, and even their distant neighbor, young James Madison, who once took shelter with them on his way back from Mr. Robertson's Boarding School, before the house burned down in 1779. It was the worst kind of fire, a ridiculous, careless fire, when the tallow Mrs. Randolph Prickett used for dipping candles flared and caught the drapes. The whole family and all their people fetched buckets of cold water from the spring that ran along the edge of the property, but to no avail. The wax caught the cloth and the cloth caught the wood and the wood caught the roof until all that remained were a few blackened studs, the iron door hinges, and the chimney. The family sent their indoor people to live with their field people, while they bedded at neighbors until a new house could be erected.

Now the cows served as its walls and the abandoned chimney looked down the hill on the second Prickett homestead, built lower on their property, nearby the stream: a whitewashed brick farmhouse in a stand of oak trees, far enough back from the water to weather flash flooding, but close enough for buckets to be passed hand to hand. Margaret took a long look at the new house (though it had been standing for two hundred years, no one referred to it as anything other than "the new house"). It was so familiar, she rarely observed it any more closely than she did her own tired face in the bathroom mirror each morning. Now, in light of the letter, she saw it as Mr. Kelly must have seen it driving up every day, as her neighbors must see it. Its old green tin roof had completely rusted out along the flashing, the verandah screens were squirrel-torn, the bricks in desperate need of repointing and a whitewash. Margaret had every intention of taking care of all those little things before they got worse, and yet, worse they got, year after year, as the money went to the more pressing disasters of crop failure and low production and drought.

She continued up the driveway toward the house, passing the geriatric tractor out in the alfalfa field, and the manure spreader, which she'd spent most of the morning trying to de-clog. With Francis gone, it was unlikely she and August would plant a crop after next year. It would make more sense to keep the pastures up and simply buy their winter feed until she could repopulate the herd. She felt traitorous even thinking such thoughts, for Margaret Abingdon Prickett was born into a proud family, a family that honored its history, that considered giving its child a middle name like Ann or Lynn or Sue as unthinkable as laying shag carpeting over hardwood floors or living out by the airport. Cows are not the only creatures of strong habits, and for many years after the fire, the Prickett sons were proud to live in the new house exactly as their fathers had in the old: planting tobacco, driving the hogsheads down the old rowling road to sell to traders in Fredericksburg, buying their furniture and throwing their barbecues on credit they carried from one crop to the next. When, after the War (and by "the War," everyone in town still meant the Civil War), the price of tobacco plummeted, and a collective feeling of urgent survivalism gripped farming communities all across the South, it seemed to the Pricketts that they must never allow themselves to become dependent again—if they could not smelt their own cannons, they could at least produce their own food. A great agricultural shift took place in Three Chimneys and the luxurious tobacco crop found itself eschewed in favor of pragmatic corn and peas; hogs for meat, oxen for labor. But of all the money borrowed during Reconstruction to coax a real farm from the brown stubble of Bright Leaf, they spent by far the most (neighbors shook their heads; far, far too much, they said) on their new state-of-the-art dairy: the dairy up ahead that, 140 years later, Margaret Prickett still used.

Omnis pecuniae pecus fundamentum.

The herd is the foundation of all wealth. It was a quote from the Roman historian Varro, and it was a clever lesson in etymology, for the Latin word for wealth, *pecunia*, comes from the word for cattle, *pecus*. It was the official motto of the American Jersey Cattle Club, and it was stenciled in strong black letters onto a sign that hung in the Prickett cheese house. Margaret's great-grandfather was even a member of the Jersey Scouts of America until 1919, when the moniker was dropped on protest by Boy Scouts of the same name. Jersey cattle were to restore the Prickett family fortune, and to that end, they borrowed heavily to raise a modern stanchion barn with new-fangled swinging headgates, and to build adjacent, over the running stream so that the icy water might cool the milk most efficiently, a cheese house, complete with floor-to-ceiling wooden shelves and ripening cave. No expense was spared on sowing the pastures and digging the trench silos, and a good thing, too, for the cows chosen to graze upon the Prickett clover and to populate the fine new outbuildings were, naturally, no common stock themselves, but descended from the First Families of Virginia dairy cattle. These mothers and daughters, sisters and aunts could trace their lineage back to the famed Tormentor family and the celebrated stud, Flying Fox. Sultana's Foxy Increase was true Jersey royalty—on one side the great-great-great-great-great-and so on-granddaughter of Flying Fox, while her distaff side wound back to Sultane, the acknowledged "mother" of all Jerseys in America. Compared with their cattle, the Pricketts joked, they were mere upstarts.

The herd is the foundation of all wealth. This motto was Margaret's inheritance. She knew it was only in the mysterious alchemy of those patrician stomachs working together to turn grass and grain and sunshine and water into the most sublime milk, hinting of fresh Piedmont air and summer's own roses, that the Prickett Dairy Farm had any prayer of survival. She would not abandon the motto—even if the herd upon which it was founded had dwindled to a mere twenty-two when, after her father died, she was forced to sell off three-quarters of the stock to recoup his bad investments, and even if the second house was collapsing around her. She was raised on homemade jonquil-colored Jersey butter and crumbly sharp Jersey cheese that her great-grandparents had given names like Manassas Gold and Wilderness Cheddar. She had been taught at her grandfather's knee how to preserve calves' stomachs at the dark of the moon and how to tell, almost by smell, the exact greenish moment that curd separates from whey, and if she'd become almost Confucian in her fealty to her ancestors' ways, then so be it. There were some things in life worth preserving.

Margaret shoved the letter deep into her pocket. Nothing so far had shaken her resolve to continue as her great-grandparents had a hundred years ago, not even when her soon-to-be ex-husband Francis Marvel packed his bags and moved out, nor when her daughter Polly wept that their life was getting so weird any minute PBS was going to show up and make a documentary about them. Registered letter be damned. At thirty-six, Margaret Prickett knew who she was and she knew what mattered. There was still a place in the world for those who did things the right way, the old-fashioned way. Sadly, for the aristocratic Jerseys napping at the old chimney, unaware they were about to go the way of all *anciens régimes*, First Virginia Savings and Loan did not agree.

At three-thirty in the afternoon, all was quiet in the barn except for the soft strains of Sinatra that Margaret left playing on the sound system for the girls. Over the years, she'd had success with Grieg and Joni Mitchell—it never mattered, classical or modern, so long as it was the same thing every day—but nothing soothed the girls like the sweet, swinging chauvinism of Frank. Their milk flowed freer when he crooned to them, they no longer kicked over their pails, but stood dreamily by like bobby-soxers, chewing their bright pink Bazooka cuds. The cows even had favorite songs. This summer it seemed to be the melancholic "It Was a Very Good Year."

Inside, she washed up and dressed for the cheese house, tying her wiry hair under a kerchief. Margaret used to be considered one of the most attractive girls in Three Chimneys, though she thought few were likely to confer the title on her now. She had no-nonsense brown eyes and a tall, vegetal figure; she wore her chestnut hair, grown long through missed salon appointments, in a single plait down her back. Margaret had devolved from attractive into that adjective farmers loved to use for thoroughbreds of any species—she was a "handsome" woman, and had become, like many of pure blood, utterly indifferent to what others thought of her. Now she pulled on her homemade white cotton shirt and pants, the scuffed white plastic boots that came to just below the knee, then tied on a white canvas apron. Before she headed over to the cheese house, she wanted to quickly check on Sultana, the only springer left this fall, since Jolly Chimney's Anna and Orange Frieda had already dropped their calves and none of the replacement heifers had gotten the job done. They were young yet, she reasoned, and might very well take next month when she got the loan of Franklin's stud again. Sultana was one of the best milkers Margaret had, so she'd give her a rest of sixty days or so after she laid down, and then bring the stud back in. They used to have a stud of their own, but with only she and August to work the farm, he had become just too much of a handful.

Margaret followed a plaintive low to Sultana's straw-filled stall, where August had brought her in early from the pasture. Like an ungainly grasshopper, he crouched with his long legs drawn up around his ears, a big red one of which he had pressed against her belly.

"What's wrong?" Margaret asked.

"Thought I heard—probably nothing," he said, rubbing the taut caramel bulge. He was trying to convince himself he had not just heard what he thought he heard. A calf's heart beats twice as fast as its mother's and so there was always a double heartbeat inside the drum of a pregnant cow. He was not positive, but he thought he detected a faint syncopation. "Might be twins."

"Don't say that," she answered grimly. "Hasn't Manda had enough to last us all?"

"She's due in six weeks." August rose and checked the calendar on the Palm Pilot he carried in his overalls. "Probably time to dry her off."

"Let's take her off her concentrates."

She gave August directions on what succulents to cut out of Sultana's feed to help dry up her old milk so that her new milk could come down, and stenciled her rump with a big, purple D in indelible marker. When she leaned over, August noticed an envelope sticking out of her deep apron pocket. She saw his eyes go to it worriedly, but in perfect August fashion, he did not ask her about it.

"I'm going to the cheese house," she announced.

He nodded numbly, and electronically punched Sultana's new feed ratio into the spreadsheet he kept on each one of the girls. "Remember, I have my program tomorrow," he called as she headed toward the cheese house.

"What time will you be back?" she asked.

"By milking time."

Margaret hosed off her boots before entering the small stone building and dunked her arms, up to the elbow, in a bucket of disinfectant she kept by the door. The whitewashed antechamber, built over a cold, underground spring, was her favorite place on the farm, especially on hot early-September days like this. This morning's small-mouthed, hooded pails bobbed like stainless steel buoys in the spring-fed tank, and Margaret checked the thermometers she had in each. Through a low doorway, she could reach the main room, where her cheesemaking equipment hung over a thirty-year-old water-circulated double-walled vat, the only real upgrade her father had made, sick to death as he was of feeding the old woodstove. She kept her cultures in mason jars on the shelf, neatly labeled *Penicilium candidum*, and

Lactococcus lactis, and *Bacteria linens.* August had repaired the old Dutch press she used for the larger cheeses and Margaret tightened the screw on this morning's creamy almond Caerphilly.

She took the ten steps down to the cheese cave, dug out behind and half beneath the house above. Because of the spring, the cave had nearly ideal conditions for ripening. It was just humid enough and a constant fifty-five degrees, winter and summer. Upstairs, she sweltered over the stove and the curd vat, but below, the sweat dried on her forehead, her heart slowed, she could make the rounds of her wheels and plump pyramids and black waxed blocks of Yellow Tavern and Mattaponi Reserve.

She began this afternoon with her day-old ten-pound Cheshires. Margaret sniffed each swaddled bundle, gently unwrapped it, and rubbed a handful of coarse salt into its sticky rind, going over every inch of her cheese like a mother cat would over her young. These larger cheeses took longer to harden, and if she wasn't careful, she could lose them all in the early days to cracks and air pockets and all the wrong sorts of bacteria. There was nothing worse than to tend a cheese six months, reverently turning it to make sure it dried evenly, carefully waxing it, only to cut into a gassy bloat of ruined milk. It happened to Margaret from time to time and she never ceased taking it as a personal failure.

Down here in the cheese cave, it seemed safe to look at the letter. She didn't need to open it to know what it said: It was the emphatic end of the conversation she'd had last week with her extension agent, the same conversation they'd had every few months since her father died. Once more, he begged her to switch to Holsteins—which though giving a far less rich milk, gave in quantities far vaster than Jerseys. Barring that, would she not at least upgrade to milking machines? No one outside of a few crackpot Mennonites, he said, still milked by hand. But Margaret never expected to turn a profit on milk alone. No, in her soul, she was not a farmer; she was a cheesemaker. She had learned her ancestors' farmstead recipes and perfected them: milking by hand into the same seamless zinc pails her grandparents used; heating the milk in the same copper cauldron; cutting it with the same wire knives. She was obsessive in her quest to keep the recipes absolutely faithful, going so far as to culture her own molds from pumpernickel and rye breads she baked herself, just as her grandmother did. And Margaret's carefulness was finally paying off. Last July, she saw her sales spike when she was mentioned beside Duke's Mayonnaise and Hanover tomatoes in *Gourmet* magazine's Southern Culinary Hall Of Fame.

If she could just hold on two months more, she thought, turning the letter over but still not opening it. Two months to keep them at bay. Those eight weeks would make no real difference in the quality of her cheeses, nor in the farm's cash flow, but two months from today was the first Tuesday in November, and on that day, the one man who had the power to make this little slip of mint green go away would be in office.

Adams stands for Amnesty.

He spoke the word over and over, a banner waving above all those other fraught mn words like amnesia and amniocentesis, an unimpeachable mouthful, a rockets' red glare of eternal pardon and utter freedom.

Amnesty.

It was what Adams Brooke promised when he was elected. An abolition of the estate tax on small farms, but beyond that, a one-time government bailout of farms earning less than $250,000 a year. That simple, he repeated nearly every night on Margaret's black-and-white television. He was raised on a working dairy farm, he had watched his grandparents struggle, and he promised—no, he *vowed*, with his forefinger raised and his hair standing on end—to redress the wrongs of four decades' worth of uncaring administrations, to wipe the slate clean, to find a place at the table for those who grew the food that was eaten at it!

Forgiveness of her dairy's debt meant everything to Margaret, and not just for her sake, but for the memory of everyone who'd come before her. Amnesty today meant forgiveness at last for Mandeville Prickett who defaulted on his British creditors, and her great-great-great-grandfather Abingdon with his worthless box of Confederate bonds, and her father who speculated on Internet stocks when he didn't even own a computer. It meant grace for all the preceding generations who had brought her to this dark, gnawing place, so burdened with her family's mistakes and miscalculations that she would never get out from under it in her lifetime, and thus would be forced, like her father, and his father before him, to bequeath it to her daughter Polly. And did she hear him? Adams Brooke demanded on the Sunday morning talk shows. Not low-interest loans, or postponements, or debt restructuring, but free and clear absolution. This was what he vowed. This was why Margaret Prickett would never again have to sign for a registered letter.

Margaret put the envelope back in her pocket and unlocked the door to an even darker moonscape of a chamber, where in semitwilight her soft cheeses bloomed blue and green, three-inch silken hair nodding faintly as she entered, tasting the air around her. She settled each upon her palm, stroking them like sightless ocean creatures, easing their crine into a velvety softshell. It was not legal for her to sell these, her favorite, secret children, because they grew from raw, unpasteurized milk and were aged under two months. But a few chefs had ferreted out her contraband and were ordering it for the best restaurants in Charlottesville and Washington and as far away as New York City. Margaret didn't mind breaking the law over something like this. These cheeses were as old as humanity itself, they were as close as you might come to circulating the earth and ether of a place, your plot of land balanced on the tongue of a diplomat in Dupont Circle or a starlet in SoHo. Why suddenly now, in this cramped corner of the twenty-first century, should our government be proscribing the established methods of thousands of years?

Adams Brooke and her cheese. To August and Polly, the two who knew her best, it seemed she cared about nothing else these days. Some people in town thought that had she cared more about her husband, he wouldn't have needed to spend so much of his time down at Drafty's with Andrew Friedman. Many said her obsessiveness about Brooke had driven Francis to his affair—what man wouldn't be jealous

if his wife spent every night down at her self-styled Election Headquarters, running off flyers and phoning complete strangers in other
counties? But then there were others in town who said it was more a
chicken-or-egg sort of thing, that they never saw Margaret out late
stumping for Brooke until after the news about Francis and his secretary broke.

"Mom!"

Upstairs, she heard the screen door slam Polly home from school.

"Mom!"

Margaret set down her mermaid *Epoisse* and raced upstairs at the
sound of panic in Polly's voice. August had dropped the bag of rolled
oats and cottonseed meal he was measuring out for Sultana's dinner
and run outside to see what was the matter. Polly was halfway down
the long gravel driveway, pointing wildly to a caravan of cars churning a pillow of dust on the old dirt road that led from Manda and
Jake's house next door. There had been a ton of cars up and down
the dirt road since the news was announced—curiosity-seekers mostly,
the kind of people who park outside the houses of convicted mur-
derers or drive to the steep embankments off which school buses have
plunged, and wait, as if to feel some emanation of the event. But the
six black Buicks and two news vans that went flying down the road
looked far more official.

"Mom!" cried Polly, catching sight of the license plate. "It's
Governor Brooke!"

"Why didn't someone tell me he was coming?" Margaret Prickett
wailed, flinging off her apron, snatching up one of the many posters
she kept in the barn, and sprinting down the driveway to stand with
her daughter. August retrieved her apron with its mint green letter,
and carefully hung it behind the door before walking down to join
them. The three stood by the mailbox while six identical black cars
with tinted windows, two white vans impaled by corkscrewing satellite antennae, and the ten-year-old, two-toned banana Cadillac
driven by Mrs. Frank, Jake's mother, rumbled past them. Margaret
waved her sign like a madwoman, shouting out his name, jumping

up and down, until all that remained was a choking cloud of dust and the magnificat of cicadas.

The cows, when they were driven in for their afternoon milking, immediately felt the full force of her disappointment. They were used to hearing her sing along with Frank—"Summer Wind," "Forget Domani"—and nothing could make them forget the terror of having stepped in a gopher hole or being barked at by a big dog like coming in from the pasture to Margaret's sweet singing voice and soothing hands. But today she did not sing. And when she milked them (not even dry—their udders ached afterward) she leaned her head against their flanks as if it were too heavy for her to hold upright.

"A man like that," August said from his own milking stool, "he must be booked solid with appointments. He must be racing around all over the country."

But Margaret didn't want consolation. She left her pails for him to empty. She had to go turn the cheese.

That night, Margaret washed her hair with borax and an egg yolk, and while it dried, she kneaded two loaves of raisin bread for Polly's breakfast in the morning. Her kitchen was dark and quiet, with only one low-watt bulb in the ceiling fixture and a kerosene lamp on the counter. The lamp cast its flickering shadow on her coffee mill, still perfumed with home-roasted beans for tomorrow's percolator, and on the crank wooden butter churn, freshly washed with sweet cream and well water, which had just an hour before yielded its new butter to the icy shelf of her old white Hotpoint refrigerator, as heavy to open as a coffin. It was a large but homey kitchen, with patina-streaked copper pots hanging from the ceiling and a brick hearth big enough to roast a whole pig. Margaret sifted flour onto the worm-knotted farmer's table in the center of the room and slammed the bread down, punching and heeling the gluten to elasticity. Polly was tucked safely into bed. Margaret had laid out her one hundred percent cotton school clothes and was preparing a preservative-free breakfast: homemade yogurt and butter in the refrigerator, hand-canned peach jam in the pantry, fresh raisin bread. While she worked, the old black-and-white TV played the ten o'clock news soundlessly in the next room: scenes of Amanda Frank's stricken face against the white hospital pillow, of Jake and Pastor Vaughn standing by like boys waiting for a ballplayer's autograph, and of Adams Brooke—her good, honest Adams Brooke—straddling the hospital room threshold like a colossus. Margaret shaped the loaves, draped them with a damp cloth, and set them to the back of her old cast-iron gas stove, where the pilot light kept everything a little bit warmer. Another day of saving her daughter from pollution. Another day closer to amnesty. Margaret sat down at her floured kitchen table, buried her head in her hands, and waited for the bread to rise.

CHAPTER TWO

The Greeks, who among ancient peoples came relatively late to complex finance, had a unique way of describing the interest on a debt. They called that which comes due *tekon,* or "child," the same word they used to name their offspring. A child is to his parents as interest is to capital, both a descendant from and a magnification of the original investment. The *tekon* of Margaret Prickett and Francis Marvel lay dreaming in her bedroom, the fruit of an obligation she was utterly disinterested in repaying. She slept soundly in what had been her mother's room as a girl, surrounded by the same faded pink and yellow rose wallpaper, trellised from floorboard to ceiling, the frame for her feather bed resting upon wide-plank floors oiled with generations of young-girl footprints. Their samplers hung on her walls, quavery alphabets behind glass, stained with blood-rusty age spots; the rugs they hooked covered her floor, ragbag ice floes adrift in the moonlight. Asleep, Polly could be all that her mother imagined— an unspoiled, natural child, as wild and fresh as the pastures she walked, a slender little milkmaid who was living outside of history, as comfortable in the twenty-first century as she would have been in the nineteenth.

But just as interest delights when working for us, and strikes horror when we see it mounting in our creditor's favor, so Polly could turn on a dime. She had grown moody over the past year since her father left, and increasingly unpredictable. One day, she would throw her arms around her mother's neck, smothering her with kisses; the next she would barely grunt hello. And she was an equal-opportunity terror. Preying on her father's guilt for having "abandoned" her, she demanded fast food, and CDs, and synthetic fibers, all the things her mother forbid. The only time either parent might trust her completely was when

Polly was asleep. With her defenses down and her hormones in the arms of Morpheus, she might at last become her honest self: a tired thirteen-year-old child, suffering through a divorce.

When the sun rose through the curtainless windows, Polly was already awake to greet it. Since classes had started this year, she found herself practically vibrating out of bed, impatient to get her chores over with and catch the bus to school. Her father thought it was about damn time she started taking things seriously, her mother didn't notice—but neither would have guessed that the reason Polly leapt from bed each morning had a name, and a face, and a slight Northern accent.

In the bathroom, Polly pulled on her work clothes and vigorously scrubbed her face with her mother's homemade soap, the first batch of which had made her skin sizzle and blister. A little less lye and a little more rose oil, and Polly could tolerate it, but she still yearned for her lost sapphire chalice of snowy white Noxzema.

Red-eyed and nearsighted, Polly peered at herself in the mirror. She had read a novel when she was a kid where the main character started off at nine and then suddenly, through the magic of ellipses, was fourteen and much wiser than her younger self. You knew she was wiser because she'd lost her baby fat and her hair had grown long enough to wear in two blonde braids, and she no longer felt the need to torment those weaker than she. Polly would have given anything to . . . away the past three years and flip the page to fourteen. Glasses were cute on a six-year-old (purple plastic frames from Lenscrafters) but on an eighth-grader even wire-rims were dreadful. Her hair, shining white in elementary school, had dulled to the color of wet hay, and lost whatever natural curl it had once had. She had a straight nose, hazel eyes, and a long, narrow body like her mother's. All in all, she was a perfectly fine, perfectly plain girl, with nothing at all to recommend her. Just face it, Polly thought glumly. He is never going to love you for your looks.

Down in the kitchen, she lit the burner of the gas stove and put coffee on to perk. Her mom had made more raisin bread, which she liked, and she slathered it with their own butter before swallowing it in two gulps. She fixed her coffee and started for the cow barn, stopping along the way to pet the narrow-ribbed, fat-pawed barn cats that tried to trip her. She sometimes squirted milk for them and they leapt high in the air to catch it in their pink mouths.

She was up so early, even August, usually the first one here, hadn't arrived. It made her feel grown-up and competent to slide back the door in the pink dawn light, everything so still and expectant. For a long moment Polly stood in the doorway, aware of her life unfolding inevitably in the way only a teenager can be. He would never love her, but she could bear it. Because she had this farm and these dear, dumb, dependent cows. She would go on for their sake. She would be alone, yes, but Joan of Arc was alone, and Queen Elizabeth. When one's people needed one, what else was one to do?

Polly flipped on the barn's sound system, and at the sound of Frank, all twenty-two cows scrambled to their feet in anticipation of being fed. And as if Polly had depressed the key marked EMPTY on an old Wurlitzer organ, together in church-choir unison, and with great seriousness of purpose, the cows collectively took a bombastic shit. It went on for a solid two minutes, the baritone splattering and tattoo of urine, twenty-two cows performing their morning's epic evacuation. It used to send Polly into fits of screaming laughter. She would hide her head in August's lap for the measure of this music and he would delight her with huge, wet mouth-farts of his own. Today, though, she merely sighed. "Love and Marriage." The irony was not lost upon her.

When they were done, Polly opened the gate on Chimney's Avis and led her to the milking station. She measured out her feed and the old girl went to work eating, while Polly stroked her flank and curried away the matted straw that clung to her velvety udder. It seemed like such old hat to her now, but she remembered when she'd first been taught to milk. As with everything else, her mom and dad fought over the best way to do it. Her mother was a careful milker, gently closing off the base of udder and using her whole hand to squeeze out the milk. On his parents' farm, her dad had been raised a stripper, which meant he used two fingers, pinching the milk down the teat forcefully. They'd each allowed the other their error, but neither would see it perpetuated in Polly. Polly would sit on the trilegged stool wanting desperately to do it both ways, to show them she could make the perfect compromise, and still fill her pail. Her father eventually walked away in disgust, her mother sat stony-faced, then roughly taught Polly the importance of gentleness with cattle.

"You're up early," August said, coming up behind her and making her jump. She hadn't even heard his truck pull in. He collected his pail and brought Tiberia's Queen over to the milking station. Like Polly, he measured her feed, then swung the old metal stanchion over her neck to keep her still while milking. They each had their own group of cows they milked in exact order every day. They'd once had four men working for them, but that was when the dairy was bigger, before Polly's grandpa died.

"Your mom okay?" he asked.

"If you call being a complete freak okay."

August smiled and settled down at his stool. He was a champion milker and could milk a girl dry in about seven minutes, while it took Polly closer to fifteen. They worked in silence, there was only Sinatra and the tinny syllables of milk hitting the pail. Polly strained the warm, frothy liquid into the taller hooded stainless steel canisters August would carry to the cheese house for cooling, and spilled a little out for the barn cats. She'd just settled down to Sultane Chimney's Surprise when her mother came in, looking like hell, Polly thought.

"I've got some flyers for you to take this afternoon," Margaret said. "I left them on the table."

Normally, Polly would argue, but her mother's swollen eyes made her hold her tongue. "I'll miss the bus," she said.

"I can give you a ride home," August chimed in, always listening, even when he seemed absorbed in something else. "I have my program today."

"Great," said Margaret, leading Orange Frieda around to her stanchion. She turned again to her daughter. "You never told me what your principal said about getting rid of the vending machines?"

"He said he'd think about it," answered Polly noncommittally.

"Because that's how it starts, you know," Margaret continued. "Put in a few soda machines in exchange for new band uniforms, then suddenly they're supplying textbooks, and the next thing you know, the school's being renamed Pepsi Junior High."

"I don't think they're changing the name to Pepsi Junior High." Polly sighed.

"Not if I can help it."

By seven, Polly was finished with her chores, showered, and stood waiting for the bus at the end of her long driveway. A tan Oldsmobile with Wisconsin plates drove slowly by, scanning the address on her mailbox, obviously looking for Manda's house. The whole country had gone crazy over these babies, but Polly didn't know what to think. Manda used to baby-sit her when she was little, but she had a hard time picturing her as the mother of twelve. She was used to Manda hiking deep into the woods with her fishing pole and her rifle, riding her three-wheeler down the abandoned railroad beds outside town, braving that whirlpool of snarling black and tan hunting dogs she and Jake raised, with a twenty-pound bag of Alpo over her shoulder and slop bucket held high overhead. Manda didn't seem made to stay in the house, wiping behinds and warming formula. She had strapped Rose onto the handlebars of her mountain bike and kept riding. How was she supposed to do that now?

Polly saw the grill of the bus with its flashing yellow lights cresting the hill, and behind it, a long line of cars choking on its dust, unable to pass on the narrow dirt road, trapped behind the lumbering tin can of screaming schoolkids. If she were able to see the license plates, she knew they would read like a road map of America: Delaware, Idaho, Kansas, Ohio. Hundreds of wise men bringing not frankincense and myrrh but used high chairs and fifty-dollars-exactly checks written out in glitter-gold indelible pen.

"The Earth belongs in usufruct to the living, that the dead have neither right nor power over it."—*Thomas Jefferson,* Mr. March chalked on the

board. Except in the window it looked like: *".ti revo rewop ron thgir rehtien evah daed eht taht, gnivil eht ot tcurfusu ni sgnoleb htraE ehT"*

The last green-mossed eponymous chimney sat across the street from the middle school, perfectly framed in the window of Polly Marvel's seventh-period history class. The Marvel Family Chimney, as it was still called, was stripped of its house during the fires that ended the Battle of Wilderness in 1864, the same week the Marvel family lost four of its five sons. Reconstruction was to mean rebuilding, but by then Mr. Marvel hadn't the heart to lay any stone beyond the markers he'd set for his boys, so the town offered up its own tribute to his loss. The council voted unanimously to change the town's name from Vaughn's Tavern, as it had been called since its founding, to Marvel's Chimney, Virginia. The gesture set old Mr. Marvel to weeping, yet he would not hear of his family being singled out when so many had suffered, and so the mantle of martyrdom was cast over the other two chimneys as well. But when the county granted money for a school, Mr. Marvel donated the plot opposite *his* family's ghostly white chimney, so that the town's children, looking upon his ruined house, might forever appreciate the price of war.

To the casual observer, it certainly appeared that Polly was fulfilling her paternal great-great-grandfather's wishes. She stared out of the window, absorbed in the whole tragic story the whitewashed bricks had to tell. A nut brown wren gathered sticks to line its nest in the chimney's flue; dark clouds gathered over the fallow field, setting it in stark relief. And yet, there was nothing in the world Polly cared about less than her chimneous inheritance. She was, in matter of fact, studying a reflection in the darkened window, a safer way of watching him than gazing upon his splendor directly.

"Does anyone know what the word 'usufruct' means?" She saw him turn back and wipe his chalky hands on his pants.

It was last period, when most other eighth-graders had elected for study hall. But Polly and nine classmates—those who were at all serious about going on to college—had chosen instead to take Mr. March's honors history class. Polly had Mr. March twice: third-period American history, and this special seminar which was going to focus, he said, on precedents in U.S. history. Not presidents. Precedents.

"Anyone?"

Mr. March had been at Three Chimneys Junior High for ten years and was by far the most popular teacher in school. He wasn't so young anymore (thirty-three) and he was starting to lose a little hair in the back, and he was not overly tall. He looked like a spy in a submarine movie, Polly thought, the one dark-haired man who didn't fit in, who might at any minute lapse into another language, even though you could never detect an accent. Maybe it was the little round steel communist glasses he wore, or maybe it was his haircut, combed across his forehead at almost the Hitler angle. Her friend Bethany had heard that he was from New Jersey originally and that he had gone to Columbia University and that he'd been in Berlin the night they tore down the wall. He had a chunk of something spray-painted on his desk, so that part was probably true.

The thing about Mr. March was that he remembered what it was like to be young. He treated them like people, like people who might just have more on their minds than the Stamp Act. He was the sort of man you hesitated before saying "Yes, sir" to, though you had been taught to say it to anyone who looked to be ten years older than you, and you certainly said it to all the other teachers, but somehow saying it to him sounded sarcastic, like "Who are we kidding." And so you caught yourself swallowing the last part, so that all your affirmatives came out like "Yes, s——." "Yes, s——." Like a hiss.

"Miss Marvel? Do you know what 'usufruct' means?"

Polly cut her eyes quickly from the window and back to Mr. March incarnate.

"No, s——," she said. "I'm afraid I've never heard of it."

"Usufruct means the right to use and enjoy something, to draw from it all the profit and advantage it might produce, provided we don't alter the substance of the thing," he explained, without making her feel stupid. "It's how our third president thought we should look at government. Instead of me saying, This country is mine, and everyone after me must do as I did, I would have to say, This country is yours; it belongs to a future generation; I am only the custodian of your country. And you are allowed to disagree with how I set things up. In fact, you almost have a duty to overthrow me."

See, even in things like that, Polly thought, even explaining some boring point of history, Mr. March made it about *them*. None of the other teachers did that.

"*One generation of men does not have the right to bind another.*" Up it went on the chalkboard.

It was really hot in the classroom and Polly found herself leaning her head against the cool pane of glass. Two nights before she'd had a dream where Mr. March invited her over to his house for dinner. Outside, the house looked just like the one she'd ridden past on her bike many times, but inside was cavelike, with stalactites dripping from the ceiling and stalagmites growing from the ground, so that there was no place to put a kitchen table, much less chairs, and they had to eat crossed-legged on the bed. She had just taken a bite of steak when he leaned in to kiss her, his glasses thick and luminous as polished moonstone. But she still had her fork in her mouth and it was embarrassing and they laughed and then she woke up. Since then, she hadn't been able to look at Mr. March directly without blushing.

"We're going to study this famous phrase of Jefferson's as it affected the infancy of the Republic," he continued, addressing the class, but looking at her directly. "How does a country create precedent when one of its very Founding Fathers favors periodic revolution?"

Mr. March had this way of holding Polly's gaze, even as his body turned back to the blackboard. She was a little embarrassed by his outfit today. Most people are not dumb enough to wear corduroy on the top and bottom. Especially when it was this hot out. Nonetheless, she liked noticing the difference between Mr. March in third period and Mr. March in seventh. How the sleeves rolled above the elbow had fallen to just below, how his shirt had come a little more untucked in back, how his pants had finally found the right relaxed placement around his hips.

Bethany passed her a note. "Eaten any good steak lately?"

Polly crumpled the note and shoved it in her backpack.

"Jefferson wrote: 'It may be so proved that no society can make a perpetual constitution, or even a perpetual law.' Do you understand what that means?" Mr. March asked, when there were no gasps of surprise forthcoming. "It means every generation has the right, almost the obligation, to create new precedent, even if that means overthrowing the existing government. Isn't that exciting?"

The class nodded blankly.

Mr. March looked about the room in disgust. "What's happened to you? Kids in my day were constantly looking for ways to rebel. This would have sent us running out into the street to smash things. Christ, by the time I was your age, I'd stolen my first car. How many of you have stolen a car?

No hands went up.

"Figures." Mr. March sighed, "We are a county founded by traitors, ladies and gentlemen. Back in 1776, we were smart-ass kids running away from home because our parents wouldn't let us do what we wanted. Then suddenly, with the stroke of a pen and a simple declaration, we recast ourselves in the role of parents. The traitors—the rebels—became the Founding Fathers; we were no longer the bad sons. Now we had to behave. But still, that rebelliousness lingers in each and every one of us. In third period, we'll study everything the State of Virginia requires for you to move onto ninth grade, but here, we're going to question. Do you understand?"

Yes, sir, they said, a little stunned by his free use of the a-word.

"The problem with you kids is that you have no personal investment in politics. Why should I be surprised you're not getting this? How often do you question your government? How many of you have even been following the election?"

Drew Powell raised his hand.

"Who do you favor, Mr. Powell?"

"The president, sir."

"And why is that?"

"Because he's most likely to win."

"A pragmatist. Anyone else?"

Shyly, Polly raised her hand.

"And who do you favor, Miss Marvel?"

"Governor Brooke, s——."

"Can you state your reason?"

"My mother says he supports the small farmer. He looks after the little man. She says it's time for a change."

"'Change.' That beloved word of every politician." Mr. March whirled to the blackboard and scrawled it like a gang tag. "Is not Change merely the watered-down version of Jefferson's generational rebellion? He proposed that every nineteen years we should sweep away the old laws and rethink them for ourselves. Now we talk about Change as if it's some radical concept, when it is only the weakest reflection of Jeffersonian radicalism."

Polly sat up a little straighter at her desk. He was so passionate. Why had she never thought of things this way? Before she knew what she was saying, she interrupted.

"But what can we do about it?" she asked. "We're not even old enough to vote."

"You are never too young to have an opinion, Miss Marvel," he retorted. "And to see things for how they really are. If you see hypocrisy and injustice, you owe it to your country and yourself to speak out. If some Northwestern University journalism students could get a man released from death row, why shouldn't an eighth-grader affect the outcome of a presidential election? It makes about as much sense, doesn't it?"

The bell rang and Mr. March stalked out of the classroom, followed swiftly by the students. Polly remained in her seat, still transfixed by Mr. March's words, issued like a challenge. Did he really believe an eighth-grader could make a difference? If so, he was the most unique adult she'd ever met.

"Come on, we'll miss the bus." Bethany tapped her on the shoulder. Polly looked down at her laden backpack, full of her mother's flyers. "I have to stay after and do something," she said with a sigh. "I'll call you tonight."

Polly waited until her friend had left, then slowly made her way down the pink halls, past the mural of her school's half-crazed mascot, the Three Chimneys Rebel: a squat, bearded cartoon infantryman in a gray slouch hat waving the Confederate flag. She passed the shut doors to the auditorium, where she knew August was playing to a handful of retired people, but she had time enough to be embarrassed by that later. Just outside the auditorium stood the cardboard boxes marked Franks Food Drive, filled with dented cans of last Thanksgiving's cranberry sauce and pumpkin pie filling, niblets, and two dusty boxes of Hamburger Helper. And beside that was the sign-up sheet for Franks Volunteer Baby-sitting Duty, only seventh- and eighth-graders allowed. Polly used the purple marker on a string to sign her name. So far, all the names were girls'.

Outside, the green sky promised a nasty storm. It was that way every September—the slow hot buildup like gas inside an oven, until the inevitable explosion in the late afternoon. The leaves showed their silvery bottoms now and the wind lifted her hair off her neck. Over by the parking lot, one of the hundreds of news trucks that had descended on Three Chimneys had navigated School Street all the way out to the actual school and was setting up a live feed. Polly recognized the weatherman from Channel 5 talking to the Pep Club members who had sponsored a Frank Eleven Car Wash. What do you think of having eleven new neighbors? the weatherman was asking, while the wind whipped his microphone cord. We think it's super! We hope to raise two hundred dollars today. Come on out!

Polly circled behind the news truck and crossed into the Arlington National Cemetery of neatly parked white cars and minivans. Everyone in town had seen the same report declaring white the safest color for driving at night, and like everyone else, Polly secretly thought that if a person were rash enough to purchase forest green or indigo, he might very well have only himself to blame should he be broadsided. Three-quarters of the white cars in the lot had "We ♥ the Frank Eleven" bumper stickers (a dollar each from the Glee Club), and many had guest passes in the front window, showing they were here for August's presentation. Her mother knew the lot would be full today, which was why she'd insisted Polly take the flyers this morning. She was even letting her come home late for milking, which was miraculous in itself and further confirmation for Polly that her mother had gone nuts.

Vote Adams Brooke, The Farmer's Friend.

Polly thought it made the governor sound like a hemorrhoid cream, but her mother was proud of the alliteration. Polly slipped a copy of the red, white, and blue flyer under each set of windshield wipers, the "least she could do" (again, her mother), since she wasn't old enough to vote. She felt like an idiot with the news van only yards away, as if she might get caught on tape doing something illegal like breaking her teachers' antennae or stealing the glass from their side-view mirrors. Quickly, she made her way up one row and down another, involuntarily noting whose inspection stickers were about to expire and whose windows needed washing. Mrs. Barker, the sixth-grade math teacher, had erected an altar to her Hawaiian vacation across her dashboard, with little hula dancers and a red plastic lei draped over her rearview mirror. Coach Emery, head of junior varsity football, had a stack of orange parking tickets on his. Each car Polly exhorted to vote for Governor Brooke, her mother's demigod, her mother's boyfriend. Polly was so sick of hearing about Governor Brooke, she could hardly wait for November.

Polly crammed another ten flyers under another ten windshield wipers, working quickly, as the wind was practically ripping them from her hand. When she came to one of the only nonwhite cars in the lot, she had raised the wiper before it registered just whose car she was about to indoctrinate. A rusted green Carmen Ghia. With no "We ♥ the Frank Eleven" bumper sticker. With a dimple in the passenger side door. With a paperback copy of *The Ugly American* and an open bag of Doritos on the backseat.

What made her test the handle? she would wonder later. Whatever possessed her, on learning it was unlocked, to open the door and slip into the front seat? Inside, the car was hot and airless from having been closed up all day, and it smelled of gym clothes left for weeks in the bag. But it was his car, and everything inside bespoke him. She ran her fingers over the cracks in the fake leather dashboard, over the lashed steering wheel cover, over the hot, black stick shift. Once, when her father was really drunk, she drove him home from a Fourth of July picnic at the Andersons'. She would never forget the terror and excitement of her headlights cutting through the black tunnel of trees, of mailboxes and road signs springing like wild animals out of the darkness. She didn't know how to move the seat closer, so she had to stretch almost diagonally to reach the pedals, and could barely see over the dashboard. From the time she was eight, she had been mentally preparing herself to drive. But the route she had memorized, that she went over nightly before falling asleep, was the twisting drive to the hospital in the event both her parents were felled by simultaneous heart attacks, not the half-mile home from the Andersons'.

A few fat raindrops hit the windshield and Polly knew she should get out. This wasn't right. But then again, hadn't Mr. March encouraged them to break the rules? When was the last time she'd felt so tinglingly treacherous?

She popped open the glove compartment to a miniature avalanche of tape cases. Arlo Guthrie, Country Joe McDonald—Polly didn't recognize any of them. He had papers, too. His pink auto registration. Harvey D. March. David? Dagobert? Creased receipts from Wendy's and Food Lion. A postcard of the Brandenburg Gate (so it said on the back) written in German, but signed most un-Germanically, Sandi. Under the seat, he had an unmarked videotape in a plain blue case that was beyond tantalizing. Was it something he recorded off TV? Was it a video postcard of Sandi kittenishly romping through the beer gardens of Berlin? Polly couldn't stand it.

Why was she doing this? She closed her eyes and leaned her head against the seat. He wasn't so handsome. He teased her and made her feel stupid. But time after time, since the first day of class, it had been her he singled out. Her he raised up. Her he put down. Back when she was a kid, she used to go over to Manda's house to play with the hunting dogs. Manda would tell her, Be careful, don't confuse them. To a dog any attention is good attention. Polly felt like that now. Like Mr. March could slap her with a newspaper and she would fetch his pipe.

It had begun to rain in earnest while she sat there—heavy curtains of water, a blinding flash, and then hail hammered the windshield. What was she going to do? Across the parking lot, the Channel 5 weatherman sprinted for his van, the Pep Club forsook its bristles and squeegees and ran shrieking for cover. She opened the door a crack, was instantly soaked with rain, and quickly shut it. But it was too late. Water puddled on the floorboards, on the armrest, on the seat. He was sure to know someone had been in his car. Frantically, Polly mopped at the water with her extra flyers.

"I didn't realize my car theft story would be so inspirational." Mr. March said flatly.

She felt the cool rush of air as the door flew open, then the surprise of rain on her skin. She traced him from his brown loafers up to his black umbrella, hail bouncing off it in flying check marks. When she made her way to his face, she saw first a flash of real dark anger, then, in an instant, a return to his familiar expression of sardonic impassivity.

"It started to pour and I just ducked in for a minute to get out of the—oh God, you must think I'm some sort of criminal breaking and entering. It was unlocked. I didn't mean—I was just putting these flyers—." Polly thrust the curled, smeared mess at him. She was trying her best not to cry in sheer embarrassment and he wasn't helping any by staring at her in that "There's a hair on my plate" way of his. Rain streamed off his umbrella like a force field protecting him from her, keeping her trapped in the car, staring up helplessly. Why was he looking at her like that? Why wasn't he moving?

"Were you giving out these flyers because you believe in Governor Brooke or were you just doing it because your mother told you to?" Mr. March asked at last. He had to shout over the rain battering his umbrella, and at first Polly couldn't be sure she heard him right.

"Pardon?" she asked.

"If you believe in him, I'll forgive you, but if you're merely furthering someone else's crusade, I'll kindly ask you to take that off my car."

He took a step back, and Polly flew out to pluck the sopping flyer from his windshield. She stared at him pitifully for the briefest of seconds, then mashed all the remaining flyers. "I'm sorry," she whispered.

"I'm trying to teach you, all of you, to think for yourselves. I don't care that you wanted to snoop inside my car. At least you did that for you."

He climbed into the spot in which she'd just sat, pulled the door shut, and rolled down the window. "Do you need a ride?" he asked, and she answered miserably that she had one. "Here, take this." He passed her his umbrella, and if he'd handed her a lit stick of dynamite, she would have taken it. "You don't always have to do what your mother tells you, Polly. Remember, we're a nation of traitors."

She clenched the shiny lacquered handle of his black umbrella, her fingerprints pressed to the echo of his warm fingerprints, and watched him pull away. She'd never been so mortified in her life, and yet she couldn't stop smiling.

Almost without trying, they'd forged a new precedent. He had called her Polly.

CHAPTER THREE

"It is July Fourth, 1826, exactly fifty years after the signing of the Declaration, and I am dead."

The large room was dark and still. Even after nearly two hours, the tall, weather-beaten man who spoke had not found comfort with his voice, never made for public speaking in the first place, which came out whistle-thin, as if someone had siphoned off half of it before it reached his lips. He had an unconscious habit when thinking of bringing his callused fingers to his mouth, lightly pinching to shape the next word out. But though his thoughts were grand, no amount of manipulating could make the voice that conveyed them larger than it was. He spoke from his Windsor chair, attired in elegantly simple period costume: white hose, homespun knee breeches, an embroidered vest over a white cotton blouse, a French blue silk jacket with deep cuffs. On his head he wore a barely powdered auburn wig. Around his neck, he wore a loosely knotted cravat.

"I died not knowing my rival John Adams was to expire only hours later with my name in his mouth," he said. "Like me, he had clung to life, desirous only of achieving that final, fateful anniversary. I left this world surrounded by faithful servants and my family, but saddened to realize they could not go on living here after me, for I was dying deeply in debt. As I closed my eyes on Martha and the grandchildren, it seemed to me I saw the twin seraphim of my beloved Patty and youngest daughter Maria, bathed in light, their arms outstretched to receive me. Lay down your life as a public man and take up your eternity as an insubstantial ghost, they seemed to say. You are safe from fame here. And even as they spoke, it seemed I heard another voice from across the same divide. I heard my rival's wife calling out to summon him with words that might have applied to us both. 'I am more and more convinced that man is a dangerous creature,' the great, wise Abigail Adams was saying, 'that power, whether vested in many or a few, is ever grasping, and, like the grave, cries "Give, give."'

"Give, give," repeated the man in soft tones, leaning over the single candle at his side. "I gave to my country and now it is time I give to God."

"Good-bye, my fellow patriots. Good-bye."

The candle guttered at the touch of his breath, and the room dropped into darkness. He would shortly be revived, he knew, with the applause that inevitably followed, but he liked, for that long hushed moment, to surrender to the undertow of his own death. The cold rush swept him off the hilltop of Monticello, back through swampy Washington, intoxicating Paris, back inside the hollow stomach of Independence Hall, where he paused with a quill in his hand before he was pulled back to Patty's bed, lay once more upon his own hard cot at the College of William and Mary, stared into the fire on his mother's rug at Shadwell, then curled back into the purple warmth of the womb. Viewed from there, a man could forget the daily struggle, the pain endured forging an important life. Would it not be a cosmic kindness, he thought, to let us return to the womb upon our deaths and see that each stage of our hard-fought lives was inevitable, like God the valet had merely been holding open successively larger coats for us to slip into?

But soon enough the lights came up and the applause called him back to life. He was once more in the middle school auditorium, where rows A through N were filled with balding men in brightly colored trousers, accompanied by patient wives, their white heads cocked in polite interest.

Thomas Jefferson gave them a deep, heartfelt bow. "That concludes my little talk, 'The Patriot in Repose,'" he said. "Now, if my kind friends have any questions for me, I would gladly entertain them." This crowd was not shy. Fifteen hands immediately shot up.

He knew the sort of questions they would pose, before they even pursed their lips to ask. How did it feel to pen the Declaration of Independence, Mr. President? How could you have written "all men are created equal" and yet still have kept slaves? Mr. President, if you had been alive at the dawn of the Civil War, would you have supported the succession of Virginia? Often he would get the amateur historian, dandruffed and bespectacled, who aspired to stump him with some bit of arcana. More often, it was men and women who had read the latest *New York Times* best-selling paperback on Lewis and Clark and were full of desire for more detail. The most painful question he ever had to answer was from a young black honor student, who addressed him politely as "sir." "Sir," she said, with the low-voiced force of a thousand lashes, "do you believe I have no right to exist?"

But he never got tired of answering their questions, even ones he'd answered a thousand times, even ones that hurt. What was old to him was new to them, and his audiences showed their enthusiasm in their endless fascination with his wine collection, with his nail factory, with the influence of John Locke on his writing. They wanted his opinion on television and the welfare state and the New Deal. They wanted to know if he thought America had lost its way.

August could never pinpoint the exact moment when his hobby had crossed over into a lifestyle, but the likeliest candidate would have to be the week, ten years ago, when the Chautauquans came to town. They set up a large tent and loudspeakers, chairs, and a concession stand on the lawn by the War Memorial, and his first thought was that a Pentecostal revival had gotten terribly, terribly lost here in Episcopalian country. But he soon learned from the public librarian that they had been invited here from out west, that they were not Do-You-See-the-Light evangelists, but living historians presenting a humanities program meant to edify and entertain. Over the course of seven nights, in period costume, and without breaking character, each Chautauquan presented a life of an eminent American: Alexander Hamilton, Harriet Beecher Stowe, W. E. B. DuBois, Jane Addams. Each began with a monologue, then moved to questions from the audience, and finally ended with a return to the self—not the historic, exalted self, but the slightly lonely, overly bookish Oklahoman or South Dakotan, who gave their reasons for why they spend a goodly portion of their lives as someone else. Teddy Roosevelt had called the Chautauquan tent shows that traveled during his time "the Most American thing in America," and August was spellbound. In his family, that which passed away was hallowed and tended and carefully maintained. But for these people, it seemed, what was dead was dead, and an identity was fair game for anyone who fit the clothes and learned the language. August left that revival—and "revival" it was for him, for he *had* seen the light—a changed man. He could not only study Jefferson, he could become him, at least for the edification and entertainment of others. What better way to learn history than to engage in a dialogue with it? Than to prod it and demand it explain itself? At first it felt almost sacrilegious to use the hallowed "I" in reference to his hero, to answer as Jefferson would have answered, to express opinions that others might very well take away as fact, and all without an advanced degree of any sort. But then, as he honed a monologue and bought his first powdered wig, it began to feel more natural. The kinship deepened until, ten years later, he had, without even trying, created a union, and a whole new filiation of self.

He called on a man in the third row, who pushed himself up and walked to the standing microphone in the left aisle.

"Mr. President, thank you so much for taking time away from your duties to speak to us this afternoon," the man began, tickled to play along. "We know what a busy schedule you must keep. My question for you is . . ."

How did it feel to write the Declaration of Independence? Hmm . . . The president turned the question over as if for the first time giving it any serious thought.

"You must remember, my friends," he began, "the question was not whether, by a Declaration of Independence, we should make ourselves what we were not, but whether we should declare a fact that already existed. As I wrote in my *Summary View* of 1774, 'The God who gave us life, gave us liberty at the same time: the hand of force may destroy, but cannot disjoin them.' We were already free men; we just needed Old King George to realize that.

"It would be difficult for you to imagine what we suffered before the Revolution, how we found ourselves emasculated and abused at every turn, by men we had never seen and could not vote out of office. You know about the paper taxes and the tea taxes, but did you know an American subject was forbidden even to make a hat for himself, though the fur was trapped on his own property? That we were forced to ship our raw iron, heavy and expensive as it was, for refinery in England so that they might sell it back to us? That a standing army was kept at our expense, so that they might with impunity take over our houses and eat us out of our winter provisions?"

No matter how many times he outlined the abuses of the British crown, he found himself still angry over the enforced infantilism of a great nation. He could hear his thin voice, calmly outlining dates and places, and yet, as in his death, he was somewhere else—alone in a close second-story room, staring at a sheet of blank parchment. They had petitioned the king over and over, like reasonable men, but the tyrant simply would not listen. And now he was forced to endure the pestilence of a summer in Philadelphia, while his wife languished at home near death. He stabbed his quill in his pot of ink. He wanted to retire from public life. This George must be made to understand. He wanted to go home.

He realized his fist was clenched deep in his pocket and that he had stopped talking.

"I'm sorry," he said. "Next question?"

A middle-aged woman in a denim jumper raised her hand. "I have a question, but I feel silly asking it," she said, blushing.

"I am your president, madame, here to answer whatever question you pose. Is that not the purpose of a democratic government? To answer to the people?"

"Well, then . . ." She screwed up her courage. "Are you by any chance related to the real Mr. Jefferson?" she asked sweetly. "You look surprisingly like the portraits I've seen." Next to her, her husband rolled his eyes in embarrassment.

"Am I related to myself, madame?" the president answered with a smile. Rule number one of the Chautauqua Living History School:

Never break character while in costume. "Who else should I resemble?"

That got a laugh.

"What made you say the Earth belongs in usufruct to the living?"

The president scanned the audience for the owner of that familiar voice, and found her in the back row, dripping wet, her eyes challenging behind her glasses. He hadn't even seen Polly slip in. She used to love his brocaded costume when she was younger and would beg to try it on, though the knee breeches came all the way to her ankles and the coat hung to her knees. Back then, she thought ponytails were just for girls, and she would snatch the lightly powdered wig from his head, and race around the stables shrieking, August is a girl! August is a girl! But since she turned thirteen—no, he could peg it even more exactly—since her father had left, Polly had been avoiding him. She seemed embarrassed by everything he did.

"The Earth belongs in usufruct to the living. . . ," he began, for she seemed to want a serious answer. "That is taken from a letter I wrote to my dear friend and protégé, James Madison, in 1789. In it I was trying to point out the inherent unfairness of one generation's forcing another to pay its debts. My wife's father, rest his soul, left me his land, his people, and his crippling encumbrances, and I spent the remainder of my life struggling with inherited debt. But I do not want to give a false impression—I was not the wisest steward of my money. I could have sold off more land to repay my loans, but I considered it beneath my dignity as a gentleman planter. I could have forgone the numerous changes to Monticello, I could have drunk less fine Bordeaux, I could have entertained fewer friends, but somehow I could not force myself to forgo these small indulgences."

He felt a stirring of the old chest-tightening panic even talking about how much money he owed, like the long bony hand of John Wayles was reaching up from the grave to rifle his pockets. He died owing over $100,000, which by today's reckoning would be several millions. It was not something he was proud of.

"When I wrote to Madison, I was thinking of the raging revolution in France and my own personal finances. What right did Louis XV have to strap a nation—or for that matter, what right did my father-in-law have to strap me—with a bill for extravagances enjoyed during his lifetime? Why should we toil and suffer to pay back money spent by men who gave no thought to us? Ten years later, when as president I became father to my countrymen, I applied this philosophy to reducing the national debt, so that generations after me would not be left in the same predicament. Unfortunately, those who followed me were not quite so conscientious."

"But I heard you wrote that no society could make a perpetual constitution or even a perpetual law because of this," she challenged him in her old sophist voice. Just like she used to quiz when she was little: Would you rather freeze to death or be burned to death? And you can't choose "neither."

What had gotten into Polly? Since when did she care about any of this? Well, he would play along. "What a good little history student you are . . . Miss Marvel, is it? Who has not entertained a youthful idealism they would rather forget?" he asked. "I did say that. And my friend, the wise Mr. Madison, quickly disabused me of the notion. How would anything get accomplished if we were constantly revising the laws? he wrote back. How soon would chaos reign? My friend had spent years of his life pushing through our nation's Constitution and Bill of Rights; I doubt he would have looked kindly on each new generation's wiping it clean. Perhaps in the end, he was right. We've done pretty well so far."

Polly sat down, seemingly satisfied, and August glanced at the clock over the last row to see it was nearly four o'clock. He needed to change and get over to Margaret's before evening milking. With great deliberation he loosened his cravat and removed his wig, setting it reverently on the chair behind him.

"Now, friends, it is time for me to relinquish office and don once more the humble mantle of August Vaughn, private citizen," the erstwhile president announced. "I hope you have enjoyed your time with Mr. Jefferson as much as I have enjoyed bringing him to you."

By the time the applause died and August had shaken hands all around, it was nearly four-fifteen and they were running late for milking. He and Polly walked wordlessly back to the parking lot, where the storm had passed on like every other summer squall, leaving the air sagging and nearly opaque. August plucked a soaked Adams Brooke flyer from beneath his windshield wiper.

"I think your mom can count on my vote," he said, but laid it flat to dry on his dashboard nonetheless.

"Since when did you become so interested in Jeffersonian finance?" August asked when they were halfway to the farm and Polly had not spoken. She had been staring out of the lowered pickup window, deeply engrossed in the gas-rainbowed puddles and cornfields flashing by.

"We were studying him in history today," she replied. "Mr. March thinks we've lost all our traitorous fire. He thinks we need a good rebellion every now and then."

"You know Jefferson was mostly thinking about his own personal debt when he wrote that letter. Don't let your history teacher twist his words around."

"Oh, you think you know everything," Polly cried, stung by his criticism. "You might wear his clothes, but you aren't really him, you know. You can't know what he thought."

Everything was a battle these days. Of course August couldn't know everything in Jefferson's head, just because he'd spent the last twenty years of his life studying every facet of the man. But he had a good idea he knew more than Polly's history teacher, whoever he was.

They pulled up the long driveway, sending gravel popping behind them. August had automatically pulled into the bald lane of grass beside the barn, where he usually parked, before he realized another truck was already there, blocking his way: Francis Marvel's navy blue pickup. For a moment after he cut the engine, both he and Polly hesitated with their hands on the door. Margaret was standing beside her husband, leaning on her pitchfork with that defeated slump August recognized as her Francis-stance, as if all her internal organs wanted to shrink as far away from him as possible. Francis waved to them, and Polly, because she was annoyed at her mother and August, decided she loved him today.

"Hey, Dad," she called, flinging her arms around her father's waist. He kissed the top of her head.

"Hey, Peanut," he replied. "How's it going?"

"Fine."

"Getting good grades?"

"Yes, sir."

"Eating right?"

"Yes, sir."

"Not pregnant yet?" He scowled at her.

"Not as far as I know."

"That's my girl." He patted her approvingly. "Your feet are younger than mine—run on inside and get your old man a glass of tea."

Polly dutifully trotted indoors, and Francis turned his attention to August.

"Hey, my friend. Finally getting that sex change you always wanted?" Francis nodded at the remnants of August's stage makeup.

"Nice to see you, Francis." August rubbed the edge of his sleeve over his cheek. "Love to chat, but I'm late bringing in the ladies."

"Don't apologize, man," Francis called to August's retreating back. "All the damn estrogen flying around this place, it's no wonder. I swear I was about ready to go into heat myself before I took off."

"We all just assumed you had, Francis." August smiled lazily over his shoulder.

"Damn if I didn't, man." Francis roared, always one to appreciate a joke at his own expense. "Damn if I didn't."

Margaret walked back to the haylage she was bailing into the girls' troughs, and her ex-husband followed her, picking up as if they hadn't been interrupted.

"So, anyway, I'm sorry. I thought you knew he was coming. I was just doing it for the publicity. Personally, I hope the cocksucker goes down in flames."

"Don't say that," Margaret snapped.

"Listen, who cares about politics?" said Francis. "Everyone saw the house on TV and the phone's been ringing off the hook. I've changed the name of the company to Chimney Eleven Contracting. I'm getting the signs printed up, and I just got the cards today. Here, take one." He thrust a white business card at her: Chimney Eleven Contracting, with nine little Monopoly-style houses running the border and two smaller ones dotting the i's. She slipped it in her pocket.

August pulled on his work boots and tried to not eavesdrop on their conversation. He had always hated the way Francis spoke to Margaret, as if she should be eternally interested in everything he had to say, no matter how painful it might be for her to hear. Her husband was still a good-looking man in his early forties, tall, with a sharp Roman nose and thick blond hair that didn't show a streak of gray (Polly, much to her mother's chagrin, had never been able to prove he was dyeing it). His complexion had the ruddy glow of outdoorsmanship or alcoholism—his burgeoning gut seem to imply the latter—and he had picked up in college that Richmond tic of wearing Docksiders without socks. August had known Francis as long as he'd known Margaret, and he'd disliked him almost as long.

"We're going to be fucking rolling pretty soon," he was telling her. "I've got a guy signing contracts tonight and I think I've finally given the zoning board enough damn money to put in the sewer line, but you know, with all the expansion, cash flow is just a little tight this month—"

"Don't." Margaret put up her hand to ward him off.

"It'll just be until next month, as soon as I finish Manda's house. Man, I couldn't have *bought* that kind of publicity."

"Francis," she warned.

"Goddamn, I said I'm gonna have it. What more do you want? I can't give you what I don't have myself."

"Your daughter needs school clothes. I can barely pay August as it is. And what are we supposed to do about college?"

"Why the hell are you talking about college?" Francis shouted. "She's in the damn eighth grade."

August wanted to jump in, to say, Don't think about me, I don't need the money. But he knew this would only put her in a worse position.

"I need to bring in the cows, Francis," Margaret said. "We have to talk about this later." She turned from him, only to nearly collide with Polly, who had appeared in the doorway holding a glass of tea.

"Bye, Peanut." Francis drained the glass and handed it back to her. "See you this weekend."

"Finish up what you're doing, Margaret," August offered as her husband stalked out. "I'll get the girls."

August followed Francis out to the driveway. He took a look back over his shoulder at Margaret, furiously forking hay into the rack, blinking back tears of rage. He reached out to put his hand on Francis's shoulder, but the other man's muscles, hard as ingot, jumped a sharp "Screw off" beneath his fingers.

"Listen, Francis. I know things are tight," August said once they were far enough away from the barn. "I've got plenty in the bank. Why don't I loan you some—you give it to Margaret and tell her it's from you. I don't need it right now."

"What the hell's wrong with you, man?" Francis narrowed his eyes. "You out to get a piece of my wife?"

August took a step back. "Francis, how can you—?"

"Aw, I'm just shitting you." Francis punched him lightly in the chest. "I can't take your money. Don't worry about Maggie. She's got more than she lets on—her dad played the stock market. They'll be fine this month, and I'll have it by next."

Francis opened the door to his new pickup, the driving-around-town not hauling-chicken-flats model, and climbed up behind the wheel. "Let me ask you." He motioned August closer. "When was the last time you took a vacation? Or even a day off?"

It had been nine years, but August didn't like to think about that. He didn't have anywhere he'd especially like to go. And besides, if Margaret didn't take off, he didn't feel he should.

"I worked a farm my entire life," Francis said. "First my daddy's, then Margaret's daddy's. I am finally free." Francis leaned in, and for the first time August could smell the hint of beer on his minty breath. "And, shit, if it took having everyone hate my guts, well, I'm sorry.

Get out while you can, man. There's no shame in buying your milk at the damn grocery store."

August pulled into the rectory at six forty-five, the same time as every evening, and parked next to the old chimney. The comforting rattle of his mother sorting heavy silverware, digging through the sideboard for summer's spindly handled ice tea spoons and flat-plated fish knives, greeted him as he walked toward the house. It was Friday, so she would have poached a salmon and made a cobbler. His favorite was blackberry, his father's was peach, but since today was the first Friday of the month, the calendar favored peach. His mother didn't have a preference; she loved all cobblers ecumenically. Inside, his father would be sitting in his recliner, reading and listening to the nightly news on NBC. He had watched no other news since the narrow-tie days of Huntley and Brinkley, though he sighed over the sharply chiseled, pretty-boy anchormen his network sported now. Throughout the broadcast, he would call out the headlines to August's mother, who would be tossing a salad or tasting the snaps for salt, and she would nod, though he couldn't see her, happy to have the world filtered through her husband. Almost everything she knew in life, from wars to peace processes to mass genocide, she had gotten from the next room.

August checked the mail and saw that the book he'd been expecting from the antique dealer in Ashfield, Massachusetts, had arrived. It was a rare monograph on crop rotation at Monticello. Not the book everyone else had, but a volume published privately in 1928, for a subscription of two hundred readers.

"How'd it go today, son?" his father called from the living room.

"We had a great turnout," he answered. "You?"

"I sat with Manda most of it. I'll tell you all about it after your shower."

"Dinner will be ready at seven," his mother said as she said every night. He would take a fifteen-minute shower. He would sit down promptly at 7 P.M. smelling of tarry Head & Shoulders and Ivory soap. He would have clean fingernails to look at when he bowed his head for grace.

August hung his costume in the hall closet, behind the winter coats so that his mother would not find it and wash it before he had the chance to do so himself. An outsider would never have found the closet door camouflaged on the Wall of Ancestors, as he cheekily used to call it as a boy, a gauntlet of neatly hung oil paintings, tintypes, and 1930s color-washed studio portraits that ran from the front door to the kitchen. From the way his parents spoke, August had grown up thinking himself little more than a jambalaya of these men and women. He had his grandfather's eyes, his uncle Clement's mouth. His mother's hair, his father's sense of humor. The similarities were uncanny, they said, and more subtle ones revealed themselves as he grew: Great-grandmother Adele's kindness to animals, Great-great-grandfather Burbidge's ability to do complicated sums in his head. Any bête noire made him just like Great-uncle Robert, who swore he hated chocolate but loved M&M's, assiduously picking out all the brown ones. Any tendency to shyness, he inherited from his mother's sister Susan, who would sit in the attic for days at a time as a child, not even coming down for dinner. It comforted him to have every angle accounted for, so that there was very little of himself left over to ruin. The only thing no one in the family could affix was this Jefferson eccentricity of his. Everyone was kind to him about it, but in their heart of hearts, no one understood how a grown man could want to be anyone other than who he was. There were no actors or even schizophrenics in the family. There was just no precedent for it.

He opened the door off the hall that led to the finished basement, where he lived. The ceiling was low for such a tall man, but that just meant the slouch he had been cultivating since high school had finally come in handy. The room was equipped with the oak bedroom set his father had owned as a boy: a narrow single bed, a writing desk with a new computer, and a cane-backed chair. If the pictures he had pasted all over the wall were of a woman, the police would have carted him away for a stalker, but luckily for his sake, they were no lascivious glossies or Peeping Tom grainy snapshots. No, the broad forehead and furrowed brow, the cleft chin and eagle gray eyes belonged to one distinguished head, reproduced in color and in black and white, formally posed and cubistically scratched in crayon by a second-grade class. It was the same face as that on the shiny nickel, and if August had had merely a nickel for every face on his wall, he would have been a wealthy man, indeed.

The walls not covered with images of Jefferson were reserved for works about him. Floor-to-ceiling bookshelves housed Jeffersonia, arranged by their Library of Congress numbers. August had nearly everything published in English on the man and his times, with many more boxes of books in the attic. He put the new entry on crop rotation in its LoC slot and headed to the shower. Exactly fifteen minutes later, he came upstairs, where his father was telling a joke.

"Father Abraham wanted to upgrade his PC to Windows 2000," Leland was saying to his wife, who had never touched a computer in her life. "His son Isaac was incredulous.

"'Pop,'" said Isaac, "'you can't run Windows 2000 on your old, slow 386. Everyone knows that you need a Pentium with at least sixteen megs of memory for that!'

"But Abraham, the man of faith, gazed at Isaac calmly and replied, "'God will provide the RAM, my son.'"

August laughed loudly to cover his mother's smiling confusion and took his place between his parents.

"Well, son, another one under your belt," his father said.

"Yes, sir."

"Die with dignity?"

"As always."

"Salad, anyone?" said Evelyn. "This is low-calorie ranch, so you don't have to be afraid."

"Thanks, Mom." August let her scoop him a bowl. "How was Manda today?"

"To tell you the truth, I'm a bit worried," his father answered, accepting his own overflowing bowl of iceberg lettuce. "She just doesn't seem herself. With all the attention, I'm not surprised—Manda was always such a private girl. But this is different. She hasn't been to visit the babies yet. She hardly says a word to anyone."

"Maybe she's suffering a touch of postpartum?" August ventured, coloring slightly. "I've certainly seen the cows go through it."

"You know, they say she was getting a little hysterical, even before the babies," Mrs. Vaughn interjected. "Throwing things and raging around, just like Mary Todd Lincoln. I wouldn't be surprised if they diagnosed her with MS."

Both August and Pastor Vaughn stared at her quizzically. Mrs. Vaughn lightly tapped her forehead and laughed.

"No, not MS," she said. "Oh, Leland, what is it called? What is it we get?"

"PMS," her husband replied.

"Yes, PMS. They think now that Mary Todd Lincoln had it, and I'll wager Manda Frank does too."

"Could be." Both men nodded and returned to their low-calorie ranch.

"I just hope I did the right thing, counseling her to have all eleven," Leland said after a while. "Seems like everything she had went into making those babies and there is nothing left for her."

"How can you say that!" Mrs. Vaughn exclaimed, "It's been a miracle right here in Three Chimneys, and you're partly responsible for it. No one thought they could all be born alive, except you, and I know how hard you prayed. Now, they're not out of the woods yet, but they will be, and Manda, when she comes back to her senses, will bless you a hundred times over for the Christian guidance you gave her."

August could tell it was what his father wanted to hear, but it brought Leland no solace. The priest dug into his salmon unenthusiastically.

"You know, I had the baby blues with you, sweetheart." Mrs. Vaughn took away the dishes and reset the table with dessert plates and coffee cups. "That's what they used to call it in my day. Maybe they thought none of us would fess up if they called it something so scary as 'postpartum.' I know I wouldn't have. I would have just kept quiet."

August tried to remember if he had detected a change in Margaret after Polly was born. If anything, August had taken her postpartum upon himself, sighing to see the three so happy together—Francis at his kindest and most goofily adoring; Margaret glowing. And in the midst of their happiness, August prowled with anguished fear, for his model of maternity was his own miscarriage-plagued mother, and then there was Patty Jefferson, lost to her husband at the height of their love for one another. August hung back in the early days after Polly's birth, sitting alone for hours in the field, worried this birth would be the event that finally stole Margaret from him completely. But of course, Polly thrived and Margaret with her, and his bachelor worries soon grew awkward and ridiculous.

His parents had years ago stopped asking why he didn't get married, settle down, and start a family of his own. They would never be willingly rid of him, but the way they watched him every time he received a letter with an unfamiliar postmark or a phone call after eight o'clock at night reminded him of how happy they would be to have him in love as they were. He looked fondly at his parents, thoughtfully scraping up their cobblers and blowing in perfect synchronicity upon the headwaters of their coffee. Married for forty years, they were in perfect tandem, barely needing to speak to communicate, united in their unconditional love for their only son. August Vaughn was the luckiest of men. Jefferson lost his father when he was thirteen and his mother when he was thirty-three. He lost his best friend and his wife and four of his children. August still had everyone who mattered. And if he didn't have them in exactly the way he desired, well, at least God would not be jealous.

He helped his mother clear the table and made her sit down to her new Mary Todd Lincoln biography while he did the dishes. He found his father's reading glasses behind the electric can opener and placed them on his head when the priest wandered through the kitchen on his way out to the old chimney. It was little more than a kudzu bump in the landscape now, but long ago, it had served its patriotic duty by providing for the likes of Washington and Madison, Jefferson and Aaron Burr. The stewardship of the tavern had historically fallen to the elder branch of the Vaughn family, while the younger shoot entered the clergy at St. Barnabas Episcopal Church next door. Between the two branches, the Vaughn family covered the spiritual and corporeal needs of the antebellum community quite nicely: A Vaughn christened a man's son, and a Vaughn poured the spirits to toast his health. A Vaughn married a happy couple, and the Vaughn next door served the nuptial dinner. For over half a century these geographical first cousins—church and tavern—pursued a convivial dialogue. That is, until the day the tavern succumbed to a "conflagration of righteous retribution," which is one of the many nicer terms arson goes by.

August knew this chimney meant the world to his father. He was the sort of man who felt almost physical pain at the thought of losing anything, even if it was something he had never had. Love letters tossed in the fire, disintegrated baby blankets, books lost or casually loaned—*never to be returned*—these were the things of nightmare for Pastor Vaughn. A family had so little, inevitably lost so much along the way; who could conceive of destroying what remained? August often watched his father pat the old chimney's thick neck when he went to the mailbox in the morning for his paper, and he knew that in the evening, when putting together his sermons, his father loved to look out his study window and see the Old Man (as he called it) standing in the moonlight, steadfast as an Indian lookout. Through the window over the sink, August watched his father totter off to the Old Man now for inspiration on this Sunday's sermon, and thought, as he did almost every night at precisely 8:30, what a good thing it was to grow old in the company of these worthy old men.

CHAPTER FOUR

When the morphine first kicked in, Manda felt like she'd been turned off the leash. Here, finally, after months of being held back, straining to run, was a wide-open field: rocks to climb, stumps to leap. Space. Now Manda slipped her collar and raced through the morning meadow, hot on a scent, tonguing her excitement. In her life she'd raised hunters who tailed and watched the others, hunters that refused to hark and move up with their running mates. Some she'd been able to correct, others continued on their stubborn way and were of no use to anybody. She'd raised quitters and babblers, and potterers and ghost trailers, but never, until the morphine, had she run alongside them, stride for stride, understanding how easy it was to get lost in the rapture of pure forward motion. Could she blame those dogs for losing sight of why they ran, when the running alone was more than enough? Nearly seven months she'd been kenneled by what was growing inside her, but at last, inside the morphine, she was free. At least for as long as they continued the drip.

But Manda was young, and her body healed more quickly than she was ready for, and she nearly wept when the nurse turned the cock on the clear plastic bag and declared, *That should have seen her through the worst of it,* and instead of renewing her blessed drip, handed her a pleated cup in which two white pills rolled lonesomely. Manda's open field shrunk to the size of a common backyard, the pain returned, and she was tied to a clothesline, allowed just enough leash to choke herself.

"I understand you're going home today," Nurse Reynolds said, checking the dressing over her incision. "Are you excited?"

Manda nodded. She was sitting up now, and taking a few tottering steps. Her voice was the last thing that struggled to come back.

Manda noticed that the nurse didn't say she'd miss her, or that it
would be sad to see her leave. All these months, Manda had just been
the pen, looked through like a chain-link fence.

"Are we feeling up to going downstairs today?" asked Nurse
Reynolds brightly, her eyes encouraging the correct answer. Manda
struggled to think. What would Pastor Vaughn say? For days she'd
been able to lie in bed without having to worry about them, and
everyone said, *Just give her time. It takes some a while to adjust.* Jake
went down and told her all about them, so it was like she had seen
them. He memorized all the confusing incantations the doctors recited over their heads, words like craniosynostosis and asymmetrical
with clonus, conditions that sounded like weed killers: RSV and NEC
and Grade 4 IVH. How did all these abbreviations come out of her
body? Manda wondered. How was she supposed to understand all this?

"I think you'd be happier if you saw them before you left the
hospital," said Nurse Reynolds.

What would Pastor Vaughn say? He would say, Yes, go see them.
They are your children. The pain would be as great here or there. Go
see them.

It was her last day, so Manda let Nurse Reynolds help her into
a wheelchair and roll her down to the Neonatal Intensive Care
Unit. The halls outside were decorated with paper pinwheels and
sick children's drawings: monkey faces, houses with yellow suns,
blood red poster-paint handprints. Inside the double doors were a
wraparound desk as one might find on a spaceship and, directly in
front of her, a bulletin board of babies' faces. Healthy babies. Fat
babies. Babies who made it and went home to those brightly painted
houses with suns, and stupidly grinning parents, canary feathers
peeking from the corners of their mouths. They had all gotten away
with something, sneaking their tiny children past death. Now they
sent pictures back of quadruplets dressed in matching kilts and first
birthday faces smeared with cake.

It was very quiet in NICU and napping dark, disturbed only by
the monitor lights and the whirring beeps of respirators. Capable
women in pink scrubs, girls who had come from backgrounds similar

to Manda's but who had done something with themselves, they'd be the first to tell you, padded silently, scribbling on clipboards. Nurse Reynolds wheeled her around to the left, where her babies were arranged in four rows of what Manda thought were incubators, but which she learned were now called isolettes. Babies A–K. Ranging in weight from 2 pounds, 8 ounces, all the way down to the smallest at 16 ounces, a size, Manda thought, more fitting for a Coke than a baby. Nurse Reynolds passed her off to one of the pink nurses, a kindly-faced but no-nonsense woman from the Islands. She removed a quilted blanket from the bubble of the closest isolette to reveal the tiniest of liver-colored babies, barely bigger than Manda's hand, but perfectly formed, with matchstick fingers, a raisin nose, and eyelids so sheer, Manda thought she could see the dreaming pupils underneath.

"It's good to finally see you," said the nurse. "Your babies were wondering where you were."

The infant inside the bubble was hooked up to a circulatory system of tubes and lines, held in place by white adhesive tape. A red light flashed at her heel—the pulse oximeter, the nurse told her—and a CPAP tube protruded from her nose. She was being fed intralipids, fats injected straight into her veins. Any activity burned off precious calories the baby needed to grow, so she was sedated, against pain and to keep her from moving. Manda remembered a conversation with one of the many doctors who saw her in the early days of her pregnancy, who had gone to great lengths to explain the heightened sensation receptors in fetuses. You know how you should speak to your children in the womb and play soothing music for them, he said; well, if you believe they can feel the good things, you must admit they feel the bad. He spoke in words she barely understood. Of the developing thalamus, able to transmit pain response by eight weeks. Sensory receptors appear on the face and genitalia by the eleventh week, he said. They spread to the palms of the hands and soles of the feet, and by the twentieth week, the baby can feel everything. He spoke of heart rates going up and oxygen saturation going down in response to pain stimuli. How some babies flailed wildly and how others, overcome by the intensity, went numb and shut down for days. Fetuses feel everything, he said; it's a medical fact. And they feel it far more intensely than even newborns do. Only after she'd thanked him and left the office did she realize that he told her all that in the hopes of dissuading her from having a selective reduction.

"Which one is this?" asked Manda, embarrassed that she didn't recognize her own child beneath all the tape and wires. She should know each one by instinct, shouldn't she? Hadn't she known Rose?

"Baby I," replied the nurse, double-checking the chart. "Infinity."

Manda winced at the name. Infinity was the name of a rich person's car. While Manda was in the recovery room, the news crew from CNN had begged Jake to let them be the first to break the babies' names, and eager to please, he went ahead and named them without her, pulling from the spiral notebook of names they'd been collecting, putting together first and middle names with no rhyme or reason— Brianna Arianna, like a cheap Italian countess, or worse, Kaylee Lea— names that obviously didn't flow, because inside his man's head he had no rhythm at all, just the jangle of his own nervousness. Manda woke to find the television broadcasting these names, she saw them printed in the newspapers and was embarrassed, because names were what you wore forever, and she felt she'd sent her daughters out in tacky rabbit fur coats when they should have been wrapped in mink.

"Would you like to hold her?" asked the nurse. "Just for a minute?"

Manda looked at the nurse in surprise. Why would they let her hold something so easy to break? The nurse took her silence as a yes, and gently untangled the tiny infant from her tubes and lines, lifted her from the bed, and placed her against Manda's chest.

In the rush of hormones returning to her body, Manda had grown a peach-fuzz beard that was now falling out. She watched a few blonde hairs sift upon the baby's forehead like the feathery clippings of her first haircut. Gently, she wiped the fuzz away, and her finger looked enormous against the tiny skull. Rose had been a big baby—nearly ten pounds—and energetic right from the very beginning. This baby moved like she was still underwater, slowly uncurling her fingers and turning her head. She opened her eyes and looked up at Manda. Glittering black fathomless eyes, full of seawater and accusation.

"She's in remarkable shape, considering," said the nurse. "Yesterday, we had to treat her for an intraventricular hemorrhage. The vessels to her brain weren't strong enough to carry the blood and it was leaking out. It happens in such small babies."

"She's all right now?" asked Manda in alarm.

"It was a level two. Not too serious."

This baby's brain is bleeding. What was she supposed to do? What would Pastor Vaughn do?

"It's going to be all right, Mrs. Frank," the nurse crooned with her comforting Island lilt. "These children have made it this far. They are born fighters."

The nurse's voice was so kind and hopeful, Manda didn't know why she started to cry. She just felt so ashamed. Ashamed she hadn't carried them better. Ashamed of all the times early on at home she'd snuck to the bathroom or the kitchen when they'd absolutely forbidden her to get out of bed. Ashamed of her children's littleness. Ashamed of their names. But most of all, she was ashamed of this numbness she felt. She felt like one of those teenage mothers who had given birth in the bathroom of her senior prom and then gone back to the business of slow dancing. She had carried eleven children seven months, even going without solid food herself so that they would have more room to grow; and yet all along, she'd felt like she was doing a very large favor for a friend. If she just got through it, she could give these children to their rightful mother and her life would finally get back to normal. In third grade, her math teacher had tried to teach them the concept of a million. They were to collect bottle caps and put them in a box. By the end of the year, they'd collected only eighty-five thousand. That's not even a tenth of a million, her teacher said, though it seemed so very many. Imagine this many bottle caps times ten. She only had eleven babies, Manda kept telling herself, but eleven might as well have been a million, for all that she could conceptualize it. And now they were out and everyone was looking at them and they were like the idea of a million and she was so ashamed.

Manda let out a single, hoarse sob and all the baby's monitors went off, the beeping pulse oximeter and the CPAPs and the temperature probe. Around her thick white respirator tube, Infinity tried to cry, but it came out just *whoosh-hiss, whooosh-hiss*.

"Take her, quick!" Manda wailed, feeling like she'd been caught trying to shoplift her own daughter. "Something's wrong."

"It's okay." The nurse swooped down and wrapped the child in a blanket to get her skin temperature back up. "She's just responding to you. You need to be strong for these little ones. They feel it when you start to give up."

Manda felt so ashamed.

She was supposed to go home in a few hours, leaving these babies behind, and the worst thing was, she was glad. She was glad to be putting thirty miles between herself and these suffering children, with their flayed maroon skin, and no-chins, and thin, splayed sea-monkey fingers, reaching up to something, reaching out to her. But how could they possibly have a concept of Mother? How, with their bleeding brains?

Manda wiped her nose on the sleeve of her gown and fell back against her wheelchair. Her milk had come in yesterday, and now it ran in two warm streams down the front of her gown and over her belly. She looked around for someone to bring her a diaper.

"Knock, knock." Pastor Vaughn was tapping on a pretend door.

"You can come over, Pastor," said the nurse, who seemed to know the minister well. Jake said Pastor Vaughn had been here every day.

"I brought the getaway car," Pastor Vaughn said, using the joke he'd tried out on his wife this morning. "I'm here to break you out of this joint."

Manda was happy to see him. Now that he was here she could let go and have him take over. He knew what she should be feeling. He would tell her what to do.

"What's wrong, Little Mother?" asked the pastor, seeing her swollen eyes.

"The baby's brain is bleeding," she said.

He peered into the child's isolette, where the baby now lay like a butterfly pinned in place.

"She's so small," Manda whispered.

"It's a shock, I know," said Pastor Vaughn. "But you'll get used to it. Why, Jake and I are old pros already. What's important is that you have come."

He stepped behind Manda's wheelchair and pushed her down the row of babies. "Look," he said, "look how beautiful. They have no idea how special they are, or how many people are praying for them. They are the most famous babies in the world, Manda, and you are their mother. You should be proud of them. And proud of yourself."

He did know what to feel. And she would do her best to feel it too.

"That one looks almost fat," said Manda hopefully.

Pastor Vaughn studied Baby C carefully before calling the head nurse. "Regina," he said, "Does Chase's stomach look normal to you?" He was sure, his smile said to Manda, that it was nothing to worry about.

The NICU nurse frowned over the obvious distention in the child's abdomen, and pulled an army green screen around his isolette. Manda heard her voice call out over the loudspeaker: "Doctor Khenesi to the NICU stat. Doctor Khenesi to the NICU stat."

"What's happening?" Manda asked, all her fears rushing back.

"The doctors are just coming to take a look at little Chase," answered the reverend, trying to keep his voice calm and even.

"What's wrong with him? Is his brain bleeding too?"

"I don't think so, dear. It's probably fine."

Dr. Khenesi, who had charge of neonatology, walked through the door and straight to the screen without even acknowledging Manda's presence. She felt like she should be doing something to help her own child, boiling water or fetching blankets, but she was just their kennel, she remembered, just a rusted old pen.

"Manda, you've trusted God this far," Pastor Vaughn said. "He won't desert you now."

"God doesn't care about these babies," Manda cried, surprising herself, for she had never spoken to her pastor like this. Everyone assumed she must be the most Christian of mothers, or why else put herself through this? But the joke was on them. She didn't always believe in God. Sometimes she thought she even hated God. She simply hadn't been able to decide what to do, and then it was too late. Everyone said it would be fine, but it was *not* fine.

Now Chase's monitors started beeping furiously, touching off the same response in Jake Jr.'s and Devon's and Ember's, and suddenly Manda felt as if every vessel in her own head was breaking. "If God had cared, He never would have given them to me. I never wanted them. Take them back."

Pastor Vaughn took a step away at her vehemence, and she was happy to see it. What could God possibly have been thinking? All she had ever wanted in life was to be left alone. When she was a girl she used to imagine herself a mushroom on the underside of a fallen tree. Away from all her brothers and sisters, she could grow, pale and hidden, shaded, unnoticed. Is she dangerous? Is she poison? people would wonder as they passed by, and because no one could be quite sure, they would leave her alone. Now God had seen fit that she should never be alone again. She would always have this menagerie of sick, helpless, beeping things, and with them the news crews back every birthday and graduation and speeding ticket until the day she died. The lights over Chase Andrew's crib was so bright, just like the camera lights, she thought her face would crack and spew spores all over Intensive Care.

"Manda." Pastor Vaughn spoke sternly to try to snap her out of her fugue. "Manda. What are we by nature?"

The girl stared at him blankly, awash in panic and sorrow.

"Manda," Pastor Vaughn repeated. "What are we by nature?"

"We are part of God's creation, made in the image of God," she mumbled.

"And what does it mean to be created in the image of God?"

Take pity on us, she begged with her eyes. "I feel like my brain is bleeding," she said.

"What does it mean to be created in the image of God?"

"It means that we are free to make choices: to love, to create, to reason, and to live in harmony with creation and with God." Once memorized, the Episcopal catechism, like her multiplication tables, had never deserted her. She repeated it by rote.

"Why then," asked Pastor Vaughn, "do we live apart from God and out of harmony with creation?"

"From the beginning, human beings have misused their freedom and made wrong choices."

"Why do we not use our freedom as we should?"

"Because we rebel against God, and we put ourselves in the place of God." For the first time, Manda thought she saw what he was trying to teach her with this quiz. The monitors were slowly starting to beep at their normal metronome pace, and her heart was calming along with them.

"What help is there for us?" Pastor Vaughn urged, his voice warm and insistent.

Manda looked her pastor in the eye and was very ashamed of all she had said. She didn't want her babies to die. They didn't mean to be unnatural. "Our help is in God," she answered, at last.

"God chose you for a reason, Manda," Pastor Vaughn said. "It is not for us to put ourselves in His place."

The NICU nurse pulled the screen away and laid Chase Andrew flat on a warming table that looked like an overhead projector. Manda perked up when she saw him. "That's a good sign, isn't it?" Manda said. "Having him in the open air like that."

Pastor Vaughn patted her hand. He hadn't the heart to tell her that only those children who require constant critical attention are ever placed on the warming table. Liberation was reserved for only the sickest of the sick.

"Our help is in God," he said.

Manda was scheduled to be discharged at 5 P.M., in time for the live feed of the nightly news. Her mother was working to get her presentable, squeezing a blizzard of Johnson's baby powder onto her unwashed long black hair to absorb the oil, and roughly brushing it through. Manda had been in a hospital gown for so long, she didn't even own maternity clothes the right size, and so she was wearing one of Jake's enormous T-shirts (just riding over her sagging whale's belly) that on the front showed a weight lifter Jesus pumping a cross, and on the back read: *This Blood's for You.* She stretched a pair of leggings over her swollen, varicosed calves and thighs, and slipped a pair of red plastic flip-flops on her feet. Her mother ordered her to sit still while she waved her mascara wand over Manda's stumpy lashes. Jake kissed his wife's cheek and told her she looked beautiful.

Everything seemed dreamlike to Manda in her wheelchair—the nurses lined up along the hallway to wave her good-bye, the bouquets of flowers thrust into her lap from the patients nonterminal enough to stumble out of their rooms, the flashbulb click and ratchet of disposable cameras. Forced roses and baby's breath slipped from her lap as the Chinesey-looking woman who pushed her wheelchair turned corner after corner in this forever hallway. Her mother ran back collecting the stray stems until she soon had a nosegay fit for a bridesmaid.

When at last they reached the main entrance, the wheelchair came to an abrupt stop. There it was, a wall of cameras, reporters and news vans, joyfully weeping women, and obvious Catholics. All the well-wishers of the world, like the faithful waiting Judgment Day in the valley of Jehoshaphat, but instead, here in the parking lot of this teaching hospital in this middle-sized town in Virginia, turning their faces to her, mother of the Frank Eleven. They did not look at Jake, grinning nervously beside her. No, he was like the groom in wedding photos, who fades behind the star in her big, white dress. All eyes were trained on her. All cameras on her. All the love and support and enthusiasm. On her.

"Mrs. Frank, how do you feel about leaving the children behind?"

"Mrs. Frank, how do you answer detractors who have called for your fertility specialist's suspension?"

"*Senora Frank, tu tienes niños favoritos?*"

Jake continued to grin, not knowing who to answer first, while her mother took this opportunity to disappear for a desperately needed Virginia Slim.

"I think I speak for the Franks when I thank each and every one of you for your support and prayers," said Pastor Vaughn. "There is nothing harder on a parent than leaving a child behind."

A thousand questions followed, but Pastor Vaughn sensed Manda's terror and steered her toward the car. With special dispensation, he'd been allowed to park his sherbet orange 1970 VW bus right outside the door for a quicker getaway (as he joked with the hospital officials, getting more of a chuckle from them than from Manda earlier). Kessler Chevrolet had donated a brand-new minivan, but it was still at the dealership, being fitted for eleven car seats.

"Don't you think we should have stayed to talk a while?" Jake asked. "I mean, all those people came just to see us."

"I think we should get your wife off her feet," answered Pastor Vaughn, strapping Manda into the front seat. The belt hit her exactly on her incision, but Pastor Vaughn had been thoughtful enough to pad the strap with an old towel. He looked over at the new mother, who was staring straight ahead, oblivious to the crowd swelling around her.

"Manda, let me tell you a little story," said Pastor Vaughn, backing out and trying not to run over Girl Scout Troop 419. Jake put his head out of the back window and told the girls please, if they wouldn't mind, he needed to get his wife off her feet.

"I once counseled a woman who had twins and decided to give them up for adoption."

"That's terrible," said Jake from the backseat. "I could never do that."

"Well, sometimes it's necessary," answered the pastor, "and in this case the boys found two fine, upstanding homes.

"One child was adopted by a family from Egypt and named Amal. The other one went to a good family from Spain and was named Juan. Many years later, Juan sent a picture to his birth mother, and she wept with joy. She came to see me in my office, and said, 'Pastor Vaughn, this photo of Juan has brought me such happiness! If only I had one of Amal!'

"'Well, ma'am, think of it this way,' I told her." And here he gave Manda, seated beside him, a little wink. "'They're twins. If you've seen Juan, you've seen Amal.'"

When that didn't bring even the weakest smile, Pastor Vaughn knew Manda must be mightily depressed.

The dogs behind the chain-link fence barked furiously when she stepped out of the bus, and for the first time that day, Manda felt a little like her old self. She used to roll cotton and Vaseline into her ears against their constant braying, but today she could have lain down among them and taken a dirt bath in their noise. The dogs climbed one another fighting to get to her face, trying to lick it through the wire. She touched their noses and hot, wet tongues with the flat palm of her hand.

"The house isn't quite ready yet," Jake explained, as if she couldn't tell by the half-hung clapboard and random rolls of roofing paper. Yet, it looked even bigger in person than it had on TV. A hedge of gifts had grown up around the house, presents from well-wishers as far away as Nigeria and Rio de Janeiro, along with cards and letters and bouquets of daisies and mums. Jake helped her up the steep-raked two-by-fours where the front steps would eventually be. "Just wait until you see inside," he said. "It's like a palace."

Rose and old faithful Turbo raced downstairs to meet them, followed by Jake's mother, who seemed chagrined to see no news vans (she'd spent twenty-five dollars that morning getting her hair done). Jake grabbed the dog's collar before she could leap on his wife, but he wasn't so quick with his little girl.

"Mama!" Rose grabbed Manda around the waist, just where the seat belt, though padded, had dug in, but Manda would not let her daughter see she'd hurt her. She bent down and showered her girl's dirty cheeks with kisses.

Oh Rose, Rose, what have we done to you? Manda thought.

Jake had brought the plans to the hospital, but Manda had never seen the inside of her new house. It was a half-finished masterpiece straight out of *Southern Living*. Inside, the kitchen floor waited for its no-wax linoleum, the blue slate counter spanned empty recesses where a paneled dishwasher and refrigerator would be fitted to umbilical pipes. Vast rooms of low-pile beige carpet stretched out before her, broken by archways and track lighting and unpainted French doors. There wasn't a normal light switch in the house; they all ran on dimmers.

"Mama, look!"

Rose ran to the top of the beige-carpeted staircase and slid down on her butt. *Bump. Bump. Bump.* Her grandmother put a swift end to it, for she was not about to put cream on anyone's rug-burnt behind.

"What are we going to do with all this room?" Manda asked, opening a door she thought was a closet, but which was another half-bath.

"Mama, look!"

Rose ran to the top of the stairs and slid down the banister on her stomach.

"Is this the way you behave when your sick mama comes home?" Jake's mother asked her sternly, pulling the little girl's arm. "Go out in the yard and play."

Manda didn't want Rose to go, but the little girl had already raced out into the backyard, which was still a churned swamp of mud and straw.

"There are nails outside," Manda said weakly.

"She's fine," replied Mrs. Frank, lighting a Merit Ultra. "I played with nails all the time when I was a girl."

"I'll watch her," Pastor Vaughn offered. "You look around."

Never in her wildest dreams had Manda imagined such a house for herself. Jake led her upstairs to the babies' rooms, hastily painted and filled with cribs. Four in one, four in another, three in the third. They passed Rose's room, where her single bed had been brought over from the old house along with her Winnie-the-Pooh lamp, whose cord trailed across the floor and found an unplated socket. Down the hall was Manda and Jake's master bedroom, with their old king-sized bed. It had the kind of shelf headboard you could store books in if you so desired, but at the old house it was always full of coffee cups and hunting magazines. With no other furniture around it, Manda noticed every scar and scrape. It looked cheap and forlorn in the new space, like someone's overweight alcoholic uncle who'd come to stay.

"Manda, look at this!" Jake steered her into their master bath, shimmering in inner-ear pink and tan. He hit the switch on the Plexiglas Jacuzzi, which because it had no water in it sounded like a garbage disposal eating a spoon. "Calgon, take me away!" he said.

His mother caught up with them in the bathroom. "I think y'all've done right well for yourselves. I don't guess you could've ever afforded a house like this on your own."

"It's too big," Manda said, backing out into the empty bedroom.

"Won't seem so big," Mrs. Frank said through a drag of her cigarette, "when you've got twelve kids running around in it."

"Mother Frank, you won't be able to smoke around the babies," Manda said. They'd taught her all about secondhand smoke in the hospital, and in her effort to do better, Manda was determined to follow orders.

Jake's mother shot her son a look that said, Hormones. She flicked the butt into the toilet.

"People've been donating clothes," Jake said, opening the walk-in closet to reveal three big moving boxes of shirts and pants. "Some are for the babies, some are for you. And here is the baby-sitting sign-up list the school sent over." Her husband handed over the multi-folded banner, purple with teenage girls names.

"I don't guess we'll need anybody for another few months, until they come home."

"Well, I hate to leave you so soon, baby, but I'd better get my route taken care of. I'll tuck you into bed when I get home."

Manda hadn't even thought that her husband might have to go to work. But of course they still needed to make a living—they had little to live on until the book deals and movie-of-the-week offers came through. She looked at the pair reflected in the mirror over the bathroom sink—her skinny husband, the man who had loved her without interruption since they were both fifteen, and herself, bloated and wide, with her unwashed hair and pregnancy acne, as miserable as she'd ever been in her life. And yet his arms snaked around her as if she were the sexiest bit of ass on the planet and he couldn't get enough of her. He still loved her. Despite everything.

"Are we staying here tonight?" she asked.

"We've got a bed and we've got electricity. I don't see what more we need."

"I can order us up a Domino's," his mother offered.

This is my new home, thought Manda, leaning back against her husband's strong arms. This is the huge place where I'll raise my huge family. We'll all eat huge pizzas and we'll all get huge.

In the backyard, Pastor Vaughn was telling Rose a joke.

"Do you know why monsters were big and hairy and ugly?" he asked. Rose's eyes were huge, and she squirmed as if she could barely wait for the punch line before exploding. "Because if they were small and round and smooth, they'd be M&M's!"

The little girl laughed and laughed and laughed, then she threw herself in his lap and laughed some more.

Manda sent them off one by one. They ate their pizza from greasy paper plates and drank soda out of sweating cans, then Pastor Vaughn took his leave, promising he'd be back tomorrow. Jake's mother stacked the stuffed animal gifts according to color and size, tied all the balloons into one smiling teddy bear zeppelin, which drifted aimlessly through the house on the central air currents; then she went home to wrap her hairdo in toilet paper and hope for better camera luck tomorrow. At ten o'clock, Manda finally convinced her own mother and sister, who had shown up just in time for the pizza, to go home, too. You'll have plenty to do when the babies come home; I can handle Rose for tonight, she said.

When they all left, Manda collected the limp plates and emptied the Coke cans, with their felty jingle of cigarette butts, into the sink. Under the table, Rose had fallen asleep on the soft pillow of

Turbo's stomach, her head rising and falling with every breath the old dog took. Jake wouldn't be back for another hour at least. No cameras peered through the window. Manda was finally alone.

It felt wrong somehow for them to have moved into this big empty house, just she and Jake and Rose, the same family she had before she went into the hospital. What entitled them to all this space? What were they without the babies? Just people who barely made their mortgage every month, who drove a bad truck, who enjoyed NASCAR and rabbit hunting. This was not her house, Manda thought. This house belonged to the babies, and she was a trespasser here. She lumbered slowly through the house again, turning up the lights, taking in all that was done and undone. It was as if Francis Marvel had taken inventory of all he would have liked in a house and tackled that first, so that there was a sound system but no dishwasher, track lighting but no bathroom door. In the unfinished dining room, she found the thermostat and cut off the frigid central air. Then she flung wide the front door to let in the late-summer night, now full of the sound of crickets and pond frogs. There was a swamp not far away where she used to go frog gigging as a girl, she and her brothers and the boys up the road, taking their burlap sacks and long poles with two nails duct-taped to the end, fixing their flashlight beams on sloe-eyed frogs in the muddy swamp grass, who knew, with the falling of the shadow, that their time was up. The great-great-great-grandchildren of those frogs called now, Welcome home. And the crickets called, and the ticks in their underbrush and the chiggers in her soil. Welcome home, Manda. Welcome home.

But she was a trespasser, and this was not her home. She turned back to make sure Rose still slept, and she let herself out through the garage, shuffling across the yard to her real home. The dogs in their cages whined as she passed by and she heard them stand and thump their tails against their plywood house. Beyond the dog pen, the old shack sat still and dark, only its Depression glass windows winking in the reflected moonlight. No one had bothered to lock the back door, even though most of their things were still inside. She turned the knob and let herself in, leaving off the lights, just feeling her way around like she had many a night when she snuck in drunk and didn't want to get it from her daddy. Manda took a deep, private, homecoming breath, letting the place settle into her and work on her confused sense of direction.

Now, this close, pungent place—this smelled like home to her. Generations of laborers and hired hands had rocked back in their dinner chairs, and passed out drunk on the rugs until their sweat just seeped into the wood walls and floors, leaving a cuss-masculine smell that all the Murphy's oil soap in the world wouldn't get out. Manda felt her way to the small kitchen and ran herself a mason jar of water, taking two of the Percocet they'd sent her home with. Her belly still screamed from the surgery and she still felt nearly as heavy as she had before she gave birth.

There was a time when six children, two parents, and a grandmother lived in this shack. As the youngest, Manda slept wherever there was space—sometimes just on sofa cushions on the living room floor, if her sisters had friends over. Now her two oldest brothers were in jail and the youngest in the military. One sister lived nearby and the other had moved to Raleigh when her husband repeatedly violated his restraining order. Both had growing families of their own. That's what struck Manda as so odd about this whole thing. If she'd spaced her children out and had eleven babies in eleven years, she would have been no better than her own mother and sisters: irresponsible, a welfare cheat, another bit of Sawdust Lane white trash. But as luck would have it, she'd had them all at once, and now she was, overnight, middle-class. And respectable. She lived in a house built by a man from one of the town's oldest families. She was cared for by a respectable minister of a respectable church. The whole town, who before would reflexively lock their car doors at the sight of a member of her family, was treating her like a favorite niece. She didn't know whether to be grateful or to spit on them all.

The Percocet was beginning to steal away a bit of the pain, and Manda settled herself in her father's old recliner. She pulled the brown and blue pilly afghan over her legs and let her heavy head fall back. It wasn't morphine, but it would do. Instead of the field, she felt a clearing open up, just a break in the woods, but someplace to run, like the place she used to run as a girl, down by the rushing creek, with its diamond mica banks and six-pack plastic logjams. In this primeval opiate forest, Manda was thin again, and racing across the red-barked pine tree that had fallen over the creek—her dog Turbo running ahead, impatient for her to cross. Manda stopped to taunt the churning, spitting water below, lifting one foot and hopping, her balance perfect, her body hawk-light. Here in the center of the log, she could say no to both worlds: to Turbo urging her forward—quick—to the other side; to her mother who from far, far away was ringing the bell she always used to call the kids in to supper as if they were wayward cattle and not her own flesh and blood. We're running away, Manda shouted to the woods; I'm not coming home for supper. But even half a mile away, she could still hear the dinner bell, which was never disobeyed without a whipping, and could picture her sharp, carcinogenic mother, the white fat on her upper arm rippling with the rhythm of that bell. Here, Bobby, Nina, Benny, Randy, Manda, Sue. Come home, I say.

Manda opened her eyes in her dark kitchen, and still the bell was ringing. She pushed off the afghan and stumbled onto the front porch, from which the sound seemed to originate, but when she got there, all was quiet. Just crickets and frogs, and the almost subaudible hum of her new house, with all its window lights blazing. Then, there it was again. The bell. And then Rose tiny in the lighted maw of the new house front door, crying, "Mama! Mama! The phone is ringing. Where are you?"

Manda shook her head hard to try and clear the Percocet fuzz and walked toward her daughter. Together it took them another twenty rings to find where the phone was hidden (in the utility room, behind the door) and answer it. It was the hospital, suggesting Mr. and Mrs. Frank come back right away. Things had not gone well with little Chase Andrew, they were sorry to say, and despite the best efforts of their seasoned professional staff, the weakest of Manda's eleven children had died.

CHAPTER FIVE

Everyone suffers with the death of a child, and Three Chimneys went into deep mourning at the sad news from Charlottesville. Citizens wore their Frank Eleven T-shirts with a new solemnity, and some especially sensitive ladies of the town stitched halos of gold thread over the tenth line-drawn child's head. The death of young Chase Andrew was an occasion for tear-streaked faces and much coming together at Three Chimneys Junior High School, where many of the girls who had signed up for baby-sitting felt especially stricken. They exchanged stories of others they knew who had died young; some told of shivering at church cemeteries before tiny tombstones whose birth and death dates fell inside the same week, while others thought it a blessing if it meant the child would no longer be in pain.

While the girls absorbed the full impact of the town's tragedy, the boys of Three Chimneys Junior High were not so evolved. They had felt the whole eleven-children thing to be as repugnant as walking in on their mothers in the bathtub, and were looking for any excuse to ridicule the sentimentality of the young ladies of their acquaintance. They made jokes like "One down, ten to go," and "Litters are for dogs and cats, not people." The girls were disgusted with the boys and told them to grow up. The boys stuffed backpacks under their shirts and waddled down the hall in a cruel imitation of poor grieving Amanda Frank.

Polly Marvel was among the crowd of distraught young women who had collected in the main hall by the auditorium to plan a candlelight vigil down School Street that night. Polly was deeply occupied with thoughts on the precariousness of her own childhood, for Manda's son was the first person she knew who had died at a younger age than she was now. It was all so fleeting, wasn't it? Polly thought, feeling adult and resigned, even as she mourned the loss of her own innocence. Childhood was not a safe place.

"Babies die all the time in Africa," Drew Powell sniggered as he walked past. "I don't see any of you crying over them."

"You're such a prick, Drew," Polly called after him. "You wouldn't know an emotion if it bit you in the ass."

"Perhaps we should watch our language, Miss Marvel," said a familiar voice behind her. "We wouldn't want our principal getting his nuts in a knot."

Polly spun to see Mr. March coming out of the men's faculty bathroom they had been unintentionally blocking. His round communist glasses were still misted with water from where he'd held them under the sink, and the short hair around his ears was damp.

"Aren't you due in class?"

It was a minute to two, and Mr. March was right. The other girls drifted away to their own classes, and the boys raced off to gym or shop or whatever boy-thing was next. Polly found herself alone, with no other choice but to walk beside Mr. March all the way upstairs.

"Isn't it just devastating?" she asked, after self-consciously adjusting the distance between them. She didn't want to hug the wall, but neither could she imagine her bare arm brushing that of his blue cotton blazer.

"Isn't what devastating?" Mr. March asked.

"Poor Chase Andrew," Polly replied, shocked that he had not heard the news. "One of the Frank Eleven. He died last night."

"Oh," said Mr. March. "You knew him well?"

"Well, no," Polly answered reluctantly. "Not well. He was only eight days old."

"But you'd been to see him in the hospital?"

"We were planning to, before . . . ," she replied, feeling a little foolish. "The Franks are our neighbors."

"Oh. Neighbors," said Mr. March.

"I just can't think of a single thing more tragic than the death of a child," Polly said, and was pleasantly surprised to hear the quiver in her voice. She'd never thought much about it, but, indeed, what could be more disturbing than a young life over before it began?

"Miss Marvel, you seem like a remarkably intelligent young lady." They had stopped outside his classroom door, and Mr. March looked down at her softly. "But until you learn to think for yourself, I fear you will remain remarkably dull."

"I don't see what's so wrong about mourning the death of a child," she said, stung, yet determined to hold on to her new-found sorrow.

"There is nothing wrong with it," said Mr. March. "So long as one does not take too much enjoyment in one's own grief. Why should the death of a child be more tragic than the death of an adult? Babies have no personalities of their own. At that age, they can be nothing more than the sum of their parents' projections. Mourning that is quite narcissistic, don't you think?"

"But babies are so innocent," insisted Polly. "They have their whole lives ahead."

"Yet how much sadder to lose someone you've grown to care about. If death should take you, with all your life experiences and potential, we should all mourn greatly, but don't ask me to get worked up over a baby.

"The concept of childhood is a recent phenomenon, Miss Marvel," Mr. March explained, with his hand on the door. "Before the nineteenth century, children were treated with far less sentiment and indulgence than they are today. They were dressed as adults and spoken to as adults, and given adult responsibilities. This cocoon of childhood is your enslavement, Miss Marvel, imposed on you by society. It is a construct, nothing more. Now, if you'll excuse me, I have a pop quiz to administer." He smiled at her over his shoulder as he disappeared inside. "Next period, I'll expect you to act surprised."

Polly watched him through the glass pane beside the door, before slowly drifting down the hall to algebra. She slipped in under the glare of Mrs. Knowles, and immediately Bethany passed her a note. *I saw you talking. Way to go. Tell your mom you're coming over to do homework, and we'll go to the vigil together.* To which Polly wrote back. *Bethany, get a grip. A vigil is just so remarkably dull.*

After evening milking and dinner, Polly climbed upon her Schwinn three-speed and pedaled back toward town. It was her favorite time of day, when the sun was just another stratum in the purple and pink sedimentary sky. She stood up on her bike, pedaling against the last exhalations of honeysuckle folding up for the night and the sweet cucumber smell of neighbors' newly mown grass. Snakehill Road wove in and out of woods, tall overhanging spruce trees canopied the road to chill her until she burst back out into the warmth of the setting sun. She raced up the rolling hills and flew down again, her wheaten hair streaming behind her, her shadow, with its night-promise pumping angles, almost beautiful, she thought, keeping easy pace beside her.

Polly took the two miles into town easily, slowing only when she was just on the outskirts, when the hay fields gave way to a final stretch of evergreen and sapling oaks that marked the last bit of wilderness before Snakehill straightened into School Street. At the white paper box and a red reflector on a stick marking a hidden driveway, she squeezed her handle brakes and coasted to a halt. A packed-dirt driveway growing a spine of scrub grass led about an eighth of a mile to a small frame ranch house. This was where he lived, she knew, from the police incident a few years back involving some failing football players who had drunkenly vandalized his house in retaliation for their bad grades. They were punished with a summer of community service, while the PTA volunteered to paint over the word JEW-FAGGOT that dripped from his doorway like lamb's blood. Before she really knew who he was, she would sometimes see a thin, dark-haired man jogging this way, his washed-to-the-point-of-transparency Columbia University T-shirt clinging to his narrow chest, his lean, hairy legs disappearing into the scantiest of terry gym shorts. He would turn into this driveway like a rabbit dashing for cover and vanish into the woods, only the rough echo of flying gravel serving to prove his existence. Polly sat for a moment on her bike, listening for those short, compact strides coming toward her through the woods. It was about this time of day she used to see him, back when he barely registered as anything other than an "older person" and thus unworthy of further scrutiny. How many opportunities had she wasted as a stupid kid, she thought, riding past his house with nothing more on her mind than an ice cream at Snow White's or a slumber party at Bethany's? If she'd only known then what sort of man he was, she would have thrown over all those childish things and ridden beside him on his nightly jog, his personal timekeeper and cheerleader and helpmeet. If only she had known.

She waited by his tubular paper box a good ten minutes, as the shadows lengthened around her and made her wish for a sweater. She memorized every nick in the white plastic box, dirty with years of newsprint and purple with bird droppings. Mr. March didn't seem to have a mailbox, which struck her as odd, for only a few people in town took boxes at the post office, and they were the sorts that seemed always to be addicted to record clubs or involved in mail-me-a-dollar, I'll-tell-you-how-to-make-a-million scams. Polly waited and listened, shivering in the twilight, until she saw the accusatory headlights of an approaching car taking the curve of Snakehill Road. Polly swiftly pushed off on her bike, pedaling furiously, trying to put as much distance between herself and the driveway as she could. If only he would jog out of the woods right now, she thought, he would catch just the glimpse of her disappearing like a fleet young nymph—a rush of hair, a flurry of limbs. Would that not be more enchanting anyway? Was not glimpsed-in-flight more seductive than doggedly-waiting-by-paper-box?

But what if that was *his* car, she suddenly thought, whose distant high beams swept over her like a prison searchlight? What if he was about to turn into his house when he saw her riding ahead and, almost against his will, felt compelled to follow her, his machine put in service of pursuing a nymph, like Apollo the god chasing a virgin until she dropped of exhaustion and succumbed? The feeling that he was there, behind the darkened windshield of his car, his eyes, like his headlights, fixed on her with a mute intensity of desire, came so strong upon Polly that when she was finally forced to stop at the town's only traffic light, she was almost terrified to turn around. She struggled to catch her breath, for she could never remember racing so hard, and she did not want to appear ragged and overwhelmed when he caught up to her. The headlights were hot upon her now, but even as the car approached, Polly knew her hopes were dashed. It was no whiny idle of a Carmen Ghia behind her, but the wide, boxy backfire of Jake Frank's mother's ten-year-old banana yellow Cadillac. No swarthy face and burning eyes behind the windshield, only a dentured smile and a friendly wave, as the car pulled through the light, leaving her behind. Polly waved a disappointed hello back to the older woman.

Trembling with exhaustion and thwarted adrenaline, Polly wearily pushed off once more, headed now toward her friend Bethany's house on Polk Street, at the corner of School. She noticed that the twenty-two trees had gone into mourning for Chase Andrew Frank—the pink and blue ribbons overfitted with deep purple sashes—but she had completely forgotten about the candle-light vigil until she saw it advancing upon her down the street. Young girls dressed in school colors, older women in comfortable slacks. The news crews walked backward filming the procession, capturing for the nation the beatific candlelit faces of the girls from Three Chimneys Junior High in front, their large blue eyes glisten-ing with tears, their hands gracefully cupped around the flames. Someone behind them was playing a flute and someone else was asking Chase Andrew in a warbling treble "Did you ever know that you're my hero?"—while others hesitantly joined in. If she didn't know what the procession was for, she might very well have been moved by the sheer simple fairylike beauty of the yellow flames. All this for a baby who weighed not even two pounds, who had barely drawn a week's worth of breath. Everyone was made serious and im-portant by candlelight; even the girls her age seemed to approach a more adult understanding of sadness merely by being removed from their native electric element. She picked Pastor Vaughn out of the crowd, touching his candle like a chaste kiss to a famous blonde reporter whom Polly recognized from when she used to watch television. She saw the weatherman from Channel 5 who had been at school the other day.

Mrs. Frank's Cadillac pulled off to the side of the road, and the grieving grandmother melted into the procession, a dozen arms reaching out to pull her in. Most of the town was here, and many strangers, all joined in one grief, solemnly advancing as one extended family down School Street. Yet as they approached, weeping, singing, holding laminated newspaper photos of little Chase Andrew, Polly couldn't shake the thought that they looked as much like a militia of colonial soldiers, evenly spaced ten across, their legions stretching back for miles. She half-expected the first row to drop to its knees, take aim, and fire, before being mowed down and replaced by the brave, fatalistic column behind it.

Bethany was standing outside on her front lawn watching the procession when Polly pulled up.

"Man, that's something, isn't it?" she asked.

"It's so predictable," answered Polly, brushing her sweaty bangs off her forehead. She leaned her bike against Bethany's front porch and waited impatiently to go inside. After another minute, Bethany tore herself away and closed the door, though the parade of candlelight went on outside the living room window. Polly reached over and drew the shade.

"Where are your parents?" Polly asked, drifting toward the huge, modern kitchen and the gleaming double-door refrigerator where the Frasers kept their three-liter sodas. Bethany rooted through the cupboards for glasses and a bag of Cheetos.

"Some reporters wanted to interview them. They're down at Snow White."

Polly rolled her eyes. Sure, Bethany's father was a doctor, but he was a hand surgeon and not at all involved in female matters. Her mom worked for the School Board, so Polly couldn't imagine what she might have to say about the Franks. The soda she was pouring foamed over the glass and onto the countertop. Don't worry, Bethany waved her off, her mom would clean it up later.

"They were saying at school that Manda and Jake had sex eleven times in one night and that's how they ended up with eleven babies," Bethany said. "My cousin was in the same grade as Manda. She said she was a slut."

"That's not how it works," Polly answered. "You don't need to have sex eleven separate times."

"I know who you'd like to have sex with eleven times." Bethany laughed.

"Shut up."

"I saw you with him outside of class. What were you talking about?"

"Stuff," replied Polly evasively. "Slavery."

"Polly." Bethany sighed. "If you want him to take you seriously, you can't waste moments like that on slavery. You have to ask him questions. Find out what he's looking for in a woman."

"He said the concept of childhood is manufactured," she replied. "That we're enslaved by it."

"Tell me about it," answered Bethany. "They expect us to buy all these clothes and CDs, but they won't let us drive to the mall to get them. If I'm old enough to have a credit card, I'm old enough to drive."

The telephone rang. "Maybe that's him," Bethany teased, lifting the receiver. "He's tracked you down. Hey, get this . . ." Bethany held out the receiver and a tinny voice spoke into Polly's ear.

"This is Governor Adams Brooke," said the pretaped message. "In the words of the undying patriot Thomas Jefferson, 'Farmers are the true representatives of the great American interest and are alone to be relied on for expressing the proper American sentiments.' As you know, I was born and raised on a small family farm in rural—"

"Governor Brooke," yelled Polly into the receiver, "what's your position on politicians invading our privacy?"

Bethany grabbed the phone from her friend and spoke into it. "Governor Brooke, what is your position on students dating their teachers?" She laughed. Polly shrieked and quickly pulled the receiver back.

"Governor Brooke, if you're elected, will you let my mother come to the White House and have sex with you?"

"Governor Brooke," cried Bethany, "ditch the toupee, you're not fooling anybody!"

"Abolish childhood!" yelled Polly. "Let my people go!"

"Yeah!" yelled Bethany. "Let my people go! Let my people go!"

". . . *corporations and give America back to the people. And so on November 3, tell Washington that Family Matters.*"

"Come on, let's go upstairs," said Bethany, unceremoniously dropping the receiver on the floor. Polly wondered if the governor was on an endless loop and would go on throughout the night, patiently soliciting the votes of Bethany's microwave and garbage disposal.

The girls took their snacks upstairs to Bethany's rock-star-wallpapered bedroom. Since Polly was not allowed to have cable television, or a CD player, or a computer to download MP3s, she was utterly dependent on Bethany for her musical education, and knew all these bare-chested young men by reputation only. Today's *chico caliente* was a twenty-year-old Cuban pop singer Bethany had discovered on Internet Radio Havana. As with so many inseparable teenagers, Polly and Bethany's friendship was in part founded on a certain knowledge of superiority each had over the other, and a certain amount of charitable pity for the other's failings. Of the two, Bethany certainly knew herself to be the cuter. She had dark brown ringlets that she wore stylishly clipped around her head, and a T-zone full of winning freckles. She had not been without a boyfriend since sixth grade, the grade when precocious girls first got boyfriends, and if some of her earlier experiments had proven themselves remedial by middle school, Polly's virtue was that she did not throw them in her face.

If Bethany was the more experienced romantically, she couldn't deny that Polly's parents' divorce had given her friend a sophistication and disaffection that she, the unfortunate daughter of parents who liked each other, could never hope to achieve. She had to acknowledge that a new glamour had settled over Polly, despite the best efforts of her mother, who wouldn't even let her daughter wear Lycra, but cruelly sent her out into the world dressed like a Pilgrim, in horrible home-made clothes. Bethany knew how Polly suffered, and how she had grown up, seemingly overnight, when the news spread around town of her father's affair with his secretary. Polly had returned to school with a secret knowledge of what boys might grow up to become—not ro-mantic lovers, good husbands, and kind fathers, but cheaters and liars and infinite disappointment. Obviously, Mr. March had picked up on her new aura of adulthood. Bethany thought only a blind man couldn't see how hot he was for her, and how they were meant to be together.

Polly pulled her reading assignment from her backpack, but Bethany had other plans before getting down to work. She reached between her mattress and box spring, retrieved a brown paper bag, and set it on her quilted bedspread. Polly could tell from the size and shape that it was a magazine, but she gasped in horror when Bethany revealed which one.

"Oh my God! Where did you get that?" she squealed.

"I wouldn't be caught dead buying it around here, that's for sure," Bethany giggled, blushing. "I got it last time we went to Charlottesville."

On the cover was a petal-fresh girl frothed with tulle and raw silk, the blush high on her cheekbones, her face half-hidden behind a bouquet of fat pink peonies. They stared at the cover for a long time, neither daring to reach out to flip it open.

"Put it away," Polly said at last.

"No, we have to look at it," answered her friend. "It cost me four ninety-five."

Polly couldn't explain the feeling at the pit of her stomach as she turned the pink and pearl pages of *Bride* magazine. It was Sep-tember's issue and young women were shot romping through mown hay fields, summer's last rays igniting their windswept veils, rakish men in tuxedos chasing gamely after them. This is not for me, Polly thought queasily, I should not be looking at this, her fingers reaching out involuntarily to reveal the next spread of carefree girls laughing into blue skies. She paused at a soft-focus picture of a young woman in a claw-footed bathtub. Her head was thrown back and her hands caressed her tanned, athletic calf, while a thousand candles burned around her. It accompanied an article titled: "How to Make Your First Night One to Remember."

"First night," Polly snorted. "No one is a virgin when they get married anymore."

"Sex is different on your wedding night," Bethany explained. "It's like starting all over again."

They devoutly flipped through every page of the thick magazine, including the advertisements—especially the advertisements, because that's where the prettiest dresses were. They were in absolute agreement about what sort of gowns they loathed (anything with puffed sleeves, anything with long sleeves, anything with too much lace), but they differed in their preferences. Bethany favored an elegant sheath with spaghetti straps, whereas Polly secretly wanted the works: tight bodice, huge skirt with train, a veil that hid her completely. If she were ever dumb enough to do it, she wanted there to be no mistake or suspicion of halfheartedness on her part. No boring bridesmaid dress ordered in white to save money, or short skirt, or modern *hat* perched ridiculously on her head. If she were ever dumb enough to get married, she would make sure the whole world knew she meant it, knew there was no turning back. But who cared what sort of dress she liked, Polly thought, shaking herself out of the pink, perfumed spell cast by the magazine. She intended to take many lovers, and who knew, perhaps even have a child out of wedlock, but as for being saddled with a husband for the rest of her life . . . well, no dress was worth that.

"Do you think if Scott and I are still going together by senior year, he'll ask me to marry him?" Bethany asked.

"Probably," Polly said, giving the answer she knew her friend wanted. "Would you say yes?"

"Probably," Bethany replied. "But have a four-year engagement through college. What would you say if Mr. March asked?"

"God! He would never ask."

"But what if he did?"

Polly was saved from answering by the sound of the door slamming downstairs. Bethany's parents were home, and the girls shoved the magazine deep under the mattress. As Bethany quickly scattered schoolbooks around the bed, Polly was left with the same guilty hangover she got whenever Bethany convinced her to try on clothes at the mall she knew her mother would never allow her to buy.

"Bethany Renee Fraser, march yourself downstairs and clean up that soda," Bethany's mother said, thrusting her head into the room, where the girls sat studiously bent over their books. "Hello, Polly."

"Hello, Mrs. Fraser," Polly answered politely.

"My daughter needs to learn I'm not running a maid service."

Bethany sighed dramatically and followed her mother downstairs, leaving Polly to wait in her room. As much as she would have liked to reach under the mattress for the magazine, she felt looking at it now would be tantamount to drinking alone. She turned instead to the limpid-eyed rock stars on the wall, their chests free of hair, their lips glistening as if just licked. She knew other girls found them handsome, but she never understood why. These boys had no character, no torment. She wanted a dark, sardonic sort of man, one who had been wounded deeply and needed someone to teach him to love again. She wanted a man whose problems made hers utterly insignificant. These boys were for children, and she wanted someone who refused to think of her as a child.

Oh, Mr. March, thought Polly woefully. What did she even know about him? Her eyes slid to Bethany's desktop computer, decorated with glitter stickers and a blue-haired pop-eyed troll. Before Bethany's parents bought a filtering package, the girls had once dared to type in the word "fuck," learning firsthand the terror of pornographic screens popping up like some perverse Whack-a-Mole. But now, logging onto Bethany's AOL account, Polly was interested in something else entirely. She glanced over her shoulder, and furtively typed in a darker secret.

Harvey March. She didn't know what she expected to find on him. He wasn't famous, after all, he'd never won anything so far as she knew, hadn't written anything or been elected to office, yet here she was tapping the floorboards of cyberspace, looking for a secret cache, some divot where a key might have casually fallen that would unlock the secret to his personality. She clicked hopefully as a handful of genealogy sites came up—some other Harvey March born in 1871 and married to some Ellen Brewster in 1903. She knew he'd taught at other schools and thought she might find his face in a group photograph as sponsor of a debate team or an old syllabus suspended like a fly in an abandoned web. He took up such a large part of her life, she was troubled to find nothing existed about him in the greater digital world. It made her feel small to care so deeply about a man no one else seemed to see.

The name Stanley March appeared over and over again in her search, however, and for lack of better results, Polly finally clicked on him. Stanley March, sixties radical (she discovered), had fled America and the draft under suspicion of planting a bomb at the uptown campus of the City College of New York. An adjunct professor, he had left behind a wife and ten-year-old son, Harvey Dylan March, then living in Montclair, New Jersey. When President Ford pardoned the draft dodgers in 1975, Stanley March elected to remain in Canada, where he had begun a new family, overlooking the small detail that he had never officially divorced his first wife. After challenging the bigamy statutes and serving three years in an Ontario minimum security prison, he went on to write many books about politics, the inequalities of the American legal system, and the impending death of capitalism, most published by Freak Tank Press (whose online catalog, Polly learned, contained such other titles as *Home Brew LSD*, *Grow Your Own Machine Gun*, and *The Cheney Diaries*). Other links gave variations on the story of this man whom she could only assume was her Mr. March's father, an assumption confirmed when she finally saw a picture of the radical Stanley, looking for all the world like her teacher, if Mr. March had lost all his hair and grown a wolfish beard.

Polly sat with this unexpected information for a long time. What she would have given to have a radical parent, one who believed in something so completely he was willing to give up everything the world thought important to follow his ideals. Mr. March was so lucky, she thought, to have the spirit of resistance coursing through his veins, to have rebellion genetically billeted in the double helix of his DNA. Like most other kids her age, Polly had only a gauzy, pop-beaded conception of the sixties as a paradise lost of teenage supremacy, one long muddy Woodstock stretching from 1964 through 1972. To have a freedom-fighting parent, one too busy burning the flag to police your artificial preservative consumption, seemed the pinnacle of romantic freedom to her. No wonder Mr. March was so cool. She didn't stand a chance.

"I hope you're going to make me your maid of honor," said Bethany, suddenly appearing in the doorway with two fresh glasses of soda. Polly swiftly closed the window on the computer screen.

"Just one word of advice," said her friend, smiling. "No matter how great he is—don't let him do you eleven times."

CHAPTER SIX

The old glass thermometer on the side of St. Barnabas Church read 92 degrees the Saturday morning of Chase Andrew Frank's funeral. It was only ten o'clock, but it felt like deep-summer midday, and the paper funeral home fans cut the air inside the church like the lifting and settling of a swarm of locusts upon a field. If the fire marshal, who was in attendance, had been a man who followed the letter of the law, he would have escorted half of the exit-blocking congregation outside; but he himself was a father of four, and would not have dreamed of denying these fine grieving people the balm of a funeral service.

The camera crews had set up before anyone else arrived, and busied themselves in the recording of the town's grief. They panned the nearly three-hundred-year-old church, taking in the clear bubbled blown-glass windows, with their chipped, black windowsills; the mahogany pews, sticky with decades of tung oil; the brass plaques hung about the walls remembering departed benefactors of St. Barnabas— the inevitable Randolphs, and a Custis or two; many, many Colonel thises and Major thats, C.S.A. It was a typically spartan, postcolonial church, with little to catch a camera's eye, and the film crews from up North found themselves, by default, focusing in on the pastel paper funeral home fans—a doe-eyed Jesus gathering to himself all the little children—to provide the expected flavor of a Southern funeral.

On a pedestal, to the right of the altar, sat a small, shiny white coffin, like a cross section of a wedding limo, its lid propped open. The last of the congregation filed past to kiss the papery purple cheek of the tiny child, whose face had been unnaturally plumped with embalming fluid. The baby's parents and oldest sister, Rose, sat in the front row, the first time they'd ever earned the right to sit so close to the pulpit, a privilege usually reserved for the oldest and wealthiest families in town. The cameras caught Manda handing Rose a miniature golf–sized half-pencil and church bulletin with which to entertain herself throughout the service. They caught Jake red-eyed and haggard, as if he had not slept for days.

When the organ music paused and Pastor Vaughn walked in, the congregation rose to its feet. Pastor Vaughn made no opening remark, but began to read immediately from the Book of Common Prayer, 1928, the Liturgy for the Burial of a Child.

"I am the resurrection and the life, saith the Lord." Pastor Vaughn's voice boomed through the church. Not only was the sermon being recorded, it was being broadcast to well-wishers fifty deep in the churchyard outside. "He that believeth in me, though he were dead, yet shall he live: and whosoever believeth in me, shall never die."

The camera lights were an additional few suns on the already sweltering cleric, and he saw that their rays had caused a shrub of microphones to take root upon his pulpit. Pastor Vaughn had the strangest feeling of being disembodied before this enormous crowd, half of whom he did not recognize, another third of whom had not set foot in his church in decades. He had gotten used to crowds at the hospital, and crowds in town, but the crowd today inside his own sanctuary made him feel little better than a televangelist, conducting a funeral before the eyes of millions. He should never have allowed the cameras in here, he thought, even as he automatically recited the liturgy. "Jesus called them unto Him and said, Suffer the little children to come unto me, and forbid them not: for of such is the kingdom of God. He shall feed his flock like a shepherd: He shall gather the lambs with His arms, and carry them in His bosom. Let us pray."

The congregation bowed their heads and joined in. "The Lord is my shepherd . . ."

It was not often Leland Vaughn was expected to perform a burial for a child. In his thirty years, he remembered burying no more than five or six children, not counting the wayward teenagers who crashed their cars on prom night or drunkenly went swimming in swift currents. He had blessed many more silent blue stillbirths, but once a child took a breath in Three Chimneys, it seemed determined to stay here. Now, the familiarity of the psalm comforted him, and by the time he had moved on to "I will lift up mine eyes unto the hills," Leland had regained his composure. What harm did the cameras do, anyway? he thought. He could think of them as exploitative, or he could think of them as the means by which new neighbors joined the Three Chimneys community. The whole world had rallied around Manda and Jake when the babies were born, and the whole world might be expected to mourn the loss of their poor lamb.

"I know a good priest should never admit his own quaking terror," said Pastor Vaughn, carefully marking his place in the hymnal and looking out over his enormous congregation, "but I confess to you here today, that is all I felt that day back in January when our dear sister Amanda came to me for help. 'My doctor says there are eleven babies in my belly, Pastor Vaughn,' she'd said, sitting here beside me on a morning a good deal cooler than this one, I can tell you. Eleven babies." The priest shook his head in disbelief. "If she had said two or three, there would be no problem, right? But eleven? No one in the history of the world had ever given birth to eleven living infants.

"She said her doctors had advised a selective reduction, which is a medical term for aborting some children so that others might thrive. It is not uncommon in situations like this, and it seemed the best solution for poor Manda. I asked her to look into her heart and see if she could live with that decision, knowing it was best for her health, best for the surviving babies. 'But how do I choose among them, Pastor?' Manda asked me. 'How do I play God?'"

"I sent Manda home, and that night I walked down to my old chimney to pray. 'Lord,' I said, 'who is playing God in this case? The doctors for having coaxed eleven seeds to sprout? Or Manda for picking who shall live and who shall die? Do I even have the right to advise her? What is Your will, oh Lord?

"I sat for a long time down by my old chimney, where most of you know I do my best thinking. I thought of a thousand arguments for keeping the children and a thousand against. And then, after many hours of back-and-forth, a passage from the Book of Ecclesiastes came into my mind, laying a calming hand over what had become a tempest of indecision. It was from Chapter Eleven, verses five and six, and it goes: 'As thou knowest not what is the way of the spirit, nor how the bones do grow in the womb of her that is with child: even so thou knowest not the works of God who maketh all.

"'In the morning sow thy seed, and in the evening withhold not thine hand: for thou knowest not whether shall prosper, either this or that, or whether they both shall be alike good.'

Pastor Vaughn took off his glasses and wiped them carefully with a cloth. The crowded church was hot and heavy and he was tired just in remembering his struggle of that night. "My great-grandmother buried six children of her own," he said at last. "It was a time when parents tried not to get too attached to their young, for back in those days, children were sown back into the earth like fistfuls of corn. My great-grandmother lost two to influenza, one to diphtheria, two were born dead, and the last came, like our poor, dear Chase, too early; sent, so it seemed, by his lost brothers and sisters to fetch their mother home with him.

"Yet before she accompanied her final child to Paradise, my great-grandmother raised five other thriving, brawling, good-hearted children, one of whom grew up to be my grandfather and great inspiration, the former Pastor Vaughn. That made eleven children. Five on earth, six given back. My great-grandmother knew something that we seem to have forgotten: It is not up to us to decide who shall live and who shall die. That decision lies solely with God. It is up to God to play God.

"So then what does a parent owe a child?" asked Leland Vaughn. "I thought long and hard about that, down by the old chimney. Perhaps you'd say he owes his child a roof over his head. Food in his stomach. Some might say a good education. For those of you who grew up during the Depression, you might think you owe it to your child to teach thrift, so that she never struggles and suffers want as you did; those who became parents in the fifties and sixties might have thought all a child required was love and an allowance ample enough to afford a Beatles album. Perhaps a parent today decides he owes his daughter organic vegetables and SAT preparation courses and a well-maintained trust fund. Give and give and give unto your child until you can give no more, says our society. Give and you shall receive.

"But I tell you here today, friends and family, as it says in the Book of Ecclesiastes: All is vanity. The things I mentioned are what we do for our children out of affection, or guilt, or out of habit. As I stand here today, and at the risk of being politically unpopular, I declare there is only one thing we absolutely owe our children, only one debt we cannot dodge. My great-grandmother understood it. And Amanda Frank understood it. Both discharged their duty faithfully, and gave their children the one thing a child might honestly demand of its parent. Life.

"Life. That's all."

The room was silent except for the whir of cameras and a few sniffling congregants. The heat and the light had nearly transported Pastor Vaughn, and he felt as light-headed as he had that night back in January, when he had driven to Amanda's old sharecropping shack and promised his help and the help of the whole community if she decided to take a chance on life. He was unsure if his advice was right or wrong, but he knew one thing—he was in no better position to decide than she was.

"I know each and every one of you grieves for poor Chase Andrew, so briefly our neighbor here in Three Chimneys. Since his death, I have asked myself a hundred times, Should I have given his mother different advice, should we have done what the doctors thought best? But then I remember that only God knows who shall prosper, either this or that, and that all of our attempts to understand His will or anticipate it or explain it—all are vanity. We can but only love and accept, my friends, and your love and acceptance of Amanda and Jake in their hour of need has made me proud. As a priest. As a neighbor. And as a citizen of this generous country.

"Let us pray."

The congregation joined in with the Lord's Prayer, and after a few more readings from the Book of Common Prayer, rose and followed the tiny white coffin out of the church and into the well-tended graveyard behind. The baby's weeping father and bowlegged grandfather were all the small vessel required to carry it, and Manda walked heavily behind, her daughter Rose riding upon her hip. The massive crowd of mourners trampled the plots of erstwhile Three Chimneyans, while camera crews further disturbed their eternal rest by driving tripods into their moldering rib cages. The baby was to be buried under a spreading oak, beside a maternal great-great-granduncle who had ridden with Mosby's Rangers and was thus awarded a hero's plot inside the wealthy churchyard. Most of Manda's other relatives were buried out on their land or in the poor cemetery six miles out of town. Jake's family were all Baptists, and were thus buried amongst themselves.

"'In sure and certain hope of the Resurrection to eternal life through our Lord Jesus Christ,'" Pastor Vaughn read as the coffin was lowered, "'we commit the body of this child to the ground.'" Manda put Rose down and told her to pick up a handful of dirt. It was to toss into the baby's grave, she said. But when the time came, Rose had so squeezed the clayey earth, it thudded on the clean white coffin.

"'For the Lamb which is in the midst of the throne shall feed them, and shall lead them unto living fountains of waters: and God shall wipe away all tears from their eyes,'" read Pastor Vaughn. "'The Lord be with you . . .'"

"And with thy spirit," replied the congregation, drowning out the small beeping in Jake's front right pocket. People surrounded the Franks after the service and at the Vaughns' afterward, so it wasn't until he checked his pager much later that afternoon that the grieving father learned the hospital had been trying to reach them for hours.

"What the hell was I thinking? Eleven babies?" Francis Marvel mopped his brow with a limp white handkerchief. Some vestige of familial gravity took over at public functions, and Polly found herself standing with Margaret and Francis at the end of the ceremony.

"We can build a smart bomb, but we can't keep one damn baby alive?" he asked. "It's just my luck."

"Believe it or not, Francis, everything is not about you," said Margaret.

"Well, it's going to be about *you* pretty soon if donations keep drying up," drawled Francis. "People don't give money to dead babies."

"Francis, you'd better not use that as an excuse," warned Margaret. "You're already five months behind . . ."

As she did whenever they argued over money, Polly tuned them out. In the year since her parents divorced, she had learned her exact worth: $490. She'd seen the complicated equation the court had used: her father's income minus any other alimony or children he was supporting, figured somehow against her mother's income plus any exceptional health care costs and day care, divided by her father's age, blah, blah, blah. The court had calculated her like a mortgage and come out with the sum of $490 a month. Not $500, a satisfying figure in her mind, the respectable burnt orange of Monopoly money, but $490, a savings to her father of ten dollars, snipped off each month like a lock of hair. She knew it was wrong, but she'd come to think of $490 as the sum she would fetch on the open market, or how much an insurance company would pay out at her death, or how much she was entitled to steal if she ran away from home. Every month when her father sent his check, *if* he sent his check, she hoped he would think to round up for her sake, just a little gesture, just ten dollars. It would have meant so much.

"It's not my fault," Francis was arguing. "Let one thing go wrong in a poor family and the whole town turns on you."

Margaret was about to answer when Pastor Vaughn appeared. "Well, this is a welcome sight," said the old priest, taking in the trio. "The death of a child makes us really appreciate our own families, doesn't it?"

"That it does, Leland," said Francis somberly. "If you'll excuse me, I want to go pay my condolences to the Franks." He kissed Polly and walked over to where Jake and Amanda stood surrounded by well-wishers. Polly watched as her father gave Jake a firm, manly hug and offered him his handkerchief to dry his eyes.

"I am so sorry my sessions with you and Francis didn't help," the priest said. "Evelyn and I have always been so happy, I think I am a poor excuse for a marriage counselor."

"Thank you, Leland," answered Margaret wryly. "Nothing could have helped by that point."

"Still," the priest said, taking her hand, "there is nothing worse than the dissolution of a family. I hope in times of trouble you will turn to your friends and neighbors for help."

"I appreciate it," said Margaret.

"We missed you at the candlelight vigil," said Leland, addressing Polly. "I thought for sure you'd be there."

"I had a lot of homework," answered Polly guiltily.

"I know you're a very busy young lady, but I'd appreciate it if you'd look in on Manda from time to time," said Pastor Vaughn. "It's hard to conceive at your age, but nothing destroys a parent like burying a child."

Pastor Vaughn was expressing the exact sentiments Mr. March had ridiculed her for yesterday, but somehow in the minister's mouth, the words sounded right and powerful. Polly found herself promising to look in on Manda and baby-sit whenever she was needed.

"I'll see you both at the rectory, I hope?" the old priest was saying. "Evelyn has baked a ham."

"Oh, Leland, I wish we could make it," Margaret answered, her voice full of regret. "But Polly and I have some pressing business down at Campaign Headquarters that simply can't wait."

Leland's face showed exactly how he ranked politics against neighborly solicitude, but he had been a priest long enough to know when to hold his tongue. "Well, I suppose we'll have crowd enough," he said, scanning the throng of well-wishers and reporters milling about the cemetery grounds. "It's incredible, isn't it, the outpouring of love in this community? Over the years we've had so many opportunities for division, but here we all are looking out for each other, sustaining each other. God has provided us a miracle, and I can't help but be proud of how our town has responded.

"Well, I should go get changed before the guests arrive. I'm about to roast in this wool jacket." Pastor Vaughn bid them good-bye, but then stopped and turned back. "Hey, that reminds me—did you ladies happen to hear the Mexican weather forecast?"

Pastor Vaughn's eyes lit up, and Polly braced herself to withstand this unbelievably stupid joke for the hundredth time in her
young life.

"No, what did it say?" she asked politely.

"Chili today. Hot tamale!" He laughed with self-satisfied delight.

"Chili today. Hot tamale." Polly smiled weakly. "That's a good
one. I'll remember that."

"And I won't even charge you for it." Pastor Vaughn smiled.

The deserted newspaper office, when Margaret let them in, was lit only
by the red exit sign over the door, and Polly was once again struck by
the smell that would forever be linked in her mind to journalism: the
stale aroma of old food and old paper, heavy pork fat (from fifty years
of sharing a wall with Snow White), decaying cloth from curtains im-
ploded by mites, the parchmenty smell of bug husks in the light fixtures. Campaign Headquarters was a tiny room at the end of a musty,
narrow hallway, cinched even tighter by stacks of Reagan-era yellow-
ing back issues of the *Three Chimneys Register* and a slag of 386 IBM
computers with 5¼-inch floppy drives that even the elementary school
refused, but which the old editor in chief could not bear to throw out.
Headquarters, which to the less politically savvy might be mistaken
for a storage closet, was filled nearly to capacity with file cabinets and
a newsprint-grimed water cooler, leaving only enough room for two
chairs, a cigarette-scarred folding table, a typewriter, and two volunteers. Margaret had been in residence here for over a year, at the pleasure of Foster Lewis, a distant step-relation of the previous editor in
chief who had bought the paper after the old man's last stroke. Foster
Lewis was unmarried and unbecomingly fond of scandal—undoubt-
edly a muckraker, if ever the town had seen one. What had for decades
been a sleepy, small-town newspaper, reporting the winners of 4-H
scholarships and pound cake bake-offs, had seemingly overnight become a broadsheet of DUI convictions and marching band embezzle-
ment exposés. Lewis was first to ferret the news of Amanda Frank's
confinement—quite by accident, actually, for he had been having

drinks with a Charlottesville General orderly in a location anonymously equidistant from both of their hometowns when the orderly, just to make conversation, mentioned that a woman from Three Chimneys had been admitted for a whole mess of babies. The "whole mess" turned out to be the unthinkable number of eleven, and despite a plea from Pastor Vaughn begging Lewis to preserve the Franks' privacy, the story became front-page news the following week. Foster immediately alerted his cousin, Patrick, the weather and features reporter for Fox News, Channel 5, and from there the *Richmond Times-Dispatch* picked it up, then the *Washington Post,* and then the world.

A four-line telephone with its chunky plastic HOLD button gave the appearance of serious matters going on inside, as did the grainy *Brooke for President* posters Margaret had photocopied from a circular. Because it went against her nature to join anything, Margaret worked unassisted by the Virginia Democratic Brooke for President organization. She had never understood the necessity of declaring a political party, or stumping for an entire ticket, when the only person she cared about, or believed in, was Adams Brooke himself. She preferred to do things her own way, outside of the machine, and though she cc'd them on all of her correspondence, she had never once asked for help or taken money from them. But her independence had come at a price; she bore the expense of her campaign efforts, including the rental of this room, and, as she learned when she missed Adams Brooke by minutes, she was woefully out of the loop concerning the governor's whereabouts.

Polly used to beg to come to Campaign Headquarters, back before the primaries, before her dad moved out. She had a kid's love of playing office, licking envelopes until her tongue went numb, staring into the corona of the brilliant Xerox as it generated galaxies of appeal letters and thank-you-for-your-contribution notes. She was sometimes allowed to answer the serious-matters telephone with the mantra "Adams Brooke for President, Three Chimneys Campaign Headquarters, How May I Direct Your Call?" before passing the receiver to her mother, the only direction in which it might go; and she was even written up as Three Chimneys' youngest little pollster.

But after her father left, everything changed. What had been a fun afternoon of make-believe once or twice a month became deadly serious business. The phone calls took on a harder, more desperate edge, the envelopes had to go out in such vast numbers, Polly's tongue was no longer an effective instrument, and was replaced by a bit of sponge on a blue plastic bottle. The past few months of her mother's election obsession had taken away any of the joy Polly used to feel, until she came to look upon Adams Brooke as a tyrannical step-father who, even in his absence, must be obeyed.

"What on earth?" said Margaret, playing back the phone messages. "Polly, listen to this."

Among the requests for bumper stickers from a local Brooke supporter, and another for fliers to pass out at next Sunday's Chicken Coop Gospel, there was a message on the machine from Sandy Jameson of the National Headquarters for Adams Brooke for President. *Your efforts on Governor Brooke's behalf have recently come to our attention*, said Mr. Jameson, *and we would love to talk to you. If you could return our call at your earliest convenience . . .*

"That's National Headquarters," said Margaret, dumbfounded. "I wonder what they want. Do you think it could be about the new slogan?"

Brooke No Opposition. It was her mother's latest, and Polly's reason for being pressed into service today. Polly had thought The Farmer's Friend was about as dumb as it got, but Brooke No Opposition, with its neofascist storm-trooper certitude, had pulled into first place.

"You know, Mr. March says opposition is absolutely necessary for our government to function," Polly said. "Thomas Jefferson founded the first opposition party. Are you against Thomas Jefferson?"

"Who is Mr. March?" asked Margaret, dialing the number left on the machine.

"My history teacher?" Polly answered. "Where have you been all year?"

"Obviously Mr. March doesn't have to run a farm," replied Margaret.

"I'm glad our Founding Fathers didn't think like you, or we'd all be eating fish and chips right now."

Margaret made the slicing "Be quiet" motion across her throat as the phone picked up on the other end. "Hello, this is Margaret Prickett from Three Chimneys Headquarters. To whom am I speaking?"

Polly couldn't have been more bored by the conversation, and turned away, idly opening a file drawer full of chronologically dated back issues of the *Register*. From what she could tell, there was a whole lot of nothing going on in this town before Manda's babies, just decades of bad hairstyles and embarrassing clothes, births, deaths, and 4-H prizes. It was the history of a town paying lip service to the passage of time, but fundamentally unchanged since its inception. Polly paused longest over the wedding photos, snickering at the seventies' limp cotton flounces and jute lace-up sandals, at the eighties' big sleeves and sequined headbands. She flipped forward through the file folders until she came to the week of October 20, 1990, seven months before her birth, and there she found a faded announcement for Francis Marvel and Margaret Prickett, two of the town's best kids, smiling formally for the photographer in a posed wedding photo. Her mother's gown was tasteful, being a modified version of her own mother's dress from the early sixties, and her father was in a traditional tux with a vest. Her parents had gotten married when they were both very young, and Polly squinted at the photo, looking for the telltale bulge of herself in her mother's waistline. But her mother was seated, snuggled up in her father's arms, and there was no trace of an unplanned child or a future divorce or a single day of trouble ahead. Polly looked over her shoulder at her mother on the phone, and contemplated waving the photo at her so that they might share a laugh. But then she remembered the day a year ago when she'd discovered some hidden love letters from her parents' first days of dating. She'd run downstairs to tease her mom and dad, and was dramatically disappointed when they did not find the letters charming at all. She learned later, that was the morning her father first admitted he was having an affair.

"I'd be happy to answer some questions, though I can't imagine what I could say that the governor doesn't already know," said Margaret, and from her exaggerated Southern drawl, Polly could tell her mother was speaking to someone more important than herself. Her accent only came out when she was trying to be accommodating. *Campaign speech!* she scribbled on the pad before her.

"What do they want?" asked Polly. Her mother snapped her fingers impatiently, pointed at Polly and then at the door. Polly closed the file cabinet and leaned against it impatiently. "Of course I understand all conversations are confidential," said Margaret with a nervous laugh. "I doubt I can give away any national cheesemaking secrets."

The conversation as Polly overheard it was full of pauses and nods as her mother answered a string of questions about the farm.

"We've been a dairy since just after the Civil War," Margaret told them. (Pause) "No, Jerseys exclusively. Holsteins are genetically engineered machines, and their introduction was the death of the family farm. My great-grandfather was a charter member of the Jersey Cattle Club, and we even have their slogan hanging in our cheese house, '*Omnis pecuniae pecus fundamentum.*' The herd is the foundation of all wealth. It's been our family motto ever since."

Margaret gave Polly a "Can you believe this?" smile as though she were talking to the governor himself. Polly couldn't imagine why his headquarters would want to speak to her mother.

"You know very well that ninety percent of all government subsidies go to five agribusiness crops," said Margaret. "We are an independent family farm. (Pause) Well, if I had to pick one thing, besides the subsidies, I'd guess it would be the estate taxes. You've just gotten out from one generation's debt when the next one dies, leaving the farm that much more burdened. You can't get out from under. The amnesty is the only thing that will save small farms like ours. (Pause) If I could speak directly to Governor Brooke? I'd tell him the individual is the only special interest any politician should answer to. Let him sell that to Monsanto. . . ."

Polly endured a few more minutes of one-sided conversation about poll numbers and good old-fashioned grassroots door-to-door before her mother finally hung up and she could satisfy her curiosity.

"What was that all about?" she asked. Margaret was staring absently into space, and Polly had to repeat her question.

"Governor Brooke's campaign headquarters has read all my letters and knows how hard it's been on our farm. They wanted permission to use us as an example in the speech he's giving."

"Us?" asked Polly.

"He knows who we are," said Margaret as if in a trance. "He knows who we are."

"I thought you didn't want to get involved with Campaign Headquarters," said Polly to snap her mother out of her reverie. "You said they were in the pocket of big business and did nothing but solicit soft money all day. You said you didn't want anything to do with them."

"I don't," answered Margaret. "I haven't. But I'm not going to ignore them if they call me."

"You're like one of those girls at school who pretends not to like a boy until he likes her, then suddenly she's in love."

"You know, you're getting a smart mouth," said Margaret crankily, turning back to her correspondence. "Why do you have to ruin everything?"

"I'm not ruining anything," said Polly archly, echoing her father. "I'm just telling it like it is."

"Polly, you are still a child. When you get older, you'll realize there are certain political realities that can't be denied."

"Like what?"

"Things you wouldn't understand."

"You know, I only act like a child because you treat me like a child," said Polly. "Back in the old days, parents considered their children smaller adults. They didn't try to protect them from everything like you do now. They entrusted them with important responsibilities."

"I let you milk the cows, and all you do is complain," Margaret answered.

"That's different," retorted Polly. "Those are chores, not responsibilities. Responsibilities require trust."

"I trust you to get working on the campaign posters," said Margaret sharply, ending their conversation. Everything was a battle these days.

The two worked in silence. Polly booted up the old computer Foster Lewis allowed for their use. It was so like her mother, she thought, to preach consistency and independence, then cave at the first nod from someone important. When she had children, she would never be like that. She would have a little integrity and set a good example. How was she supposed to respect a woman who constantly changed her mind?

Polly opened up Photoshop to the picture of Adams Brooke's fat, smiling head. The only reason her mother brought her along, she knew, was because Polly understood how to work the computer; if she didn't she would be utterly useless. She took out the text reading "The Farmer's Friend" and replaced it with "Brooke No Opposition" in blocky, black letters. When she reached for some paper to feed into the printer, she accidentally knocked a stack of mail from the table.

"What's this?" asked Polly, picking up the green-tagged certified letter from First Virginia Savings and Loan. Margaret had brought it to the office so that it wouldn't constantly reproach her at home, but she still had not been able to bring herself to open it.

"Put that down," said she. "It's nothing."

"Mom, it's dated. It says 'Open Immediately.'"

"I know what it is, it doesn't concern you."

"God, do you hear yourself?" asked Polly hotly. "'*You wouldn't understand. It doesn't concern you.*' You're always harping on Dad for not facing up to his responsibilities, and you're too afraid to even open a letter."

"Do you want to know what's in that letter, Miss Smart Aleck?" Margaret stood up and smacked her hands so angrily against the card table, the telephone fell with a Lucite thud upon the floor. "Your house. And your clothes. And your college education. That's what's inside that letter. And they are all about to disappear." Margaret hadn't meant to share any of her money troubles with her daughter, but the girl was so sanctimonious sometimes. "I have liquidated my pension. I have sold every stock and bond we own. I've taken out as many mortgages on the farm as they've been dumb enough to give me. But we are broke. Do you understand? We're going to be on the street and you are going to be sold into white slavery because your drunk, irresponsible father certainly can't afford to take you in, and the only person who stands between us and ruin is Adams Brooke, and if his campaign needs our help, then I am damn well going to give it."

"All you care about is money," yelled Polly. "I'm sorry Dad doesn't pay you, but it's not my fault."

"You know, I'd like to have fun sometimes too. I'd like to go out for a beer or take a vacation or do something other than worry about money, but how can I?" Margaret's voice cracked, and the tears that she was always fighting for Polly's sake threatened to overwhelm her. "Who is going to take care of you? Who is going to take care of the farm? All I want is for someone in this world to keep his promise. Is that so much to ask?"

"I'm sorry I'm such a burden," cried Polly. "I know you wish I were dead like Chase Andrew."

"Polly, that is a horrible thing to say," exclaimed Margaret. "How can you possibly believe that? That is a horrible, horrible thing to say."

To Polly's great satisfaction, her mother broke down in tears. The room was silent except for Margaret's soft weeping and the telephone, splayed across the floor like a murder victim. *"If you would like to make a call, please hang up and try again. If you need help, hang up and then dial your operator."* This message cycled through three times before the maniacal dial tone, scientifically engineered, in Polly's opinion, to manufacture as much anxiety as the human body could withstand, took over. This *was* what she wanted, wasn't it? To reduce Margaret to tears and make her hurt as she hurt? But even as she dispassionately watched her mother, an insidious, creeping fear stole over her. If her mother was afraid, perhaps she should be too. Polly remembered the night her father moved out, the evening she sat in her bedroom window, watching Francis load cardboard boxes and bulging green trash bags into a rented U-Haul, taking with him objects that had seemed, like herself, native to the house—the leather recliner, a framed print, the grandfather clock from the hall—but that she now learned had a specific owner, that had in fact come with, and would now leave with, her father. When at last he was gone, blowing her a kiss from the front yard, she had walked downstairs and through the eerily silent house to find her mother screwing a sliding chain lock onto the front door, a door that like every other door and window on the farm had been perpetually left unlocked the entirety of Polly's life. Until that moment, she had never once considered there was anything outside that might be in need of locking out. But that night in bed, she began listening for sounds—a creaking floor-board, the unexpected rustle in a bush—suddenly aware they were two women alone and unprotected. Polly was a clever girl, and she thought she knew all that could go wrong in this wide world, but her mother's tears today, like a locked door, said she didn't know the half of it. Slowly, she retrieved the phone and placed if back on the card table.

"I'm sorry, Mom," she said, through the rising lump in her own throat. "What can I do to help?"

Margaret cried all the harder and held out her arms for her daughter. Damn Francis who never has to go through this, she thought. What got into her to terrify Polly like that? She murmured a hundred apologies into her daughter's hair, hugging her as fiercely as if her epithets had in fact summoned a white slave trader, who was even now waiting in the hallway.

"I'm so sorry, Peanut," she said, using Polly's father's name for her, and Polly knew then that her mother must be very sorry. "It's the stress of the election. Things aren't as bad as all that."

Polly gently dried her mother's eyes and poured her a glass of water. "Leave it to me," she said, "Adams Brooke will win this election. I know he will. I'll do anything it takes.

"Don't worry, Mom," said Polly, gathering her mother into her arms, as she herself had so often been gathered. "Leave it to me."

CHAPTER SEVEN

Balanced budget, six years standing.
Ran clean campaign.
Ordered drug dealers out of town.
Opened his arms to the poor.
Kept at it, even when all seemed lost.
Embarrassed by wife's shoplifting? Not at all!

Near-death survivor.
Organ donor, and regular giver of blood.

Organized youth center for troubled teens.
Pardoned Jimmy Sands, an innocent man.
Put ducks in a row.
Orchestrated amnesty for
Small-time farmers and vowed to abolish excessive
Income tax for those who took the Family Matters Pledge.
Tough on crime.
Is one of us.
Oh haven't you guessed? The
Next President of the United States is Adams Brooke! Vote the
    Farmer's Friend!

She had no one to blame but herself. She had come up with the acrostic. She had carefully handwritten it in tall red block letters down two sides of a sandwich board sign. She had fashioned the straps and lifted the thing over her head. She had, of her own free will, offered to parade it down School Street, beneath the shade of the overhanging oak trees, from eleven on Sunday through three o'clock, when her mother would come pick her up and kiss her gratefully, and that kiss would make up for the utter humiliation of it all—all her own fault, she knew—but the kiss of pride and gratitude would make it all worthwhile.

"Brooke No Opposition. Adams Brooke for President."

Last night, it had been like old times between Margaret and Polly. She slept in her mother's room, curled inside her mother's arms, pulling Margaret's freshly washed, long wet hair over her own like a wig. She lay quietly on Margaret's stomach, letting her breath find the rhythm of her mother's, just drifting, as close to climbing back inside as a long, lean girl of thirteen could get.

"Vote the Farmer's Friend this November."

I would never want you dead, Margaret had whispered to her in the darkened bedroom. *I never want you to say a thing like that again. I would die a thousand deaths before I would ever let anything happen to you, Polly. I love you more than life itself.*

If her mother had been here, the two might have made a game of it: imagining Polly as a pair of dancing legs beneath a box of Lucky Strikes, hoofing it on *Ed Sullivan*, or pretending to be a singing telegram for social change. Last night, they'd been a team, coloring in the block letters and stapling buckram straps to the poster board, but today, her mother was entrenched in the cheese house and Polly was on her own, with only the heat of her own self-consciousness to keep her company. Did she think that up? asked Mrs. Vaughn on her way to Sunday school and taking an eternity to read each line. My, how clever. The priest's wife popped open her purse and handed Polly a wintergreen Life Saver to suck. You must be awfully hot in that thing, dear, she said. What a good girl you are.

With most of Three Chimneys sitting in the pews of St. Barnabas at one end of School Street or First Baptist at the other, the sidewalks were mercifully deserted. Polly handed flyers to a few aimless newsmen, who were so very bored with this nowhere town that a girl in a sandwich sign actually pricked their consciences. Most of them would much rather have been part of the election coverage than stuck on a dumbed-down human interest story anyway, and if even a kid, for Chrissakes, could care so much about politics, could they continue to believe they were anything other than infotainment sellouts? The thought drove several of them into Drafty's for a round or two, despite its being not quite noon.

She walked past Tinton's Grocery, closed on Sunday, in accordance with blue laws that had long ago been repealed. She walked past the feed store and the Community Center, with its white obelisk War Memorial. She paused and read the neatly chiseled names of the Confederate dead, boys who fought with the 13th Infantry, others who died with the Gordonsville Greys. Her mother told her that every Memorial Day in her girlhood, the older ladies of town would lay a grand rose wreath, larger even than what they awarded the winning horse on Derby Day, at the foot of this obelisk, a practice that had been discontinued at about the time of Polly's birth. Even the dead had a place to be on a Sunday afternoon, thought Polly fleetingly.

A little after noon, the red doors to St. Barnabas swung wide, discharging the overheated congregation. Polly was just past Snow White when she saw Pastor Vaughn in his black cassock step outside to shake hands with everyone who left. Her father was not a churchgoing man, and so her family, more often than not, had stayed home on Sunday—there was plenty of work to do, and church seemed just another chore—but secretly, she'd always envied the girls whose parents got them up and then turned them out ironed, combed, and polished. It was another form of solidarity, she thought, seeing, even now, some of the girls from school descending the church steps in their lilac and navy sweater sets, wearing panty hose, even though it was about a hundred and fifty degrees outside. The girls looked dewy and respectable, with their parents walking behind them, far enough behind to give them freedom, but there, nonetheless, watching over them, keeping them within sight. They cared that their children got into Heaven. But where was her mother? Fighting on another front, Polly thought loyally, working to better society instead of mouthing platitudes about it. But still, she had to admit, those families looked so untroubled and certain about themselves. These were girls who lacked nothing, who shared among themselves, like a sugary soda, the knowledge that all would go well in their lives, moving effortlessly from Homecoming Court, to an all-girls college, to the crisp, understated pages of *Bride* magazine. There was nothing messy in their lives, no registered letters or unpaid child support, and when the time came, they would produce tidy, happy, equally entitled smaller versions of themselves who would begin the whole cycle over again. Polly was only thirteen, but she understood, as surely as she wore this sign, that she was marked down as different from everyone else in this town. As she watched, her friend Bethany bounded down the stairs with her parents in tow, saw the other girls from school, and ran to join them. These were the people she went to when Polly wasn't around. Even between herself and Bethany, there would always be this great divide.

Polly suddenly felt like a homeless drifter in her jeans and cardboard, as though she might be advertising a strip bar instead of a political candidate. She remembered her defiant words to Adams Brooke's recorded voice, and didn't want Bethany to see her in this thing. Not knowing where else to go, she quickly ducked inside Snow White.

The restaurant felt cool and dark inside as the screen door swung shut on the stiff heel of her sandwich board. She took a seat at the counter next to a state trooper and settled the stiff slices of her sign over the stool. When after a few minutes Lucille took her order, Polly brazenly asked for a contraband Coke and chocolate cream pie with Cool Whip. The waitress clucked over so much sugar so early in the day, but if young ladies wanted to rot their teeth, that was their own business.

Snow White had not changed so much as a napkin dispenser in the thirteen years Polly had been alive, and if she'd ever bothered to ask her parents, she would have learned that the same greasy clock had hung upon the wall in their youths, that the same blocky hot sauce and vinegar cruets graced the same twelve Formica tables that had been placed there opening day 1947. This restaurant had

befuddled the out-of-town newspaper reporters, who found it perpetually closed whenever they sought to eat here, but the locals
knew the schedule, and kept the place as full as it could handle.
Everyone understood that Mrs. Hawks, the owner and sole cook, was
staunchly loyal to her stories, despite how smutty they'd become over
the decades, and opened her restaurant according to the ABC daily
lineup. Monday through Friday, she served food from 11 till 2 in the
afternoon, closed during *One Life to Live* and *General Hospital*, then
opened again from 4 until 6:30. Saturdays she was closed altogether
because she usually visited her out-of-town children, but Sunday she
opened for lunch after church, serving from 12 until 3. The hours were
posted nowhere, nor was there a menu to be found in the establish-
ment. Everyone knew what she had. Barbecue with or without slaw.
Navy bean soup. Egg salad sandwich. Fried chicken on Sunday with
pressure-cooker green beans and potato salad. Pies of three varieties.
Coke but not Pepsi, in glass bottles, for which she charged only 65 cents,
and which you had better not try to take out of the restaurant or she
would lose her deposit. No matter how cantankerous Mrs. Hawks had
grown over the years, no matter how tyrannically she set her hours,
Snow White was never without customers during its brief, gaudy hours
of operation. And everyone was perfectly content to wait.

At noon, the restaurant was full of churchgoers from the morning sermons, Baptists and Episcopalians alike, all gnawing legs and
thighs and center breasts. Polly was grateful not to know anybody too
well—there was no one under retirement age eating lunch so early,
unless you counted the toddlers with their grandparents, perched like
little despots upon their red plastic molded thrones.

"That'll be three dollars, sugar," Mrs. Hawks's Lucille said, and
Polly awkwardly pulled her arm inside the sign to get to her pocket.
It would be so easy to shrug off this sign, she thought, and leave it
like a shed skin here in the restaurant. Maybe she could tell her
mother she had been mugged, or was a victim of political sabotage.
But she knew that too many people had seen her come in with the
sign, and that someone would helpfully run after her if she left it. She
dug into her pie glumly.

Because my mother
Really
Ought to see a psychiatrist
Or other mental health professional, I am stuck in this hell.
Kill me, somebody.
Enough already!

Nobody cares about stupid
Old Adams Brooke,
Or his stupid campaign.
Please kill me now.
Please, somebody,
Or else I'll have to commit
Suicide.
I mean it!
Torture, is what this is.
I know a secret about Adams Brooke:
Old cow shit turns him on. Vote for cow shit lover!
Nature Calls!

Polly shoveled the last forkful into her mouth and left 50 cents by her plate. But there was to be no escape for her today. Just as she was rising to leave, the Frasers stepped in and waited to be seated. She could not avoid passing them; with no back exit through which she might vanish, there was nothing to do but awkwardly maneuver between the crowded tables and try not to embarrass herself further by toppling any unwary water glasses.

"Why, hello, Polly," said Mrs. Fraser.

"Hello, Mrs. Fraser," the girl replied. She glanced at Bethany, but her friend was staring at the floor, in deference to Polly's obvious discomfort.

"Having a relaxing Sunday?"

"Yes, ma'am. And you?"

"Just came from church," said Mrs. Fraser, making no reference to Polly's signage. "It was about a million degrees in there."

"I'm sorry to hear that," said Polly. "It seems summer just won't end."

"Seems so."

"Well," Polly said after a long, uncomfortable pause. "I'd better get going."

"Give our best to your mother," said Mrs. Fraser. "Tell her we're dying to have her over for margaritas sometime soon, if she can find the time."

"I will, thank you, Mrs. Fraser." Polly wiggled through the door, ignoring Bethany's wan smile of encouragement. Back on the street, the hot sun was high overhead, but Polly still had nearly three hours before she could go home. Try as she might, she couldn't summon last night's magical camaraderie. *I would never want you dead. I would die a thousand deaths . . .* , she heard her mother say, but the words now seemed to lack conviction, sounded cynical to her ear, as if this had all been an elaborate trick, one big joke on Polly. Why else would she be out here alone, while her mother hid at home behind her cheeses? What sort of mother sent her daughter out to be publicly humiliated?

"Hey, Francis, isn't that your girl?"

Polly was just passing the hot beery doorway of Drafty's when she heard a voice call out from inside. She squinted in to see who had recognized her, before realizing that she should have immediately run and precious seconds had been wasted. But it was too late. Her father was weaving his way to the screen door, a pint of Bud Light in his hand, though the glass said *Guinness*. Unlike the fathers in church, hers was unshaven and dressed in shorts and a University of Richmond sweatshirt.

"What in the hell are you wearing?"

"Adams Brooke for President." She smiled weakly, handing him a flyer. She could see behind him into the twilight of Drafty's, a beer joint she'd never dared enter. A television hung over the bar like the one in Manda's hospital room, tuned to the Redskins preshow, while the purple and red jukebox beneath twanged "Ghost Riders in the Sky." Several of the news reporters were eating popcorn from a plastic wood-grain salad bowl. Her father balled up the flyer and tossed it over his shoulder.

"Shrinky, will you come here," he called. "Have you ever seen anything so goddamn stupid?"

Andrew Friedman, the psychiatrist who shared office space with her dad, joined him in the doorway. He was a thickly bearded man with glasses, and as unlikely a friend as her father could have found. Like many Northerners who had moved south to stay, in a desire to assimilate he had enthusiastically taken up Southern ways, like frequenting beer joints on Sunday and eating grits. Her father used to say he would have hung a goddamned Confederate flag in his office, if he hadn't been told that no one clearing over $18,000 a year did that sort of thing anymore. Neither man was on his first beer, Polly could tell.

"What the hell has your mother put you up to this time?"

"For your information," Polly said, "I'm proud to represent Adams Brooke. He's committed to saving the small farmer."

"The only thing he's committed to is his own damn career," scoffed her father, "and if your mother can't see that, she's got her head even farther up her ass than I imagined."

Here, Andrew Friedman, psychiatrist, intervened. "It's important for teenagers to have role models, Francis. It's productive for her at her age to be interested in the world at large."

"Is it productive for her to be parading around town like a goddamn monkey?" Francis asked, and his face was a deeper shade of purple than normal. When he lived at home, he wouldn't have been able to make it to the bar this early, Polly thought. He would still be hosing down the milking equipment or spreading manure. How nice that he'd been able to more conveniently arrange his schedule.

"Dad, this is a free country. I am under no obligation to discuss my political convictions," Polly said primly, and turned to go.

"Don't you walk away from me, young lady. I am under no obligation not to whip your butt." He lurched a step toward her before Andrew Friedman stopped him.

"You can't take that beer outside," the psychiatrist reminded.

Francis stopped, his body outside, but his beer hand just inside the door of Drafty's. "Business is bad enough without you two making idiots of yourselves all over town," he said.

"You're working real hard right now, I see," Polly said with as much sarcasm as she could muster.

"For your information," said Francis, "I am meeting with a client. Shrink Wrap here is thinking of building a house."

Andrew Friedman chuckled at Francis's nickname for him. All her father's friends had nicknames for each other. Bethany's dad, the hand surgeon, was called Quack; Coach Emery, who graduated the same year as her dad, was Jock Itch; and Mr. Crenshaw, from First Virginia Savings and Loan, was known simply as The Jew, though his family had been Presbyterian for generations.

Her father stuck his head inside the bar to take a swig off his beer, and Polly used the distraction to walk away.

"Where the hell are you going? I'm still talking to you," he shouted.

He wanted to come after her, Polly could tell, but that would mean setting down his beer, and he and she both knew it wasn't worth it to him to take a step farther. He quickly shifted tactics.

"Come on, Peanut," he called, wheedling this time, "take that damn thing off. You look like a moron."

Polly stiffened her back and kept walking. Everyone on the street was watching her, having overheard the exchange. Beer, she thought. And friends. She moved them into the column of things that mattered more than her, along with ten dollars extra a month. Cheese. And Adams Brooke. When she was little she had foolishly believed herself to be the center of her parents' lives; nothing was her rival, nothing better loved or preeminent. But the older she became, the more surely she was learning her worth, and it was less than an amber glass of beer, and it was less than having her father's friends think him funny. It was less than a campaign slogan.

Polly had been brave all day, but now she felt self-pity threatening to overwhelm her. She walked to the War Memorial, where she figured she might as well sink down among the other casualties of war, for despite her mother's words of last night, Polly knew if she disappeared into the ground and never rose again neither of her parents would miss her.

"What sort of opposition is this?" a familiar voice called out from across the street. She looked up, and to her dismay saw Mr. March rolling down the passenger window of his green Carmen Ghia. His words were sarcastic, but his voice was more tender than she'd ever heard it. How long had he been there? she wondered. Polly swiftly wiped her hot, red face.

"You look like you could use a ride home," he offered, reaching across and opening the passenger door from the inside. "Come on, get in. I'll give you a lift. . . . though I'm not sure that sign will fit."

It was all the permission she needed. With a vengeance, Polly ripped the sign from her body and tore it in half. She left the letters scattered all over the sidewalk and defiantly slid into the passenger seat of Mr. March's cramped car.

"Polly Marvel, you've littered!" he exclaimed. "It feels good to be a lawbreaker, doesn't it?"

Mr. March pulled back onto School Street and headed out of town. For the first time in their acquaintance, Polly didn't even try to speak. She stared straight ahead through the bug-bespeckled windshield and simply breathed in the smell of him, of his stale navy polo shirt, slightly citrusy with Old Spice.

"It's been a rough year, hasn't it?" Mr. March filled the silence, and Polly merely nodded. "A divorce forces you to grow up fast. It exposes all the flaws of the two-party system, if you know what I mean. My parents split when I was ten. I acted out. Ran away from home. Stole a car."

"I think about that sometimes," she said. "Acting out."

"I can tell you're the rebellious kind."

Now he was making fun of her again, and Polly turned her face back to the windshield. What did he know about her? They drove past his driveway, and Polly involuntarily glanced over.

"That's my house," Mr. March said, noticing.

"Is it?" she asked disingenuously.

She felt his eyes on her then, though she kept hers fixed straight ahead. She had given herself away, and now he must know, without a doubt, that she was a pathetic, twisted stalker. Polly shrunk back against her seat miserably.

"You know, you're welcome to stop by anytime," he said, "if you ever need to talk."

Polly nodded, for her tears were too close to the surface to trust her voice. He was so good and generous and she was so unworthy. She couldn't believe how everything had turned against her. Finally, to be alone in the car with him, to have him speaking so gently, and for her to be swollen and red-faced, as humiliated an insect as ever crawled on the planet.

"I don't know why you agreed to wear that sign in the first place," he said.

"My mother was upset and I wanted her to feel better," she said. "It was my idea."

"One thing I learned from my own parents' divorce: Adults have their own agenda. You need to look out for yourself."

"She's my mom," said Polly. "I owe her."

"You don't owe her anything. Just because someone feeds and clothes you does not mean they own you. That is the very definition of slavery," he said earnestly. "You were born into a tradition of rebellion, Miss Marvel. When your forefathers saw oppression, they rose up against it. They threw off the shackles of tyranny and created a new nation. You are not an extension of your parents. You are not their instrument. You are you. In all of your Polly Marvelousness."

He was coming out of the canopy of trees on Snakehill Road and fast approaching the turnoff to her house. Polly Marvelousness. If she didn't tell him which driveway was hers, maybe he would just keep driving and they could go on like this forever. But he was already putting on his blinker and taking the left-hand turn.

They pulled into her driveway and rode the last quarter mile in silence. The cows were sleeping out by the old chimney and the fields were Sunday afternoon–still. The sunbaked smell of manure rose up to meet them, and Polly hung her head at the rusted farm equipment out front, like some redneck's old Camaro raised up on cinder blocks. When they reached the front of the house, Mr. March stopped the car, and once more reached across the seat to open the passenger door. As he leaned over, his face was nearly in her lap, and she could count the thin strands of dark brown hair arcing from his scalp. His arm casually brushed her shoulder as he sat back up. She felt the entire day's humiliation worth this unintentional caress.

"There is no better time than *childhood* to learn these lessons, Polly." Mr. March smiled kindly at her. "Jefferson said, '*The time to guard against corruption and tyranny is before they have gotten hold of us. It is better to keep the wolf out of the fold than to trust him drawing his teeth and talons after he shall have entered.*' Keep the talons out of your flesh. I don't think it's too late for you."

Her mother's truck was not out front. Nor was August's. Polly stood in the empty driveway as Mr. March pulled his car forward and peeled around. It didn't occur to her until much later that she hadn't had to tell him where she lived.

Harvey March did not drive straight home after dropping Polly off, but aimlessly turned down a succession of country roads in an effort to clear his mind. He didn't get out this way often, and was surprised to see the same trapping of grief echoed in the country homes as in those he was more familiar with in town. Nearly every mailbox was tied with a dark purple ribbon to honor Chase Andrew Frank, the fallen of the Frank Eleven. Every picture window sported a single Christmas candle screwed with a blue bulb, that like an eternal flame burned even in the daytime. How did these people instinctively know what to do? he wondered. Was there a guidebook to grief and grieving, some *Public Mourning for Dummies*?

The roads turned from unlined pavement to gravel to dirt the farther out he drove and the more spontaneous turns he took, until at last he considered himself officially lost. It was not such a bad feeling, and not one he was unused to. When he was a student at Co-

lumbia, he would sometimes take different subway lines to their ter-
mini just to wander an unfamiliar neighborhood, the more deserted
or dangerous the better. He liked being a stranger in a place no one
else would think to go.

Though Harvey March had lived in Three Chimneys for ten
years, he still felt himself as much an alien here as he had wandering
Canarsie or Van Cortlandt Park. Three Chimneys was, in fact, a sort
of self-imposed end of the line for him. While certainly no native
questioned as to why a young man of twenty-four with a master's from
Columbia University would have chosen to make a home in their
lovely town, his friends back home were mystified. Harvey's future
had seemed so bright. He had studied political science and interned
with a senator. He was peripatetic and urbane, able to order cocktails in five languages. But he was also a little unstable, and apt to get
into trouble. He sometimes spoke his mind to the senator, when even
the dullest clerk would have recognized the need for silence. He had
a bit of a reputation for creating his own bad luck, so when he was
dismissed from his internship, though everyone was sympathetic, no
one was truly surprised. Harvey had taken a midyear replacement job
teaching government at a private school in New Rochelle, and when
he was dismissed from that, people assumed it was more of the same.
Overqualified and too big a mouth.

And then he shocked his whole circle of friends, by abruptly
leaving town. No one even knew where he went, until he dropped
his mother a birthday card, postmarked from some nowhere town in
Virginia, of all places. No explanation, no promises of return. Just
the news that he'd taken a job teaching U.S. history to eighth-graders
and was renting a house. There was some speculation he'd met a
woman down there, but nothing more was heard about it, and after
a few years Harvey March was forgotten, so much so that even the
alumni fund-raisers no longer bothered to call.

He drove too fast for the narrow dirt roads, raising mushrooms
of dust and sharp chips of gravel that snapped at his windshield. The
woods around the road thickened as he slalomed downhill, the
bramble of kudzu and thorns tangling into a narrow green tunnel

around his car. He took a swift hairpin turn on the dirt road and pulled up sharp at the bottom of the hill. The road, without any warning, had whittled to a single lane that splintered into a wooden bridge over the lazy, orange Rapidan River. Shit, thought Harvey March, wishing he had turned around at the last fork in the road. His perverse desire to get lost had disappeared almost the moment it was achieved, and he was bored and ready to go home. Now he had no choice but to continue straight over this rickety bridge until he came to the next road or driveway or thickening wide enough for a three-point turn. The bridge was low and the water not even high enough to cover the sticks and discarded beer cans of its muddy bottom, but neither fact mattered to him. He was raised in the city and moreover had seen too many Amazon jungle movies to trust any crossing made of plank. He inched his car onto the bridge as gingerly as he would have led a spooked thoroughbred, and didn't realize he had shut his eyes until he looked up to find himself squared off against a large white minivan, its massive black bumper self-congratulatorily stickered with "My Child Is a Three Chimneys Elementary School Honor Student" and the ubiquitous, but now outdated, "We ♥ the Frank Eleven."

The huge vehicle bore down on the bridge, and for a second they were at an impasse. Neither car could move forward on the single lane, and neither was so discernibly past the middle as to claim precedence. Harvey looked into the windshield of the other car and saw a large smiling woman with four soccer-jerseyed kids—three husky boys in the back, watching cartoons from a television suspended in the backseat, and up front a girl rhythmically bobbing her head to the headphones covering her ears. Their mother shrugged at Harvey as if to say, What can you do? You're outnumbered, and waited patiently for him to back up.

For a moment, the history teacher considered resistance. Why should he make way for this minivan full of soccer hooligans? Because it was larger? Because such was expected of him as a gentleman, no matter how vertiginous it made him? Because he mustn't dare delay the soccer practice of a Three Chimneys Elementary School honor student, whichever of the four it might be? But then he realized why he would inevitably be the one to back up—because this woman, with her four kids and 2.9 percent–financed van with removable cargo seat, would never dream that he wouldn't. She perfectly understood that the past must give way before the future—her shiny van trumped his rusty Carmen Ghia, his sad bachelor existence was dust before the warm flesh of her progeny, and thus by divine right, she was entitled to put him in reverse, then back him off the bridge, onto the shoulder, and nearly into the ditch. His foot hovered over the gas pedal, ready to slam down and send her smiling face into the windshield, her kids flying over the seat like the Wile E. Coyote cartoon they were watching. It would be worth his own death, wouldn't it, to spare the future this bunch. But of course, when he did finally step on the gas, he was in reverse, and the woman in the van tooted her thanks and bowled on her thoughtless way.

Harvey sat for a long while, shaking in his car. Thank God for girls like Polly Marvel, he thought; they were the only reason to stay in such a godforsaken place.

Though the road was too narrow, he backed his Carmen Ghia into the ditch, whipped the steering wheel around, and floored it.

Then, as if it were a trail of crumbs left in the woods, he followed the minivan back to civilization, breathing its dust the whole ride home.

Sometimes Polly wished for the kind of house where a radio was left running. Or where a television blared the day's headlines in an endless loop of overwrought music and droning voices—anything to break the eternal quiet of her house when no one was home. After Mr. March left her, she walked inside to the still, hot kitchen. A trio of flies rose and circled and settled back on the wooden countertop, where they had been feasting on a puddle of tomato juice spilled when Margaret canned some of the season's last Better Boys. The jars still sat in their water bath on the stove, slowly cooling for storage in the pantry. Through the open window, she heard Sultana's pregnant lowing complaint. When her dad still lived here, he played bluegrass records on her grandfather's old stereo console. But after he moved out, her mother had given the stereo away. And she now kept the television in the closet, wheeled out for the late news and special occasions only. Her mother might find the silence peaceful, but it left Polly feeling marooned, afraid to make noise and disturb the heavy somnambulance of the quilts and hanging baskets and cluttered artifacts of Prickett relatives, buckets of their stripped hardware and toe-stubbing antique irons used for doorstops.

She would be in trouble when her mother got home, she knew, but she didn't care. Her parents had no problem being unreliable, why should she hold herself to a higher standard? She stood in front of the old Hotpoint refrigerator, staring vacantly at what there was to eat. Margaret had baked a gooseberry pie and left her homemade ice cream in the freezer, but Polly reached for the rasher of bacon and wound a raw piece around her index finger. She gnawed it while she poured herself a glass of vinegar and sprinkled in a little salt. It was her secret snack when her mother was not around to police her. She glanced at the kitchen table, where Margaret had left a to-do list.

Shipment to Philadelphia
Order cheesecloth
Copy more flyers for Polly
Note to S. Jameson
Buy yarn, winter hat Polly
Remind Polly Farmer's Market Saturday
Election Day—sample ballots. Polly?

While she was making an idiot of herself on School Street, Margaret was planning her life through the autumn. Mr. March was right. Her mother saw her as nothing but a way of being in two places at once.

Upstairs, something thumped like a tennis ball thrown against the window. Polly stood motionless in the kitchen, waiting to hear the sound again. *Thump.* She heard it. Then again, a panicked patter. She set down her glass and climbed the narrow servants' staircase that connected the kitchen to the upper floors. The noise came from one of the unused bedrooms at the other end of the long hall, on the east side of the house. Last winter, the wooden eaves had rotted, and unable to afford to replace the roof, Margaret had simply shut the doors and avoided those rooms altogether. They were too expensive to heat, she said, and anyway, there was more than enough space for the two of them on the sunnier side of the house. With its bulbless light fixtures and sour carpet runner, that wing had become like the dark side of the moon, and Polly now found herself treading nervously. The thump came again from the white paneled door at the end of the hall, where her great-aunt Louisa had slept when she was alive. Polly knew her only from a few faded Christmas photos, for she had died long before Polly was born. But she had left behind a wonderland of fancy gloves, feathered hats, and costume jewelry that Polly used for dress-up, back when she played at that sort of thing.

Polly immediately felt a draft when she turned the white porcelain knob. Unattended, the leak in the roof had only gotten worse, and a deep brown water stain ran from the ceiling to the warped pine plank floor. She could see blue sky through the rotten section of roof, and beneath it, the feathers and twigs of a mourning dove's nest. One of the pale gray birds had become trapped inside, and fluttered madly around the room, knocking into her great-aunt's vanity mirror, the heavily carved rosewood chifforobe, the shut and locked uncurtained windows. Polly ducked as the bird skimmed her head, banking sharply to avoid the door and crashing dully once more into the mirror. Polly raced across the room and threw open the window, prying up the screen and pushing it out into the yard below. The dazed bird lifted up but seemed unable to find its escape, for all Polly's shooing. It flew drunkenly around the small bedroom until finally it hit the window ledge and bounced outside. Polly watched it fly to the corner of the east chimney, where it hunkered in the shadows, puffing itself to twice its size.

What a mess, she thought, surveying the water damage and dropping-streaked furniture. The pale pink and green wallpaper hung in strips, and the old iron Franklin stove that once heated the room had scaled with rust. It looked like no one had set foot in here for decades, rather than months. When she was little, she used to play inside this chifforobe, opening its many miniature drawers and rooting through its artifacts—cut-glass drops from an extinct chandelier, rolls of gauze bandage, red Lucite and rhinestone buttons snipped from a threadbare coat. She would drag blankets from the hall closet and read for hours, curled inside the armoire, falling asleep and alarming her mother, who searched the farm for her in vain. Now Polly instinctively opened the door and saw the goose-down comforter she had brought here well over a year ago, exactly where she left it; only it had been gnawed by something, for a cloud of feathers rose up to greet her. There was a family myth of silver hidden from the Yankees that, once the war was lost, never reappeared. Polly used to tap the walls for it and paw behind the canned goods in the cellar, until her mother told her that if such silver had ever existed, it had certainly been sold long ago to pay off debts. Still, she could barely stop herself from opening drawers and burrowing into pockets, and over the years, she'd mined the house of thirty-five dollars in loose change and stray bills.

The drawers of the chifforobe she knew well. One held nothing but linen napkins and browning lace tablecloths that Polly recognized from Christmas photos. In another were a few grimy toys, including a sky blue windup toy telephone that played haunting, off-key music in a minor chord that for some reason had terrified her as a child. She was tall enough now to reach the top drawer, and was rewarded with a cracked leather snap purse, hung by a thin gold chain. Inside was a plastic rain bonnet given out by the local funeral parlor, a few sticky bobby pins, and a small pink bud-shaped cup of something called Rose Milk. But Polly felt something inside the torn silk lining, and fishing around, came out with a folded blue airmail envelope bearing the postmark "Mecklenburg Prison, Mecklenburg, Virginia." From inside, she drew out a letter, typed double-spaced on an old-fashioned manual typewriter.

Though her great-aunt was long dead, Polly paused and looked behind her. Money was one thing, but the plunder of private correspondence made her hesitate, as if discovering an old letter or even a discarded grocery list might lay bare some dark family secret, like an illegitimacy or the fact that she was adopted. She had especially avoided love letters since the fiasco with her parents', but in the end, her curiosity got the better of her, and she began to read.

Dearest Rudy, it said, *How I miss you. It is hell in this house with Momma and Daddy and Abingdon and now Martha, for she has moved in and acts like she owns the place, lording it over me who has lived here all her life. I can't wait until you are home and we have a house of our own, for being here is killing me, Rudy, and I count the days until I see you again. Do they treat you well? Do you want for anything? Daddy sold off some acres to those Franks to pay for what you and Winston have done and he never lets me forget it. Day and night. I count the days, dearest Rudy, until I see you again and we are out of here, for it is killing me . . .*

The letter went on in this vein, but in the blank space between the lines, her aunt had received a reply in masculine cursive. *Dearest Lou, You know paper is hard to come by here, so I am sending this back to you with these lines. How are you, honey? I am hurting for cigarettes here and $20 would sure go far. Yes, $20 would sure help a man out . . .*

Polly folded the letter and shoved it back in the purse. She knew her great-aunt Louisa had never gotten a house of her own, but spent the rest of her life here with Polly's grandparents and Margaret, and had died in this room, which was now white with bird droppings and ruined by water. The smell of dry rotted wood and wet plaster was giving her a violent headache, and Polly suddenly found it difficult to breathe. She thought of this house sucking in anyone who came too close. Her grandmother Martha. Her great-aunt Louisa. Her own father. She tried to imagine herself married to Mr. March and inviting him to come live here with her mother and the cows and all these ruined rooms, but the thought was too ludicrous. Yet taking over the farm was exactly the life her mother planned for her, as surely as if she had scribbled it on her to-do list. Polly started at the sound of footsteps in the hall. When she spun around, her mother, like a prison guard, loomed in the doorway.

"Where have you been?" Margaret asked in annoyance. "I've driven all over town looking for you. I saw your sign on the ground, and I thought something had happened."

"*Keep your talons out of my flesh,*" Polly yelled, pushing past her mother to her bedroom, then slamming the door angrily.

Dumbfounded, Margaret stood beside the old carved chifforobe, while from somewhere uncomfortably close came the panicked flapping of doves.

CHAPTER EIGHT

After Polly's mutiny, Margaret abandoned Brooke No Opposition. She tried to keep her enthusiasm for the slogan, going so far as to take out a full-page ad in the *Three Chimneys Register*, fifty dollars she could ill afford to spend, before admitting that she, too, found the phrase a little awkward and somewhat musty. The Farmer's Friend had a lilting bounce, and she retreated to it, but when she was being honest with herself, she had to admit Polly's defection had swayed her. She couldn't look at the words without remembering the acrostic and the fun they'd had making the sign. Whatever the reason she'd turned against it—and her daughter steadfastly refused to talk about the day she ripped up her sign and abandoned her post—the slogan simply didn't work without Polly.

The last honorable man in America. On Channel 5, the mid-afternoon anchor was interviewing a former schoolmate of the governor's, asking if there was anything the American people should know about the man behind the candidate. *He's the last honorable man in America*, repeated George Shearling of Pittsboro, North Carolina. *I've known him all my life and I trust him like my own brother*. In the background, a clip played of Adams Brooke's high school graduation. In it, a tall, gawky teenager was reaching for his diploma and flashing the peace sign to the camera. Two years later he would enlist for Vietnam and be nearly fatally shot. *It changed his life*, said classmate George. *Before he'd been a regular farm boy, but after that he became a crusader. I've never known anyone like him*.

It was the third week in October, and Margaret had all but given up on hearing any mention of herself. It had been three weeks since National Headquarters called, and yet there had been no reference to Prickett Farm and its struggles in any campaign speech; in fact, she'd heard nothing of the amnesty at all, but instead a good deal of talk about health care and oil prices and our enemies abroad. No one had promised her she'd be mentioned, she had to remind herself, and for all she knew, she could have been one of a hundred farmers interviewed. But still, the phone call had felt like a promise, and now she was left with the hollow, queasy hangover that comes from hoping for too long. With her constant checking of the newspaper and television news, she felt like a moonstruck teenage girl obsessively calling home for her messages. She didn't want to believe, as Polly had taunted, that she played hard-to-get only when nobody wanted her. Margaret watched for several more minutes, until she was sure the election coverage was over, then unplugged the television and put it back in the closet.

She had no choice now but to make her reluctant daily trek to the mailbox, a walk she'd come to dread even before the last registered letter from First Virginia Savings and Loan. She'd identified a pattern to her collection notices—a review of the delinquent account on the 15th and a subsequent threatening missive fired off. By the 20th or so, the letter would arrive: *Attention Margaret Prickett: Because you have failed to act on our earlier notices, we have been forced to turn your account over to our collection agency for immediate action . . .* Each new letter took a line from the one that went before, building on its threats like a harmless bit of string evolving into a rattlesnake, until the final strike: stationery from a lawyer, the threat of repossession, the certified letter. After a while, she simply left the letters unopened, telling herself that the clock began ticking not when she received the letter, but when she read and could no longer deny its contents. Today, when she reached in she found the usual, and something else: a handwritten, plain white envelope with a crooked stamp. Inside was a piece of spiral notebook paper and the tortured block printing of Conrad Marcus, the man who picked up her cheese for delivery. His truck was so old and rusted, its tailpipe was held on by duct tape, and he himself was even older and more broken-down than his truck. *I am sorry, Miss Prickett,* he wrote, *because I have worked for your daddy and your granddaddy, but I really need you to pay what you*

*owe because gas has gotten so dear of late and its hard for a man to make
ends meet.* Margaret's face burned. She took a certain defiant pride
in holding off the credit card companies, but to have overlooked a
bill from Conrad Marcus made her sick with shame.

"August, I need to drive a check over to Conrad's place," she
called into the barn when she got back. "Can you watch things for a
minute?"

She looked down the long row of empty stalls, the floor still holding puddles from its recent hosing, giving off that clean, riverbank smell
of wet concrete. Only heavy-bellied, swaybacked Sultana moved inside her pen, brought inside for the last few weeks of her pregnancy to
rest and store up her reserves for the delivery. *August?* she was about to
call again, when she heard someone speaking overhead in the hayloft.
It was August's voice but not August's voice—a mellower, sadder baritone, different from his reedy Jefferson, the one that conjured ripping
tinfoil no matter how accurate he told her it was. She followed the voice
up the ladder to the wide-planked loft, where August was getting the
place ready for a winter that seemed determined not to come. He had
spent the morning restacking bales to make room for what was drying
in the field, and had moved on to tarring the many hairline cracks in
the ceiling. There was still so much seed and pollen swirling in the air,
he was painting on a field every time he lifted his brush, and there some
future archeologist might be able to determine what Virginia dairy cattle
ate, circa the beginning of the twenty-first century, by bits of haylage,
trapped like bugs in amber.

"And after she was gone," said August, ministering to the cracks
in the ceiling, "His Heart cried out: 'Deeply practised in the school
of affliction, the human heart knows no joy which I have not lost,
no sorrow of which I have not drunk! Fortune can present no grief of
unknown form to me! Who then can so softly bind up the wound of
another as he who has felt the same wound himself? But Heaven
forbid they should ever know a sorrow!'"

He was unaware of her presence, she knew, for he rarely spoke at
length when they were alone together during the day, unless it was to
pass on information about one of the girls. She stood for a moment at

the top of the ladder, watching him work. He had tied a red cotton bandanna over his nose and mouth to filter the pollen, but a less-threatening bandit she couldn't imagine. He was simply too tall and gangly to take seriously, with hay poking like Indian feathers from his wavy red hair. His ears were red too, from the exertion of reaching for the rafters, and she could see where his loose white shirt drooped from his shoulders, from his ruddy farmer's tanned neck. He spoke again, this time changing the clip of his voice to one more impatient and didactic.

"And the Head replied: 'I often told you during its course that you were imprudently engaging your affections under circumstances that must have cost you a great deal of pain: that the persons indeed were of the greatest merit, possessing good sense, good humour, honest hearts, honest manners, & eminence in a lovely art; that the lady had moreover qualities & accomplishments, belonging to her sex, which might form a chapter apart for her: such as music, modesty, beauty, & that softness of disposition which is the ornament of her sex & charm of ours; but that all these considerations would increase the pang of separation . . .'"

August dipped his paintbrush in character and splashed tar passionately against the roof.

"'. . . In time, my friend,'" he continued in the same exasperated voice, "'you must mend your manners. This is not a world to live at random in as you do. . . . The art of life is the art of avoiding pain: & he is the best pilot who steers clearest of the rocks & shoals with which he is beset. Pleasure is always before us; but misfortune is at our side: while running after that, this arrests us. The most effectual means of being secure against pain is to retire within ourselves, & to suffice for our own happiness. Those, which depend on ourselves, are the only pleasures a wise man will count on: for nothing is ours which another may deprive us of. Hence the inestimable value of intellectual pleasures. . . .'"

He turned to dip his brush again, and in doing so caught sight of Margaret's wondering face. He immediately dropped his brush and retreated into mortified silence.

"That was quite a conversation you were having," said Margaret, climbing the rest of the way up the ladder. She was enjoying his embarrassment.

"That was Thomas Jefferson," August rushed to explain. "In Paris, he fell in love with a married woman, a painter, and to get over her, he wrote a dialogue between his Head and his Heart. I was just practicing parts of it."

"Oh," said Margaret.

"I'm giving a program for the Richmond chapter of the DAR next week. I thought a little romance might please the ladies."

"I guess election year is an especially busy time for Founding Fathers."

"I'd better go down and check on Sultana," August mumbled, unable to meet her eyes. "Let me get out of your way."

Margaret regretted mocking him and put out her hand as he walked past. "Is that what you do, August? Do you live your life avoiding pain? Do you only value intellectual pleasures?"

He dared a glance at her, unsure if she was being kind or still teasing. "I'm definitely more of a Head," he replied slowly.

"A head *case* is more like it." Margaret laughed. "Why do you spend so much time being someone else?"

He struggled for an answer. "Who else should I be?"

"August," she said, and this time there was no trace of teasing. "That heart of yours is wilting away here on this farm with us. I'm sorry that I've been monopolizing you so much since Francis left."

"I don't mind," said August, hesitating at the ladder. "I like it here."

"Still," she replied. "I'm going to start giving you more time off. But only if you promise to go out on a date every now and then and tell me what it's like."

She had meant it to sound lighthearted, but a bit of the hollowness she had been feeling all afternoon crept into her voice. August looked at her sharply.

"You know I could never do that," he said in a rush. "You know—"

"Margaret! Are you in here?"

Neither of them had heard a car pull up, but when Margaret went to the loft window she recognized the leased gold Lexus in the driveway. "It's Crenshaw from the bank," she whispered, sitting heavily upon a bale of hay. "Oh God, what am I going to do?"

"What's he come about?" asked August, immediately remembering her unopened letter.

"I have no idea," Margaret lied. "Listen, will you go downstairs and tell him I'm not here?"

"Your truck is right out front."

"Tell him it broke down and I'm out with a friend. Or that I was kidnapped by aliens. August, please, tell him anything," Margaret hoarsely pleaded. "Just don't make me talk to him. I can't face him today."

For all his Jeffersonian affinity, August had far more in common with George Washington where veracity was concerned. He could conceal, but he could not confabulate, and the idea of lying to a man from a bank especially filled him with horror. But then he looked into Margaret's frightened eyes, and knew it was in his power to take a little bit of that terror away. His Head told him it might very well be a crime to lie to an officer of a federally regulated institution, but his Heart led him to the ladder, where he descended like a martyr to the lion's den. He gave Margaret a brave smile and called out with forced cheerfulness, "Hey there, Bob, that you?"

The bald little man below threw up his hands in mock terror when August leapt down. "Don't shoot! I'd give you all my money but I left it at the bank."

August realized he hadn't untied the bandanna over his nose and mouth, did so, and hastily shoved it in his pocket. "Aw, come on," he joked to cover his nervousness. "A powerful man like you must carry a spare thousand or two."

"Wish I did, my friend," said Bob Crenshaw, laughing uncomfortably along with him. "Times are hard for everyone."

Like August, Robert Crenshaw had been born and raised in Three Chimneys, and like August, he himself had been more than a little in love with Margaret growing up. But his family had moved here within the last century, and moreover, had always been tied up in money, so they had neither Vaughn nor Prickett standing in the community. Still, despite their social inequality, young Bob Crenshaw had often fantasized about stealing off with the dreamy Miss Prickett and showering her with love sonnets, for like T. S. Eliot, he considered himself a banker-poet, and saw no incompatibility between love and lucre. He was here today on an unpleasant mission, though, and wanted to get it over with as quickly as possible.

"Where's Margaret?" he asked, peering behind the taller man. "I need to talk to her."

The lie came far more easily to August than he had imagined it would. "She's giving my mother a driving lesson."

"Your mother's learning to drive at her age?"

"The hospital's idea. They're running short of patients."

"Margaret's truck's in the driveway," Crenshaw said, skeptically. Margaret had received the bank's letter nearly a month ago and had never responded. He knew she had good reason to avoid him.

"They took our car. Margaret's is a stick shift. We want to teach the old lady, not kill her."

"Know when they'll be back?"

"They just left." August began to warm to his deceit. "I'm surprised you didn't pass them on the road."

Crenshaw nodded, and August could see the tiny furrows of hair transplants budding on his shiny scalp. He looked so utterly out of place in this filthy barn—scrubbed and plump and pinstriped, his polished wing-tip shoes sinking in the manure. Though the man made a pretense of believing August's story, he showed no inclination to leave. Instead, he walked away from his leather briefcase and peered into the cow stalls.

"This one pregnant is she?" Crenshaw asked, nodding at the lowing Sultana.

"Should lay down any day." August followed him nervously. "Good thing, too. Margaret can hardly keep up with orders from New York. Business is really turning around."

"Too little too late, I'm afraid."

"Don't say that, Bob." August wanted to uproot every blade of hair on the barren pink pate. How dare he stroll around this barn as if already taking stock for the foreclosure sale?

"She'd be better off filing Chapter 11 bankruptcy. At least then she could keep possession."

"Come on, it can't be as bad as that."

"August, you don't know the half of it." Crenshaw gingerly patted Sultana's fawn-colored head, and the cow lowed all the louder. "Her agent and I told her after the old man died, she'd better mechanize and join the co-op, but she wouldn't hear it. None of us blame her, mind you. Old man left her with a heavy load, but she won't do what it takes, and now she's going to lose it all."

Margaret file for Chapter 11? Admit to the world she was a bankrupt? August knew she would sooner sink into her grave than dishonor her family like that.

"How are your programs going?" Crenshaw asked to take the scowl off of August's face. "Will we see you on Election Day?"

"What's Election Day without Thomas Jefferson?" he asked.

"I sure do love your programs," said Crenshaw. "Though I must say, I'm a Civil War man myself. You know, my great-great-grandfather was wounded at Chancellorsville. It's important to keep the past alive. So long as you don't get stuck living in it."

Crenshaw looked once more around the barn, and his eyes rested briefly on the hayloft. "When she gets back from her driving lesson tell her to give me a call. She can't avoid me forever." At times like this, the banker wished he wore a hat, for he felt the end of their conversation demanded a polite tipping of one on his part. "Tell her what I said about Chapter 11," he said over his shoulder as he picked his way out of the barn. "I'm happy to help her with the paperwork if she can't afford a lawyer."

"Will do," said August, telling his last lie of the day. He watched the banker slip into his leased Lexus, with its white leather upholstery and its global navigation system, as if Crenshaw were likely to drive anywhere he might get lost. His briefcase was expensive, and his suit was expensive, and his car, which he didn't even own, but would upgrade every other year, was expensive, and August felt such a rage against money it nearly choked him. He stood up beside Margaret every day, saw how hard she worked, and how little it rewarded her. He knew she didn't sleep most nights from gnawing anxiety, and yet she was never too exhausted to make her daughter's breakfast, or say a kind word to a frightened cow, or pay her help, a personal check every other week, written in her fine, no-nonsense hand, in homemade black ink that faded to purple if not cashed promptly. He had never known a richer woman with less money in his life.

"Well, I have to get that check to Conrad," she said, climbing down the ladder.

"Did you hear any of that?" asked August, surprised by her nonchalance; he'd expected a tirade or defiance. Margaret looked at him sharply.

"We still have two weeks," she said. "He's out of his mind if he thinks I am going to do anything before Adams Brooke wins this election."

My Dear Madam—Having performed the last sad office of handing you into your pickup, and seen the wheels set to motion, I turned on my heel & walked, more dead than alive, to my own carriage, where I drove in suffering silence, home.

My father was not at the table at the usual appointed dinner hour, and my mother had not heard from him since he had received a summons to University of Virginia Hospital earlier in the day. She was in a most melancholy mood, much given over to talk about the "old days" and how complicated things had become in the intervening years. "Take me, for example," she said. "I tried for years to have more children after you, dear, but the good Lord did not will it so. And did I rush out and buy some eggs or have your father do his thing into a cup? Heavens no! We might all be a good deal happier if we were more content with our fate."

I thought long and hard about what she said—what it meant to be content, and how tricky that one word: fate. I thought of you, dearest madam, fated to carry the load of many spendthrift generations and perhaps, I feared, to sink under it. Then I thought of myself, destined to stand eternally at the leeway of your life, to watch impotently and offer undesired help. I wondered if contentment must forever pass us by, when with only a few words, all might possibly be different. Thus engrossed in thought, I sank into my father's living room chair. As luck would have it, PBS was running a Founding Fathers marathon, and so seated by my television, solitary & sad, the following dialogue took place between my Head & my Heart:

Head: Well, friend, you seem to be once again in a fine state.

Heart: I am indeed the most wretched of beings. One who touches me deeply is in the gravest of trouble and I am forced to sit helplessly by.

Head: And yet that trouble is not your trouble, so why do you disturb our equilibrium with it? Has your friend in question given you any cause to think she would desire your help?

Heart: She has in fact done just the opposite, and bid me not concern myself.

Head: Then as the voice of reason, I would advise you to obey her.

Heart: Oh, that is easy for you to say! You who live cloistered like a monk, never having felt the pang of admiration for another.

Head: If I do prefer the pleasures of solitary scholarship over crass carnality, is it really so surprising? Have I not been taught by a thousand different lessons that longing brings only pain? Have you already forgotten that day in our youth when you won me over to your side, when we called a truce to our perdurable war, and united in our devotion to the woman in question? She was not even a woman then, but a mere girl of sixteen, thin and ripened by the sun. We had spent a summer working for her father just to be near her, while she, lazy nymph, read novels in

the hayloft and sunbathed on the new-tarred roof of her porch.
She had no thoughts of responsibility back then, her narrow
shoulders were unbowed by debt or disappointment, and we
loved her in her indolence. How often did we pause in our
journey from stable to cheese house, sweating can upon bony
hip, just to adore her gorgeous inactivity? Then how often shy
away, when her eyelids fluttered in our direction? On the day in
question, just as summer was setting and the chill wind of a
school year gathering, we screwed up our courage and invited
her to climb the hill behind her house, where the old chimney
flared. This had always been our favorite spot on the farm, and
we learned it was hers, too, as we hiked up, our bare paired feet
sweaty in our sneakers, the rhythm of our walking in perfect
partnership. You and I spread a blanket we had found, full of
fleas it turned out, but they were a cause for much merriment
and slapping, and it didn't matter that she had come along out
of boredom more than anything else, because all of her real
friends were off at the beach or touring in Europe. She was
speaking to us as if we were one of those friends, as if we had
shared secrets and might do so again. It was a magical afternoon, if you recall, as we bit into acid-sweet tomatoes like
apples and wiped the juices from our chins. We passed a ther-
mos of iced tea back and forth like a jug of whiskey and pretended to be drunk. Then you, my friend, emboldened me to
slice a wedge of her mother's sharpest cheddar and hold it to
the daughter's lips. Our eyes met as she slowly bit it from the
knife, and it seemed in that suspended moment that all we had
so desired might very well come true. . . .

Heart: Ah, what joy your words give me! How blissfully I remember that day.

Head: Shall I remind what grew out of that cherished moment on
the hill? Nothing! You had not the courage to kiss her then,
and I argued it was premature. And then the school year
started, and then she met that boy, and Polly sprang a few years
later, and she never glanced again.

Heart: Why must you torment me so?

Head: To show that you have barely changed! You still yearn like a lovesick boy and yet are not man enough to act.

Heart: But now I would declare my love, yet you hold me back!

Head: If I gag you, it is to spare you, friend.

Heart: But we must help her! You have been hoarding money in that trust account of yours for years.

Head: She will never accept a loan from me. Not even to save her farm.

Heart: Not from a friend . . . but perhaps from a closer relation . . . ?

Head: Surely you cannot flatter yourself that she will marry you?

Heart: Why should she not? Could she find a more devoted servant than I? Could she find a more adoring father to her daughter or more tender minister to her fields?

Head: You read too many novels, my friend. True love often goes down in defeat when not protectively pressed between the pages of a book.

Heart: We hesitated once before and lost our opportunity. You cannot stop me now. Not when we must lose her for good if she herself loses the farm. I will speak to her, and when I am ready, you, sir, must open your mouth to let my words pass through. There will be no barring of the gate this time.

Head: You are a fool! There is nothing but heartache ahead—!

"Dear, do you mind if I flip over to Channel 12? I was hoping to catch the eleven o'clock headlines."

August started from his reverie at the sound of his mother's voice. How long had he been sitting in this recliner, fighting his internecine battle? The credits were cycling past and that aching Appalachian fiddle that had come to stand for all American music pre-1920, melancholically filled the room. His mother was in the doorway, backlit by the kitchen lamp, wiping her hands upon a shadowy dish towel. August flipped over in time to catch the top story: The presidential race was too close to call, with a few key states hanging in the balance.

"I do wish your father would phone," Evelyn Vaughn said, not staying to watch the headlines, for she had suddenly remembered some cherries that needed pitting if there was to be a pie tomorrow. "I worry about his driving at night. Especially in that beat-up old van."

"I'm sure he's fine," said August, still caught in the undertow between Head and Heart.

"It's only held together by rust and the Lord's Prayer," she called from the kitchen.

August kept up an abstracted conversation with his mother, grunting and "hmmming" enough to be polite. But his thoughts were all given over to Margaret and his bold new plan to speak his mind. If only he could woo as Jefferson had—courting his beloved with the strings of a violin instead of his own weak, tuneless words. When they'd overheard the two lovers in perfect accompaniment on fiddle and piano, suitors to the young Martha Wayles Skelton had thrown up their hands and walked away, knowing their cause was lost.

"In local news," the television anchorwoman was saying, "two more of the eleven children born to Amanda and James Frank of Three Chimneys, Orange County, are dead tonight. Doctors at University of Virginia Hospital state that Baby B and Baby F succumbed to complications following surgery. They were among the largest of the children at birth and had received a better-than-average prognosis. The other eight children remain in critical condition. As you recall, Amanda Frank made history last month with the first-ever recorded live birth of eleven infants. She was being treated with the fertility drug Pergonal."

The rectory door opened just as a grim-looking hospital spokesperson appeared on the television to give a statement.

"Leland!" Evelyn cried, racing to take her husband's jacket and briefcase while August vacated his father's recliner. Leland Vaughn leaned in the doorway like a man just returned from war, grateful to be out of the trenches, but still wearing the sad dust of all he had seen. He let himself be led to his favorite chair and deposited into it heavily.

"Oh, dear," Evelyn fussed. "We had no idea. We just heard on the news."

"Can I get you anything, Dad?" asked August.

"A cold beer if we have it, son, would be great," the priest answered.

"How is poor Manda?" asked Evelyn.

"She is holding up about as well as can be expected," the priest said, allowing his wife to remove his clerical collar and loosen his top button. "She has to be strong for the other children. Jake is taking it mighty hard, though."

"I should make them something," Evelyn said, thinking of the cherry pie that moments before she had been planning for her own enjoyment. It would go straight to Manda and Jake's in the morning, along with a second of blueberry.

August returned with a Heineken that had spent the past two years sandwiched between Worcestershire sauce and sweet relish in the refrigerator door. It foamed up Pastor Vaughn's nose as he tried to drink it, but the priest barely noticed. He downed it in four long swallows.

"I've never seen anything so sad," he said at last, wiping the corners of his eyes. "They had to fit both children with shunts to draw away the spinal fluid leaking into their skulls. There was no way they were going to escape severe brain damage, but the doctors thought they might still live . . ."

"You don't have to tell us about it, Leland," said Evelyn, patting his shoulder. "You should rest."

"I gave them Holy Unction this morning, and then we spent the rest of the day waiting. Watching the doctors treat their seizures, watching them go cyanotic. They had to sedate Jake—he was raging around like a wounded bull— but Manda just sat there, holding their tiny blue hands and waiting for the inevitable. I tried to comfort her, but she seemed beyond reach, like she'd put away some part of herself or, I hoped, given it over to a higher power—I couldn't tell which. The worst thing is, Evelyn," he said, reaching up for his wife's hand, "I don't know if it's strength or despair that's driving her. She's so stoic, and she won't talk. I'm beginning to think we should get Dr. Friedman in to see her."

"Oh, Leland! A psychiatrist?"

"Mom," piped in August, "if she is depressed she could harm herself or the children."

"Manda would never do that," Evelyn replied, scandalized that her own son could think so ill of a neighbor. "Shame on you."

With a deep sigh, Pastor Vaughn hefted himself out of his chair and took his beer bottle to the kitchen, where the fluorescent strip under the cabinet gave off a thin blue light. In the deep porcelain sink, a paring knife lay bleeding beneath a colander of stemmed black cherries; on the counter, carefully filmed in saran wrap, a dinner plate of roast chicken and mashed potatoes awaited him. Everything seemed so normal and familiar compared with the beeping, whirring chaos of today. Leland rinsed his bottle and dropped it in the recycling bin. From the kitchen window, he could see the old kudzu-covered chimney shining in the moonlight, its brick bench beckoning him to sit a while. Evelyn was calling him to come along to bed and August was bidding him good night, but he felt if he just had a moment or two alone, he might be able to make sense of this awful day.

"You all go on, I'll be up in a minute," he told his family, unlocking the back door and stepping out into the overripe night. It shouldn't be this hot so late in October, he thought, and maybe that was part of what had him so unsettled.

Sometime early in life, so long ago he couldn't even remember when he'd heard the tale, a cousin had told him that this plot of land had once been an old Indian burial ground. He didn't doubt his cousin's story, though the boy was an inveterate liar, because over the years he'd found gnawed obsidian arrowheads alongside the broken crockery and melted nails from the tavern fire. Leland had cut his teeth on the history of his family's tavern, yet in his imagination, its chimney had been standing just as it was long before any white man had ever set foot here. He even imagined a legend for it, like the legend of Virginia Dare turned into a white doe, but in his tale, an old Indian chief refused to abandon his post during an attack from an enemy tribe. He guarded his camp faithfully, allowing many women and children to escape, and did not budge even when about to be hacked to death by naked young warriors. Then, in good

Ovidian fashion, just as the enemy hatchet was about to cleave his head in two, the Indian gods took pity on the old chief and turned him into a funnel of stones, a ghostly sentinel to forever watch this plot of land. When the boy Leland shared his hopes and fears with that ancient pile of bricks, he more than half-felt he was whispering them in the wise Indian's ear, and that no matter what, the chief would watch out for him.

He brought a heavy heart out to the Old Man tonight. Ever since he could remember, he had been imagining his home the site of great events and adventures. It seemed so long since anything of note had happened here. His great-grandfather could remember bloody Confederate engagements fought nearby, and *his* great-grandfather lived among older relatives with recollections of James Madison and Thomas Jefferson. Leland knew from the crop in his backyard that history had passed by his very house, for splinters had broken off in proof. And yet all day, ever since he had oiled crosses onto those two small swollen foreheads, he had been fighting the fear that he had pushed too hard for history to once again pay a visit to Three Chimneys. What if it was his desire to see his town once more at the center of things that had pushed his parishioner Manda Frank to have all eleven babies, when every doctor she consulted was against it?

Had he not for years now felt a spiritual drift in his community—felt the modern world, with all its allurements and inevitable tensions, pulling at his congregation, leaving more pews empty every Sunday, putting up walls between neighbor and neighbor? Had he not prayed for some cataclysmic event to unite them all in a common cause, as once a war or a flood might have done? Manda had been the answer to his prayers: a modern miracle to reclaim those adrift, a natural disaster in which no one would be hurt, but instead, lives saved, and even better, before the eyes of the whole country. Looking back on it now, after the deaths of three of those innocent, unsuspecting children, Pastor Vaughn couldn't believe he had thought his advice victimless. Yes, he'd convinced himself he was saving those babies from the abortionist's needle, but had he not become a more vicious murderer? He had thought he was leaving it up to God to play God, but now he felt Satan had come to his church that day in the guise of a confused young mother, and Leland had counseled her out of his own ennui and desire to bring glory to a forgotten town. Manda and her children had been his means to his selfish end.

It was in this position of despair that August found him, leaning his cheek against the Old Man and staring at the moon. August had scared up another beer from the refrigerator, thinking his father might be in need of it.

"The Old Man giving you any inspiration?" August asked by way of letting his father hear his approach. The pastor seemed so lost in thought, his son didn't want to startle him.

"He seems pretty silent tonight," replied the priest.

"Dad, you know it's not your fault."

"I wish I did know that, son."

The two men were quiet for a time while Leland drank his beer and offered the occasional sip to August. For all Leland's skill in counseling parishioners, there had always been an uneasy silence between him and his only child, and Leland often felt, without his wife to act as mediator, a shyness around his son. He was grateful the young man had come out to console him, but he didn't exactly know how to say so.

"I have to write a sermon for those two poor children," the priest said at last. "What can I possibly say about them that I didn't already say about their brother?"

August shook his head. For that, he had no answer.

From the one lit window on the back of the house, a lone figure was watching the men below. Evelyn had wiped the cold cream from her face and neck, then slipped her recently salon-styled hair into its protective net and pinned it at her temples. She had brushed her teeth and thought guiltily about flossing as she did every night before deciding she was too tired and would most definitely get around to it tomorrow. She had exchanged her poplin shirtwaist dress for a thin, faded flannel nightgown, and now she sat in the window seat of the bedroom she had shared with her husband for the past thirty years, listening to the metal box fan rattle against the wooden sill. Around the corner of the fan, she could see the two of them out there by the chimney, passing a beer back and forth. (*Two* for Leland? He only drank at Chinese restaurants, and then only a small glass of plum wine to keep her company.) Not until she saw her husband rise to leave would she abandon her post and slip under the cool sheets of their pencil-post bed, pretending to have been reading the whole time. Until then, she would sit and watch, and if they needed her, she could be outside in a second.

Evelyn put her mouth close to the fan blades and spoke slowly, "Aaaaaaay. Eeeeeee. Iiiiiiii. Oooooooh. Youuuuuu. And sometiiiiiiiimes Whyyyyyyyyy?" She repeated her drawn-out vowels, savoring their robotic choppiness inside the fan. "Aaaaaaaay. Eeeeeeee. Iiiiiiii. Oooooooh. Youuuuuuuu. And sometiiiiiiimes Whyyyyyyyy." Ever since she was a girl and had discovered the joys of reverberation, she could barely pass a fan without whispering something into it. She used to croon Bobby Darin off-key when she was alone, or recite the Preamble to the Constitution, or like tonight, simply say her vowels and listen to them come back to her in a stranger's voice.

She wished her men wouldn't take things so hard, sitting out there alone in the dark as if their worlds were coming to an end. August had seemed preoccupied all night, and she wondered if he wasn't nursing some heartache that he was reluctant to share. She tried not to put pressure on her son, but the one thing she desired more than any other in the world was a grandchild to spoil before she claimed her small plot of God's green acre. She had wondered off and on if her son might be gay, and had tried to discuss it with him, noting, for instance, just how charming those Village People were or pretending to seek his opinion on a new sofa fabric. But he had never taken the opening, and Evelyn had never had the courage to ask outright. She'd noticed that his moods had been more erratic over the past year, since Francis Marvel and Margaret Prickett had separated, but she hoped his heart did not lie in that direction. Margaret was a hard woman, for all of her good qualities, and one who had never shown the slightest interest in her son. It would be a shame for him to break his heart against those particular rocks.

And as for her husband, downstairs suffering for his part in poor Manda's tragedy, Evelyn felt the fiercest loyalty. He had done absolutely nothing wrong, she believed, in counseling Manda to have all eleven children. As a man of the cloth, was he to encourage her to murder half of them in the womb? Where should he have drawn the line? At four? At three? At two? Any self-recrimination, she felt, should be saved for the doctor who got her into this mess in the first place. Evelyn was a firm believer in "What is done is done," in its being best not to dwell on what might have been. Everything had its own inevitable rise and fall. Over the years, she had developed a personal cosmology to suit her way of looking at the world, one that she was convinced Science would eventually prove correct. Like the seasons, everything in life followed in cycles. She believed not in reincarnation per se (that would be un-Christian), but in the endless rise and fall of life and life energies. She believed that one day they would find proof that other advanced civilizations had existed long before this one, that they had flourished, become proud, and annihilated themselves, as this one was bound to do. The Earth's molten core was made up of the souls of all these men—well, not so much their souls (those were in Heaven), but their life energies—like one giant nuclear explosion, or electrical coal pressed into fiery diamond. She had once broached this view with Leland, who hadn't taken her seriously at all and had tried to argue her into line with periodic tables and Scripture. But though Evelyn was as God-fearing a woman as the next, she knew, as Leland obviously pretended not to, that there was much in this world unaccounted for by the Bible. And if he wanted to argue science, she might say that life was like Newton's third law of thermodynamics, which she had learned all the way back in high school: Matter is neither gained nor lost, it is only transformed. Leland might feel the lives of those poor young children were wasted, but Evelyn knew they were ultimately part of God's grand recycling. They would pass through the crucible at the center of the Earth and eventually, along with Atlantis, and Ancient Egypt, and Medieval Rome, give their energies back to the world.

"Aaaaaaaay. Eeeeeeee. Iiiiiiii. Oooooooh. Youuuuuuuu. And sometiiiiiiiimes Whyyyyyyyy," she repeated, letting the blades chop her words and fling them across the humid night. Out by the chimney, Leland and August had ceased talking, and each now stared off into his own corner of night. Evelyn would have laid down her life to make these two men happy, and yet looking upon them from her vantage, her heart ached with something akin to the pain of unrequited love. After only a minute more, she pushed herself up from the window seat and crawled slowly into bed. What was done was done, and no amount of watching was going to transform those dreamy, anguished faces. She knew, with a wife and mother's intuition, that a woman occupied the thoughts of both her husband and son. And yet she also knew, with a wife and mother's infinite, recycled sadness, that in neither case was that woman her.

CHAPTER NINE

Block by block, and tree by tree, the banners came down along School Street. One child dead was an honest tragedy, but three children dead had become, by unspoken agreement, a source of public embarrassment. No candlelight vigil celebrated the short lives of Baby F and Baby B as they were eased into the ground by their brother's side. As Leland presided over the funeral, the family was in attendance, a few curiosity-seekers, and no one else.

With the Frank story taking such a mournful turn, the television crews, too, were gone, having packed up their cameras and headed off in search of other news. A pretty blonde five-year-old had disappeared in California, and a prominent senator was a close, some say too close, friend of the family's. A heretofore-unknown mosquito had materialized in Mississippi, bringing in its whiny wake an outbreak of suspiciously malarial symptoms. And of course there was the election. All the reporters not assigned to missing children and tropical outbreaks went into the scandal-digging business with the gusto of resurrection men.

A thick warm drizzle was falling on School Street a few days before Halloween as Leland squinted through the ineffective windshield wipers of his old VW bus. It hadn't rained for weeks and he drove especially carefully, minding Evelyn's warning that the lightest rain was always the most treacherous, and out of deference to the blinding headache he'd had since this morning. It was the barometric pressure, most likely, or the fact that he needed new glasses, but he had been so distracted of late, he'd missed his last two eye exams. Slowly he crept past the fog-shrouded War Memorial, the empty Drafty's, the empty grocery, the empty hardware store. The spreading oaks, out of decorum, had renounced their brilliant fall foliage, which withered yellow on the branch and fell in diffident soggy barrows along the storm gutters. Leland supposed downtown had always been this quiet and lonely during the day, but he had grown so used to seeing people on the street and cars parked tightly together like happy sunning flocks that normalcy now seemed meager and undernourished by comparison. Neighbors had begun to avoid one another, crossing the street so as not to have to say hello, giving each other wide berth. They were behaving like the sheepish victims of a pyramid scheme or survivors of ergot poisoning, rubbing their eyes as if waking from a collective bad dream. He'd noticed the change today in Snow White when he'd had his morning cup of coffee; faces had darkened at the mention of irresponsible Amanda Frank, giving birth to eleven children she couldn't possibly afford, and hints had been dropped about her extended family's dependence on the State. And then there were the mercenary regrets of the town's businessmen, who'd sat sullenly eating their breakfast. For all the disruption the news crews had caused, profits had risen 40 percent while they were here, and local merchants had begun to look forward to an elevenfold life span of remunerative notoriety. Notorious was how Three Chimneys felt now—famous not as the birthplace of the Frank Eleven, but, instead, as their ill-omened grave site.

Pastor Vaughn was on his way to the Franks this afternoon because of a phone call he had received from Jake last night. Every day since Manda's discharge, the parents had driven the thirty miles into Charlottesville to sit with the babies. There they stayed until lunchtime, after which Jake would make his rounds collecting tin and paper while Manda worked with her hunting dogs until Rose came home from kindergarten. But for the past few days, Jake told him on the phone, Manda had refused to go to the hospital. She wouldn't say why, she simply wouldn't get in the car, and Jake had been forced to go alone. Not that he minded, he explained, but the nurses were telling him that with any luck the strongest babies would be able to go home soon—that is, if the family seemed emotionally ready. Would Pastor Vaughn, if he had a minute, if it wasn't too much trouble, mind coming out to have a few words with his wife?

The dogs in their wet skins set up a furious racket when the minister pulled into the driveway. In the beginning of her pregnancy, Manda, not yet enormous, had tried to keep working. She bred her best hunter and intended to get one last litter in before the babies came; but the dog delivered while Manda was on bedrest, and with Jake too busy to do much more than feed them, they had grown like wild animals—black and tan missiles that launched themselves upon the unwary visitor, too steeped in their dog chaos to take and follow a command. From what Jake told Pastor Vaughn, Manda had been out in the pen working with them every day since she got home from the hospital, hoping to undo the damage, and that was where the minister found her, ankle-deep in mud, scrubbing down the kennel's rusting corrugated tin roof.

"Shut up, you," shouted Manda over the yelps and howling. "*Shut up*, I mean it."

Manda fixed the twelve compact beagles with her stare. The dogs squirmed to an uneasy silence, whining and pawing at the ground, but even sitting still, their skins jumped and their ears vibrated; they were barely domesticated, Leland saw, holding themselves together out of desperation only.

"Hello, Manda," said Pastor Vaughn, and she clapped her hands to release them. The dogs rushed the fence as she closed the gate behind her.

"Hey, Pastor Vaughn," said she, walking to the shed behind the pen. She was wearing nothing against the rain, just an old flannel shirt, gray sweatpants, and a pair of plastic boots. Her lank black hair hung about her pale face, still swollen from all the extra weight she'd put on. Before the pregnancy, any two of the dogs could have knocked her over, but now she seemed like an unassailable stone wall.

"Where's Jake this nasty afternoon?"

"On his rounds, I expect," she answered, still not looking up. She was emptying a thirty-pound bag of Buckeye Hi-Performance into a trash bag–lined steel bin. Pastor Vaughn rushed to help her.

"Shouldn't you be laying off the heavy lifting?" he asked. She shrugged.

"And where's Rose today?"

"In school. Mother picks her up."

"So you're here all by yourself?" he asked. "I guess you should enjoy it while you can."

"I guess," answered Manda, measuring out each dog's ration. She planned to run them on some swamp rabbits in a few weeks and had put them on their conditioning feed.

"So Jake told me the good news that some of the children might be coming home soon," said Pastor Vaughn, a bit too brightly. He found himself unexpectedly nervous around the silent mother, who robotically measured two cups of food into each of the twelve stainless steel bowls. "Will you be happy to have them home?"

Manda looked grimly over the pen, lost in thought. "I think these dogs are ruined," she said at last.

"Manda, could I trouble you for some Tylenol? I have a vicious headache," said the preacher, wanting to break the depressing spell cast by the wet dogs and the musty food, the unmucked pen and the relentless drizzle. He was getting soaked, and a dull pain was blooming behind his left eye.

"I've got Percocet if you want it," she said.

"No thanks, Tylenol will do."

He followed her through the garage, where she stepped around a large pile of donated toys, many still in their original packaging, many more obviously used: a chipped train set; a doll bruised with dirty fingerprints, her joints arthritic with Cheerio dust. She didn't bother to take off her muddy boots, but tracked brown sludge across the new white carpet on her way into the kitchen. She ran a glass under the tap and placed two round, red pills on the counter.

"Thank you," said Leland.

Manda's old dog Turbo lumbered in from the family room. Her thick nails clicked across the plywood floor as she made her slow, stiff way over to Manda and sat down just where Manda was standing at the sink. Pastor Vaughn's eyes strayed to the unwashed dishes stacked in the sink and the dried cereal stuck to the countertop.

"Why are some dogs house dogs and others outdoor dogs?"

Manda asked, reaching down to rub Turbo's wiry gray muzzle. The dog's formerly brown eyes were now blue with cataracts. "Why do I let this one come inside while I make the others stay out in the rain?"

It was the most Manda had said since he'd arrived, and it gave Leland hope. He took a seat on one of the torn vinyl kitchen chairs and beckoned for her to do the same.

"She could track a swamper four or five hours without ever giving up. With the pack. On her own. She always got her rabbit. If I could have bred her, we'd have had state champions," said Manda, rubbing the old dog, who had flopped heavily onto her side. "But she just wouldn't take. She's one of a kind."

"Manda," said Pastor Vaughn, willing her to look at him. "These have been rough days, I know. No woman should have to go through what you've been through. But you can't lock away your feelings like this and expect to get by alone. You need to reach out. To your husband, your doctors, your church, your neighbors. We are all here for you."

Manda nodded, then took the minister's empty water glass to the sink. She set it in the pile of dirty dishes.

"Jake says you've stopped going to the hospital," he continued. "Do you want to talk about it?"

"I have a lot of work to do, Pastor," said Manda, looking out the window toward the pen. "You see what shape they're in."

"But your children need you most of all," said Leland gently. "They need their mother."

Manda looked at him quizzically. "They've got all those doctors and nurses. These dogs've got nobody."

"But these dogs are just dogs. Your children are your children."
Manda nodded.

"So you'll go back to the hospital?" asked Leland. "You'll be strong for your children?"

"Yes, Pastor Vaughn," said Manda.

"Manda, everyone is praying for you. Everyone wants to help you and Jake through this." Leland tried to make the lie sound convincing, wanting to believe it as much for his own sake as Manda's.

"Once the children are home, you'll see. You'll have more help than you know what to do with."

Manda nodded.

"Three Chimneys is a family," said Leland with finality. "We won't let you down."

Manda rubbed Turbo's belly as if to raise a genie from a lamp.

"Is there anything I can get for you?" asked the priest. "Anything you need?"

"I don't think so," said she. "I think we're good."

"All right then," he said, not wanting to go, but having no real pretext for staying. Despite what Evelyn said, he thought it best to give Dr. Friedman a call. "I'll check in on you later this week."

Manda led him back through the utility room, where piles of Jake's work shirts and pants were heaped atop the washer. If she was this overwhelmed now, he feared the worst for when the babies came home. Manda noticed his frown and automatically stuffed the clothes inside the machine, but didn't bother to turn it on. As she led him to the garage, the phone in the utility room rang.

"Aren't you going to get that?" asked Leland when she kept walking. He imagined the hospital calling or Jake anxiously trying to get through. Manda stopped at the door, but made no move to answer the phone.

"It's just going to be another one of those," said she, without elaborating.

Pastor Vaughn lifted the receiver. "Frank residence," he said.

"*God has cursed you!*" screamed the shrill voice on the other end. "*It's unnatural what you did and now you're being punished. I hope they all die, I hope—*" Leland slammed the receiver down in horror.

The sound of barking dogs, high-pitched and insistent, followed him down the road, so far that he knew he must be imagining it, but then again, maybe it was a trick of the fog, which like a feathery set of gills exhaled every sound and smell in this stretch of woods. His heavy breath obscured the windshield, but when he turned on the defroster, it made the bus so hot, he had to switch it off again. This would be the weather in Hell, Pastor Vaughn thought dully. Not an infinite inferno, but one long unsettled day in between seasons, too hot to wear a sweater, too rainy to go without one, a muggy, clammy, oppressive sort of day, when all the world's sins would stick to a man like dust from the road.

The world was full of hatred, he knew, but out there, not inside his house. His community was a helpful community, not without its foibles, but generous and kind and open-minded. The call obviously came from that vast wilderness beyond, where the Devil had wedged himself between men and their better natures. That world was full of inconstant people, he knew, ones who promised warmth and support but who, when things became difficult, had their own hearths to tend.

When he returned to the parish house, Leland determined, he would get back on the phone himself and make yet another round of calls to all the book agents and movie scouts, the PR firms and Website designers who had contacted him in the early days of the Frank Eleven. His attempts so far had been greeted with embarrassed silence from the assistants on the other end, or, worse, with blithe good cheer. *"Certainly, Mr. *** will get in touch with you right away. He has the number, right?"* Leland would dutifully leave it again, and stress how deeply the Franks needed support in light of their recent tragedy. He understood the story would be a more difficult sell, but all of those people couldn't possibly turn their backs, could they? He thought about the signed contract he had FedExed for that movie-of-the-week, though now he realized gloomily that he'd never received the countersignature.

Fog wrapped the road in a sticky, white cocoon, and Leland was forced to pilot Snakehill Road by instinct alone. Only once before had he ever seen fog so thick, rushing down from the mountains like soup overboiling a pot. It was the night he drove Evelyn home from the hospital in Charlottesville, the long terrible night she miscarried their first child, a girl, not quite five months. The doctors had performed a D & C, and Leland wanted to rent a hotel room rather than face the long drive home. But no, Evelyn had insisted quietly, she wanted to sleep in her own bed; and so he had driven in the worst fog of his life, weather that caused a kind of hysteria, with elderly women stopping their cars in the middle of the road, too afraid to drive on, and young men speeding around them to their near-deaths in oncoming traffic. His wife had fallen asleep in the overheated car, the chocolate brown Plymouth they had back then, her pale cheek resting against the cold window, her young face slack and tired. Now, driving home from Manda's, Pastor Vaughn could barely tell if it was day or night, for it seemed the fog had stolen into the bus and behind his eyes, filling his brain with cobwebs. His headache had assumed the form of a deep red pitcher plant, luring whatever random thoughts crawled near. It was so hard to concentrate. Mary Todd Lincoln suffered from migraines, he thought incongruously. Maybe I have MS.

Leland blinked, and a figure separated itself from the fog directly in front of him. A dog, of all things, dead center in the middle of the road, just inches from his bumper. The black and tan beagle sat unconcerned and serene, like a grinning canine incarnation of the Buddha. Leland slammed on the brakes and turned the wheel sharply to the left, but felt the sickening lurch of his tire going over something brittle and softly resistant. And then he was woefully off balance, the nose of his bus angled into the ditch, where it hit with the wicked retort of a discharged rifle, sending him sharply into the steering wheel. With a gulp, the pitcher plant swallowed his eye and vomited it out again.

From somewhere far off in the woods, Leland heard a mournful howl; it took him a long minute to realize it was not animal, but the echo of the VW's horn, depressed by his bleeding cheek. I hit that dog, thought Leland weakly. I hit that dog. But even as his eyes were shutting and his fingers losing their grip on the steering wheel, he thought he saw, from the corner of his throbbing eye, something black and tan wriggle out from beneath his bus and bound joyfully off into the mist.

For the final presidential debate, Margaret broke her rule about watching television during dinner. She wheeled the small set out of the closet and into the kitchen, where she and Polly watched the proceedings in black and white, through static not quite controlled by the coat hanger over the antenna. Night had gathered, but the two sat cozily at the long kitchen table, safe inside a yellow circle of lamplight. The room smelled like a Norman Rockwell painting of dinner: Margaret's home-made meat loaf, mellow orange winter squash baked with butter and cinnamon, an apple crumb. Polly ate hers over her history homework, her textbook opened to the Election of 1800—one of the most bitterly contested in American history, Mr. March said. Jefferson created the first opposition party, and factionalism was born.

Margaret thought that so far, Adams Brooke was clearly win-ning the day. Though he was dressed identically to the president— in a dark suit, white shirt, and yellow tie—he came across as someone who had pulled on his clothes in a hurry and couldn't wait to get out of them again. His tie was infinitesimally askew, loosened moments before he went on the air; his hair, too, was not worn laquered to his head, as per Beltway fashion, but rumpled rakishly, as if he'd just re-moved a John Deere cap after a hard day's work. His lack of pretense was what she admired most about him. When Adams Brooke rolled up his shirtsleeves you saw, rather than the pale extremities of a leg-islator, the tan, muscular, pre-melanoma arms of a man who'd spent his life outdoors, on the farm, on the battlefield, in the service of others. The current president played golf. Adams Brooke built houses for the homeless. Maybe no one else noticed these things, but Mar-garet did, and it sometimes seemed to her that this close race could come down to something as subtle as that—were you the sort of voter who wanted your president comfortable in a suit?

"Mom, do you think August is in love with you?" asked Polly, looking up from her textbook.

"What?" exclaimed Margaret, taken completely by surprise by the question.

"He spends an awful lot of time here," said Polly, helping herself to more acorn squash. Her mother now only allowed them to eat what was grown locally and in season, so there would be no more juicy to-matoes or sweet corn until next year, unless she ate what they'd canned. The pollution created from trucking vegetables, even organic vegetables, all the way across the country was simply not worth it, her mother said.

"August is an old friend," replied her mother. "I've known him longer than I have your father."

"I can't imagine August in high school." Polly laughed. "Did he wear his Jefferson costume back then?"

"I don't remember much about August in high school. He worked for Grandpa. He seemed completely normal."

"Well, I think he's in love with you."

Margaret frowned at her daughter. "Pay attention to the debate," she said. "This is history happening."

The two turned back to the television, eating in silence. Adams Brooke was explaining his Family Matters Pledge. *We are all a family,* he was saying. *Those within our own houses and those outside our borders. We must discipline fairly and we must forgive and embrace, even the prodigal son. As a superpower, we should be a benevolent father, but as a member of the global family, we must also be a respectful brother, listening to the voices of others. First and foremost, both at home and abroad, we must understand that Family Matters—*

"Mom," asked Polly, interrupting. "How can you tell?"

"How can you tell what?" asked Margaret, with one eye still on the television.

"If a man is in love with you?"

Margaret turned to face her daughter. So this was what all her erratic behavior had been about. Polly was in love. Of course, she should have seen it months ago, but it had never occurred to her that the moodiness and rebellion might be the by-product of her first crush. She had much to say to Polly on the subject, and much to warn her against, but she really wanted to hear the debate.

"There are a lot of ways to tell," said Margaret, waiting until the governor finished speaking and the president began. "He pays attention to you. He makes you feel important. When others are talking, he listens out for you, and answers as if you were the only one in the room. But Polly, you are too young to be thinking of love. You have your whole life ahead of you."

"I'm not thinking about it," said Polly defensively. "I was talking about you."

"Don't worry about me."

"It's just that you haven't been on a date since Dad left," Polly said, then added under her breath, "and Adams Brooke is already married."

"Why is it," asked Margaret, "that everyone thinks if you admire and believe in someone, you must be in love with them? Adams Brooke is an honest and morally upright politician, and one who stands to help us. I'm no more in love with him than August is with me."

"If you say so," replied Polly skeptically. "But don't you think it's funny that you and I will start dating at the same time?"

"You're not dating for several more years," said Margaret, "and I'm never dating again. I'm done with men. Now, be quiet. I want to hear this part."

Adams Brooke was talking again, answering the president's challenge about his stance on homeland security.

With terrorist threats against our water and food supply, Adams Brooke was saying, *now, more than ever, we need to turn our attention to the predicament of the American farmer. In these troubled times, it is irresponsible to have our nation's agriculture concentrated in a few megafarms owned by centralized agribusiness. If for no other reason than our own safety, we need to return to the ways that made our country great—by growing and eating locally. And that can only be achieved by supporting America's small farmers.*

"Hear! Hear!" said Margaret, pounding the table in approval.

Let me give you an example, said the governor, lowering his voice and speaking into the camera. *There is a family farm in Three Chimneys, Virginia, owned by a struggling young mother named Margaret Prickett—*

"Mom!" cried Polly. "Oh my God! That's you!"

Margaret paused with her fork halfway to her mouth. He said her name. On national television. Not in a stump speech in a cornfield somewhere, but during a national debate, watched by millions of people across America. Campaign Headquarters hadn't lied to her—he really did know who she was. Margaret felt her cheeks burn as if the entire country had suddenly swung around to look at her.

Margaret is struggling to keep her dairy farm afloat in the face of mounting debt and government indifference, continued Adams Brooke. *Her family has worked the same piece of land for two hundred years, since the founding of this great country, but she is about to lose it all. It's for small, hardworking farmers like Margaret Prickett of Three Chimneys, Virginia, that I am proposing my onetime amnesty under the Family Matters Act—*

"Mom! Oh my God! He's talking about you!"

Margaret barely heard her daughter through the roar in her head, the thunderous applause of the House and the Senate and all their invited guests as she stood up to be recognized during President Brooke's first State of the Union address. *"It was for people like Margaret that I worked so hard to see this amnesty through, and now that you have passed it in a tremendous show of bipartisan support, her farm, like that of so many other brave Americans, is safe at last."*

I understand the pain of farmers like Margaret, because my grandparents owned a small dairy farm in North Carolina, Adams Brooke continued on the TV, telling the story Margaret cherished above all others. It was how she knew he would follow through on this promise, even if he broke all others. *I worked there every summer of my boyhood and let me tell you, it's hard work. It's backbreaking work. But it's also rewarding work, and it should be lucrative work. My grandfather had a saying, one he repeated so often he put it over the door to his milk house. He used to say to me, "Adams, Omnis pecuniae pecus fundamentum." And I'd say, "Papaw, in English, please." And he'd translate, "The herd is the foundation of all wealth." Small farmers in this great country should be able to earn a living wage, and if I am elected in November, I will see to it they do!*

"Mom?" Polly said, aghast. "Did you hear that? Did you hear what he said?"

But Margaret wasn't listening. She could not take her eyes off Adams Brooke's kindly face and easy, gap-toothed smile, his eyes crinkling at the corners as he joked about his grandfather's gift for Latin.

She was suddenly seized with the same pit-of-the-stomach feeling she'd had the day she glimpsed Francis in his pickup, a woman's head, so very obviously not her own, nestled on her husband's shoulder.

"Mom," cried Polly. "He stole our saying."

"Be quiet," Margaret snapped, needing desperately to think. "We don't own that saying. It's from the Jersey Club. Maybe his grandfather was a member too."

"They called you a few weeks ago," Polly said. "I was right there. You told them all about it."

"Everything you heard in that room is confidential," said Margaret swiftly. "It's like a doctor's office or a confessional. You swore."

"I didn't swear."

"It's got to be a coincidence," said Margaret, trying to calm her pounding heart. "Adams Brooke has his own family history. Why would he need ours?"

"If he'd lie about his own grandfather, what else is he lying about? Mom, you've got to tell somebody."

This brought Margaret up short. A few reporters still lingered from the Frank Eleven story; the last thing she needed was for one of them to overhear Polly talking to one of her school friends. "Polly, don't tell anyone about this," she said.

"You can't censor me," retorted Polly. "I have rights under the First Amendment."

"You have no rights in this house," said Margaret hotly. "Too much is riding on this election for you to be childish right now. I need you to give me your word."

The two stood locked in mutual defiance, neither willing to back down, neither willing to call the other's bluff. On the television, the president was saying that our enemies were developing weapons of mass destruction and it was only a matter of time before they used them.

"Hello," a muffled voice called from the back door, causing mother and daughter to flinch at the same time. "Is anybody home?"

Reluctantly taking her eyes off Polly, Margaret strode across the kitchen. The fog was so thick outside, she couldn't make out who was standing there, until she opened the door and Leland Vaughn all but fell inside. His face was pale and a thin line of dried blood ran from a cut on his forehead down to the corner of his mouth.

"Oh, my God, Leland!" cried Margaret, helping him into the room. "What happened to you?"

"Just a little run-in with the ditch," he said, joking weakly. "Long time since I've seen fog like that."

"Where is your bus?"

"About a mile up the road toward town," he answered.

"Let me call you an ambulance."

"No," said Leland swiftly. "August will be home soon. He had a program tonight. I'll phone him to come get me."

"For goodness' sakes, Leland," said Margaret, thinking swiftly, *August had a program. He won't have seen the debate.* "I'll drive you home. But I think you should see a doctor first."

"It's nothing, really," said Leland. "Just a little bump."

Over his protests, Margaret led the priest to the sink, where she found a clean cloth and ran it under warm water. All the wrinkles invisible from the pulpit revealed themselves under her kitchen light, a busy network of laugh lines and crow's-feet, the decoration of a life well lived. Leland was getting old. She held his familiar face in her hands, gently washing the blood from its folds and creases—the cut was only a superficial head wound, but everyone knew how badly those bled—and he shut his eyes, drifting almost to sleep, letting Margaret take care of him as he never would have allowed an emergency technician. It's all about trust, she thought. Just as Polly said. Gingerly, she painted his cut with the dropper from her tiny vial of iodine, and brushed his silvery bangs forward. If he didn't tell, no one would even suspect he'd been in an accident. Still, when she was done, Leland's eyes remained closed, and his head rested heavy in her hands.

"Leland," asked Margaret gently. "Are you sure you're all right?"

The priest opened his eyes and looked around the kitchen slowly, unsure, she could tell, as to where he was. What was this wet, warm cloth? This kerosene lamp? This counter with its butter churn and coffee grinder? Then his eyes lit on Polly, watching worriedly over her mother's shoulder, and he seemed to come back to himself.

"Just let me catch my breath," said Leland with a reassuring smile. He walked unsteadily to the kitchen table, and with a sigh lowered himself into the chair Polly had vacated. The priest stared appreciatively at the leftover food steadily cooling on the young girl's plate.

"That looks like some mighty delicious. . . . some mighty delicious . . ." They waited for him to continue, but instead his tired eyes went to the old black-and-white set, where the debate, completely forgotten by the two women, was wrapping up. In one of those tricks of science whereby a person's own electricity clears the picture, as Leland leaned forward, Adams Brooke's face emerged from the static, as wholesome and inviting as a fresh-baked pie. Leland smiled at the screen.

"I sure do hope he wins," said the priest. "That Brooke seems like a boy to make his father proud." Polly shot a wry glance at Margaret, who did not respond. On the television, the moderator thanked the participants for a lively and informative debate.

"Meat loaf," said Leland, his eyes lighting up, as if the very syllables of the word he suddenly found in his mouth contained all the flavor of the thing itself. "That looks like some mighty delicious meat loaf."

CHAPTER TEN

"So he really mentioned you in the debate?" asked August over the scarred card table at Campaign Headquarters. "I can't believe I missed it."

"It was no big deal," said Margaret.

"How can you say that? He singled you out—you, out of all the people in America."

"They do that. It's politics."

"I meant to be home to watch it," August said. "My program ran late."

"Really, you didn't miss anything," Margaret said, dialing the heavy four-line telephone. "How is your father?"

"They towed the bus, which was mostly fine," he replied. "Only a crushed bumper. Dad said he hit a dog, but we looked and didn't find a dog. Thanks for driving him home."

Margaret nodded, but she was barely listening. She was extremely grateful August had showed up, but she was in no mood to talk. The polls had not agreed with her that Adams Brooke had trounced the president in last night's debate, and so the race, on this, the eve of the election, was still maddeningly deadlocked. Margaret's solution was to personally phone every name in the thin county phone book. She had made it up through the Ks and was about to start on the Ls, with only three hours left before people would be in bed, when August, her savior, had showed up and, on his private cell phone, begun working backward from the Zs.

"I finally convinced him to see the doctor—" August broke off as the answering machine at the number he was calling picked up. "This is a reminder from the Friends of Adams Brooke." He spoke slowly and deliberately, as to an especially dense child. "Tomorrow at the polling booth, show America that Family Matters, and check the box marked 'Governor Adams Brooke for President.'"

He pushed END on his phone and looked at his watch. "It's past dinnertime. I know a lot more people are home, but no one is answering the phone."

"If you can take some constructive criticism," said Margaret, "you're not putting a lot of heart into it. Listen to me . . ." Her line picked up, and she began enthusiastically: "Hello, this is a neighborly reminder from the Friends of Adams Brooke—No, wait, don't hang up, I just need a moment of your time—" Margaret found herself speaking to the dial tone. "Screw you, then."

"Yes, that's much better," August said, smiling.

But Margaret was in no joking mood. Since the debate, everything felt like it was unraveling. They needed a hook, something to convince people to listen past the first "Hello."

"August," she said with sudden inspiration. "Why don't you phone people as Thomas Jefferson. Adams Brooke is always quoting him, and what better endorsement could he get?"

August was silent as he dialed the next number. "Go ahead," Margaret urged. "Do your Jefferson."

"This is a neighborly reminder from the Friends of Adams Brooke . . . ," he began, speaking into yet another answering machine.

"No," whispered Margaret. "Your Jefferson. *Your Jefferson.*"

August tried to continue, but Margaret's frantic gesturing threw him into confusion. Without finishing his speech, he hung up the phone. "I can't 'do' Jefferson. It doesn't work that way."

"What do you mean?" asked Margaret in annoyance. "Don't tell me you need to get into character. You're not one of those method actors?"

"No, I mean I've never used Thomas Jefferson. When I became a living historian, I made a compact with myself—never to put him in the service of anything other than history. I don't want to turn him into just another pitchman."

Margaret sullenly watched him dial the next number, get a busy signal, and hang up. She continued to stare at him until he squirmed uncomfortably in his chair. "Why don't I go next door and get us some coffee," he said. "I think I can catch Mrs. Hawks before she closes."

"I'm sorry I snapped," Margaret said wearily. "With the race so close, I was willing to try anything."

"I know," he said, slipping around the card table and out the door. "It's just that some things are more important than politics."

For her part, Margaret couldn't think of any. Every night except last night when she stayed home to watch the debate, she'd been in this cramped, stale office until well after midnight, making phone calls and typing letters; or driving around in her car, nailing *Brooke for President* posters on people's trees. Some nights she didn't get to bed until well after 2 A.M., after she had finished baking cranberry muffins, or composting, or washing clothes. And then she had to be up by 5 A.M. to start the day all over again. Today, she'd been on the phone since milking this morning, with only the briefest interval for milking this afternoon. Chores around the farm had fallen far behind, and the girls were on a subsistence diet of whatever they could forage from the field, supplemented with a few hastily baled forkfuls of hay. Their milk production had dropped off with the disruption of their familiar daily routine. They were used to being coaxed and sung to, carefully curried and practically tucked into bed. For the first time in her life, Margaret regretted having so lavishly spoiled her cows. She was merely quick and efficient with them these days, yet they were punishing her as if she had suddenly started beating them and taken away their television privileges. It was like having a stableful of teenagers as ungrateful and difficult as the one who slept down the hall from her in her house.

". . . Hello, as you know, tomorrow is Election Day, and the race is neck and neck. Adams Brooke hopes every American will exercise his or her sacred right and come down to the polling booth to vote. And he hopes when faced with four more years of corporate greed, you'll say, 'No, my *Family Matters. I choose Adams Brooke, the Farmer's Friend.*'"

"Maggie? Is that you?"

What had she done? Margaret frantically ran her finger down the tight lines of the phone book until she hit the name Marvel. In her haste and fatigue, she had inadvertently dialed the seven poisoned digits belonging to her husband.

"Never mind, sir," she said coolly. "I know how you are going to vote."

"I'm voting for the man whose grandfather is a whiz at Latin."

"You saw the debate?" she asked queasily.

"Of course I did. Congratulations. You're a celebrity."

Margaret had forgotten about her ex-husband, who, of course, remembered the sign in the cheese house. "Listen, Francis," she said sternly, "his campaign headquarters called me and I gave them that motto. They had my permission to use it."

"Whatever gets you through the night, Maggie." Francis said, laughing. "He's just a lying scumbag like all the rest."

"What are you going to do?" she asked.

"Do?" he asked. "I'm not going to do anything. I just want you to remember my generosity next time I'm ten minutes late with a check."

Margaret slammed the receiver into its cradle, then lifted it and slammed it a few more times for good measure. August stepped into the room with a cup of steaming coffee, fixed just as she liked it, extra milk and no sugar. He stood still and watchful, waiting for her to calm down before he spoke.

"You need to go home," August said with quiet authority. "We don't have that many more people to call, and I'm happy to stay here and finish up."

Margaret looked at him through the sweaty tangle of her hair. She hadn't gotten more than three hours of sleep any night in nearly a month, and she was beginning to hallucinate. Was that a golden light around August's head or just a weird refraction of the compact fluorescent?

"You drive yourself home and go to bed," he said, daring to order her. "Tomorrow is going to be a busy day and you need to be rested."

She thought about fighting with him, but tears welled in her eyes at the idea of eight whole hours of sleep. "You really don't mind making the calls?" she said at last.

"Not a bit."

"And you'll make them all?" she couldn't help but add. That extra nudge would have sent Francis off the handle, but August merely smiled patiently and swore he would make every last call before he left the office.

"I don't know what I'd do without you," Margaret said, rising and giving his rough hand a squeeze. "I'll see you tomorrow?" she asked, gathering her pocketbook and sweater.

"What's an election without Thomas Jefferson?" He looked up briefly, for he was already dialing the next M in the phone book.

Margaret left her full cup of coffee cooling on the table and drove herself home.

She knew, when she nearly hit her daughter, who was running along the edge of the stubbled field like a panicked rabbit, that there would be no full night's sleep tonight. Before she could even roll down the window, Polly had ripped open the passenger door and breathlessly told her that something was wrong with Sultana. She'd tried to reach her at Election Headquarters, but August said she'd left already. Margaret fought the urge to back down the driveway and leave the old cow to deliver her calf all alone. She could get a hotel room somewhere on the Interstate, unplug the phone, drink a fifth of Jack Daniel's, and let nature take its course. Instead, she told Polly to get in, and together they drove up to the barn.

They found the expectant mother laying awkwardly on her left side with her thick gelatinous eyes rolled up toward the tarred barn roof, vainly seeking heavenly intervention. Her other stock waited dully through labor, panting and grunting and each delivery seemed to take less time than the last. But Sultana, her prized milker, was as dumb and nervous as a new heifer. She had been bred six times already, yet each birth presented a new horror and opportunity for bovine melodrama. Sultana had been lowing loudly ever since Margaret left, Polly told her, and had broken her water about an hour ago. Polly knew calves came relatively quickly if all was well. Most calves arrived unassisted in the middle of the night, and by the time she arrived for morning milking, the fresh-licked little one was lustily nursing or bucking about. She had never seen one of her mother's cows in such distress before. She feared that sweet, stupid Sultana was dying.

After just a brief glance at the downed cow, Margaret ordered Polly to fetch the iodine soap, then went to wash up in the barn's splash sink. She was so tired, she just stood there scrubbing her nails and forearms, chaffing the skin all the way up to her already reddened elbows. The hard plash of the water, mixed with the cow's piteous bellowing, seemed to carry with it the pleas of her own epidural-free, torturous delivery of Polly and the cadence of her newborn daughter's first-breath wails. The sound of a female in agony had its own hypnotic power, Margaret thought, soaping and scrubbing with the mindless repetition of a hospital resident at the end of a thirty-six-hour shift. It was the first, most reliable sound any child born would ever hear.

"Mom, wake up."

Margaret shook herself. She had to deliver this calf. She dried her arms, stripped off her good shirt so that she was wearing nothing more than her white cotton bra, and fitted herself with a fresh pair of plastic OB sleeves. Polly placed a pair of Plexiglas welder's goggles on her mother's nose and, carrying the bucket of iodine and a Coleman lamp, followed Margaret to Sultana's stall.

"It's okay. It's okay," Polly whispered to the miserable cow, who scrambled to her feet at their approach. She followed her mother's orders to slip a halter over the animal's neck and tie her to the stanchion. "We're just here to help you."

The lights were low throughout the barn and the Coleman lamp threw a shadow herd against the wall. Sultana's restless sisters paced their pens, rattling their feed trays and craning their shaggy necks to see. They watched Margaret lubricate her arm up to her shoulder and approach their sister's washed backside. Tails switched and pink grapefruit uteruses clenched in sympathy.

With her arm deep inside the cow, Margaret felt for the calf's position. She should have been able to grasp two front fetlocks and make out the calf's cone-shaped head. To her dismay, however, instead of a muzzle Margaret felt a bony ridge of tail, and instead of the front knees, the hocks. It was as she feared—the calf was turned completely around and was coming out back legs first.

"We're going to have to pull her out," she announced wearily, resting for a minute on a bale of hay. "I'm going to need you to help me."

"Shouldn't we call August?" Polly asked. Margaret glanced at her watch and figured that he could only be up to the Ps in the local phone book. It was more important for him to remain where he was, she decided. They would have to do it without him.

She dispatched Polly for the calving chains, while she inserted both arms deep into the cow and worked to expand the birth canal. She had never delivered a posterior calf alone, though she had assisted her father twice, tugging her length of chain at his command, easing off when a contraction let up. They had saved one calf and lost one calf, when the umbilical cord kinked and the animal gasped too much fluid in utero. She and Polly would have to work fast once the legs presented, and pray they had the strength to tug a fifty-pound infant from its mother's flesh. It would be a bloody and dangerous business.

Why was this happening tonight? Margaret railed to herself, using twine to tie the animal's tail to her collar so that it did not lash the midwife blind. While other campaign workers were drinking coffee and laughing over doughnuts, locked in the punch-drunk confraternity of a college all-nighter, she was up to her armpits in gore and placenta, easing a life into being that might very well be snuffed if those same hypercaffeinated, sour-breathed soldiers in headquarters across America didn't take tomorrow's election. Somewhere in the sky above block-printed states, her Adams Brooke was napping on a plane, resting his voice for his final twenty-four-hour campaign blitz—a rally at midnight for night-shift workers at an Arkansas Toyota plant, a 3 A.M. call to arms in a Kansas cornfield, 5 A.M. pancake breakfast sermon with United Garment Workers Local 215 in Seattle. As she relubricated her arms and looped the birthing chains over the stuck calf's rear dewclaws, she pictured herself there beside him in the roomy airline cabin, watching him in the dim half-light, pinpricked with reading lamps others had forgotten to turn off. Instead of hooking easy-grip pull handles to a link of chain, she was leaning over her candidate with a blue plaid wool blanket; instead of calmly explaining to her daughter the necessity of working with each contraction until the legs emerged, she was easing his bifocals from his nose and folding them into his pocket. She might be pushing Sultana onto her side to give the calf a better angle, but in reality, she was easing herself into the seat beside her candidate and gently tugging a corner of his blanket for her own cold, weary body. *"I'm sorry I stole your family history,"* he whispered, just as she was falling asleep. *"As soon as I win, you can have it back."*

"Mom, are you okay?"

Margaret focused on her anxious, excited daughter. She had never allowed Polly to help with a birth before, and now together they were going to tug another creature into being. She made Polly grasp the handle at one end of the chain and on Sultana's next contraction gave the order to pull—gently but forcefully, the bottom leg only. They felt the calf give internally an inch or two before the contraction eased and Sultana closed her eyes to rest. They didn't have long before the next pang, and this time it was Margaret's turn to pull upon the chain, coaxing the top rear leg as far along the birth canal as Polly's had come. They took turns this way for nearly an hour, not daring to pull too hard and risk tearing the mother or injuring the calf. They traded off, barely speaking, watching the cow for the first signs of tensing, then tugging up to follow the natural curve of her cervix, before they would tug down to arc the calf all the way out. After about half an hour, the sharp dark hooves presented. Another fifteen minutes and a set of flopping blue hind legs dangled from the mother's vulva like a second slimy tail.

Only then did Margaret order Polly to pull with all her might and not wait for the natural rhythm of the contractions to aid them. They dug in their heels and planted their rumps on the stale wet straw, arched their backs, and pulled like biblical oarsmen, tugging for the life of this calf, who would suffocate if they didn't get it out quickly once its cord was pinched. Margaret's arms trembled and screamed, and she couldn't imagine how her much younger daughter was bearing it, but when she glanced over, Polly's eyes were clenched in concentration and her knuckles were white around the grips. She was not going to let this calf die any more than Margaret was, and the older woman was overcome with a love so fierce and all-consuming, it took all her will not to drop the birthing chains and embrace her sweating, blood-smeared daughter. "*Pull*," she heard herself grunt like a boatswain, "*Pull*," and they gave one last final heave before the tension evaporated on the chains and a limp, helpless animal slithered out onto the straw. Margaret didn't know where she found the strength in her used-up arms, but she immediately hoisted the blue calf by its back legs so that the fluid might drain from its lungs, even as she yelled at Polly to dump a bucket of cold water over its head. She grasped its skull as if to kiss it, and ran her trembling thumbs from the bridge of its nose to its muzzle to expel any mucus in its sinuses. Polly followed her mother's instructions to tickle its nostrils with a piece of straw, and was rewarded with a bombastic sneeze and the new calf's first terrified bellow.

They'd done it. And it was a heifer. Margaret's first cautious thought concerned the profitability of the herd. But August's fear of twins was still with her and she knew she needed to examine Sultana again for signs of a second calf. She'd have to wash her arms and Sultana's rump before slathering herself with more lubricant and starting the process all over again. She looked over at Polly to tell her they were not done yet, and saw that her daughter had turned away.

Margaret crawled on her knees to where her daughter sat spilling hot tears over the sticky new calf. Sultana was too exhausted to clean her, and Polly was gently wiping the cheese-bloody afterbirth from the baby's soft hide. Laughing and crying at once, Polly looked up at her begrimed mother, much as Margaret herself had done when the doctor had placed the hard-won infant Polly on her naked chest.

"How can you stand to love something so instantly?" Polly asked.

Sultana was lowing again, and Margaret feared what she would find when she once more groped the recesses of the cow. She tried to prepare Polly for the possibility that another calf was still inside and that it might well be a male, and that if so, it would mean the heifer she now wept over, the one they had struggled so hard to deliver, was a freemartin, and thus sterile. She tried to explain the biology behind opposite-sexed twins in cattle, how their blood mingles as they float in their mother's womb, how the heifer drinks of her brother's testosterone and in so doing unsexes herself. She might look perfectly normal on the outside, Margaret went on, but inside she is blighted and undeveloped and unable to have offspring or give milk. She is an utterly useless creature.

Polly nodded her impatient comprehension, but Margaret could see the girl was unconvinced. There was no such thing as a useless creature to a thirteen-year-old. Polly could not accept, Margaret saw, that the life of one must sometimes be spared for the survival of the herd. Maybe she had been wrong to shield Polly from the realities of the farm for as long as she had, but she remembered her own attachments to certain of her father's stock and how heartbroken she had been to see them culled and shipped away. After what they had just been through together, Margaret didn't have the heart to deny her daughter's weeping request: If Sultana did have twins, they would keep them, wouldn't they, Mom? They would never kill something they had worked so hard to save, would they?

It was nearly midnight before she'd cleaned up and forked fresh bedding into Sultana's stall. She had waited to make sure the mother was letting the twins nurse their critical share of colostrum, and had only left when each infant was firmly fixed to an udder. She had sent

Polly in to wash up and go to bed over an hour ago, but as she herself was scrubbing her chest and shoulders at the kitchen sink, she spied a washtub of laundry she had forgotten before she left for Election Headquarters however many hours ago it was now. A pile of whites had been washed and blued and wrung and left to wait hanging on the line when she got home. If she didn't put them out tonight, they would mildew and she would have to laboriously wash them all over again tomorrow. With her last bit of strength, Margaret tugged a thin cotton house shirt over her stained white bra and dragged the metal tub of laundry out into the yard.

The air had finally cooled some, though it was still twenty degrees too warm for the beginning of November. She shivered under her open shirt and stopped to button it, but her fingers were too stiff and she gave up. The porch light had burnt out a week ago, and so she followed the moon to where it dusted the clothesline and felt in the dark for the pins she left hanging there. Margaret shook out a cold damp bedsheet and flung it into the dark, pinning instinctively at precise lengths. Polly's simple cotton underwear and ribbed cotton tank tops. A slip that had belonged to Margaret's mother that she herself now wore as a nightgown. She remembered, almost as if it were a dream, a night just like this when she was a girl: the night of the comet. The same anticipation hung in the air, the same thrilled foreboding. The wind lifted her hair just as it was doing now, while she and her cousins raced like blinded bats across the field between her grandmother's house and the railroad tracks. There was supposed to be a comet that night and they were going to stay up to see the fiery red ball streak across the sky and set the world on fire.

They ran and shrieked and played until something moved in the air, and the moon went dark, and collectively, like animals huddling before a storm, they came together in a clump at the center of the field. A strange electricity tickled their skin and caught in their lungs and they knew as sure as they lived, the comet must be at hand. Far away, as far away as Richmond, thunder grumbled. The cousins held hands and waited with an anticipation and desire so great it seemed to lift them off the ground and leave them hovering over the mowed stalks of field corn. What would the comet look like when it came? Would they be instantly combusted and tossed as sparks through the black night sky? Would they ever be the same? Then suddenly, just as the anticipation threatened to explode them from within, there was a flash, and a streak of lightning, emerald green and thick as a girl's arm, hit down just in front of them. The cousins scattered. Margaret, cheated of her comet, opened her mouth to cry *What happened?* but all she tasted was metal on the railroad tracks.

A set of headlights swung up her driveway, and Margaret blinked in the glare. She paused with her mouthful of clothespins to see who could possibly be driving up at this hour and was greatly relieved to see August Vaughn step out of his truck and come toward her across the yard. He looked as tired as she felt, and she realized for the first time the sacrifice he had made in staying behind at headquarters, for talking on the telephone surely took as much out of a man like August as delivering a whole herd of breech calves. He didn't speak at first, simply took the wrinkled sheet from her arms and gently eased it over the clothesline.

"Sultana had her calves," Margaret said as he fished in the tub of women's underclothes for something less personal to hang.

"Polly called right after you left. I came as soon as I finished up. I thought that's what you'd want."

"Thank you," said Margaret. "It was a great comfort knowing you were there."

"So it was twins?" asked August.

"Male and female. We should sell them for veal, but I promised Polly."

"Promised her what?"

"They were the first calves she's ever delivered. She's in love, but she doesn't understand how hopeless it is."

August nodded, took a deep breath, and hung a lacy slip. Margaret laughed at his obvious discomfort.

"I thought you would be in bed by now," he said. "I was just going to see about Sultana."

"I needed to get this on the line."

"Why don't you go up and let me finish," he said, confronting the remaining pile of soft white underwear and bras. "I'll come up and check on you in a minute."

She had already asked so much of him today, and still he kept giving. But it was a blessing to be able to surrender the last task of the day and finally creep up to bed. She thanked him gratefully and limped inside, leaving him in the moonlight with her soft, ghostly laundry. It wasn't until she was upstairs that she realized her shirt had been unbuttoned the whole time.

Margaret took a scalding shower, brushed her teeth with baking soda, and crawled naked under the clean sheets. She heard August moving around downstairs in her kitchen and wondered briefly what he was doing. She didn't pay him nearly enough to deserve such loyalty, but she would remedy that the first chance she got. As soon as Adams Brooke was elected, she would find a way to give August a raise, and more time off, because he was such a nice man and such a good friend to her. She heard him coming up the stairs and saw him standing in her door, filling the frame with his own gangly frame and long, sweet head. In his hands he carried a mug of hot steamed milk, fresh from her cow's udder, just in case she needed help unwinding. He gently set it on the oak table beside the feather bed her grandfather had hewn for her grandmother as a wedding present, and tucked the sheets more snugly around her freckled shoulders. He looked so tenderly down upon her, looked, in fact, for all the world like he had something desperately important to say to her, that Margaret struggled to keep her heavy lids from closing. *What is it?* her eyes asked. *I'm about to tell you,* his replied. *Best be quick about it,* her eyes blinked once. *I'm trying,* he opened his mouth to say, but sadly, he simply didn't get it out fast enough.

Within a minute she had lost her battle, shut her eyes, and fallen deeply, soundly asleep.

CHAPTER ELEVEN

Margaret overslept on election morning and awoke hungover from a dream that had been playing all night, resetting itself every time she rolled over or opened her eyes to look at the clock. Adams Brooke had won the election and Margaret had been invited to his inaugural ball. She arrived, clutching her engraved invitation, but no matter how hard she tried, she couldn't get to him through the crowd of wealthy supporters. She spent the whole night shouldering through men in tuxedos and women in sequins, but never seemed to inch any closer to the stage, where he was dancing in endless two-step circles with his wife. Rough hands shoved her back, disgusted faces turned away, and when she looked down, she realized she had never changed out of her barn clothes, that she was still painted with blood.

Polly was not in her bedroom when Margaret peeked in. Nor was she downstairs at breakfast. Margaret poured herself a cup of strong coffee and took it to the barn, where she could hear strains of Sinatra already playing over the loudspeakers. In their stalls, the girls lowed miserably, but Polly was not at her stool, either, which explained the swollen-udder lamentations down the row. Margaret knew where she would find her daughter, and sure enough, she was there, in the calves' pen, sitting watch over the brother and sister, who were themselves curled in a warm, brown embrace. When Polly saw her mother she smiled conspiratorially, but Margaret had to shake her head and make her get up. It was the hardest lesson to learn about motherhood, and one Margaret was not always sure she had yet absorbed; it was too easy to become lost in the miracle of childbirth, while the rest of the world stood by waiting, forgotten and miserable.

August arrived a few minutes later, and the three of them went about their milking as if today were just any other day and not the one that would decide the balance of their lives. August tried to be cheerful, trotting out some of his father's less moth-eaten jokes, but Margaret's mind drifted southward to the governor's mansion, where Adams Brooke would be sitting down to breakfast, pushing his food around his plate, scanning the morning newspaper for the latest poll numbers. Still too close to call, he would be reading, feeling, like her, the hopeful dread of the day. Margaret finished milking her cows, and when she carried the heavy, sloshing buckets to the cheese house to cool, she averted her eyes from the sign above the door, the words that reproached her like a neglected grave site or a grandparent sitting alone in a nursing home. "Foundation." "Herd." "Wealth." They were only words, she told herself. Keeping silent was no desecration. But even as she ducked beneath them she asked herself, as she had so many times since that infamous debate, *Why?* Why make up a detail that didn't add a thing to his public persona, that could easily have been omitted, that if revealed as the plagiarism it was would only get him in trouble? It was almost pathological, Margaret thought, like a boy who couldn't stop himself from taking a cherry when he walked past a fruit stand. It wasn't his, but it was no big deal. And who, he'd probably figured, would turn him in for such a minor infraction? Margaret, the injured party? Margaret, his biggest supporter?

An hour later, Polly and Margaret were on their way to Three Chimneys Junior High, where the school cafeteria's yellow plastic bucket chairs had been stacked into corners and the long Formica tables folded away; where the red, white, and blue bunting left over from Fourth of July helped, but did not completely, distract from the faintly sickening milk-and-pizza-mildewed-mop smell of the echoing room. Two tables had been left out, and here the matronly volunteers sat, vainly searching for a name in the roll register until it was helpfully pointed out to them, brightly smiling as they eviscerated it with their mechanical pencils and straightedges. Polly insisted it was inhuman to drag her to school on a day it was officially closed, but it had long ago been decided she would accompany her mother to pass out sample ballots, and so she waited next to Margaret in the long, slow-moving line of prework voters.

All around them, people were talking and laughing. Election Day in Three Chimneys was not some grim, gray affair with steely boxes and sour-faced volunteers sitting under limp American flags; this was no soup line of a day. No, the town believed a nation's patriotic privilege could only be celebrated rightly with brownies and Brunswick stew, raffle tickets and free cholesterol screenings. In stalls set up outside, all across the front lawn of Three Chimneys Junior High, the Fire Department and the Police Department and the Rescue Squad and the American Lung Association vied with representatives from the Republican and Democratic parties to claim the attention of each registered voter. Yes to the president. Yes to the governor. Yes to two quarts of the most delicious Brunswick stew cooked this side of the Rappahannock; it was a shame the Fire Department made it only once a year—judging by the line at their stall, they could have bought six new ladder trucks if they sold it every week. Yet for all the festivities, fewer people turned out each year to vote, and the midterm elections found the polls nearly deserted. When Margaret was a girl, voting had been as ingrained in the populace as waving hello when you passed a car on the street, or phoning the sheriff if a strange person walked through your neighbor's backyard; and that little needling "Have you voted yet?" asked only to shame coworkers on election morning in other cities, was invariably answered, "Of course—you?" by anyone hailing from Three Chimneys. But now, few in line beside her were under sixty, and no one, certainly, appeared as haggard and nauseated as she, wearing the desperate face of an all-night gambler, someone who had literally bet the farm on the outcome of a single contest. She inched forward in line.

"Hello, Evelyn," said Margaret to August's mother, when at last it was her turn.

"Hello, dear," Mrs. Vaughn replied. "Sign here, please."

And then it was time. Margaret stepped into the confessional of the voting booth and drew the silky blue curtain behind her. Somewhere in his local precinct, in a public school or a library, a hundred flashbulbs exploded as the governor disappeared into a booth just like this one, where he would face a similar dizzying array of names and parties, State Supreme Court justices and initiatives; and where, in that brief moment of privacy, perhaps his only one of the day, his finger would come down on the little red flag (checked and rechecked, then checked again), and Adams Brooke would confidently choose himself. Since the debate, Margaret was no longer confident of any-thing, but she, too, would choose—her future, her farm, her family—in the person of Adams Brooke; and so, with a trembling hand, she pulled back the heavy red lever that looked like the brake on an amusement park roller coaster, and heard the satisfying, permanent *chunk* of her political will be done.

"I'll be back in a few minutes." Polly called to her mother the mo-ment Margaret stepped into the polling booth. It was the one time all day Polly could be sure of making a getaway, and she used the opportunity to skip out of the bright cafeteria and through the doors that led to the darkened school beyond. Margaret hadn't heard her, and was mystified to find Polly gone when she stepped out. Under normal circumstances she would have looked for her, but today she couldn't waste a moment, and so stepped the required forty feet from the polling site to pass out her *Brooke for President* sample ballots.

A school was a public place, like a church or a restaurant, and Polly found it especially lonely now, emptied of its student body. The low sun slanted through the front door windows, piercing the upper half of the blue and gray metal lockers, highlighting dust motes as if they were swirling plankton. Polly was hyperconscious of her hard-soled shoes' echoing down the freshly buffed granite hall; she paused at the corner, where the hall doglegged off toward the English Department and the sign for play rehearsal might as well have been written in Arabic and pointing the way to Marrakesh, so exotic did it seem without four or five overly emotive students standing next to it for context. One of her earliest memories, from when she was no older than four or five, was of coming to this school to vote with her father, being taken in his arms inside the booth, where he pulled the curtain on a wonderland of buttons and levers and windows and knobs. *Hold tight*, he'd said as he reached for the big red lever to record his ballot, *we're in a time machine*. He pulled it and Polly screamed, surrendering to her child's sense of vertigo and the sensation of hurtling backward through space to that place where her mother and room and toys were not.

After a brief hesitation, she took the stairs leading up, and was swallowed in shadow before coming out onto the sun-drenched, overheated second floor. From the second-story window she could look down on her school's front yard. *Rebels Homecoming 11/7*, read the large white letter board, and below: *Pray for Peace*. Polly told herself she would walk by his classroom without cutting her eyes to see if he was there. If he called out to her, she would go in, and if not, she would use the rest room upstairs and return to her mother. It was a childish game, for she'd seen his car in the parking lot, and knew, almost for certain, he would be sitting behind his desk grading papers. Still, she took a deep breath and pretended to be studying her nails as she walked past the illuminated door.

"Polly Marvel!" She felt the flush of triumph when she heard the familiar voice. "Is that you lurking in the hallway?"

"Oh, hi, Mr. March. I didn't realize you were here."

"And yet you somehow found yourself outside my classroom." He smiled. "Well, come in. Would you like to help me make up your midterm exam?"

He was dressed more casually than he would be on a school day, which made him look younger, but less comfortable somehow. He wore a pair of faded jeans and a dark red V-neck sweater over a white T-shirt, from which peeked a few strands of corkscrewed chest hair. Still, he was freshly shaven and smelled like limes.

"I think you should make it really hard so that only I will pass," she joked.

"Polly, you will always deserve an A," he responded gamely, "so long as you maintain your charming criminal activity. 'Trespassing on school property,' added to 'littering' and 'breaking and entering.' I'm eagerly awaiting what you'll do next."

"I'm too tired to get into trouble," she said, somewhat melodramatically. "I was up all night helping my mother."

"Not campaigning, I hope."

"Oh, no," she rushed to say, but then became suddenly embarrassed at offering up the story of Sultana and her calves. He had never expressed the least interest in the natural world, and suddenly the intimate details of the story felt bloody and forward.

"So what kept you up till all hours?" he asked, leaning his chin in his hand. "Dreaming of me?"

"Mr. March!" squealed Polly, blushing furiously. "Our cow Sultana had twins. And we had to help her."

"Oh, I'm so disappointed," he said with a sigh, returning to his paperwork. "Even an old man likes to be admired, you know."

He was teasing her again. Polly drifted over to the window, where below, her mother accosted her neighbors with ballots. She had been thinking of Mr. March a great deal since the night of the presidential debate. He would be deeply disappointed in her not having spoken up.

"Polly?" he asked, looking up at her long silence. "Is something wrong?"

"Our twins can't give milk. One is male and the female is sterile," she said at last. "Usually, Mom would ship them off for veal, but she promised me we could keep them. I love them so much, I can't imagine being without them."

She had said the word "love." Even though she was talking about her calves, she had used the word in the same room with him. He watched her closely, and covered in confusion, she turned back to the window.

"Did you come all this way to talk about your cattle?" he asked.

She shook her head in embarrassment. Down below, on the front lawn, she saw August pass her mother on his way to his makeshift stage. As on every other Election Day, he was dressed as Thomas Jefferson, and now he bowed ceremoniously to Margaret before turning to the small crowd gathered to hear him. Her mother might not see that he was in love with her, but it was obvious to Polly. Poor, pathetic August, she thought. Didn't he know her mother had no room in her heart for anyone other than Adams Brooke?

"What are your parents like, Mr. March?" she asked.

"My mother was small, Jewish, very quiet. She died five years ago," he answered. "My father disappeared when I was ten."

"I thought he was in Canada," she said, before remembering she'd learned that bit of information off the Internet. Mr. March looked at her sharply.

"Yes, Canada. I didn't realize it was such common knowledge."

"It's not," Polly stammered in an effort to recover. "I just thought your father might be Stanley March, the writer."

"You've heard of him?" asked Mr. March archly.

"I was doing research for a paper on conscientious objectors, and I came across his name," said Polly.

"How fortuitous."

"You must be very proud that your father followed his conscience and left the country," she said passionately, turning back to the window, where below, her mother was pushing another ballot on another neighbor, stumping for Brooke as if the lie of the debate had never been uttered.

"'Proud' is one word for it."

"At least he was brave enough to make a stand," Polly insisted. "That takes a great deal of courage."

Mr. March pushed aside his paperwork and gave her his full attention. "Miss Marvel, what is on that prying little mind of yours?" he asked.

"Do you remember once you told us even an eighth-grader could affect the outcome of a presidential election?" she asked.

"I remember."

"Adams Brooke is a liar and a thief and I can prove it," she confessed. "But I haven't told anyone because my mother asked me not to."

"She has asked you to go against your conscience?" he queried. Polly nodded. "She has asked you to lie for him?"

"Not so much lie, as keep quiet," said Polly.

"But you're telling me," he said.

"I shouldn't be."

"It's right that you do," he answered gravely. "This is how people in power remain in power. Through fear and intimidation. If you go along with your mother, you are a collaborator. Do you know what that means?"

"It's not that big a deal," said Polly swiftly, seeing how seriously Mr. March was taking her. "It's not a huge lie or anything."

"You know a secret about Adams Brooke, and suddenly she allows you to keep two calves she would normally sell for veal?" he asked. "Don't you find the timing interesting?"

Polly looked down onto the school's front yard as if seeing her mother for the first time. Who was that stern, grim woman handing out flyers with the funereal sobriety with which one might distribute rocks for a stoning? Would she let anything stand in the way of getting Adams Brooke elected? Polly looked over to where August stood on his stage. He was addressing the crowd, but his eyes were on Margaret, speaking to the only person out there he cared about. We are her slaves, Polly thought suddenly. August and I live to serve and protect her. And she counts on that.

"Eventually, you are going to have to develop a system of values separate from your parents," said Mr. March. "You are going to have to start making decisions for yourself."

Polly nodded miserably.

"The old cliché," said her teacher, "is that history is destined to repeat itself. Those with power have always sought to enslave those without. They frighten, they coerce, they bribe, all to retain that power. But once in a great while, someone special comes along, a person who rises up and says, 'Enough. *I won't follow the herd. I will think for myself.*' It is lonely to be that person, but, in the end, it is she who makes the difference."

Mr. March studied her over the rim of his steel-framed glasses. She felt him drinking in every atom of her face and body: her gray wool jumper and black oxford shoes, her prim white blouse, smocked along the collar with needlepoint turtles, her red hairband, her bitten nails. She felt him measuring her as if whether or not to find her worthy of an appointment or grand commission, like Meriwether Lewis being tapped to tackle the dark, vast American interior.

"The question for you, Polly Marvel," said Mr. March, after a long and thoughtful pause, "is which do you choose to be? The cycle or the precedent?"

As he did every election year, to crowds increasingly smaller, August stood up as Thomas Jefferson and delivered the third president's first inaugural address. In 1800, Jefferson had won the most closely contested election in American history. John Adams, his former friend and ally, quit the White House bitterly, refusing to see his successor sworn in. He left in his wake a series of midnight appointments, including John Marshall, Jefferson's cousin and bitter enemy, as Chief Justice to the Supreme Court. The election had been dirty, and cruel, and violent, yet Jefferson considered it a triumph of democracy, a second American Revolution, for power had changed hands without bloodshed or rebellion, and the infant American experiment, which he'd feared might be stillborn, seemed destined to thrive.

Dressed in his powdered wig and deep-cuffed coat, August mounted the hay trailer that served as his stage on these occasions, and spoke passionately to the handful of his neighbors who had shown up to vote.

"'It is proper you should understand what I deem the essential principles of our Government, and consequently those which ought to shape its Administration,'" he quoted, catching Margaret's eye. She gave him a brief, distracted smile before handing a *Brooke for President* flyer to Dr. Fraser, Bethany's father.

"'Equal and exact justice to all men, of whatever state or persuasion, religious or political; peace, commerce, and honest friendship with all nations, entangling alliances with none; the support of the State governments in all their rights, as the most competent administrations for our domestic concerns and the surest bulwarks against antirepublican tendencies; the preservation of the General Government in its whole constitutional vigor. . . . a well-disciplined militia, our best reliance in peace and for the first moments of war till regulars may relieve them; the supremacy of the civil over the military authority; economy in the public expense, that labor may be lightly burdened; the honest payment of our debts and sacred preservation of the public faith; encouragement of agriculture, and of commerce as its handmaid. . . . ; freedom of religion; freedom of the press, and freedom of person under the protection of the habeas corpus, and trial by juries impartially selected. These principles form the bright constellation which has gone before us and guided our steps through an age of revolution and reformation. . . . Should we wander from them in moments of error or of alarm, let us hasten to retrace our steps and to regain the road which alone leads to peace, liberty, and safety.'"

Every difference of opinion is not a difference of principle, Jefferson had said upon his inauguration in 1801. *We are all Republicans, we are all Federalists.* August watched Margaret gravely distribute her flyers. He wondered what Jefferson would have said had he lost.

They came home briefly for afternoon milking, but Margaret was far too restless to remain at the farm, and so she left Polly with her calves and accompanied August back to the voting station, where they stayed until the polls closed at 7. At 7:30, with 70 percent of precincts reporting, the projected winner of Virginia was announced, and at 7:31, Margaret knew the worst. Afraid to leave her alone, August drove her to his house, where he said they would watch the results together. Virginia didn't mean a thing, he pointed out, not with all the states out west still to go.

The television was on in the darkened living room when the two arrived at the rectory. Leland was at the Franks, but Evelyn, taking one look at Margaret, immediately ceased cleaning out the refrigerator to brew a pot of crisis coffee. With twelve states reporting, only Vermont and New Hampshire had gone for Brooke, while the entire South, including the governor's home state, belonged to the president. The cheesemaker stared numbly at the red rash creeping across the U.S. map. She had felt him slipping away from her all day, from the moment they diverged at the polling booth, as if the very action of flipping the lever next to his name had let the air out of his campaign and begun its slow, inexorable deflation. As determined as she had been that he should win, she was now that fatalistic about his defeat. She should have known that someone as idealistic as Brooke could never win the country, that big business and special interests and corporate greed would take the day. And yet, whispered an insidious little voice in her head, wasn't it in some way fitting that he be punished? Could she not take comfort that lying and thievery went unrewarded, and the universe was just? As if to punctuate the sentiment, Georgia abruptly turned red.

"The chef of Montrachet in New York once offered me a job in his cheese cellar." Margaret turned to August. "Do you remember his name?"

"Don't talk like that," said August sternly. "It's only eight o'clock."

But they watched with mounting dismay as one state after another fell to the president. West Virginia. Kentucky. Tennessee. Rhode Island registered for the governor. With its two electoral votes.

Margaret had not been in Pastor Vaughn's living room since the death of her father two years previously. She had the same sense of unreality then as now, sitting on the Vaughns' pale blue chesterfield with a cup and saucer on her lap, nodding numbly as the minister told her what to expect at the funeral—a hymn, an anthem, a eulogy; a collect, a lesson, a psalm. During the whole time he spoke, her eyes had drifted to the daily artifacts of his life—the framed family photos on his mantel; Evelyn's green and red needlepoint cushions. Behind his head, inside his glass-front bookcase, she saw the family's heavy, embossed family Bible perched like a tombstone. So, when do we get to the grave? she wanted to stop and ask him. Everything else was preliminary, wasn't it, merely a way of easing the family toward the inevitable, like a long and pointless bedtime story for a child afraid of the dark. Now she watched

August's lips move as he reassured her about exit polls and closing times, but her mind had skipped ahead to the end, and she sighed with the sort of fatigue and loneliness that she had not felt so strongly since the last time she was here.

"Margaret?" asked August, when he noticed her staring into space.

Slowly, she reached into her front pocket and removed a folded envelope. It was warm from resting against her body all day, and its seal was slowly coming unglued. She had brought it with her to rip into pieces when Adams Brooke gave his acceptance speech, but now she finally slipped her finger inside and loosened it the rest of the way. "I guess I might as well open this," she said.

"Margaret, don't—," began August, but she cut him off.

"It doesn't matter, it will be public soon enough." She removed the letter from the envelope and smoothed it on her lap. "August, I'm afraid you are going to be out of a job."

They both stared at the paper, with its lurid red header. "Can't you restructure?" he asked, helplessly. "Consolidate bills?"

"I did that last year," she said. "It's over. Adams Brooke was our last hope."

"Children," called Evelyn from the next room. "I have some pot roast still warm in the oven. May I serve you some?"

"No thanks, Mom," answered August impatiently. He lowered his voice. "There must be something."

"I'm just so sorry to put you in this position," said Margaret. "I wish I had some sort of severance package to offer you. I don't know what we would have done without you over the years. Especially this last one."

"Margaret," called Evelyn. "Pot roast?"

"No thank you, Mrs. Vaughn. I've got to get home to Polly." Margaret stared at her foreclosure notice for a long minute, then rose and reached for her pocketbook.

After missing his chance last night, August was determined not to let her walk away tonight without declaring himself. He cast a quick look into the kitchen. If only he could go down on bended knee without his mother barging in with a tray of food.

"I know you don't want to take money from anyone—," he began.

"I would take money from an orphan right now"—she tried to laugh—"if I could just get Bob Crenshaw off my back."

"Then take it from me," August said, summoning his courage. "I've got plenty in the bank. I live at home, I never go anywhere. I don't have kids. I've got plenty saved, and it's yours if you need it."

But Margaret was waving him off even as his passion built. "I cannot take money from you, August," she said. "I *pay* you. Or at least I did. If I took money from you, you'd be working for free."

"Let me work for free," he offered.

"I won't hear of it. I'll file Chapter 11 first," she said.

How he wished he'd had the courage to ask her last night in the twilight of her bedroom, her body naked beneath the sheets, as vulnerable and approachable as he'd ever seen her. How much easier to ask her to marry him there than here in his parents' living room, sitting awkwardly in his mother's chintz chair, the singularly unromantic smell of pot roast wafting from the next room. "Would you take money from a relative?" he asked, as suggestively as he dared.

"A relative?" She laughed. "Who, Francis? Oh wait, I have a second cousin in Durham; I'll give her a call."

"No," said August quietly. "What if you remarried?"

"I'll never marry again," Margaret declared, patting his shoulder as she walked toward the kitchen. "It's not worth it. The smartest thing you ever did, August, was stay single."

He knew Thomas Jefferson would never give up so easily. He would find just the right elegant phrase to stop her from walking away; with truths self-evident, he would open his heart and declare his desire to form a most perfect union. He watched her kiss his mother's cheek and thank her for the coffee. He tried to picture his strong, capable Margaret bent over a cheese board at some fancy New York City restaurant, calmly explaining the subtle interplay of aromas to drunken bond traders, who snaked their arms around her waist and murmured endearments, and the idea filled him with despair. For all the years he'd played Jefferson, August had never

understood politics on a personal level. He had studied the philoso-
phies and embraced the theories, but until tonight, he had never
experienced the loss of a cherished dream. There must be something
he could do to save Margaret. He could not let her walk out of his
life.

"Hello, all," called Leland wearily, coming in the front door and
hanging up his coat. "Who's winning?"

As August turned to bid his father hello, he glanced over at the
television. For a moment he couldn't believe his eyes. Hope had come
from a most unexpected quarter.

"Margaret, put down that letter and come here," August said,
excitedly.

Margaret and his mother stepped into the living room, where a
flashing boot of blue filled the television set. In a shocking upset that
was taking even the veteran newscasters by surprise, Florida, with its
twenty-five blessed electoral votes, had gone for the governor.

"Florida," cried August. "He took Florida!" If he could take
Florida, thought August, Illinois was almost certain. New York and
California had been guaranteed from the start. If he could take Michi-
gan and the other farming states, the day would be his.

Margaret dropped her pocketbook on the floor and sank back
onto the couch. It was going to be a long night.

Just after one o'clock, Adams Brooke ascended the platform erected
on the front lawn of the governor's mansion to address the red, white,
and blue crowd of supporters and press who had been camped there
all night. He looked haggard and when he began to speak, his ragged
voice backfired like a rusted carburetor. He thanked his rival, the
president, speaking of their spirited battle and the will of the people
and the wonders of the democratic system. He thanked his supporters and his wife and two grown daughters. He thanked God for allowing him to be born into this great country. Then he promised a
bright new era of bipartisanship and prosperity and, with a fervor that
whipped his sea of supporters into a typhoon of delirious cheering,

vowed that his first act in office would be the introduction, by God, of the Family Matters Bill!

Margaret missed most of the president-elect's acceptance speech because she was crying too loudly, her head buried in August's chest, racked with the kind of sobs she hadn't experienced since she was a little girl. She was grateful in the way a person pulled from a fire is grateful, or in the way a woman who has just pushed through her last contraction is grateful; she was grateful in a full-bodied, gut-wrenching, lie-down-and-die sort of way. To August's chagrin, his parents had remained downstairs to watch the election results; Margaret's sobbing now woke them both where they had been dozing in their chairs.

"Oh, Margaret, dear," said Evelyn, instantly misreading the situation. "I'm so sorry."

But Pastor Vaughn saw things more clearly. There was no mistaking the look of bliss on his son's face as he held his cheesemaker and gently stroked her hair. He was so quiet about matters of the heart, the thought had simply never occurred to Leland: August was in love. He watched his son spin Margaret across the living room floor, in imitation of Adams Brooke and his wife on TV, twirling her into an awkward dip. How happy they all seemed, he thought, with a momentary selfish pang. Before Margaret woke him, he had been dreaming of the Frank children, laid side by side in their shared tiny coffin. It never failed to bewilder him how the Lord could smile on some, while seeming so indifferent to others.

"If only there were some way to thank him," said Margaret, pulling away from August at last and wiping her streaming eyes. "I need to let him know how much this victory means to me."

"Send him a dozen roses," said August. "A singing telegram."

"Make him a cheese," said Evelyn, clapping. "The world's largest cheese!"

"Yes, a cheese." Margaret laughed. "That's what I'll do."

"A Mammoth Cheese," said Leland, abruptly sitting up in his chair. No one had noticed he was awake, and the three started at his sudden proclamation. From his dozing in the leather recliner, the minister's silvery hair stood on end and a long crease scarred the length of his cheek. For a moment August thought his father was talking in his sleep.

"Dad?" said August worriedly.

"You must make him a Mammoth Cheese," Leland continued. "You must make it and take it to Washington."

"Leland," asked Margaret gently, "what are you talking about?"

"August, tell her the story," ordered his father, now completely awake and growing more excited by the minute. "Tell her the story of Jefferson's Mammoth Cheese."

"It's late, Dad," said August slowly.

"Tell it," Leland commanded.

"It's a very funny story from Jefferson's first term," August said with a sigh, humoring his father. "Some Baptist patriots in Cheshire, Massachusetts, were so thrilled with Jefferson's election and his promise of religious freedom that they made him a one-thousand-two-hundred-thirty-five-pound wheel of cheese and took it to Washington."

He told Margaret that it took a day's milking of nine hundred Republican cows—no Federalist milk allowed. That it took six months to make and transport—by sled, by sloop down the Hudson River, and by cart to the nation's capital. One man joked that by the time it reached Baltimore, it was strong enough to walk the rest of the way. Jefferson's friend Charles Wilson Peale had recently discovered the bones of a mastodon, back then thought to be a wooly mammoth, and thus the cheese was immediately dubbed the Mammoth Cheese by Jefferson's detractors who observed it on its way to Washington. Ballads were written in its honor, tickets sold for its viewing, fine speeches delivered. And on New Year's Day 1802, its instigator, Elder John Leland—now called by some the Mammoth Priest—delivered as fine an oration on the virtues of Republicanism and cheesemaking as August dared say had ever been heard.

"That was Orange County's Elder John Leland," Pastor Vaughn told Margaret. "The one I'm named for. The one from Leland-Madison Park."

A small bust and marker off nearby Route 20 commemorated the spot where the same Massachusetts preacher then living in Virginia, had sat under a tree with James Madison in 1788. If Madison would bring an amendment guaranteeing the tenets of religious freedom, Leland would deliver Virginia's Baptist vote to ratify the Constitution. It passed, and Leland had preached for many years in Orange County before retiring home to Cheshire and becoming more famous as the maker of Jefferson's Mammoth Cheese.

"If you want to thank the president," said Leland, "we could stage a reenactment. People love reenactments—just look at how many show up for the battles at Gettysburg and Manassas every year. A new cheese for a new president."

"Leland, that's a lovely idea," said Margaret kindly, "but I could never make a cheese like that."

"Why not?" he asked.

"I don't know how to, for one thing," she answered. "I don't have anything to hold that much milk."

"We could build something," said Leland.

She smiled sympathetically. "A lot goes into making a cheese. I would have to set it and cut the curd. How would I press something so big?"

"How did they do it in Massachusetts?" Pastor Vaughn turned to his son.

"They used a cider press, but—"

"Alan Franklin has a cider press," said the priest. "It's collecting dust in his barn."

Margaret was growing a little annoyed at his insistence. "A twelve-hundred-pound cheese would take over twelve thousand pounds of milk, and I only have two dozen cows."

"But that's what's so beautiful about the original cheese," insisted Leland. "It wasn't about any one farmer. The entire community brought their day's milking. They came together like a family and worked in service of a single ideal," he exclaimed. "Medicine and science have brought nothing but tragedy to this town. But—history. History is something Three Chimneys understands."

"Dad," interposed August, alarmed at his father's perseverance, "a cheese that size would take months, and Margaret doesn't have a lot of time. Her farm is in foreclosure."

"Oh," said Evelyn, blushing on Margaret's behalf. Margaret frowned at August for alluding to her difficulties, especially since Adams Brooke's winning the election would now solve them.

"I didn't know," said Leland soberly. "But all the more reason to pull together. If you file an appeal, you are guaranteed a hundred fifty days before any action is taken."

"That's only five months," said Evelyn.

Margaret had instantly dismissed Leland's wild proposal until August had challenged her by suggesting it couldn't be done. Five months. That gave Brooke three months once he took office in January to pass the Family Matters Act, and with it the amnesty. His birthday was just about five months from now, on April 6, and it would take just about that long to ripen a young Cheshire cheese.

"I could preach a sermon next Sunday to ask for donations," urged Leland. "You'll only bear the cost of your labor. Think about it, Margaret, won't you? Not just for Brooke or yourself, but for Three Chimneys? For us all?"

Margaret's agitated brain spun back on itself, and she couldn't believe she was considering saying yes. A twelve-hundred-pound cheese? She knew larger cheeses had been made, but in factories and by people who knew what they were doing. She was insane to contemplate it, but Leland's shining, hopeful face seemed to be willing her to try. She turned to August, who had grown very quiet.

"Mr. Jefferson, you were the first recipient," Margaret said. "Is this an utterly crazy idea? What do you say about it?"

August could have said many things, for much was in his heart. He could have said that the first Mammoth Cheese became a nationwide joke and Elder Leland went home too depressed to preach for many years afterward. Or that along the way, the cheese generated maggots at its core, and most of it had to be cut away, dumped into the Potomac. Or he might have declared honestly and with great heaviness of heart that this was a country wherein anything was pos-

sible, that America loved a large and pointless gesture, and that the
orders generated by the publicity might very well save her farm. But
then where would that leave him, poor ridiculous farmhand, with his
useless proposal of marriage? His opportunity to save her would have
passed him by. He could have said all this and more, but how could
he, with good conscience, take away her last, long-shot chance to
save herself?

"I guess it depends on how grateful you really are," he finally said.

That night, in the bed hewn by her grandfather, under the quilt sewn
by her grandmother, Margaret Prickett dreamt not of dancing with
the new president at his inaugural ball as she had the night before,
but instead of meeting Brooke's long-sought eyes at last, over a giant
wheel of cheese.

II

THE CHEESE

"Heaven above looked down, and awakened the
American genius, which has arisen, like a lion,
from the swelling of the Jordon [sic], and roared
like thunder in the states, *We will be free; we will rule
ourselves*."

—Elder John Leland

CHAPTER TWELVE

"Though we rarely think about it," said Pastor Leland Vaughn from his pulpit at St. Barnabas the Sunday after the first Tuesday in November, "a word, like a person, has a life span. Some die having outlived their use, while others are born to take their place."

Pastor Vaughn looked out over his congregation, who sat in warm wool sweaters and carefully pressed blazers, a wash of color in the pews like a child's paint-by-number. After a few fitful starts, the weather had turned, and a cold November rain beat against the clear panes of glass in the chapel windows. Far off in the distance, he heard morning thunder; not a boom, but rather a long, low rumble like a large herd anxious to get home. The dark gray sky pressed in, serving only to heighten the contrast between the world outside and his bright and welcoming church.

"So, in 1801, when Elder John Leland set out to make his cheese for President Jefferson, he could not have conceived of it as *mammoth*. Large maybe, or imposing, but not mammoth, in the sense we know it, for that word was only just taking its first toddling steps into the world. You see, earlier that year Charles Wilson Peale began displaying the reconstructed skeleton of the woolly mammoth he found in upstate New York. He sold tickets to see her in his museum of curiosities, took her on the road to England, even hosted a dinner party inside her massive rib cage. Single-handedly, he created a craze for all things mammoth.

"Now, when Thomas Jefferson's political enemies, who considered the president's archaeological leanings frivolous, got wind of the enormous cheese in Massachusetts," he continued, "they immediately snatched up the word 'mammoth' and flung it against the Elder Leland's heartfelt gift. The Republican Cheshire became the

Mammoth Cheese; the patriotic John Leland, the Mammoth Priest. The Federalists meant it as a joke—see how stupid these backwoods zealots can be? Their gift is as absurd as the reconstruction of a pile of old bones. And yet the joke was soon to be on them. This homespun, heartfelt, *mammoth* gesture appealed to the populist spirit of most Americans. The Federalists' elitism foreshadowed their own inevitable extinction, as must be the case for any group who does not instinctively understand that this is a country that likes its gestures large."

Pastor Vaughn was gratified to hear the chuckles from his congregation. He had surprised them this morning by calling on their help to make a 1,235-pound wheel of cheese for transportation to Washington. He asked them for provisions. He asked them for money. He asked them for their time and enthusiasm in aid of a neighbor whose farm was struggling. His parishioners, grateful not to be reminded of the poor Franks, were sitting up straighter and listening intently. Pastor Vaughn looked down at his sermon notes, and spoke sincerely.

"Now, friends, it might interest you to know another familiar word entered the English language only a few years ahead of 'mammoth.' It is one you might imagine had been with us always, and yet it made its first appearance in the Federalist Papers, which argued our duty to our country. That word is 'responsibility.' Certainly 'burden' had been with us a good long while, and we had even been 'responsible' for each other as early as the late sixteenth century, but it wasn't until 1786, when wrestling with what our nation should become, that the term 'responsibility' meaning a charge, or a trust, or a sacred duty—came to be used. Thanks to our neighbor James Madison, we now have a *sense* of responsibility, a state of being, and a place in which to dwell.

"I tell you today, friends, we have a mammoth responsibility to aid one another. I know not all of you voted for Adams Brooke, and here I am asking you to participate in a project that will magnify him. But like the Confederate and Union war veterans who donned their tattered uniforms and re-created Gettysburg, we should understand, as they did, that more important than which side you fought on, are Life's defining battles.

"So I say, let's invite the cameras back! America deserves to see the real soul of Three Chimneys, not weighted down with death and tragedy, but lifted up in celebration of all that is natural and fruitful of the earth."

From the upturned, excited faces, Pastor Vaughn knew he had them. He bowed his head.

"Let us pray," he said.

November 21 was the day set for the cheesemaking, and that morning Polly woke stiff from sleeping curled tightly in a ball. Every winter, her mother promised to get heat upstairs, and every winter they continued to make do with the single oil stove in the living room that exploded on every twenty minutes or so. Polly pinched the tip of her numb nose and tried to visualize her morning routine so that she could get through it with no wasted moments of indecision. Leap from the bed and race to the bathroom. Warm your shins before the space heater—front, then back. Wash your face, but not your hair, (a rule she'd learned after running her brush once too often through crisply frozen locks). One, two, three, go! she told herself. But her body refused to move. Instead, she longed to nestle deeper under the quilt and return to the dream she was having of Mr. March—not even a romantic dream, just the two of them eating breakfast together at a small red table. She was having pancakes and he was eating cantaloupe. Her stomach growled at the memory.

"Polly!" called her mother from downstairs. "Get up!"

Mr. March set down his spoon, and reluctantly, Polly flung off her blankets. She ran to the bathroom, where Margaret had thoughtfully left the space heater running by the sink, but it took her only a moment to realize this was no maternal act of solicitude. Damn it, Polly cursed as she tried first the hot and then the cold tap. The pipes had frozen. It was her responsibility to keep a lightbulb warm against the leaders in the pump house, and she had let it burn out. The morning was not starting well.

"I don't ask that much of you," Margaret said when Polly, unwashed and fully dressed, slunk downstairs. "What are we supposed to do if someone needs to use the toilet?"

Her mother didn't look up from the cheddar biscuits she was rolling on the long kitchen table. She slammed the rolling pin, raising a cloud of flour; rolled and dusted, turning as she went. She punched out twelve perfect circles with an old tin can and slid them onto a greased pan. The kitchen smelled of melting cheese, which, so early in the morning, made Polly want to gag.

"I didn't realize it would get so cold last night," she said.

"It's been below freezing for a week now," answered Margaret. She took the biscuits to the oven and swapped raw for cooked. When the hot biscuits cooled, they would join the mountain she'd baked last night; poor recompense, Polly thought, for the farmers donating an entire milking. She walked to the kitchen pantry and rummaged for a hundred-watt lightbulb.

"Today of all days," said Margaret.

"Okay, I'm sorry," Polly snapped, and pulling on her boots and coat, left her mother furiously pounding.

Outside, across the yard, August kindled a fire in the rusted old oil drum they used to burn their trash, the gristly smoke blending with the gray dawn and darker gray silhouette of the looming cheese vat nearby. Within days of Pastor Vaughn's sermon, her mother's Mammoth Cheese had replaced the Frank Eleven as the favorite topic of conversation at Three Chimneys Junior High. The Pep Club printed buttons that read "More Cheese Please" (illustrated with a holey slice that Polly felt compelled to point out was Swiss, not Cheshire), and even the boys, who had mercilessly ridiculed poor Manda and her family, were intrigued by the prospect of meeting the president. Anything was possible, they decided among themselves, and maybe, if they were lucky, they'd be there the day the president took a bullet. After enduring hours of cheese talk at school, Polly would come home to find August digging a pit in the side yard, or her mother fielding calls from neighbors: Alan Franklin offered up his large cider press—little good it did him now that the government had gotten so prickly about E. coli; and Speedy Sheet Metal promised a homemade vat and form. Margaret swallowed her pride and took donations of lumber and rope, pulleys, and burlap. Then every night she left Polly to do the dinner dishes while she went to the cheese house, trading in her intuition for the safer methods of science. From the window over the kitchen sink, Polly watched her mother, in her white apron and boots, puzzling like a scientist over the best way to impregnate thirteen thousand pounds of milk.

"Morning," called August.

Polly waved dully as she worked the stiff wooden latch to the lean-to pump house. Inside it was dark and cold as a crypt. August watched her sympathetically.

"Pipes freeze?" he asked. She nodded.

"Yard's frozen, too," he said. "I'm going to lay down some straw."

She watched him head back to the warm barn while she lowered herself to the ground. Above her head ran a circulatory system of lead and copper pipes leading from the ancient mechanical pump into the kitchen and up the wall to the bathroom. She sucked in her breath and shimmied beneath them, catching her hair on bug husks and bits of broken plaster. Her nose brushed the icy pipes; she blinked against sleepy, unseen spiderwebs, feeling rather than seeing the panicked weavers hoist themselves out of reach. Something had died, for the small room smelled like an unwashed meat locker. Gingerly, Polly felt around until she found the socket where the old light had burned out, and screwed in its replacement. Now, in the naked glare, she could see the long shadows of spiderwebs and the mouse carcass in the corner. Sharp, short icicles dripped from the main water lead like a row of teeth. Sometimes she wondered if her mother gave birth to her solely to relieve herself of jobs like this. Adams Brooke got a cheese while she got buried alive.

She quickly slid out at the sound of a truck in the driveway, then brushed the droppings from her coat. The donating farmers weren't expected until after their own milkings, sometime after seven. As she watched, a white van with a corkscrew antenna and side-panel logo pulled up close to the house. She recognized it from the early weeks of the Frank Eleven.

"Mom," Polly called, "someone from Channel 5 is here."

In the kitchen, Margaret was sprinkling homemade cheddar into another batch of biscuits. She had been baking since last night but was afraid to stop, unsure of how many people would show up today. When she heard Polly call, she pulled on her heavy wool jacket and stepped out to join her daughter. Channel 5? What could they possibly want? A tall, bright-toothed man she remembered seeing at Chase Andrew Frank's funeral stepped out from the driver's side. Then the passenger door swung open, and out leapt smiling Pastor Vaughn.

"Look who I brought," he exclaimed, escorting the driver around to meet them. "Margaret, Polly, you know Patrick Lewis, Foster's cousin?"

Patrick Lewis, weatherman and features reporter for the local Fox affiliate, had the same handsome, saturnine features as his first cousin, though years in front of a lens had kept his fleshy physique vertical, in contrast to the newspaper editor's slowly spreading horizontal. He stretched out his hand, and Margaret reluctantly took it.

"Patrick was kind enough to inquire after Manda," Pastor Vaughn explained. "So I told him all about our cheese. He wants to feature us on the nightly news."

"I'm sorry for your town's loss," said Patrick Lewis, gravely. "It's been a difficult autumn." Before Margaret could respond, Patrick directed a cameraman who had followed him out of the van to begin filming. He pointed his camera at the enormous vat in the yard. Margaret pulled the priest aside.

"Leland, what is this all about?" she whispered.

"He wants you to give Channel 5 an exclusive. He'll check in every few weeks, and come along to Washington—he wants to follow this cheese from beginning to end.

"I don't think that's a good idea—," she began.

"Nonsense. Why not let the world see how excited we are about our new president?" exclaimed Leland. Then, leaning in, he conspiratorially added, "And if they find out we have a world-class cheesemaker in our midst, well, that's fine too."

"This is supposed to be a thank-you," Margaret said, "not a publicity stunt."

"I know, I know," the priest assured her. "But why shouldn't you benefit a little? You've worked so hard, and we're proud of you. Anyway, who could we trust more than Patrick? He's practically family."

From across the yard, Margaret watched the reporter warm his hands over the fire August had kindled. Behind him, his cameraman circled the vat, taking in its cedar slats, its reinforced barrel rings, its polished, modified beer tap. He panned her barn and made his way over to her whitewashed stone cheese house. His hand was on the door before Margaret remembered the sign above the door.

"That's just where I keep my supplies," she said quickly, rushing over to stop him from trying the knob. "Please turn the camera off."

The cameraman looked to Patrick, who, with a sigh, gestured for him to comply. The reporter reluctantly left the fire and walked up to Margaret, fixing in place his most winningly apologetic smile, the one he used to announce freezing rain the day of the Christmas Parade or thunderclouds for the Fourth of July.

"Of course we don't want to trouble you," he said. "Leland warned me you might not be so gung-ho about our little idea. It's just that when I heard about your cheese, I thought, This is exactly what our country needs right now. Something wholesome and patriotic after all we've been through. I thought it was the perfect story."

"I appreciate that," said Margaret, relieved to see the red camera light go dark. "But it's important to me that this cheese not be misconstrued. It is merely to thank Adams Brooke for his belief in the small farmer, nothing more."

"Of course, I understand," said Patrick sadly. "It's a shame we didn't even get to meet Mr. Jefferson."

"What do you mean?" she asked.

"I told him about August, too," confided Leland, more subdued now than when he'd bounded out of the news van. "He never thinks about his future, and I thought if he got on TV, he'd surely get booked into every veterans' hall and high school in Virginia."

Margaret stood guiltily before the priest. "I don't think August wants that sort of attention," she said.

"I suppose you're right," said Leland. "You probably know him better than I do."

"Why don't we ask him ourselves," said Patrick, catching sight of August in the barn door, bent under a heavy bale of straw. He beckoned for Leland and his cameraman to follow. "Excuse me, Mr. President! Fox would like to request an interview."

"You're not considering letting this man film us?" asked Polly when she and Margaret found themselves alone.

"Of course not," said Margaret crossly. Through the back door window, she saw the kitchen tap shudder, belching air and rust. A moment later, hot water gushed into the sink.

"Go inside and wash up," Margaret told Polly. "We have a lot to do before everyone arrives."

Polly marched inside and slammed the door, and Margaret turned to August, who held his bale before him like a shield. Every night for the past few weeks, he had worked at the farm until nearly twelve, digging in frozen ground, fashioning tools for Margaret's use. She had to bring him plates of food when he wouldn't break for dinner. He had been against it, but once he saw Margaret was determined to make the Mammoth Cheese, he had stood by her every step of the way. Now Patrick was explaining his idea—Thomas Jefferson would present the new Mammoth Cheese to President Brooke. A passing of the torch, so to speak—August would be half the story. Patrick would see to it, he said, that August became the second most famous president alive today.

"No thank you," said August, shaking his head in embarrassment. "I could never use Jefferson that way. It goes against my philosophy."

"What's a philosophy, son," asked his father, "when you could not only help yourself and Margaret, but bring happiness to an entire town?"

"No, I respect your son's opinion," said Patrick sadly. "It's just a shame. You know congressmen watch a good deal of TV. If they saw how greatly their constituents favored the amnesty, I would imagine they might have a pretty hard time voting against it."

The reporter's words brought August up short. Congress. He hadn't even considered that he and Margaret, so far from power, might somehow affect the outcome of the amnesty. He glanced over at Margaret, who now stared at the reporter with a little of her old campaign intensity. Is this what she wanted? he wondered. If he was with her, was he not with her all the way?

"Your costume is in the truck, isn't it, son?" asked Pastor Vaughn. "Why not put it on. It would be such a help to everyone."

"Margaret?" August asked, willing her to look at him. What do you want from me? he silently asked. But Margaret appeared as confused as he, looking from Patrick Lewis to the ground, to her cheese house, and to the ground again. For a long moment she didn't speak.

"I wouldn't want you to do anything you didn't feel comfortable doing," she said at last.

He couldn't read her expression, but there was no mistaking the look of eagerness on his father's face or the calm assurance on Patrick Lewis's. Who wouldn't want to be on TV, the reporter seemed to be saying. It was every American's dream.

"I suppose it could make a good story, " replied August slowly.

"Great!" said Patrick Lewis. "So, Margaret—Mr. Jefferson is on board. Won't you please let us film your cheese?"

August watched her closely. Looking away from them, she gave a curt, miserable nod.

"Well, then, let's have an interview before everyone else arrives," said Patrick, clapping his hands. "America is going to love this!"

It happened so quickly, August could barely comprehend it. He walked back to his pickup truck like a man condemned and retrieved his costume from where it hung, just back from the dry cleaner, in the passenger-side window. *This will be great for him,* he overheard his father tell Patrick Lewis. *The thing about my son is that he never thinks of* himself.

August stepped into the kitchen, where something was burning. With the arrival of the news van, Margaret had forgotten her last batch of biscuits; when he opened the hot oven, their tops were deep golden, but the bottoms had burned black. He slid them from the oven and left them to cool on the counter. Slowly, he made his way up the back staircase to Margaret's bedroom and there undressed before her pier mirror, stepping out of his crusty overalls and into the white hose and buckled shoes of a president. He pulled on his blue silk jacket and draped his cravat around his neck. All that remained was his wig, resting forlornly on the bed. It was silly, he knew, but ever since he'd begun portraying Jefferson, August had felt a nearly mystical connection to his wig. In the breeches and hose, he was still August Vaughn, but once he fit that powdered wig into place, he felt himself, oddly, slipping into the head of his hero. And he continued to be Jefferson until he took it off at the end of his program and reluctantly returned to himself. Now, with a feeling of treachery, he picked it up.

"Knock, knock." Margaret stood in the hall, fearful of barging in on him naked. She inched open the door.

"Come in."

He glanced at her in the mirror. She was wearing his favorite sweater, an olive turtleneck she'd knit herself. He'd been unable to take his eyes off her all morning.

"Are you sure you're all right with this?" she asked.

He smiled weakly. "If it will help you . . ."

"I want it to help *you,*" she said. "If I lose the farm, you should have something . . ."

"Don't," he said.

She reached up and gently wrapped his cravat, once, twice around, adjusting the knot as she would have her husband's tie. "You've thrown your lot in with me," said Margaret softly. "You should get something out of it."

He closed his eyes. "I feel weird using my costume this way."

"You shouldn't," Margaret said, smiling at him. "You look very handsome in it."

She took the lightly powered wig from his hand and placed it rakishly on his head. "Come on, Mr. President," she said, raising on tiptoe to kiss his cheek. "Let's go make some cheese."

Farwood Purdy from Hollywell Farm and Sam Abbott from all the way down in Hanover were the next to arrive, their pickup trailers rattling with ten-gallon capped pails like buoys in a storm. Soon after, in a steady stream, came all the stringy farmers of Pastor Vaughn's wide acquaintance, men who still maintained their adolescent habit of chewing Red Man long after everyone else's gums had freckled with cancer. With their prematurely gray crew cuts and pond water eyes, they appeared an entire generation ahead of Margaret, rather than a scant few years. In the seats beside them sat their disapproving wives, only a few of whom helped out physically, most opting instead to manage the books and look after the kids. Some of the kinder wives pitied Margaret her hard existence, left without a father or husband and forced to do all the filthy work herself, while a decided majority thought she got just what she deserved. A woman who didn't own a washing machine and was too proud to microwave a baked potato from time to time was a woman married to her own misery. And now it was up to their overworked husbands to help her out of trouble.

Margaret shook their hands hello, passing out cheese biscuits and coffee like party favors. None of the other wives made cheese, and so they wondered at Margaret's vat, her paddle for stirring, the knife August had rigged from two-by-fours and baling wire. She patiently explained to them how she would heat the milk and add the culture, drain off the whey and transport the cut curd by bucket to the modified cider press in the barn. All the while, she watched the farmers pass pails of milk down a chain like water to a house fire. Over fifteen hundred gallons she needed. By ten o'clock, to her amazement, her neighbors had provided it.

More people arrived, and more press. The *Richmond Times-Dispatch* sent a stringer, and Foster Lewis sent his photographer from the *Three Chimneys Register*. Margaret had borrowed an industrial-sized thermometer from a candy factory in Richmond, and August let her know the milk had reached its proper temperature. The time had come for her to step forward and take over. As the cameramen recorded, Margaret climbed the stepladder and stared down into the deep, white, steaming pool. Who knew what her neighbors fed their livestock? Or with what they were injected? For all that she appreciated and desperately needed their assistance, Margaret couldn't help but worry that this melting pot approach (some of the farmers had provided Guernsey milk, some Brown Swiss, but most had donated thin, insipid Holstein) might be the undoing of her finished cheese. She would do her best with what she had to work with, but perfection, she knew, might very well elude her. An inferior cheese could be her Faustian bargain for having any cheese at all.

It's too late now, she told herself, feeling the camera lens trained on her face. For all her skill, Margaret knew she could only stand back and watch this cheese take shape, stepping in to guide it when she could, urging it along, but ultimately, for all her nurturing, at the mercy of its nature. She took up her sterilized canoe paddle and stirred in her carefully prepared culture. Crouching in his jacket and breeches, August worked a set of bellows to raise the temperature and fed more wood to the fire. Margaret drizzled in a quart of annatto for coloring—another concession to Pastor Vaughn and Patrick Lewis, who swore America would never accept anything but an orange cheese—then stirred in a steady stream of her carefully measured sharp, brown rennet.

Margaret looked across the vat to August, who stood with his wig askew. He studied the steaming pool anxiously, knowing as well as she the prankish property of milk to appear almost unchanged while undergoing its metamorphosis until, without warning, it set in an instant. Had she calculated correctly? Would they be humiliated on the nightly news? Margaret looked for success in August's eyes as he continued to scan the surface of the cheese like a cat after fish. An eternity seemed to pass, magnified by the polite cough or the restless shifting. A smaller batch would have set already, and as the minutes passed, Margaret steeled herself for failure. Forget it, drain the vat, she was about to tell him, when just then a wide smile spread over August's face and, to her infinite relief, Margaret looked down to discover something new and wonderful, fully formed between them.

When Polly was four, her grandfather threw a barbecue for his sixtieth birthday. It was among her earliest memories—neighbors scattered on blankets in the dappled shade, the ladies tucking their bare legs under their skirts. She ran in the hayloft with the older children, sipping lemonade in a can through stray bits of straw that stuck to her lips. Her grandfather had dug a pit in the side yard, just where August excavated his for the cheese, and outfitted it with a heavy iron spit. All morning and into the afternoon, her grandfather turned a whole pig, its bristly hide boiled and shaved, its front and rear hooves nailed to a plank. Throughout the day, until one of her parents would shoo her away, Polly returned to watch the pig roast. In the morning, it was an opaline pink; by late afternoon, a deep charred mahogany, dripping fat onto the glowing coals. As the pig's slanted eyes turned, she would follow it with her head, trying to imagine what it saw. The canopy of trees. A cloud shaped like a smiling crocodile, then the slow devolution to roots, and feet, and budding clover. Polly's father and grandfather lifted the finished pig from its spit and laid it on a wooden picnic table, where oily juice dripped down into the grass. Then the neighbors—those hard-drinking bachelors picking bluegrass by the creek, those boys and girls playing spin the bottle in the dusty hayloft, their tired mothers with late-in-life dozing babies— all gathered around the pig. Its skin had been scored every eight inches or so and peeled back from the flesh as if it were a prickly pineapple. As Polly watched, her grandfather sharpened his carving knife and sawed through layers of skin and fat to reach the succulent white meat below. She stood in line and held out her paper plate like all the rest, but the heavy slice bent her thin wrists backward and her plate fell to the ground.

That barbecue was the last time Polly had seen so many people at Prickett Farm at once. But now Mr. Tinton and Mrs. Larette, the church organist; Coach Emery and Bob Crenshaw all watched in awe as her mother drew her oversized wire knife through the mass of curd, slicing it into a checkerboard of small squares. The curd released its whey and August tapped the vat, siphoning the river into another tub from which Margaret would make whey cheese later. Now instead of lining up for barbecue, her neighbors queued up for the buckets August filled, ferrying the curd like the shuttle run Polly had endured in grammar school. Pick up pails from August, limp it across the frozen yard to Margaret at the mouth of the barn, where she eased it into the massive cheesecloth-lined form donated by Speedy Sheet Metal. Run the empty buckets back to August, where two more neighbors took over, the loop continuing for hours. And always there was the camera. Her mother the purist, who wouldn't let her watch TV, who was so afraid of commercialization she brought her own Band-Aids to Polly's pediatrician rather than risk Mickey Mouse being taped to Polly's butt. Her mother the hypocrite. Polly watched Patrick Lewis pan their farm, instructing his cameraman to zoom in on the cows in the pasture, the rusted pitchfork leaning against the cheese house. He focused on the farmers as they spat their chaw rather than the neighbors who drove up in expensive cars, and took an extensive amount of footage of one of the barn cats intently licking its privates. She overheard him laughing with Bob Crenshaw. *Curd. It even sounds funny, doesn't it?* he said. *Curd?*

Polly wandered away from the crowd, up to her old chimney. From her perch high above, she could watch Mrs. Winston and Mrs. Dickinson, whom she had last seen in a heated argument on School Street over the bill for a fruit basket sent to Manda Frank's hospital room, now race each other with heavy buckets, slipping and falling, and laughing like schoolgirls. Their husbands stood nearby, arms folded, leaning in, sharing a joke at their wives' expense. To Polly, the yard had become a long, chaotic dinner table, anchored at one end by August, doling out his curd like a first course, and by Margaret at the other, emptying plates. But how could Margaret accept favors from these people? Down in the yard, Polly watched more cars arrive, their greens and reds shining through their crusts of road salt like nuggets in a dusty creek bed. She stared dully and only barely registered one smaller car pull in behind a row of mini-vans and pickups. Dressed all in black, its owner moved through the purple and teal parkas of the crowd like a speck of antimatter, carving a channel toward the house. She watched curiously until suddenly she recognized the figure; then Polly was up, and racing down the hill.

"Mr. March!" she cried. "Mr. March!"

"Here you are," he said, when, out of breath, she finally reached him. "I was worried I'd come all this way to find you conveniently absent."

"If only," gasped Polly. "Oh, Mr. March, it's been awful. Much worse than a candlelight vigil."

Her teacher wore a black pea coat over black jeans and a black sweater. His black baseball cap was the only one, she saw, that sported the name of a team rather than a tractor company. She stood help-lessly before him, unable to believe he was here.

"Well, I have braved the hordes," said Mr. March. "Am I to be denied a glimpse of the Mammoth Sleaze?"

Polly collected herself and boldly led the way. Glancing over, she watched him take in her farm—the exfoliated bricks of her house, and the botched operation of her screened porch, where Margaret had attempted to repair the rips with wire and the metal mesh from their fly swatters. She saw his eyes range over the crush of neighbors in the side yard, their bulky, unfashionable clothes and grinning faces. Pastor Vaughn stood by Patrick Lewis, encouraging two of her school-mates who were staggering under the weight of their pails.

"Is that the weatherman from Channel 5?" asked Mr. March.

"Mom's letting him film the cheese. He wants to go with us to Washington."

"Indeed?" Mr. March's raised eyebrow managed to convey all the contempt Polly herself was feeling. She led him to the side yard, where August now hung over the rim of the vat, reaching for the last shovelfuls of curd. All across the yard, spilled steaming whey had cooled into long white finger lakes, which the barn cats lapped eagerly. Here it is, she said, nodding to the vat. Her neighbors had kicked dirt into the pit to kill the fire beneath it.

"I once had a most enjoyable party in a hot tub about that size," said Mr. March blandly.

Polly blushed, imagining herself and Mr. March naked inside the cheese vat. August stood up at that moment, and seeing her, gave her a bright smile.

"And who's that?" Mr. March asked, nodding to August. "I saw him in the schoolyard on Election Day."

"That's just some guy who works for my mom," she said, quickly turning away. "He likes to dress up as Thomas Jefferson."

"Ah, a Founding Father fetish," said Mr. March with a wicked smile. "I've seen the type before. I bet he doesn't know Ho Chi Minh was a Jefferson buff as well."

Mr. March leaned in, and Polly could smell the cigarettes on his wool coat. She felt wildly daring speaking about communist leaders, with her neighbors standing just out of earshot. Her mother had tried to make this day as miserable as possible for her, but now Mr. March was here, and Polly felt reborn. In the doorway to the barn, Polly noticed, Margaret was taking a rest from the marathon curd transfer. Sweating even in the cold, she had stripped down to a thin white T-shirt, and was lifting her wet hair from the back of her neck. Mr. March turned and followed Polly's gaze.

"There's my mother," said Polly, with the sickening realization that Margaret and Mr. March were exactly the same age. Her teacher made no response, but continued to stare as Margaret drew an elastic from the front pocket of her jeans and secured the loose bun she'd made.

"Do you want to meet her?" Polly asked weakly. He turned back to face her.

"I'd rather meet your calves," he said.

He could have made no better answer, and Polly fairly danced to the barn, leading him not past her mother and the crowd by the press but through the side lot, into the back. The barn was dark after the bright sun outside and it took a moment for their eyes to adjust. Beside her, Mr. March breathed deeply, and Polly, so used to the grassy smell of hay and manure she didn't notice it any longer, quickly apologized. "I'm sorry it stinks in here," she said.

"No, it's nice," he said.

She led him past the wooden stalls and the curious older girls, past Sultana, who swung her head and pranced away when Polly reached out to stroke her. The two moon-eyed calves lay curled together in a corner, wedged under their feed trough. Though they watched warily from the shadows, neither rose as Polly let Mr. March into their stall. He hesitated, not having touched livestock since the infant petting zoo at Central Park, and then it had been a goat with intrusive lips and blank, rapacious eyes that he'd gingerly approached. Polly told him not to be afraid, they wouldn't bite. He crouched down before them and slowly stroked their necks.

"They like you," she said.

"So this is what you do when you're not in class?" he said.

"Mostly," she replied, then asked boldly, "What do you do?"

"Wonder about my students." He smiled. "Mostly."

Mr. March scratched the twins behind the ears and squirmed when the female licked him with her long, velvety tongue. "It was a good bargain you made," he said. "These calves for Adams Brooke."

Adams Brooke again. Polly scowled at the name. In the doorway of the barn, the bright light of the camera captured the last few relays of curd. Those in the yard cheered the weatherman as he gamely joined in the cheesemaking, mugging for the camera and letting the priest get ahead of him. She looked back to Mr. March, kneeling before her calves. Mr. March dressed all in black like a partner in crime. Mr. March, the only person who had thought of her all day.

"Come with me," she said. "I have something else I want to show you."

She led him through the side lot, skirting her mother, who was unfurling a sail of filmy cloth and draping it over the face of the cheese. Everyone in the yard gathered round as August lowered an enormous

wooden disk cut to fit the form. He and Margaret each grasped an end
of the screw's handle and tugged, raising a groan from the ancient cider
press. Tighter and tighter they screwed, forcing whey from the bottom
in a thousand tiny trickles. Polly led her teacher to the old stone cheese
house and let them inside, pulling the door behind them.

It was easily ten degrees colder inside the thick-walled building
than it was outside, though a slanted beam through the window warmed
a single pane on the floor. Polly had been inside the cheese house a
hundred times, but never without her mother, and she felt more like a
thief here on her own property than she had breaking into Mr. March's
car or the empty school. Margaret's glass jars of cheese knives and her
hand-labeled specimens of culture gave the room the feel of a mad
scientist's laboratory, not helped by the portentously ripe aroma coming from the cellar below. Outside, a muffled cheer rose from the crowd,
but inside, all was still and cool, and expectant.

"Do you remember a few weeks ago, you said I was going to have
to start making decisions for myself?" Polly asked, leading him farther into the small room. They were up against Margaret's long
wooden shelf, upon which stood a tightly clamped Caerphilly. "Take
a look," she said.

For as long as Polly had been alive, their motto had hung from
a square-headed nail. *Omnis pecuniae pecus fundamentum*, flowed the
words in a perfectly fluid antique cursive; indeed, it had been said no
one in Three Chimneys could match Polly's great-grandfather for
penmanship. If her mother wanted to invite the television cameras,
she thought, let them have something to film. Together she and Mr.
March would take down this sign and present it to Patrick Lewis in
the yard, and Adams Brooke would be exposed, once and for all. Polly
turned and swept her arm toward the space above the door, but to
her astonishment, all she saw was the iron nail, like an obscene whis-
ker. She glanced swiftly around the room—into the dark corner where
the mop was propped, beneath the counter stacked with white plastic buckets and lids, and back to the nail again, as if her eyes had betrayed her and it had been there all along, safely encased in glass,
mounted in its prudent black frame.

"What am I looking at?" asked Mr. March softly.

But for the moment, Polly had forgotten her teacher. In two long steps she was at the door, which she flung open so forcefully, it shook the jars on the shelves. Over in the barn, August and Margaret each took hold of a rope August had rigged from the rafters and, on the count of three, heaved the half-ton cheese high above the crowd. They caught their breath and heaved again, tugging it higher on its straining ropes, blinking against the warm white rain.

"Polly," Mr. March repeated. "What am I looking at?"

By the time Margaret and August finished cleaning up, it was long past dark. Their shoulders throbbed from hefting buckets, their faces ached from smiling for the camera. At ten o'clock, August fell limply onto Margaret's battered old sofa, while she pulled the black-and-white TV from the closet. Polly had gone to her room hours ago without speaking to them, and when Margaret crept upstairs to ask if she wouldn't like to watch herself on television, she said no. To August's surprise and delight, when she returned, Margaret threw herself down beside him and settled her head in his lap. August strained not to move a muscle that might cause her to shift, his arms glued to the armrest of the sofa in an attempt to seem casual. She was filthy from the cheesemaking, sticky with dried milk, dusty and sour, but she had never been more beautiful to him than tonight, lit by the vacuum tube glow of the old television set.

"I don't know what I'm going to do with Polly." She sighed. "She's getting more defiant every day."

"She's a teenager," August said. "Remember what you were like back then."

"Not like this."

"I worked here, remember." August smiled. "I recall more than a few slammed doors over the years."

Margaret smiled in acknowledgment and stared up at him. He had long ago stripped off his deep-cuffed jacket and had worked in his waistcoat and breeches, his long cravat slowly unfurling from his neck. His wig lay with his jacket and his own damp, longish hair curled across his forehead.

"I wish men still dressed like this," she said.

"I do too. I kind of like it."

"It suits you," she said.

A double homicide in Lynchburg dominated the headlines and while the newscaster droned, Margaret closed her eyes. The blue light of the old black-and-white television bleached her skin to marble, and her lightly veined lids appeared heavy and serene as an effigy's. A scab of milk dotted her right eyebrow. August moved to brush it away, and she opened her eyes.

"Look, there we are," she said.

Tightly edited, the segment showed a montage of the day, from the milk's arrival to the pressed cheese's ascent. Patrick Lewis explained the project, promising frequent updates on the cheese throughout the winter. He closed with the interview August had given. Too bright and earnest, August thought; he sounded to himself like an eager student trying to please his teacher. *The greatest cheese in America for the greatest man in America,* he heard himself saying. *That's what they called it in my day.*

"I can't watch," he said, turning his face away. "I hate the sound of my voice."

"Don't be silly," she said. "You sound great. Very presidential."

The segment ended, and Patrick moved on to weather. Margaret sat up and gave August a pat on the knee. "I don't know about you," she said, "but I could sure use a cup of coffee."

"If I have the energy to lift it," he said, forcing a smile, not wanting her to leave.

"I'll start the water if you don't mind locking up the barn." She sprung to her feet as though they had not spent a punishing day of lifting and stirring. With great reluctance, he hoisted himself from the springless sofa.

Outside, the temperature had once again plummeted, and he stirred the fire they'd kept burning all day in the argus-eyed old oil drum. August looked back to the kitchen window, where Margaret moved behind a screen of flying sparks. Briskly, she ran her kettle under the spigot, struck a match, and ignited a burner. He watched her take matching coffee cups from the cabinet and gently blow them free of dust. It was in the everyday moments he loved her best, watching her when she was unaware, for she went through her life with such confidence, with the assurance that whatever she was doing at that instant was the one thing in the world that needed to be done, that and nothing else. He yearned for a life of such easy conviction, unclouded by doubt or crippling self-consciousness. In a moment she would fill the cup she had taken down for him and he would drink her hot coffee and then he would have to go home, their perfect day together ended. Another opportunity wasted. When Martha Jefferson lay on her deathbed, she had copied out a line from her husband's favorite book, *Tristram Shandy*.

> *Time wastes too fast:* she wrote, *every letter I trace tells me with what rapidity life follows my pen. The days and hours of it are flying over our heads like clouds of a windy day never to return . . .*

To which, Jefferson finding the incomplete line upon her counterpane, added:

> *. . . And every time I kiss thy hand to bid adieu, every absence which follows it, are preludes to the eternal separation which we are shortly to make!*

Jefferson had burned everything of Martha's—every letter, every likeness, every book—but he kept that one sentence he had finished for her, to remind himself that he and his love had once been the beginning and end of a single thought. Margaret passed from the window into the next room with what somehow seemed the finality of passing from his life altogether. He thought what it would mean to lose her as Jefferson had lost the only woman he had loved.

In the open barn door, August saw the suspended cheese, wedged between the thumbscrews of the cider press, suspended from the rafters like a cow airlifted from a forest fire. Once Jefferson himself had stood before an identical cheese and thought it a joke, but if he had been present at its creation, he too might have been awed by the massive scale of what they had made, its deadweight heft and dripping bottom, its pulsing ferment, as alive as any cell-dividing creature. If August held his breath he could almost hear it devouring itself, swapping liquid atom for solid, hardening into an entity that could crush him like a plinth from Stonehenge. He imagined, with a certain satisfaction, Margaret returning to the barn to find him flattened beneath it.

A bat flew down from the rafters, circled his head, and flew back again. His every sense was on fire tonight; he was keenly aware of the burning wood in the drum outside, the wet hay beneath his feet, the leathery hides of the sleeping cattle in their stalls. All day, he and Margaret had passed the pen between them, composing their cheese like a long, organic poem. Did he now dare ask her to complete the sentence he most longed to speak? Would she give the answer he desired? Under the great orange moon, August felt more hopeful than he ever had before, and in that vulnerable state, his Heart stirred and whispered to his Head, Release me, friend. We will never have a better chance than this.

Margaret stepped into the barn with two steaming cups of coffee. The shadow cast by the megalithic, suspended wheel fell over her face, giving her an almost sibylic countenance. How mysterious and chthonic she appeared to him at this moment, as if, should he ask her to, she might very well pronounce his fate. August did not know what had come over him, what sort of spell had been cast by the interplay of shadow and steam and rich, ripening smell of whey dripping like groundwater in a cave. Yet, even possessed as he was, he could not declare himself directly: I love you, Margaret. Will you be my wife? Instead, he picked his words carefully, and tried his best to sound lighthearted.

"This cheese came along in the nick of time," said August, his voice catching. "If you hadn't come up with a plan, I was going to ask you to marry me."

And then the infinite stretch of silence, more awful than any encounter with Jefferson's Megalonyx whose eyes were two balls of fire ranging in the darkness. Margaret stood motionless, holding her two cups of coffee as if cast in stone. He saw clearly the progression of emotions across her face. Surprise and confusion gave way to distress before resolving itself into what he could only interpret as pained compassion. She took up his pen, as he desired, but with a single, sad stroke, she struck him through.

"Lucky we made the cheese," she said at last, smiling weakly. "How could I have ever lived up to my role as first lady?"

She had meant to be kind, but he felt humored like a fanciful schoolboy. For the first time in his life, he wanted to rip the breeches and jacket from his body and fling them into the fire. He wanted to see the powdered wig go up in a hiss of acrid smoke. Far worse than laughing at him or despising him, she pitied him.

"It's late; I'd better get going," he said, needing to be out of there as fast as possible. She took a step to the side, blocking his exit, wordlessly commanding him to look at her. When he did, her large moist eyes were those of a merciful veterinarian who had just administered a lethal injection.

"Here," she said, holding out not a needle, but a cooling cup of coffee. "Take this for the road. You can bring the mug back tomorrow."

"Okay," he said, ducking past her. "Thanks."

"August—," Margaret called as he made swiftly for the exit. He tried to keep the hope off his face when he turned back to her, tried to damp down the redness in his cheeks.

"Adams Brooke will like this cheese, won't he?" she asked. "He won't think it's ridiculous?"

Ridiculous? Ridiculous? How on earth, thought August, could anything be more ridiculous than he?

CHAPTER THIRTEEN

"I can't believe I forgot to change the oil."

August drove silently down Interstate 64, casting a glance at his distraught father in the passenger seat. Leland was easily as religious about his oil changes as he was about his religion, and he attributed his bus's long life to his fanatical maintenance routine. To have forgotten an oil change amounted to an automotive venial sin.

"Dad, you didn't do any lasting harm. The mechanic said he could take care of it."

"But it's the principle," countered Leland. "It survived going into a ditch."

"We'll pick it up tomorrow. It will be fine."

"I need to keep that bus running long enough to take Margaret's cheese to Washington. She's counting on me."

August winced at the name and looked guiltily at the unreturned coffee mug from last night. It had rolled onto its side and wedged between the dashboard and windshield, where inside it he could see the last slick of undrunk grounds, her own slow-roasted brew, which last night had tasted bitter as hemlock, without the redeeming results. The mug was unreturned because he, himself, was unreturned. He had called Margaret this morning and told her he needed to take his father to the hospital for an MRI. Of course he wouldn't leave her in the lurch—he'd arranged for Glenn Mullins, a high school boy and treasurer of his Future Farmers of America chapter, to fill in for him. No, he didn't know if he would make the afternoon milking either—it depended on what the doctor said. But Glenn was willing to help out for as long as necessary.

After the phone call, he spent his morning lying in bed, listening to the second hour of a documentary on the Founding Fathers on his VCR—listening only, for no amount of will could turn him away from the wall at which he stared, noticing for the first time the uneven texture of its plaster and the thick raised vein that ran from floor to ceiling like an engorged esophagus. It had been years since he'd been in bed at this time of day, when the wan sun nudged through the transom window of the basement apartment and illuminated all the room's imperfections. Most of the spider cracks were covered by the spines of books, but this wall against which his bed rested was a Rosetta stone of nicks and hairline fissures, any one of which might be widened to reveal the room's former brick face. It was a converted cellar, after all, with all the damp, harkenings-back that cellars possess. You could put a skin of plaster over a thing, the very walls seemed to say, but you couldn't change its nature.

As he lay in bed until the extravagant hour of 8 A.M., August was denied even the solace of hating Margaret. No matter how hard he tried, he could not blame her for this numbing inertia, this fixed esophagal staring, this droning on of documentarians reading transcripts of letters in mock-urbane cadence some producer had decided signified "Colonial." August had only himself to blame. All his life he'd known that if he never spoke, he would never receive an unwelcome answer. He had lived by this truism since he was sixteen years old, and in one instant, one unguarded, hypnotic instant, he had thrown it all away.

"You must be awfully pleased to have the whole town take part in one of your Jefferson episodes. To be finally doing something useful with it," said Leland, returning his son's attention to the truck.

"What do you mean by 'useful'?" asked August. "When have I not been useful?"

"Oh, son, you know what I mean," said his father bluffly. "Using your costume and wig to help a neighbor instead of standing up there in the auditorium just talking about things. I'm simply saying it must feel good to get into some action."

August had never imagined his father saw him as so passive. Had he not spent the last eight years of his life educating and instructing his fellow citizens on their civil liberties? Did his father think his lectures had been nothing more than one long dress-up party? For a moment, August wondered how what he did was so very different from his father's putting on a cassock and every Sunday quoting a man dead these last two thousand years, but then he remembered he was driving the frail person beside him for an MRI.

"It just amazes me I forgot that oil," said his father.

They pulled into University of Virginia Hospital half an hour early so that his father could fill out his paperwork, but Leland insisted on stopping by the pediatric ward first, to check on the Frank children. Of the eight still alive, five had gained considerable weight and been moved to the step-down nursery, but three were still struggling in the NICU. Leland had not spoken to Amanda and Jake in nearly a week, and was surprised to find them at the hospital with five car seats in tow.

"Good to see you, Pastor," said Jake, pumping the cleric's hand. "Can you believe today's the big day?"

August saw the look of confusion pass over his father's face, and then the dawning of embarrassed comprehension. The strongest five children were to go home today, and he had utterly forgotten.

"I'm sorry not to be able to put my bus at your service," said Leland regretfully. "It's in the shop."

"No trouble, no trouble," replied Jake. "You've done so much for us already."

Behind the glass, Manda strapped little Brianna into her donated EvenFlo infant seat, then adjusted the puckered elastic bow that denoted gender for bald female babies. She waved gravely to the priest.

"Manda's a little nervous bringing them home," said Jake. "With the oxygen and monitors and all. I told her the doctors wouldn't release them if they were worried, but you know how mothers are . . ."

"You have help lined up?" Leland asked. "I'm sure I put today's homecoming in the church bulletin."

"Manda's mom and my mom and her sister and a few ladies from the congregation. We'd had a whole lot more sign up, but it's three months later, and, well . . ."

"I'll stop by as soon as I'm done here," assured Leland.

"We couldn't put you through the trouble," said Jake.

"No trouble at all."

"We should see how your appointment goes," August chimed in, herding his father toward the door.

"Just cracked the old noggin." Leland waved off Jake's look of alarm. "Nothing to worry about. I'll see you all this afternoon."

They walked in abstracted silence to the lab, where Leland was handed a thick questionnaire to fill out. August settled himself on one of the interconnected narrow molded bucket seats such as one might find at McDonald's or a domestic airport, and picked up the only magazine in the room. October's cover of *American Child* magazine sported a milky-toothed, blue-eyed girl dressed as a pumpkin or a piece of candy corn, he couldn't tell which. Inside were an article on just how much Halloween candy a three-year-old should be allowed (one carefully chosen piece after dinner, treated as a dessert— even childless August had to chuckle at that one) and one titled, "What Every Parent Should Know About Latex Mask Allergies." On page 89 "Spooky Snackables for Young Ghouls" presented him with photo after photo of mellow orange American cheese dishes: oily rounds cut like jack-o'-lanterns and thin slices rolled into witches' fingers. He wondered how Margaret was getting along with Glenn Mullins, and if he was, even now, helping her tighten the screws on her ripening Cheshire. August gave himself a firm shake. He wasn't going to think about Margaret today. That was the point of not going to work.

"They ask here about glaucoma," Leland said, peering over his reading glasses. "Your great-uncle had glaucoma. Do you think that's relevant?"

"I think they mean mother or father."

"You're probably right," Leland said, nodding, and continued his inky scratching.

The inside back cover of October's *American Child* magazine was devoted to a full-page color photo of three last trick-or-treaters: two eight-year-old boys and a girl dressed as the Spirit of '76. They were freeze-framed as in the old painting, banging their drums and piping their fife, but something was different about this trio, August quickly realized. Their heads were wrapped with oozing bandages, and fake blood trickled from their mouths. A makeup artist had blackened the eyes of the towheaded girl in the middle and traced railroad track scars across the cheeks and foreheads of her two companions, so that they resembled nothing so much as battlefield corpses recalled to life. Who wanted to dress up as a boring old patriot for Halloween when you could be Zombie Liberty, or Rotting Freedom? The casualties of Independence out begging, August thought, and then tossed the issue aside in embarrassment. What was he doing looking at *American Child* magazine anyway? What right did a loveless, rough bachelor have reading a parenting magazine?

Leland shuffled up to the receptionist and handed over his medical history. She made a Xerox of his insurance card and told him to have a seat.

"I can't believe I forgot the Frank children were coming home today," Leland said, settling into the hard chair next to August. "What has gotten into me?"

"You've had a lot on your mind," replied his son.

"No more than usual."

"You're getting older, Dad," said August kindly.

"Look at these youngsters," said Leland, reaching for the magazine August had just discarded. "A couple years ago, you wouldn't have seen anyone dressing patriotically. Makes you feel good, doesn't it?"

But it didn't make August feel good. Any more than having the town rally around the cheese made him feel good. What was wrong with him today?

"Mr. Vaughn." A narrow-hipped nurse dressed in street clothes called the priest to the back. That she looked barely older than Polly did not inspire confidence in August.

"Do you want me to come in with you?" he asked his father.

"Just wait here," Leland answered. "I'll give you the grisly details when I'm done."

August sat with his hands in his lap and his long legs crossed at his bony ankles. He could get used to seeing himself in the kind of khaki, pleated dress pants he wore to the hospital today, letting his body slowly adjust to the newness of them like tender gums to a set of false teeth. He could wear crisp white poly-cotton shirts and rayon ties and thin-ribbed dress socks and shoes with tassels. He could trade in both his farmhand blue jeans and his Jefferson breeches and "join the world," as his father had urged him to do so many times in the past. Would it be so awful to let the horny calluses on his palms soften into kinder keyboard-reddened fingertips? Could he not take any number of office jobs where the most stressful decision he would face was choosing between Choco-Mints and Cheese Nibs from the break room vending machine? Margaret's debt was not his debt, after all; her needs were not his needs. He was a simple man, nothing more, just trying to get through this life with the least amount of pain, and here he had arranged his life to maximize his misery. Margaret Prickett stood for everything he hated: She was uncompromising, she was protectionist, she was positively Federalist in her worldview, and, worst of all, she expected the same level of absolutism from those around her. Why, with all this against her, should he love her?

"Excuse me, are you done with that?"

Lost in thought, August had not noticed the woman sitting opposite him. He hoped his face had not given away his furious internal diatribe.

"That magazine," she repeated. "Are you done?"

"Oh, yes," August apologized. "It's last month's."

"*American Child?*" she noted ruefully. "You'd think a hospital this size could at least afford a *Sports Illustrated* or *Malpractice Digest.*"

August smiled at her joke. He could tell she was the sort of woman who had heeded her mother's advice to cultivate her personality, for her looks were quite plain. She was as pale and linear as a sheet of graph paper, with a long square face and shingled bangs, and a shelf of shoulder pads overhanging bony arms. Yet there was something familiarly appealing about her, August thought. She reminded

him of his one and only relationship beyond what he'd suffered with
Margaret, another Chautauquan, who had portrayed Emily Dickinson
and whom he'd befriended years ago at a summer retreat. Letta had
been thin like this woman, and soft-spoken, lost in her crinolines and
bonnets and as awkward as he throughout their first sexual encounter, which had nearly foundered under the stress of stiff eyelets and
too many hooks. They had corresponded for several months after their
passionate Chautauquan weekend, but her too-obvious hopefulness
and his painful discomfort on the telephone had doomed the relationship to failure.

"I hate to bother you," she said, taking the magazine. "But
haven't we met before? You look very familiar."

"I'm from Three Chimneys, over in Orange," August replied politely. "Do you get down that way?"

"Can't say I do," she answered. "Where did you go to school?"

"Georgetown. You?"

"Purdue. So that's not it." She shook her head. "Oh well."

"I must have one of those faces," August said.

"They say the same about me."

The woman opened the magazine and idly flipped through it,
automatically plucking out the subscription cards as she went. She
looked up to see August watching her. "I hate these things," she said.

"Me too."

"I'm Gillian," she said with a smile.

"August."

"Wait a minute." She laughed. "Now I know. Weren't you on
TV last night?"

It hadn't even occurred to August that she might have recognized him from the news. What had come later with Margaret had
completely crowded out the memory of Patrick Lewis and the television cameras. "That was me," he mumbled.

"You're out of uniform," she said.

"I only dress that way when I'm presenting a program," said
August. "Yesterday was an exception."

"So you make cheese for a living?" she asked.

"I was helping a neighbor. I'm a Chautauquan Living Historian."

"That's quite a mouthful."

August would have given anything for something to hide behind. He glanced nervously around the room, but the only other reading material concerned yearly mammograms and hepatitis B screenings.

"I've always been interested in history myself," said Gillian, not bothering to pretend with the magazine any longer. "British history mostly."

"Then I guess we are mortal enemies." He smiled.

"I can't believe I'm sitting here with an honest-to-God celebrity." Gillian shook her head. "Wait until I tell my mother."

So this was how men met women, August thought. They got themselves on television, then sat in doctors' offices waiting to be recognized. He wasn't sure what to do with this woman's enthusiasm, so he steered the conversation back to her.

"And what do you do?" he asked.

"I'm an assistant librarian at the University. Rare books."

"I'm surprised we haven't met," said August. "'I spend a lot of time in Rare Book rooms. Check your bag. No ink pens. White gloves.'"

"I have a stack of them." She smiled.

"They're always so clammy," said August. "Every time I put them on, I think of Jefferson railing against 'the dead hand of the past.'"

"I'll never look at them the same way again!" When she laughed, her nose crinkled and she looked like a mischievous schoolgirl. "So why Jefferson?"

"Why Jefferson?" August echoed. "Oh, it's a long story."

Gillian glanced around the waiting room. "I'm not going anywhere."

People often asked August "Why Jefferson?" but very few honestly wanted to hear his answer. They asked so that they might interrupt with why *they* had always been interested in Jefferson (or Benjamin Franklin, or King Arthur) or with the news that Jefferson was a moral reprobate and a sham. August had the short get-in-before-their-eyes-glaze-over version, and the slightly longer, invite-them-to-tell-their-story version, but this woman, perched on the edge of her chair, seemed genuinely interested in *him*, a welcome change from last night.

"Well," August said, "Jefferson was cripplingly shy, but when he believed in something he found the courage to speak out, even if it meant standing up before an entire nation. He was cursed with having no ego and an enormous ego at the same time. He was a very flawed man, but he thought America and Americans were infinitely perfectible."

"You don't seem very shy to me," Gillian said, and August realized she was right. It was actually fun talking to Gillian, he thought with surprise. He couldn't remember the last time he'd had fun talking to a woman. Surreptitiously, he checked her finger for a ring.

"So, what are you in for?" he asked. Immediately, he knew he'd said the wrong thing, for Gillian's face fell and she reached once more for the magazine.

"Oh, they've found another lump," she said uncomfortably. "You know."

He understood it now—her thin arms, the boyish flatness of her chest. What kind of monster thinks about picking up women in a doctor's office? He tried not to picture a mold-gray fractal growing beneath the pink silk blouse she covered with *American Child.* He couldn't bear to imagine this nice, plain young woman laid out in a coffin, her hands quiet inside a pair of white gloves. Leland emerged from the doctor's office and Gillian's name was called. She gave August a weak smile good-bye, and he wished her good luck.

"She seemed nice," said Leland, observing the exchange.

"What did the doctor say?" asked August gruffly, brushing aside his father's curiosity.

"He treated me like a drunk," said Leland, with the moral superiority of a man who had never once sat behind the wheel of a car after so much as a sip of brandy. "He made me close my eyes and touch my fingertips to my nose."

"What does that mean?"

"And he made me walk a straight line—heel, toe, heel, toe."

"He thinks you're an alcoholic?"

"No," replied Leland, handing over his ten-dollar co-pay to the receptionist behind the window. "He thinks I had a stroke."

"A stroke!" August nearly shouted in alarm. He couldn't believe how casual his father was being about this.

"Just a little one. Not even a little one—a forerunner, a John the Baptist stroke. They call them TIAs. It's a transient isch-a-something attack."

"Ischemic?"

"I think that's right. He said it was nothing to worry about, I just need to start taking it easy and watch my diet. Lay off your mother's cobbler for a while."

"Dad, an ischemic attack is a serious thing. It means you're primed to have a real stroke at some point."

"And I could be hit by a bus tomorrow," Leland replied, leading his son out of the office and down the hall. "Son, I sat by Manda Frank's two innocent babes and watched their skulls fill with blood. I am sixty-five years old and experienced a twinge. Now, let's go home. I want to get over to the Franks before lunchtime."

"The doctor said you had to rest," said August in exasperation.

"Time enough to rest when I'm dead, son," said Leland simply.

August followed his father to the truck and waited for him to buckle himself in.

"I've never had such fun as yesterday," he was saying as August pulled into Charlottesville town traffic. "It's kismet, isn't it, son? I'm named after that John Leland—all the Lelands in the family are. He was bosom friends with your great-great-great-great-grandfather, and he must have made quite an impression for one of our family to overlook his boreal origins and unfortunate choice of denomination. It's the greatest of Southern honors, son, to have one's name incorporated into a family tree. It's an honor not given lightly."

August drove down University Avenue past the redbrick Rotunda. The founding of the University of Virginia, Virginia's Statute of Religious Freedom, the Declaration of Independence—these were the only accomplishments Jefferson wanted listed on his gravestone. Not his time as governor. Not his two terms as president. It was a cold morning, and students scurried across the quad. August headed for the Interstate.

"I'll tell you, though," said Leland, "with my luck, I'll drop dead just as the president reaches out to shake my hand. It's the Vaughn curse to be ten minutes too early or too late for any real greatness. We've all suffered under it. Remember your great-uncle St. John? He used to say he wanted to have two thousand books on his shelf before he died, and if he hadn't developed pneumonia in his lungs when he was sixty-eight, he would have made it. In his will, he left his entire collection to the University of Virginia and when they counted, they came up with one thousand nine hundred and seventy-seven. Twenty-three books shy. Isn't that just a shame? Don't you think if he'd lived, he would easily have bought twenty-three more books? If he bought just one book a month, he would have only had to live two more years to have made it. It seems such a shame to have come so close and still ended up twenty-three short."

Who wanted to be remembered for being twenty-three books shy? thought August sourly. For that's all anyone remembered about Great-uncle St. John. Not that he hated his eggs over easy, or preferred his coffee with four sugars. Nor that he'd once taken morphine recreationally or that he had read, cover to cover, each of the one thousand nine hundred and seventy-seven books on his shelf. No, he'd been reduced to a single anecdote of twenty-three volumes shy, just as crazy old Great-uncle August would be reduced to his wig and breeches by those who came after. If anyone *did* come after.

What had gotten into him? August wondered, cracking the window of his pickup to let in some fresh air. He was utterly dissatisfied with everything in his life today. And in under an hour, he would be pulling into the driveway of a house where he'd spent his entire life, and descending the steps to his room like a prisoner to his familiar dungeon. And tomorrow, he would have to face a woman he had loved for too many years, and step back into a routine that, after last night, seemed unbearable to him. His father was still chuckling over poor, shortchanged Great-uncle St. John, when they crossed the narrow trickle of the Rapidan River. As a boy, August used to ride his bicycle out to this stretch of water, where the Manahoac Indians had long, long ago erected a burial mound like an ossuary landfill, a junk heap for bones that would have been originally stripped clean and buried elsewhere. A hundred years previously the river had shifted, and with every spring freshet, earth dropped from the mound, exposing blanched strata of bone—men and women, old and very young. Little remained by the time August found the spot, but he had spent many days of his boyhood picking along its rim, finding pot shards and what might have been soft bits of white teeth; marveling at the capriciousness of history, that it would take a tribe whose name meant "They Are Merry" and doom it to extinction. As an eight-year-old boy, Thomas Jefferson had followed a party of traveling Indians as they left the main road and trekked six miles through the woods to visit a mound like this on the bank of the Rivanna River. They had found it with no instructions or inquiry, and Jefferson never forgot the sorrowful expressions they wore as they stood above the mound for many hours before retracing their steps and continuing on.

The Manahoac burial mound lay just through the woods off the road they were on, and August squinted to see if the river had finally reclaimed it. Scrub underbrush and saplings made it nearly impossible to tell, but just as he was driving past, his eyes lit upon something he'd never noticed before—a faded sign, nailed to a pitch pine, just off the shoulder. *For Sale, Ten Acres*, it read, and gave a real estate agent's name and number in type so faint it could have been there for years. Though August had driven this route to the hospital often enough, he'd never had eyes for a sign like that. What did the availability of a place matter to him? His life was spoken for.

But now, almost without thinking, he found himself silently repeating the number on the sign, over and over, committing it to memory. His father continued on about Great-uncle St. John's book collection and how the University of Virginia had said it wasn't worth much—it consisted mostly of subscription novels by authors who had long since lost their currency—but August shut out the sound of his voice, worried he might transpose numbers or lose one altogether. That sign might have stood for months or years, but to August, it was brand new, and already he feared he might be too late. Someone might at this very minute, while he was stuck on the road, be picking up the phone to call and ask that agent about those ten acres. He found himself, without meaning to, driving faster, ignoring his father's hints that he take it easy, where was the fire? How awful it would be, he thought, to lose by minutes what he had just, at this moment, finally found.

His mother had lunch waiting for them when they finally pulled in at one o'clock. It was such an unexpected treat to have both her men home in the middle of the day, Evelyn had been unable to allow the event to pass uncelebrated. August's heart sank at the sight of chicken and dumplings, carrot salad, fresh yeast rolls, and coffee in the silver urn. He would have to disappoint her, and he could tell she was already vulnerable, waiting as she had been for a phone call to tell her the outcome of the doctor's visit, a call he and his father had each forgotten to place.

"You-all start without me," August said, kissing the top of his mother's silvery head. "I need to take care of something."

"Couldn't it wait until after lunch, dear?" his mother asked. "Your food will get cold."

"I'll just warm mine up later." The food smelled so good and the room was so warm, he had to fight the impulse to fall back into his old routine and forget all about that phone number. "Really, Mom, I'll just be a few minutes."

"Don't pay him any mind, Evelyn," August heard his father say as he bolted for the basement. "He had ants in his pants the whole ride home."

August's hands were trembling as he dialed the number from the sign and waited four rings for someone to pick up. Mentally, he went over the sum in his savings account, money that only the night before he was intent on laying at Margaret's feet. If she didn't want him, well, so be it, thought he; she wouldn't have another opportunity. From what little he knew about the price of real estate, he calculated he should have enough for the parcel by the river with some left over to build a modest house. Nothing fancy, just a small cottage with a bedroom and a study. And a front porch overlooking the water. And maybe a shed. He could save money by clearing the land himself, then when spring came around, he could plant a vegetable garden, an abundant patch without a single sprig of alfalfa or clover to be seen. Nothing that smacked of fodder or hay. Just ripe red tomatoes and cucumbers, sweet peas, and yellow squash. And at night he could sit on his porch and breathe in the grassy smell of ripening vines and the ferrous smell of a muddy river bottom, and imagine himself the protector of all the Manahoac spirits that still flitted, merrily or not, through those woods.

A machine picked up on the other end, and August left a rather breathless message, knowing even as he spoke that his excitement would put him in a bad bargaining position. The land was probably sold long ago to some hunt club that had never bothered to take down the sign, he told himself; don't go getting your hopes up.

But it was no use. Once the idea of buying that piece of land presented itself, August realized he could no longer be happy here in this room, surrounded by these seven hundred and sixteen books, eating yet another decade of meals with those too-familiar people upstairs. Of course, it was an inexcusably selfish time for him to think of moving out. His father had just had a stroke, after all. And Margaret had never been in more need of his help. But somehow their dependence on him was precisely the reason he needed most to leave. It frightened him, this newfound defiant rebellion. Maybe this was the reason he had never taken a day off. Maybe deep down he knew that if he ever took a single step back, he would find himself in full-scale retreat.

The smell of chicken and dumplings wafted down the basement steps, and for a moment August felt the urge to bound up the stairs and beg his mother's pardon for missing her tenderly prepared luncheon. The whole time he had been plotting his escape, she had been thinking of what he might most like to eat on a chilly November afternoon, and how she could most graciously serve it. But then the phone rang on the bedside table, and for the first time in years, his first thought was not *I hope that's Margaret,* and he knew that, no matter how lovingly his mother had set the table, it was time for him to go.

CHAPTER FOURTEEN

The night of Pastor Vaughn's doctor's appointment, the sky let forth a fantastic autumn thunderstorm. Maybe it was the sycamore tree lashing his bedroom window that woke him, or the clatter of hail on the tin roof. Maybe it was easier to blame the weather than the black cat of his own mortality hunkering on his chest, stealing away his very breath. Whatever the reason, Pastor Vaughn started awake at four in the morning, rigid beside his dreaming wife, acknowledging for the first time since he saw the doctor that he was going to die.

As a man of the cloth, he knew he would have to be a terrible hypocrite to dread his own passing. He had a hundred pious illustrations and a thousand theological expectations of what he might find on the Other Side, and yet all he could think of, lying there in his bed, was that the intersection of Life and Death was nothing but a sort of celestial abacus, waiting for the businesslike flick of the Divine Finger. How horrible it was to realize that upon his passing all of his family's beads would be stacked in the column of the dead, with only a single remaining soul left among the living. And when August was slid over to join them—with that final, fatal click—the Vaughn strand would be null, a zero, a holding place in the great heavenly equation.

He rolled over and looked at Evelyn, her face slack against the pillow, just barely visible by the light of the digital clock. She had done a lot of crying in the bathroom after lunch, carefully reapplying her powder so that he wouldn't be able to tell, but he always knew. Evelyn's default was laughter, and anything short of that meant serious depression. He never realized how much he counted on her good mood until something snatched it away, and he'd spent the day trying to joke her back to herself. *How many Episcopalians does it take to change a lightbulb?* he'd asked. *Ten—one to screw it in, and nine to say how much they liked the old one.* But it was no use: She'd snuck off to the bathroom several more times before bed.

Now he looked at his beloved wife, her curls tucked beneath their net like a school of silvery minnows, her lips still pink with traces of lipstick, and wondered how they had gotten to this point. He remembered their years of trying and miscarrying, before and after August, Evelyn's cautious early optimism and her stricken face when eight to ten weeks later yet another child bid them farewell on its journey to eternal rest. After a while the cycle became too hard on her body, and after that it didn't matter anymore, she had grown too old. And yet looking at her now, her face smooth in sleep, could he not be forgiven for wishing her another Saint Elizabeth, blessed with a child in her blameless old age? Was she not, in the larger sense, barren, denied a child of her child? He knew it was irrational to think this way, as irrational as it had been for him to rejoice in the birth of a son so that the Vaughn name would not die with him. But what a cosmic joke to father a son that never marries and produces no son of his own! Funnier than the Mexican weather report.

Evelyn sighed and rolled over in her sleep. Leland fleetingly considered waking her, but he knew she would be horrified by his line of thought, and while the company of her horror might salve his own, there was no point in having them both awake, listening to the rain on the roof. He kissed her shoulder and slid out from under the warm covers, into the clothes he had taken off earlier. He made his way through the deeper dark of the house, girdled by night and rain clouds, and downstairs to the kitchen. He wasn't really hungry, but eating seemed to be the thing one did once up, and so he made himself a bowl of gray chicken and dumplings and poured a glass of milk— skim. He sighed. Evelyn had gone to the store and bought it immediately upon learning he'd suffered a stroke, pouring all of their good whole milk down the sink. She'd rid the house of cookies and ice cream, emptied the shakers of salt and replaced it with something called Mrs. Dash. She'd gone to the back of the pantry and flushed

out of hiding his supposedly secret stash of Halloween Reese's peanut butter cups, and had banished the tin of sugary, creamy Interna-
tional Coffee. He was amazed the chicken and dumplings had been
spared, but they had been saved for August, who'd never materialized from his room, and once midnight had struck, Leland had pro-
nounced them fair game.

He hadn't told Evelyn the entire story of his doctor's visit: that
he'd never known he was claustrophobic until he was swallowed by
the round sucker mouth of the CAT scan, with its swimming, nib-
bling X-ray machine, how he could feel the iodine molecules creep
through his body slowly enough to count, like sheep before sleep or
air bubbles in an IV line—a slow, trudging march toward his com-
promised brain, where they settled in his weak spots and then lit up
like Christmas tree lights on the final readout. He had guiltily with-
held his doctor's desire to schedule a consultation with Evelyn and
August to ask them questions about Leland's increasing vagaries and
memory lapses; the doctor wanted to identify a pattern, like an elec-
trician tracing a wire in the basement back to its short circuit. But
the priest could not forget the note of gravity in his physician's voice,
a tone that said, Get your ducks in a row, my friend, you know not
when your time is near.

He finished his snack and washed his plate. Outside, the great
green hedge of storm imposed itself between his house and those of
his neighbors, its furious wind shaking the sign at the end of his
driveway: Three Chimneys. Population 781. It was appropriate weather
for Proper 29, the last Sunday in the church's liturgical calendar,
the end of the long stretch of Pentecost known as Ordinary Time.
After this Sunday would come the frolic and rejoicing of Advent,
with its pageants and nativities and adoring magi. But the sermon
he had to compose for this week would be a doleful one, its readings from the Book of Luke, a meditation on Christ's sufferings upon
the cross. In 1970, the Church had tried to lift this final week out
of the grave by renaming it Christ the King, but that came with its
own baggage for American clerics. Theirs was a country that fought

to be rid of a king, that associated monarchy with tyranny and despotism. Proper 29 was always a difficult week for Leland, and just to make it harder, he now realized he'd left his notes back at the church, on the edge of his desk, peeking out from beneath his Lectionary for Year C.

I should go back to bed, he thought, even as he felt his way down the dark hall to the closet, where his galoshes and mackintosh were buried amid unused tennis rackets and fishing poles, plus gift boxes Evelyn obsessively saved even though she'd forget they were there and invariably buy new ones. He pulled the string and blinked against the naked bulb of the hall closet, knowing it was crazy to go to the church at four o'clock in the morning, knowing he should get back to bed so that Evelyn wouldn't worry. But some stubborn corner of his moth-eaten brain refused to give in to this new forgetfulness. He was not some sick, feeble old man who crawled back under the covers when there was work to be done.

Leland pulled on his rain slicker and immediately found one of his black galoshes, but a quick kick around failed to produce the other. Just his Vaughn luck. With a sigh, he dropped to his hands and knees, pushing aside the clutter in the closet, years' worth of accumulated junk—unmated snow shoes and singular gloves, a wall of coats that crashed from their hangers at a mere touch, a ripped butterfly net. Like water filling a hole in sand, every time he scooped his way toward the bottom, more junk flowed down, until he found himself impatiently tossing into the hallway hand weights and a tackle box, August's high school track letter jacket and something he thought was a smokeless ashtray. Evelyn should never have let the closet get this bad, he thought, refusing to admit there was no injunction against him cleaning it himself. Pastor Vaughn pawed and panted, laboring as if there were nothing in the world more important than finding this shoe. He did not even recall why he was looking for it, or consider that he might make do without it. Tomorrow, he decided grimly, he would speak to Evelyn about the importance of order, and how if she really wanted to help him, she would direct her expulsatory energies away from all the delicious food in the house and onto the massive amount of crap in this closet. Leland had been rooting and muttering for a full fifteen minutes before he gradually became aware that he was not alone in the hallway. He felt eyes on his bent back and uplifted rump, and realized that with all his thumping and grunting, he had succeeded in rousing the whole household.

"I'm sorry," said Leland, turning to face his worried family. "This closet is completely out of hand."

But he spoke to an empty hallway. His wife and son lay in their beds, their individual dreams like chimney smoke mingling above the house to tell the confused narrative of a woman with breast cancer sinking to the Center of the Earth. There was no one in the hallway but Leland and the Wall of Ancestors, as August always called it, two hundred years' worth of framed uncles and aunts, fourth and fifth cousins, men muttonchopped and mustachioed, women with stern Depression-era finger waves, each generation having taken deeply to heart its duty to record itself. He would have thought a family made up predominantly of clergy would have shrunk from the vainglory of personal iconography, but his seemed to relish it, gaining momentum with each passing generation until simple Revolutionary oil paintings became finely etched copper daguerreotypes became squirrels' nests of paper photo albums, each Kodak Brownie snap carefully transcribed with the sitter's name and date taken. This sense of entitlement, this refusal to be forgotten, had been passed down like blue eyes or left-handedness until he, Leland, had inherited the lot of them. Until now, he'd always thought of these pictures on the wall as kindly genii, watching over his hearth, offering a familial bosom into which he might fall come his day of reckoning; but now, in the semidark, in the furious rain, their obsessive memorializing felt almost malevolent. A faceless past was easy to disappoint, but the Vaughn family—compulsively sketching and painting and snapping—bequeathed itself wholesale to the next generation, so that it might feel the weight of those who had come before.

Leland abandoned the closet and strode to the front door in his single boot, turned up his collar, and ran, splashing through his yard, across his gravel driveway, slipping on the churchyard grass and catching himself awkwardly. He fumbled with the key and let himself into the front door of St. Barnabas, newly painted red to symbolize . . . what was it again? The blood of Christ? Sanctuary? The mandate had come down, and his handyman had dutifully painted over the doors, which had been, since the church's founding, walnut-stained wood. The church was cold and dark inside, its thick stone walls muffling the storm outside. Leland stood dripping on the black and white tiled floor of the vestibule behind the center aisle, the staging area for so many nervous fathers and daughters. How often had he dreamed of officiating at August's wedding—"I now pronounce you . . ."— and watching his boy slip away like the tide, arm in arm with his tulled and veiled future. It seemed this was never meant to be, but he rarely entered by this door that he didn't think of his son leaving by it, returning with a bundle in his arms to take to the font, where Leland might trace a cross on his grandchild's forehead, saying, "You are sealed by the Holy Spirit in Baptism and marked as Christ's own forever. Amen."

He limped down the center aisle, his one wet sock leaving its ghostly footprint, and unlocked the hall door to the Parish House. He flipped on the bank of fluorescent lights that lit the gauntlet he still had to walk before reaching his office, the long double row of St. Barnabas pastors who had come before him, mostly men of his own kin, each in his own egalitarian black frame, hung from the picture rail with the forthright simplicity of a grammar school alphabet. His own official church portrait hung at the end of the line, just over a water fountain, taken fresh out of divinity school, a serious face made somewhat less imposing by his square plastic glasses, long sideburns, and bushy mustache. He looked like a priest who would drive a Volkswagen bus, and strum a folk mass on his acoustic guitar; a priest you could "rap" with and to whom you could confess to having smoked pot. His cleric's collar looked wrong on someone so ungroomed, he thought now, as if they'd buttoned up a stray dog, and he was embarrassed that this was how the line would end, that the Vaughn priest coda at St. Barnabas was this clownish photo.

Leland unlocked his office door and switched on his warm yellow desk lamp. His secretary, who worked only two days a week, had left him a mound of unopened mail, thirteen phone messages, and a stack of correspondence to sign. He sat heavily at his desk and played back the crackly answering machine, listening to his parishioners, their voices disembodied and uncanny in the predawn silent church. Wednesday night's potluck was in jeopardy because Mary Planer had ruptured her eardrum. Alice Barlow, vice chair of the flower committee, needed to know ASAP what sort of flowers the pastor preferred for the Christmas service, because if she did not get the order in on time they would be forced, like last year, to buy foil-wrapped baskets of poinsettias from the Food Lion that were overpriced and, moreover, were likely to once again wilt by the midnight mass. Abraham Johnson, the church's woefully underpaid handyman, left a shy, quiet message asking for an advance on his meager wages because his son had fallen afoul of the law and needed to be bailed out of jail. The last message on the machine was from the nurse in his doctor's office asking if he had picked a date for his family consult.

Proper 29. Christ the King. Leland had reached the end of the line. His notes were right where he left them, but the energy that had gotten him out of bed and into his single galosh and down the aisle had deserted him, and he lay his cheek upon a stack of hymnals. His eyes fell upon his own handwritten notes, the Old Testament passage for the dying of the church year, Jeremiah 23:

> Woe to the shepherds who destroy and scatter the sheep of my pasture! says the LORD. . . . It is you who have scattered my flock, and have driven them away, and you have not attended to them. So I will attend to you for your evil doings, says the LORD.
>
> Then I myself will gather the remnant of my flock out of all the lands where I have driven them, and I will bring them back to their fold, and they shall be fruitful and multiply.

Knock, knock.

Leland looked up at the rap upon his office door. His mind really was going, he thought. It was four-thirty in the morning; the church was empty.

Knock, knock.

"Who's there?" Leland answered hesitantly.

"Dead."

Dead, who? He almost laughed as the door creaked open. This is how it would end, he thought, with a shadow in the doorway on a dark, rainy night.

"Dad," repeated his son. "What are you doing here at this time of night?"

"August?" His son stood in the doorway, clutching a dripping umbrella and a cell phone in case he needed to call emergency personnel.

"I heard you banging around upstairs and I followed you over," said August, relieved. "It's four-thirty in the morning. You should be in bed."

"I forgot my notes," explained Leland.

"Are you all right? You look like you've seen a ghost."

But he hadn't seen a ghost, thought Leland with relief. The shadow he thought was coming for him was nothing more than his own flesh and blood, the very antithesis of a ghost. "No, no, I just had a lot on my mind. What are you doing here?"

"I couldn't sleep either," his son admitted.

The two remained as they were—August in the doorway, Leland at his desk. Outside lightning flared, and each mentally counted down the thunder.

"I made an offer on a piece of land today, and it's been accepted," said August, abruptly breaking the silence. "I'm going to build a house."

Leland stared at his son, unsure if he'd heard right. "A house?" he asked. "You're not moving to the farm?"

"What do you mean?" asked August, confused.

"The farm has been in her family for generations. I figured you would all live there."

Understanding slowly dawned on August. "I'm not moving in with Margaret," he said.

"Oh. I just assumed," stammered Leland, realizing his mistake. "I saw you on Election Night, and it seemed so natural. . . . I'm sorry, son."

"There is nothing to be sorry about," said August sternly. "Margaret and I are good friends. Nothing more."

"It's just that—," Leland turned away, surprised by the rush of disappointment he felt. He straightened his papers and reached for his Bible.

"What?" prodded August.

"I was just thinking how we've become a family of only children," Leland said slowly, slumping in his chair. "I look at our family tree and there's you, and your cousin Julia, and that's about it. All along we've had branches lopped off by disease, and the odd bachelor or spinster. But nothing compares to this generation. I worry we've pruned ourselves into extinction."

"What am I supposed to do about it, Dad?" August asked, more defensively than he'd meant to. "Get married just so you have something to record in the family Bible?"

"No, son," said Leland quickly. "That's not what I meant."

August didn't want to argue. He looked down at the floor, and caught sight of Leland's wet foot. "Where is your other shoe?" he asked.

"I couldn't find it."

"Well, let's get you home. And pray Mom's asleep, or you're in for it."

Pastor Vaughn collected his notes and turned off the light. "Perhaps you'd better wait a while to tell your mother about the move," he suggested. "You know she'll try to talk you out of it."

"The bid's been accepted," said August.

"She'll buy it out from under you," his father said with a smile, "to keep you at home."

Leland locked his office door behind him and looked down the vanishing horizon of St. Barnabas clergy. This church had been the mainstay and life's work of every man on that wall, and yet they were little more than hatch marks to this building, just another way of keeping time.

"Do you ever wonder if this church will miss us when we're gone?" asked Leland. "Do you think it misses any of the people who sat in its pews or the young girls who walked down its aisle? Do you think a place has a memory?"

"Dad, we should go home," said August, patting him gently on the back. "You've had a long day."

"I'm fine, son," said Leland. "I'm just thinking of my sermon. *'When they came to the place that is called The Skull, they crucified Jesus there with the criminals, one on his right and one on his left.'* It's always amazed me that pilgrims flock to worship at a place associated with our Savior's humiliation. They take home handfuls of everyday dust because they believe it remembers Christ's suffering and is sanctified by it. I just think of strangers preaching here in this church that has been such a part of our family for so long, and it would comfort me if somehow the stones in the wall or the tiles of the floor remembered us Vaughns for having been here, for having tried our best."

"I think that's all anyone wants, Dad," said August. "To be remembered."

"You know, I heard a funny joke the other day, son," Leland said, leading them back the way they'd each come, past the inscrutable, patient faces and into the shadowy womb of the church. "A man who was about to be hanged said to the sheriff, 'Say, do I really have to die swinging from that tree?'

"'Course not,' said the sheriff. 'We just put the rope around your neck and kick the horse away. After that, it's up to you.'"

August heeded his father's advice and did not speak of the move to his mother. Weeks passed as he filled out the loan application secretly, Xeroxed his check stubs in the next town, and worried himself sick she would learn he was moving out from Bob Crenshaw or someone at the bank. Finally, on the morning of his closing, he could put it off no longer. He found his mother on her hands and knees under the sink, taking up last year's contact paper, which she suspected was about to peel.

"Well, Mr. Jefferson, don't you look nice today," she said when he tapped her on the shoulder. "A special occasion?"

"I'm giving a program in Williamsburg this afternoon," he said. "The president of William and Mary saw me on TV and asked if I'd speak to the Board of Visitors."

"That's very impressive," she said.

"One step down from Monticello."

"Should I expect you back for dinner?" she asked. "It's tofu night."

August still had not gotten used to his mother's poring over low-fat, no-salt cookbooks, or puzzling over the wok she'd bought at Sears. She hadn't quite gotten the hang of Asian cooking, substituting Worcestershire for soy sauce and candied for fresh ginger. He and his father smiled bravely through those meals, but no one looked forward to tofu night.

"I think dinner is included," he said.

"Well, have a good time," she said, ducking back under the sink. "Call when you get there so I know you're all right. It's raining again."

August hesitated. Was it imperative he tell her today? he wondered. After all, it was only a closing; the house wouldn't be built for several months yet. But he was ashamed of the cowardice that had kept the news from her this long, and taking a deep breath, he informed her, as gently as possible, that he had bought a little piece of land on the Rapidan River and would soon be moving out.

"What?" Evelyn gasped, pulling her head from under the sink. "What do you mean you're moving out?"

"It's a very nice piece of property," August explained, trying to sound enthusiastic. "You'll love coming there."

Evelyn stared at her son in disbelief. All the reasons he shouldn't leave right now deserted her, and she heard herself stammering out the first thing that came to mind. "But you can't move to the river," she said. "Convicts live down there."

"What are you talking about?" asked August.

"I've heard a man who served seven years for armed robbery keeps a trailer down by the river and who knows what sorts of escaped criminals he has living with him." Evelyn rushed to explain. "I wouldn't feel comfortable with you coming home late at night."

"Mom, I'm sure I can handle the convicts."

"And the river floods. Every year, someone's carport is ruined."

"I'm building far enough back. You don't have to worry."

"But your father—," Evelyn began, instinctively turning to look for her husband, who had already left for work.

"He knows. He's happy for me."

"You spoke with him first?" Evelyn asked, trying to keep the hurt from her voice. "Were you just going to move out without telling me?"

"I'm telling you right now," said August, suffering every bit as much as he'd imagined he would. "It will be several more months before the house is built. Today is only the closing."

"You're closing already?" she nearly yelped. "With no discussion?"

"There is nothing to discuss," he said as firmly as he dared. "It's a done deal."

Evelyn couldn't believe this was her son standing before her. He had never displayed such treachery in his life. What about your father? she wanted to yell at him. What about his stroke? But her anger at her son had fallen into such disuse over the years, she barely knew how to recognize it now. Instead it took the form of a pounding headache that would send her to bed and keep her there for the rest of the afternoon.

"We'll talk about this when your father gets home," she said sternly, crawling back under the sink. She could hear him behind her, shuffling helplessly in the kitchen, not wanting to leave with her angry at him, but she would not give him the satisfaction of further discussion. After a minute during which neither moved, she finally heard August pick up his car keys and lean over her.

"I'm sorry," he said to the Brillo pads and Bon Ami, the rusted cans of muriatic acid, the stacks of worn blue rubber gloves. "I love you."

Evelyn realized she was gritting her teeth. "You should think about what you owe your family," she said, not caring how petty and demanding it sounded.

"It's all I ever think about," said August flatly. Evelyn ripped the backing off her clean new contact paper and tearfully pressed it into place.

"Mr. Jefferson!"

Bob Crenshaw met August at the door of First Virginia Savings and Loan and, with a deep, theatrical bow, ushered him inside. "It is an honor and a privilege."

"Just August today," said August, patting his wigless head. "I'm only dressed because I didn't know how long the closing would take. I have a program in a few hours."

"Oh, come on, play along," whispered Bob. "Everyone saw you on TV. You're a celebrity around here."

The banker ushered him past the grinning security guard and into the open, wood-paneled lobby. Even on a Saturday morning, the teller line was long at First Virginia Savings and Loan, for most of its customers looked on the ATMs with the same suspicion they would have a row of slot machines. A few of those waiting August recognized from his programs—elderly couples his parents' age cashing social security checks, a young mother who had once diapered her son in the front row during his talk at the public library. Everyone turned to look at him as he stepped in, and he felt immediately self-conscious, as if he'd come to the bank to rob it.

"Mr. President, may I introduce you to some of my colleagues," Bob said, leading him over to the tellers. Behind the soundproof glass, three women in name tags waved enthusiastically. "Carole, Janice, and Yvonne—our third president," he presented. "Mr. President— the hardworking staff of First Virginia Savings and Loan."

August tried to swallow his mounting discomfort. "Ladies," he said, with a slight bow.

"It's not often we have a personage of your stature here at First Virginia," said Bob loud enough that the customers in line could hear. "Thank you for trusting us with your business."

August ducked his head as Bob led him past the long line and around to the bank's glassed-in conference room. "This is fun," the banker said.

"Bob, let's take it easy," said August. "Jefferson had a problematic relationship with the banking system."

"Sure. Sure," said Bob, pausing with his hand on the knob. "But while I have you here, I wanted to ask your opinion about something. I've been thinking about a series of commercials to attract kids, you know? Something along the lines of 'Save your nickels, boys and girls, and you can grow up to be president just like me.' What do you think?"

"I think it sends a pretty mixed message. With campaign finance reform, and all."

"No, I mean, what do you think about starring in it?"

"Maybe we should start the closing," August suggested. "I have to be in Williamsburg by three."

"Of course, of course!" Bob said, opening the door at last. "But think about it."

August stepped into a small room crowded by bookshelves, a desk, and a long, scarred oak-laminate table. At the end sat a broadly smiling, large-boned, middle-aged woman, whom Bob introduced as Mary, the bank's notary public. She wore a tight leather miniskirt and a gold ankle bracelet underneath her pantyhose. "Mary has been dying to meet you," Bob said, with a wink.

"Mr. President, it's an honor." Mary rose to greet him. "We'll try to make this as painless as possible."

August took a seat between the two of them as Bob collated stack after stack of paper, each closely worded document shot through with sticky red arrows. Sign here. And here. And here. He tried to listen while Bob explained his title, his title insurance, his state taxes, his escrows, but all the while Mary was talking. I didn't know you made cheese, Mr. President. I didn't, August explained, puzzling over something called a recording tax. I was only helping a friend. Oh, she said, stamping her own stack of papers. A close friend? How's our cheese coming, by the way? asked Bob, pointing out a spot August forgot to initial and reaching into a bag of baby carrots he had begun compulsively eating after seeing himself on the news, huffing red-faced across Margaret's yard with a bucket of curd. You know, I've been helping Margaret with her foreclosure extension. We have our hands full with that little lady, don't we?

August nodded, wishing he could make them both disappear. The room was close with dry-rotting old law books and a vase of dying roses perched upon what he took to be Mary's desk in the corner. Manila folders and framed photographs littered its top. Mary with a golden retriever. Mary with a man older than herself, who could have been a boyfriend or could have been her father. Mary lifting a mixed drink from a cabana chair on a cruise ship just as the maraschino sun sank into the waves behind her. What was he doing here? August looked down at the thick stack of papers Bob continued to shove at him. Now that it was too late, he wanted to take everything back— erase his name from the contract, rescind his bid, which on second consideration seemed foolishly generous and far more than the seller had expected to get. Why hadn't he used a real estate agent? What did he know about clearing a lot, or getting electric hookup, or building a house? August paused in his marathon signing, and Bob recognized the sick look on his face.

"Chin up, old man," the banker said kindly. "It's just like getting married. Drive out there when we're done, and you'll remember why you fell in love."

August nodded blankly and reached for his checkbook. He was about to sign his name to the largest check he'd ever written, one that would nearly drain his bank account. "Wait," cried Mary as he reached for his pen, "I have something perfect for the occasion. Why didn't I think of it before?"

She rummaged in her desk drawer and came up with a flossy white ostrich quill pen, a souvenir from her trip to the Liberty Bell three years ago. "I think this is more presidential, don't you?" she asked.

But August wished he'd stuck to his reliable old Bic. The quill, stiff from disuse, skipped terribly, and the signature at the bottom of his check, even to him, looked halfhearted and unsure.

August left the bank at noon and drove home to Three Chimneys.

Lot 5608, ten acres, riverfront. He tried to remember what he'd found so special about it, for in his memory, it was now nothing but a tangle of scrub and brier, a marshy bit of land doomed to flood with every heavy rain, just as his mother had predicted. Had he only been like other men in the throes of a midlife crisis, he would have bought a motorcycle or jumped from an airplane, but instead he had avoided his job and destituted himself for a parcel of unworkable swamp.

August felt as gray and unsettled as the sky outside. It had rained sporadically all morning, once so hard they could hear it inside the bank; but now it had slowed to a drizzle, just enough to require his wipers. There must be some way to remedy this horrible mistake, he thought, automatically driving the familiar road home. He could contact a real estate agent first thing tomorrow and put it back on the market. If he had to sell at a loss, it would be a fitting punishment for having acted so rashly in the first place. In fact, he secretly *hoped* he would lose money: $10,000; $20,000. It needed to be a sharp slap of a sum, sufficient for him to remember his folly and never seek to repeat it.

Sunk in despair, August sped through town and up winding Snakehill Road. He hadn't meant to come this way, it was not the most direct route to his new property, but as he neared Prickett Farm, he found himself slowing to a stop. From the road, August could see only the roofline of house and barn and the high white chimney beckoning from the hill. A mist hung low in the hollows of the pasture, following the meandering line of the small creek. In the stubbled fields, a flock of intrepid crows picked through the waste of September's mowing. She would be washing down the cream separator about now, wouldn't she, scrubbing each individual disk and spout? Or crating up a shipment of soft cheese for delivery to New York next week? August killed the ignition at the driveway's edge, where a few stray pieces of gravel broke for the open road. He had almost three hours before he needed to be in Williamsburg, time enough to find her and apologize for being gone so long. After he spoke to her, he would drive home and inform his mother he'd put the property up for sale. Everything is back to normal, he would tell her. I'm not going anywhere.

August sat for a long time in his truck, willing himself to turn up the driveway. He sat for so long, a small gray dot appeared on the road behind him. As he watched in the rearview mirror, it became gray sweatpants and a hooded jacket, a slight man who looked familiar to August, though he couldn't say from where. The man ran past his truck to the edge of the paved road, turned at the Franks' driveway, and jogged back, his glasses wet with rain, his breath a white cloud around his head. To August's surprise, he slowed when he reached the truck, walked over, and tapped the window.

"Hey, you're Thomas Jefferson, aren't you?" the man asked. He had olive skin and dark hair plastered to his forehead by the rain. The tip of his nose was bright red in the cold.

"I'm August Vaughn," August answered politely.

"Oh right," teased the other man. "*I'm not the president. I only play one on TV.*"

"I'm sorry," said August. "Have we met?"

The man stuck a wet hand inside August's window. "I'm Harvey March, Polly's history teacher. I saw you the other day at the cheesemaking."

Now August remembered. Polly and this small, dark man standing in the crowd, watching him shovel curd. He shook the teacher's hand. "It's awfully wet outside. Can I give you a lift somewhere?"

Mr. March shook his head. "I jog out this way every day. Rain or shine. Polly's told me a lot about you."

"All good, I hope," said August. Mr. March remained silent.

"Polly's an exceptional student," her teacher said at last. "I expect great things from her."

"We all do," answered August.

"It's a shame to see her eclipsed by a cheese."

"That's not likely," said August seriously.

"Still," said Mr. March. "It's quite an undertaking staying faithful to history. The original cheese read *Rebellion to Tyrants Is Obedience to God.* Do you think Polly's mother will put that on hers?"

"If you know your Jefferson," said August, bristling, "you know that not all sources quote that. Only a few."

"I suppose it is pretty radical by today's standards," said Mr. March, "to overthrow one's tyrants."

It had begun to rain harder, but he showed no intention of jogging on. For some reason he seemed to be sniffing August out. This Harvey March reminded him of a black lab he'd known as a boy who tried to mount all the other dogs in the neighborhood.

"*'The tree of liberty should be watered from time to time with the blood of patriots and tyrants,'*" quoted Harvey March. "*'Rather than that revolution should have failed, I would have seen half the earth decimated. If there were one Adam and one Eve alive in every nation and alive free, that would be greater than the present.'*"

"These were things Jefferson said as a young man. After he witnessed the French Revolution," responded August. "He gave up those notions when he matured."

"Should we give up what we believed strongly in our youth?" asked Mr. March. "I sometimes think maturity is what has doomed us to this slavish mediocrity."

"You can call it mediocrity, or you can call it progress," replied August. "People are more comfortable now than they ever have been."

"But I think we can both agree," he said, "we are not what Mr. Jefferson hoped we might be."

August fell silent as Harvey March bent to tie his loose shoestring. It was raining in earnest now and water poured off the teacher's slicker in two heavy streams. He stood up wearing the friendliest of smiles.

"I should get going," said Mr. March. "You know, I've always had the greatest respect for you impersonators. How do you ever find costumes that fit?" He patted the truck door then, and took off, running steadily and without haste through the cold November rain. August watched him go, gray sweats dissolving into the wet sky.

The teacher's words stayed with August a long time. No, he was not the man Jefferson would have wished he might be. But more important, August knew, he was not the man he himself wished he might be. He stared up Margaret's driveway, rain crashing now on his windshield, obscuring everything outside. At times of uncertainty, he used to go through his program, taking comfort from the peaceful undertow as he was pulled back in time, back to childhood, back to the womb, there to lie suspended and safe for that infinitesimal moment. August closed his eyes against the rain and surrendered to the tug of memory—the White House, Independence Hall, the woodland wild of unbuilt Monticello—but something was missing, and no matter how hard he tried to summon it, Jefferson's life would not come. His eyes closed, his breath suspended, August saw, instead of John Wayles, his own father wearing one wet shoe, alone in the darkened Parish House; instead of Patsy's transparent hand on the counterpane, Margaret, strong and vital in the barnyard mist, backlit by a swinging moon. And then the tide drew him even farther out, and he found himself back in the cradle, the white wicker one he recognized from his mother's carefully preserved picture albums. His parents stood over him, smiling as they did in every snapshot, as if unable to comprehend their great good fortune, but when August looked down at the sleeping child, he saw the cradle was full of nothing but photographs, yellowed around the edges, worn from fond handling, their sifted daubs of color like the strokes of an impressionist painting of a baby. *I thought he would move to the farm,* he heard his father say. And then his mother: *He should remember what he owes his family.* What's happening to me? August thought, wildly, feeling himself unexpectedly choked for air, struggling like a man caught in the current of a real and present death.

He cracked the window, and rain wet his blue silk jacket. August unfastened his seat belt and struggled out of the jacket, throwing it down next to his wig on the seat beside him. In the rearview mirror, he glanced away from his sorrowful face.

August started the truck and solemnly drove the eight miles to Lot 5608, ten acres, riverfront. From the road, he was just able to make out the faintest of paths through the winter-thin forest, tamped most likely by boys such as himself who had come to visit more recently than had any member of the long-extinct Manahoac tribe. He tapped the hazard lights, raised the umbrella, and plunged into his woods, pushing aside wet, bare dogwood branches and arching briers, tramping the leafy forest floor, raising puffs of mushroom smoke. His property was rich in poison sumac, running cedar, bright red holly berries, decomposing fallen oaks, their geode hearts dark and compelling with shelf fungi. He kept his eyes on the suggestion of path, deafened by the rain on his open umbrella, not recognizing the burial mound until he'd almost walked right past it, for the bunker it had been in his boyhood had been ground down to a low molar on the riverbank after all these years. The outline was the same, however, a long oblong rise, artificial on the landscape, yet as fixed a part of it as an ax swallowed by a growing tree. He stood at the mound a good long while, listening to the river rush behind him. This is my stone dropped in the pond, thought August. Everything will emanate from this point. First he would build a circular rock wall to keep the rising river from further theft. Then he would clear concentrically outward and upward. Where the ground swelled to his right, there he would place his house. To the left, where the rain seemed to have melted a meadow, he would plant his vegetable garden. He would situate his life so that no matter where he stood, or worked, or relaxed, he could see this point and remember whose land he was on, and to whom he owed his independence.

August stood by the Indian mound until his feet were soaked and his white stockings soggy. For better or worse, I own this, thought he. It was no Monticello. But then again, he was no Jefferson.

CHAPTER FIFTEEN

Three nights in a row, Manda had the same dream.

Her dog Turbo was finally going to have her puppies. Poor Turbo—she had been pregnant for twelve years, ever since Manda first tried to breed her, and no one, not even the vet, recognized her condition. Day by day and year by year, her belly had grown inexorably bigger. Her swollen teats brushed the ground, leaving trails like a party of weary slugs, her head hung heavy between her shoulder blades, and she lowed mournfully. In her dream, Manda went to the utility room to check on the dog and found her gnawing at her bottom, the dog-fond, flea-ridden yellow rug stained with blood. In her dream, Manda waited as each puppy slithered out, then one by one, she wiped them clean and collected them in a cardboard box. She sat for a long time beside her dog, stroking her leathery ears and making her lick water from her fingers. The puppies climbed blindly over one another, anxiously searching out their mother's milk, and Manda knew she should let the puppies nurse, but Turbo was so tired, it seemed she was asking Manda with her sad dog eyes to spare her just a few hours longer. So Manda carried the cardboard box into the woods. In her nightgown and bare feet, she walked the red pine needle path down to where the creek bank shone with silver moonlit mica and nuggets of quartz. In her dream, Manda kept walking until the icy winter water came up to her knees, then one by one, she set the puppies in the water and watched them float away, like Moses toward the bulrushes.

Three nights in a row, Manda had that dream, yet she couldn't remember sleeping since the babies had come home from the hospital three weeks ago. Manda and Jake and Jake's mother and Manda's mother and sister Nina each took a different baby in rotating shifts, passing the infants around like a game of hot potato, hoping some new combination might settle them down, but with no luck. Not even Jake's mother, who prided herself on surviving three colicky infants, was able to console them for more than a few minutes at a time. Manda kept waiting for them to exhaust themselves, with their red faces and their hot scalps and their rigid torsos, but only when their tiny rosebud mouths wrapped around the manila nipples of their bottles were they quiet, and even then, she had to listen to their desperate gulping of milk and tears. For several minutes after their stomachs were full, they would lie limp and dreamy, only to start whimpering as if in the throes of night terrors, then ratchet their way up to full-blown screams. In the NICU they had lain peaceful for weeks under the care of a team of nurses, gathering their strength for this homecoming. But now that they were here, their home oxygen lines became tangled and crimped, their nasal cannulas slipped loose, and all the monitor alarms went off at once. Premature babies are a good deal fussier, they had told her before she left the hospital, and these babies have been through quite an ordeal. It's going to be rough going for a while.

The children deemed strong enough to release still came home with medical challenges. Ember Cheyenne and little Devon suffered with bronchopulmonary dysplasia and were still noosed to tubes, one for feeding and another fifty-foot length that would allow them to be carried anywhere in the house without being disconnected from their oxygen tanks. Infinity and Kaylee experienced bouts of reflux and had stopped breathing twice. Little Adams Brooke had such severe diaper rash that his skin cracked and bled, keeping everyone fearful of infection, and all the children needed to be dosed with medicine every eight hours. Manda felt especially ill-prepared for this chaos because Rose had done nothing but smile and sleep the first few months of her life, slept so deeply, in fact, she would drift off in the middle of her feedings, feedings she'd had to be awakened for in the first place. If Rose fussed it was because she wanted her bottle or was finally protesting a diaper Manda had gone six hours without changing. She never complained when Manda bundled her into a backpack and took her rabbit hunting, nor when she was carted to loud, smoky concerts, nor when the dogs brayed outside her bedroom window late at night. Manda used to scoop Rose up on her way out the door along with her purse and car keys—she was that portable—and even as a toddler, she would sit wherever she was put, happily sucking her pacifier and looking at the same *Sesame Street* board book over and over. But now Rose was as shell-shocked as her parents by this invasion of babies. One night when they had cried without interruption for three hours, Rose gathered her Barbies and Etch-A-Sketch and Elmo and blue plastic Rollerblades and threw them in the babies' nursery. Here, she cried, covering her ears with her hands, they can have it all, just make them stop!

But they never stopped. This was what Manda was learning. As soon as she was done feeding one baby, there was another to burp and another to change and a fourth and fifth to give medicine to before it was time for the first one to eat again. Day and night had no distinction anymore, except that some innate sense of right and wrong forbade her from running the washing machine after midnight. Laundry belonged to the daytime world, she believed, and if she crossed that shadowy line, she might as well surrender any last hope of control.

It was three o'clock in the morning when Manda woke from her dream, shivering and numb from having drowned the puppies. She didn't remember falling asleep in the rocking chair feeding Infinity. The baby's eyes were shut, though Manda could tell from her shallow breathing that she was not deeply enough asleep to be put in her crib without her waking up. But Devon was whimpering in the next room, which meant Jake must have fallen asleep in his rocking chair, and she would have to see to him, and Kaylee was starting to cry and box the air. Manda's sister Nina was supposed to arrive for the midnight-to-six shift, but she'd already missed one night with a sore throat she "didn't want to pass on to the kids"—illness being the only excuse that couldn't be challenged—and Manda knew she was bagging out again tonight. She hated her sister Nina in that moment for her flimsy lie and her freedom.

Manda eased her daughter into the crib, and immediately the child's eyes popped open. There was nothing to be done about it, though, for Kaylee had begun to wail, and Devon was now crying loud enough that Jake could surely no longer sleep through it. Manda checked the babies' feeding chart and saw that Kaylee was not due to be fed for another hour; it was Ember's turn, but Ember was the one baby who was not awake, and Manda did not want to disturb her. The nurses had encouraged her to establish a militaristic schedule for the babies to keep herself sane, but the babies refused to follow any set rhythm. She had two choices: feed Kaylee early or wake Ember, but standing there in that shadowy hyperreality of the nightlight-lit room, she simply couldn't make a decision. She hesitated between the two cribs, trying to concentrate. She was so tired. Couldn't somebody else decide?

"Babe?"

Manda opened her eyes in a panic. She had been back on that pine needle path through the woods, carrying her box of squirming puppies, but suddenly here she was in the girls' nursery and there was Jake standing in the doorway holding both boys. She could only have shut her eyes for a second, yet hours had passed in dream time. Kaylee was still crying and Infinity had now joined her, yet, through all the noise, Ember, the one who needed to be fed, still slept.

"I've fed both the boys but I can't get them to go back to sleep," Jake said. "Should we take them in the car?"

"I guess so. Why don't you go warm it up."

Manda pulled her winter coat on over her nightgown and gathered up poor baby Ember, who, with Devon, had to be connected to the portable oxygen tank in order to go in the car. The other babies wailed as Jake returned to strap them into their car seats, fitting themselves to one another's cries until they had established that metronomic rhythm that was somehow harder for Manda to bear than their pandemonium. It seemed purposeful and spiteful and designed simply to drive her mad. Ember woke up and added her voice to those of the others. Manda figured she would break the law and feed Ember on her lap while they drove around.

Manda stepped barefoot into a pair of fleece-lined winter boots while Jake ferried the children out into the garage and snapped them into place. He, at least, had pulled on a pair of jeans and a sweatshirt, though his hair stood on end and he, too, wore the glazed expression of a sleepwalker. While he loaded the portable oxygen tanks, Manda went back upstairs to let Rose know they would be gone for a little while. She had neglected to do this once, thinking someone in this house should be allowed to sleep, only to come home to a hysterically crying daughter who was certain she'd been abandoned.

Manda pushed open the door to Rose's room, made softly aquatic by her blue nightlight. Despite the chill, Rose had tossed the covers off, and slept as she had when she was a baby, open and vulnerable with her arms thrown over her head. Her purple lips were parted and when Manda bent down, she could smell the sugary grape Kool-Aid Rose had drunk before bedtime. Since the babies had come home, Manda had given up on a nightly bath for her older daughter and had lost all sense of when she'd last brushed her teeth. She would have to be better about that, she promised herself, pulling the bedspread up over the little girl, and suddenly realizing why Rose had kicked the sheets away. They were soaking wet.

"Rosie, get up." Manda tugged her daughter from the bed. "You did it again."

She knew she should strip Rose and put her in a hot bathtub and strip the bed and put the sheets in the washing machine and remake the bed and re-dress her daughter and not be mad. But the minivan was full of screaming babies and Jake was waiting for her, and Rose was beginning to whimper, for she had not wet the bed in two years before these babies came to live with them, and it was all just too much for Manda right then.

"Lie here on the floor until Mama and Daddy get home," she told the little girl, pulling the dry bedspread onto the ground and easing Rose onto it. She rolled her up like a sausage and kissed her on her dewy forehead and promised they'd be back very soon, they just had to get the babies to sleep.

If Manda could have foreseen how these new brothers and sisters would have affected Rose, maybe she would have done everything differently. Not have gotten the Pergonal shots in the first place, maybe, or not have turned the morality of the thing over to Pastor Vaughn and her faithless neighbors, or not have given in to Jake's needy hound look that said, "We can do this, babe, you and me." Once she found herself pregnant, it had seemed so much easier to go along and let God or Fate or whatever you called it make the decisions for her. So much easier than plotting how to kill some while letting others live, than facing neighbors who would forever see her as a child murderer, than explaining to her surviving kids that they had grown strong in the vacuum of their aborted siblings. So she had let God or Fate or whatever you called it have its way and still she was seen as a killer who should have known better and still she would have to explain to each of the children that lived that they were one of eleven, not one of eight, and who was to say if they would not curse her from their wheelchairs and out from behind their thick glasses and with their slow-moving thoughts for ever having brought them into this world weak and defective in the first place. And for this surviving, spiteful gang, she had sacrificed the happiness of her true daughter, her firstborn, who had never signed up for any of this, who was nothing more than a sacrificial lamb. And where were those neighbors after all, the ones who'd demanded these children of her, then tricked her with false promises of help and money? Everyone had deserted her. She was alone with her husband and her poor bewildered firstborn and this plague of children.

Manda's thoughts were dark as she opened the door to the warm minivan, where Jake was resting his forehead against the steering wheel. Infinity and Kaylee and Adams and Devon and Ember were screaming with a vengeance now, but experience had taught her that three miles down the road they would begin to whimper and six miles into the drive their lids would droop. Jake had a circuit he drove—straight down Snakehill, through deserted School Street, past the dark, hulking junior high, and deep into the country, where no lamps lit the road and only the occasional lonely porch light promised any other human life. He would drive the route they used to take as teenagers on Friday night, pushing deeper and deeper into rolling hillside until they would come upon the spot where they used to make out, an isolated field overlooking a branch of the Rapidan planted with three Calvary crosses, just visible from the road. He would drive the van in circles, headlights slicing the foggy field, as if part of a futile search party, then he would turn around and silently drive home again. She didn't know how much more of this dead-of-night driving they could take. Jake had to go to work in the mornings, and she was too tired to spend time with the new litter of beagle pups, who were on their way to becoming ruined and untrainable. Now, with the donations already drying up, they needed the money more than ever.

Outside, it had begun to flurry, and snow flew hypnotically out of the darkness. Manda leaned her head against the cold pane of passenger-side glass and watched the watery albatross moon trail her family like more bad news. If only she could do it all over again. She would do everything so differently. Manda surrendered herself to the rhythm of the windshield wipers chipping frost like brilliant bits of bone and the halfhearted in-out, in-out choral wailing of the drowsy children. The van was doing its work. In five minutes, she was asleep.

Polly knocked on the Franks' door right after Saturday's morning milking, armed with two wheels of cheddar and a plate of biscuits. Why grown-ups thought food solved all of life's problems, Polly did not know. If she had three dead children, the last thing she would want to look at was greasy cheese and some cold, salty biscuits. But birth and death seemed to bring out the baker in women around here, and when she asked her mother about it, she was told to give it a rest, one day she would understand.

The house Polly's father had been building for the Franks was in pretty poor condition, she thought, eyeing the place while she waited for someone to let her in. Her father told her that work naturally slowed down in the winter, but she'd noticed that nothing had really been done since the last funerals. There were still no steps up to the front door, just a pair of snow-covered two-by-fours over a concrete foundation where one day steps would go. The doorbell bristled with wires, and the windows, which should have had wooden trellises to give them the appearance of being paned, were just smooth, blankly reflective sheets of glass. The frozen earth of the yard swam with deep, sharp ruts from where curiosity-seekers had pulled up to see the house, then backed out again. It seemed to Polly that if her father intended to use this house as a showplace to jump-start his new business, he might want to finish it.

"*We use the back door*," said Manda when she finally answered Polly's knock. No "Hello" or "Thanks for coming." No "Wow, some cheese" or "Let me at those biscuits." Manda looked like someone had punched her in both eyes and like she hadn't bathed in a week. Polly thought people shouldn't have children if they were going to get so stressed out by them.

She wiped her snowy boots on a wet towel that served as a welcome mat and followed Manda through the house. Inside, she saw, was no better than outside. Manda and Jake's ratty brown plaid sofa had been moved from the old house so that they would have something to sit on, but that and the TV were the only pieces of furniture dedicated to adults. Everything else was baby crap, so thick Polly had to pick a path into the kitchen. Bassinets, swings, plastic bathtubs. There were three weird quadruple strollers parked where a dining room table should have been, and the kitchen sink was piled high with unwashed bottles left to soak in cold, gray water. Manda and Jake had finally dragged in the refrigerator that had been sitting boxed up in the garage waiting for Francis's men to install it, but they had been unable to fit it into its recess. It hulked awkwardly in the middle of the room for people to bruise their hips upon.

"Mom sent you some cheese," Polly said, looking around for an inch of empty counter space.

"Thanks," said Manda, taking it from her and reaching for the refrigerator door.

"Mom says never put cheese in a cold refrigerator. It ruins the character."

Manda ignored her and added the cheese wheels to a half-empty jar of Ragú and ten premade formula bottles that constituted the entire contents of the sleek donated Jenn-Air.

"I'm glad you're here," said Mrs. Sawyer, Manda's mother. She was on her hands and knees before the television watching a bubbly woman pitch clothes on QVC while she diapered the tiniest baby Polly had ever seen. It was a pale, bald creature with a fetusy face and stumpy arms and legs, dressed in socks and one of those snappy undershirt things. Her mother had warned her that the babies were premature and might appear undeveloped, but this baby looked positively extraterrestrial.

"Here you go," said Mrs. Sawyer, pointing the squirming alien in Polly's direction. "Adams Brooke is all yours."

Polly started at the sound of the name before she remembered Jake's suck-up to the president. She had come here this morning after much badgering from her mother to make good on her promise of baby-sitting, but now she deeply regretted it. She had never held a baby before, much less one so fragile and weird-looking.

"Come on, be quick about it," commanded Manda's mother. "I need a cigarette and someone won't let us smoke in the house . . ."

Polly inched forward and held out her arms as if to receive a pile of linen. Mrs. Sawyer passed off freshly diapered Adams Brooke, who immediately let out a cry of complaint. Polly didn't even get a chance to ask how to soothe him before Mrs. Sawyer was out the back door and lighting up a Virginia Slim.

"Manda?" Polly asked weakly, looking around for the baby's mother. His head was hanging at an awkward angle and Polly was afraid to reposition it, terrified of somehow pushing on his soft spot, the one thing she knew would instantly kill a baby. "Manda, the baby is crying. I think he might be hungry. Manda?"

Polly followed the sound of more crying around the corner and up the stairs. She passed an empty nursery painted green and an empty nursery painted blue, until she arrived at the pink nursery, where

Manda was rocking another fetusy child with a tube up its nose, while three more screamed around her. Polly held out her own crying baby and asked what she should do.

"Put him over your shoulder," Manda said wearily. "He might need to burp."

Polly carefully repositioned the child, avoiding his head. "I think he's hungry."

"He just ate," said Manda. "Check the chart. And write down the time of his diaper change, would you?"

How was she supposed to hold the baby and write something down? Polly thought Manda must not be a very good mother, to have all these babies crying at the same time. She really needed someone more experienced than Polly to watch the kids; in fact, the girl thought, she was probably doing more harm than good, and maybe she should leave and let Manda's mother take over again.

"All these people promised to help, but no one has come," said Manda, nodding to a box of greeting cards that sat atop the babies' dresser. Inside, Polly saw the sign-up sheet that had hung outside her school's auditorium and knew her own name was one among many. "It's just the grandmothers, Mrs. Vaughn, sometimes my sister Nina. And now you."

Reluctantly, Polly swallowed the excuse she'd been forming and resigned herself to staying a few hours. She couldn't believe that all the people who had marched in Chase Andrew's candlelight vigil had backed out. "What about the presents downstairs?" she asked. "People are still sending you stuff."

"Strangers," said Manda. "Only strangers send things anymore. You know, the town wanted these babies and now they won't do a damn thing for them. I don't know how much longer I'm supposed to baby-sit."

Baby-sit? thought Polly. Manda was losing it. "Where's Jake?" she asked.

"Jake is working," replied Manda, standing up to return Devon to his crib. She wrapped a long line of plastic tube around her arm like a garden hose. "And he's going to have to take a second job soon if things don't get better."

Polly looked around, disgusted. Why a woman would want to have one baby was beyond her, much less be burdened with eleven. Or eight, she corrected herself. No, nine, when you counted Rose. What was Manda going to do when the other three came home from the hospital?

Manda returned to the girls' nursery from down the hall, and Polly heard the baby she had just laid down begin to cry. "Did you see Rose in the yard when you came in?" she asked. "She's not in her room."

Polly shook her head.

"Rose?" she called, making a quick pass of the house. "Rose?"

Manda returned to the nursery and angrily punched a number into the portable phone. Polly could only overhear one side of the conversation.

"Listen, I really need you to come over right now," Manda was saying.

"I'm sure you're not contagious."

"That's the fakest cough I've ever heard."

"Listen, Nina, I can't find Rose. I need to look for her."

"Well, fuck you then."

All the babies were crying, but Manda seemed oblivious. She dialed another number.

"Hey, it's me. Did you see Rose this morning?"

"No, she's not in her room."

"No, I haven't seen her since last night."

"Yes, can you come home right away? Mother's here."

Manda hung up and threw open the window of the nursery, letting in a rush of cold air.

"Mother," Manda shouted. "I need you to come watch the babies until Jake gets home. Rose is gone."

"She'll turn up," Polly heard faintly from the backyard. "She's probably playing in the yard."

"Mother! Please!"

Polly pictured Mrs. Sawyer angrily stubbing out her cigarette and muttering to herself. She was more than a little afraid of Manda's mother, who had twice been arrested for drunk and disorderly and once for assaulting Manda's father. Not wanting to get stuck alone with Mrs. Sawyer and all these babies, she quickly offered to help Manda search out Rose. After all, she wasn't so old herself—she remembered the kinds of places little kids liked to hide.

After returning Adams Brooke to his crib, the two made quick work of the house, searching under what little furniture there was and taking an inventory of all the closets, crawl spaces, and clothes hampers. Mrs. Sawyer told Manda she was crazy, that kids disappeared and kids turned up, but nothing seemed to calm her agitated daughter. Manda pulled sheets off the bed and turned over the sofa cushions. She opened the refrigerator and even looked inside the oven. After a futile twenty minutes, they took the search outside, where the granite sky threatened more snow.

"Rose!" Manda called. "Rose, where are you?"

"Rose!" echoed Polly.

Manda headed off toward the woods that separated the Franks' property from the Pricketts' as Polly moved across the yard to the old iron pump and well. It was the way of little girls, was it not, to end up down wells? A low brick wall surrounded it and a rough piece of plywood capped the top. Rose would have had to fall in and slide the wood back in place on her way down; still, Polly pushed the slimy board aside, lay down on her belly, and stared into the black hole. "*Rose,*" she whispered. "*Are you down there?*" She imagined herself narrating the events for Mr. March, the only audience she cared about. *My voice dropped like a ribbon, unfurling in the dark, until it reached where she lay, still and broken inside the water's cold, green box.* The well smelled metallic and peaty, like a chimney sprouting up from some ancient, underground dwelling. "*Rose?*" she whispered.

Beyond the well, like a stump someone had forgotten to clear, sat Manda's old house. She never knew why her mother forbade her from setting foot inside, only that Manda's people were not her family's sort of people, and while the Franks might be called on to baby-sit or help out on the farm, their property was corruptive in some unspoken way, like a dirty-movie theater or a superfund site. Once, when she was seven, she had to wait on the front porch while Manda took a phone call from her boyfriend, the whole time in desperate need of a bathroom. And though Mrs. Sawyer had yelled at her to come on inside and use the damn toilet, what was wrong with her? in the end she had run all the way home, losing her battle on the top step before she reached the safety of her own bathroom. After that, her neighbor's house had become a source of shame as well as terror.

A little of that old dread still lingered as Polly hoisted herself off her belly and climbed the cinder-block steps up to the porch. It was nothing but a cheap shingled cottage, full of cheap ugly furniture. It was no scarier than a shriveled spider to her now, she told herself, empty of its menacing boys and ozone of blue cigarette smoke. She tried the front door but it was locked, and so she stepped around to the Depression glass windows that ran from the floor of the porch to its roof. She put her face to the cold pane to see past her own reflection and jumped as a mouse skittered off the inside sill and hung suspended for what seemed like a lifetime, its wiry tail twirling like a windup toy, its finger-joint legs flailing, until it came down on the dusty old recliner and disappeared between the cushion and afghan.

Walking to the side of the cottage, Polly found the back door unlocked, and reluctantly let herself in. Like the room of a favorite child killed in a freak accident, the house, with its gaping La-Z-Boy and still-ticking driftwood clock, its molding coffee cups on the mantel and magazines on the floor, had a preserved-in-amber sort of feel to it. Nothing in the living room had been disturbed since Manda and Jake had left. Polly scanned the room for signs of Rose, and had the sudden queasy premonition she would find her, not in the well at all, but here in this house, half-hidden by the recliner, lying in a pool of blood. Wouldn't Mr. March feel sorry for her then, a young innocent girl coming upon so gruesome a discovery? The police would be called, and the news crews, and he would see her on television sitting in the backseat of an ambulance with a blanket wrapped around her shoulders, bravely waving away the paramedics' offers of oxygen. She was almost disappointed to find no child on the living room floor, only a faded braid throw rug, no more frightening than a throw rug should be.

The only place left to check was the hall closet, and Polly strode to it, determined to be done with this house. She yanked the door open, and leapt back in alarm as a long metal bar crashed at her feet. No, not a bar, she saw immediately. It was Manda's old shotgun, the one she took rabbit hunting. Polly stared at it, not knowing if it was loaded and poised to explode the moment she touched it.

Manda had once nearly used this gun on another human being, Polly knew, for she remembered when her baby-sitter was arrested for having placed it against the chest of a teacher. It was a long time ago, but Polly retained the half-held memory of watching television one early winter night while Manda sat at her kitchen table. Manda let her watch as much television as she liked, encouraged her, even, to stay up long past her bedtime, for her baby-sitter was afraid of the huge, groaning Prickett house, and desired Polly's company. Francis had wanted to go out that night and no one was available except the newly acquitted Manda. Polly remembered her parents' argument over it. But Francis must have won, for she clearly saw her baby-sitter bent over the kitchen table, an open history book before her.

Polly pinched the end of the long-barreled gun where she'd been taught to grab a snake if ever she was attacked by one, and carefully set it back in the closet. She shut the door and left the cottage, circling back to the dog pen, where Manda's beagles were barking furiously. Manda was there already, checking to see if Rose had crawled inside one of the rough wooden dog houses.

"Manda," Polly asked, coming up behind her, "you had Mr. March for history, didn't you? He was here when you were in eighth grade?"

"I had him," answered Manda flatly. "He replaced Mrs. Haney."

"What was he like?"

Manda stared vacantly off into the woods, high into the canopy where Rose could not possibly be. All around her the dogs leapt, leapt and scratched with their dull, bruising nails, whining and barking with the insistence of a car alarm. Polly thought she would go insane from the chaos of the noise, but then Manda clapped her hands sharply once, and the dogs instantly quieted down.

"Dogs respond best to silence," she said as if Polly had not spoken. "You don't say 'Sit' or 'Come' or 'Heel' until you teach them how to do it. You have to make them think it's their idea. Only after a dog's learned a command do you put a name to it."

What did Polly care about Manda's stupid dogs? She hadn't answered her question about Mr. March.

"I take the trouble to start these dogs," said Manda, "spending hours with them, teaching them how to hunt. I tell the men who buy them, 'Don't shoot anything the dog hasn't trailed, you'll undermine his instinct,' but they don't listen. They shoot the first thing that jumps out of the bushes, and then they blame the dog."

"Manda," Polly urged. "What was he like?"

"He failed me," said Manda in a tone that invited no further questions. Polly stared at her baby-sitter, and there seemed to be something dull and ugly like Manda herself hanging in the air between them. For a brief, horrifying moment the queasy thought crossed Polly's mind, *He was in love with her*, but then she dismissed it—how could her Mr. March ever love white-trash, crooked-toothed, sallow Amanda Frank? Amanda who had never made above a C her entire life, who skinned her own game and had the dirty fingernails to show for it. Polly turned away in disgust. "Rose," she called. "Rose!"

The two moved deeper and deeper into the woods, following a snow-dusted pine needle path, property that had once belonged to her family, Polly now knew. These woods were connective tissue, yet off-limits, and like Manda's old house, full of dark enchantment. Here among the tall, lanky pines, fires might be started and girls fondled; here, in Polly's childhood imagination, traps of all natures were set. The woods were nothing more than a topographical feature, she knew, setting apart almost identical pieces of land on either side, but as if it were a mustache hiding a cruel mouth, she worried that if she ever wandered through, she'd be swallowed up whole and never seen again.

"What's that noise?" Manda asked, turning her head toward a rustle in the deadwood briers. An animal bounded out of the brush toward them, and it took a moment for Polly to realize it was Manda's old beagle, Turbo, leaping about like an excited puppy.

"She's by the creek," Manda said, and began racing after the dog, who had turned back into the woods and was running along the snow-slick path. Polly followed behind and caught up with them at the edge of the rushing creek, far angrier on this side of the woods than what ran through their pasture. Over the icy rapids, an old tree had fallen, creating a makeshift bridge, and halfway across sat Manda's daughter, playing contentedly with her shaggy red doll.

Rose looked up impishly when she saw her mother. "Mama, why are monsters big and hairy and ugly?" she shouted to Manda over the greedy water. The tree wore a treacherous frozen skin, making it impossible to walk across, and Manda was forced to creep out on her wounded belly, her knees gripping the slick bark to keep from plunging the four or so feet into the icy creek. Just out of reach, Rose straddled the tree as if it were a wooden horse, her snow boots kicking merrily over the chasm.

"Mama, why are monsters—?"

But Rose never got out the punch line to her joke, because her mother swiftly grabbed her around the waist and with a strength Polly couldn't have imagined, arced the little girl over her head and thrust her back onto the solid bank, where Polly grabbed her. Manda teetered as she crawled backward to safety, then once on land she shook her daughter roughly, while Polly watched in dismay.

"Don't you ever, ever run off again," sobbed Manda, burying her face in her daughter's damp, caramel hair. Her dog Turbo barked wildly, licking the mother and now-crying daughter at once. "You're all I have left, Rose. You're all that's mine."

CHAPTER SIXTEEN

Margaret had not thought it possible for someone to be quieter even than August, but then she met Glenn Mullins. He was everything you might expect from the treasurer of the high school Future Farmers of America, a position requiring him to open his mouth only once per meeting to mumble that the club's current budget stood at $254.17, up six dollars from the month before. He was a tall, well-built boy of seventeen, with an application in at Virginia Tech to study dairy science, and he went about his chores with a shy grin on his face as if Margaret had asked him to model his underwear instead of muck out the stalls.

No, Glenn Mullins worked quickly and efficiently, and Margaret had nothing to complain about. But it seemed to her the fragile solar system of the farm was splintering apart without August's steadying gravity. The left rear wheel of the manure spreader, already a crazy quilt of rubber patches, finally blew when she was off in the fields and as far away from the barn as she could be. Then one morning last week, she'd discovered that the single uninsulated pipe in the cheese house had frozen and burst, turning the concrete floor into an ice rink. And now, looking up, she noticed that two more bricks had fallen from the top of her chimney, a structure growing lacier by the month and in desperate need of repointing. If she wasn't careful, soon she would have a full-scale collapse on her hands. Margaret was afraid of heights, and under normal circumstances simply would have asked August to remortar the loose bricks, but now, with him on "vacation," she would have to dip into her nonexistent supply of petty cash to pay a handyman. She might ask Glenn Mullins to deal with the tractor and broken pipe, but she couldn't very well ask him to repair the chimney of her house.

With August the border of farm and residence had been comfortably blurred, she realized, and it had seemed as natural for him to fix a running toilet as it had for him to oil the barn door.

"Glenn, it's time to turn the cheese," she called to the boy, who was refilling the hayrick above the girls' stalls. "Do you think the two of us can handle it?"

"Sure, Miz Prickett." The boy grinned, wiping his hands on his clean dungarees. He always showed up to work in freshly laundered clothes and smelling of Mennen aftershave. He was prompt and polite and always ready with a "Sure." There was nothing about Glenn to dislike, she told herself.

"You get on that side and I'll take this one. We could really use Polly."

The trick of turning a cheese the size of a Volkswagen required that two people should upend it while a third positioned himself on the opposite side to ease its fall. If in the process of flipping, however, the cheese was not caught quickly on the other end, the momentum of the turning might tear apart its fragile, cheddared fabric. Margaret wished she had waited to send Polly over to Manda's.

"On the count of three."

Glenn lowered the cheese to shoulder height and Margaret positioned herself beneath it. She closed her eyes against the vision she had every day of the cheese slipping its pressboards and ropes, of an avalanche of curd, months of wasted time, thousands of wasted dollars. If that happened she would slink away to another state and change her name, for she would never be able to face her neighbors again.

"So, I finally see the famous cheese firsthand?"

Margaret turned at the sound of her ex-husband's voice and saw Francis Marvel leaning in the doorway, shaking his head over his wife's latest folly. She saw him just as Glenn pulled the guide rope. "Come help me catch this," she said quickly.

He jogged around and stood over her, catching the cheese with a grunt and easing it down. Margaret ducked out from under his arms and adjusted the wrinkled cheesecloth.

"You never cease to amaze me," said Francis.

"Glenn, why don't you start measuring the girls' feed," said Margaret, dismissing him.

"So where is August?" Francis asked when the boy ducked his head and left. "Don't tell me he's finally come to his senses?"

"August is taking some vacation time."

"Vacation time?" Francis repeated incredulously. "August? What did you do to him?"

"I didn't do anything," Margaret snapped. "He had a lot of time saved up and he simply wanted to use it. Why does everything have to be my fault?"

Francis threw up his hands in surrender. "I didn't come to argue with you. I came for Polly. Is she ready?"

"Ready for what?"

"It's my weekend, remember?" said Francis hotly. "You're always on my back about taking her—well, here I am. So where is she?"

Margaret had completely forgotten that this was Francis's weekend when she'd sent her daughter over to help out poor Manda. "She's at the Franks'," she said, sighing. "You can pick her up there."

"Oh great," said Francis. "Just the place I want to go."

Her husband took off his heavy shearling coat and strolled over to the cheese. "I didn't believe it when I saw it on TV," he said. "I thought, A twelve-hundred-pound cheese—what the hell is she going to do with that?"

"Take it to Washington," said Margaret.

"You getting good publicity from it?" he asked. "Orders up?"

"That's not why I'm doing it," said Margaret, hoisting the cheese protectively back to the rafters as if Francis were an undesirable strain of mold.

"Crenshaw told me it was a first-rate publicity stunt."

"Crenshaw can believe what he wants," said Margaret tartly. "I'm doing it because I believe in Adams Brooke."

"I looked for you in the cheese house." Francis smiled, "Where's your granddaddy's sign?"

"Francis," warned Margaret.

"Don't worry, your guilty secret is safe with me," he said. "I couldn't give a fuck."

Smiling over his shoulder, Francis walked deeper into the barn to where Margaret had tethered the two new calves. "Whose are these?" he asked.

"Sultana's."

"Both of them?"

Margaret nodded, wishing she had lied. "Male and a freemartin. I know I should sell them, but Polly is so attached."

"That's your problem, Maggie," said Francis, "You don't know when to let things go."

Margaret gazed at him steadily. "That's not *your* problem, obviously."

Francis ignored her, tugging the male's ear playfully. "Sultana sure does produce some fine-looking calves. You know, every now and then I miss the old girls."

"Well, good," said his wife. "You can milk them while I'm in Washington."

"I don't miss them that much."

"The girls know you. Glenn will help."

"I can't believe you're really going to take that thing to Washington. You've done some dizzy shit over the years, but this is the dizziest yet," said Francis.

"So you'll do it?" she said, ignoring his insult. "You'll milk them while we're gone?"

"We'll see," said Francis. "A lot can happen by March. I might be on my honeymoon."

It was hard for Margaret to believe there had been a time when she was in love with this man, when she found his humor earthy instead of vulgar, when he couldn't keep his mouth off her—off her lips, her shoulders, from between her thighs. He had always been rough and irresponsible, but that's what she liked about him, even when he joked about his inconstancy and said, as he often did, he wasn't the sort of man a woman should ever get cancer on. She never believed him until the day her father died and they learned just how deeply in debt he'd left them; then suddenly their whole married life metastasized. He wasn't going to turn slave for any beast or man. He expected her to sell the farm, and when she refused, he started fucking his secretary, as if to say, See, I told you when it got hard, I would be gone. For if nothing else, Francis Marvel was a man of his word.

"I gotta get going," he said. "I thought I'd take Polly to the matinee of the space movie she wanted to see."

"I don't want you taking Polly to the movies," Margaret said. "Every time you go, it's a week before I can deprogram her."

"What has happened to you?" Francis asked, finally fed up. "You used to be fun. Now you won't even let your daughter enjoy a movie."

"I don't want my daughter growing up polluted, that's what's happened to me," said Margaret vehemently. "I don't want her to have an attention span of a music video. I don't want her to give it up to the first boy who kisses her because that's what she sees on TV. I don't want her weighing four hundred pounds because it's easier to take her to the McDonald's drive-through than to fix her a healthy dinner. Everyone is out to get her, the whole world is out to get a little piece of my daughter, and I want to protect her for as long as I am able. And I don't like you undermining me."

"Maggie, take a breath," said Francis, pulling on his coat. "We've been through some hard times, but I still love you. You gotta let go. Of her. Of this place. Look at you, holding on to calves who won't even produce. Do you think that's kind? You'll have to sell them sometime, and then it will be that much harder on Polly."

Francis climbed into his pickup truck and rolled down the window. "Listen, I'm going to take our daughter to the movies and I'll bring her home tomorrow. And if you smell Dunkin' Donuts on her breath, don't go calling the cops. And by the way," he said, giving her a softly ironic smile, "happy anniversary."

Margaret watched her ex-husband's truck pull out of the driveway. Thirteen years she was married to him, and she had forgotten their anniversary. Glenn Mullins was watching her from around the corner of the barn. Behind him in the yard, twenty-four dumb, needy faces looked up at her anxiously.

"Don't you have work to do?" Margaret asked angrily, and the boy ducked out of sight.

Little Kaylee Lea had peed on three clean diapers in the course of a single change, and Polly was on the verge of tears. What was with this baby? she thought. It was like she took perverse enjoyment in single-handedly choking up the landfill. Polly had just taped the fourth diaper in place and decided to ignore the juicy abandon with which the little girl had a moment later let go from the other end when she saw her father's truck pull into the driveway. Thank God, someone had heard her desperate prayers and come to rescue her. She couldn't get out of here fast enough.

"Well, well, the place is coming right along," she heard Francis say to the children's father down below. By the time Jake had gotten home from work, Rose had been found, and Manda had gone to lie down in her darkened bedroom. Jake was outside feeding the dogs when Francis pulled up in his new, navy blue truck—bought, unbeknownst to Jake, with some of the donations that were supposed to go toward his house. A builder had certain start-up costs, and respectable transportation was one of them; after all, how could a man instill confidence in his clients if he was still driving his eight-year-old Ford F-series?

"Yep, it's a mighty fine house if I do say so myself." Francis barely spared a glance for the skeletal front steps or the blank windows. "A few little finishing touches and we'll be all set."

"There's just a thing or two inside—," Jake began, but the sense of being undeserving of such largesse was so strong in his voice that it was as if, to Francis, Jake had not spoken at all. Over the years, Polly's father had become adept at filtering out all but the most strongly inflected complaints, and so the subtle reproofs by which Southern society was run, and which was the only language Jake spoke, seemed to bounce right off him.

"You know, those fixtures didn't come cheap," said Francis. "State-of-the-art refrigerator, that one is, with dual humidity control.

And man, that sound system. And the hot tub! I hope you've been making good use of the hot tub. But not too good—you got to let the rest of us catch up, you coon dog, you."

"No, it's more the siding," Jake tried again, "and the steps—"

"A lot of people told me, 'Francis, go easy, you got to make a little profit for yourself,' but I said 'Shit, the man's gonna have a dozen kids, and half of 'em girls. If anybody deserves a break, it's Jake Frank."

"Well, thank you, Francis," said Jake. "I've just got a little list—"

"How are the donations coming?" interrupted Francis.

"Well, sad to say, they've been trickling off," admitted Jake. "After the last two didn't pull through. Times are kind of rough."

"I'm sorry to hear that, man," said Francis, and Jake wasn't sure if he was sorry about the children or the donations. "Damn stock market's going to be the death of us all."

"Hey, Dad!" called Polly, racing out of the garage with her coat and backpack.

"Hey, Peanut," called Francis, opening his arms for a hug. "How's about a movie?"

Polly gratefully threw herself into her father's embrace and breathed in the cool, irresponsible scent of him. Except maybe for Mr. March, no one could have pleased her more than her father today. Their breach over the *Brooke No Opposition* sign had long ago been mended with a trip to the mall, and now her father had come to rescue her. She asked Jake to say good-bye to Manda for her and wished him the best of luck with the babies. Father and daughter were in the truck and down the driveway before Manda's mother could get outside to yell at them. She had a laundry list of things wrong with the house and Polly was supposed to stay until Manda woke up. It figured the girl would cut out, thought Mrs. Sawyer wrathfully. There was one fruit who obviously didn't fall far from the trifling tree.

"Oh, thank God you showed up," Polly said, cranking up the truck's heat. "I couldn't take another minute in Baby Land."

"Yep, babies are a royal pain in the ass, there's no two ways about it," her father agreed. "How's Manda making out?"

"I think she's going crazy," Polly said, flipping through her Dad's CDs. "She acted like a complete zombie except for when Rose wandered away from the house. Then she freaked out. Her mom had to give her a pill and put her to bed. She's worried about going broke."

"How do you think *I* feel?" Francis asked sourly. "I put up half of my own money to build that house, based on all these donations. Well, what the hell happened to them?"

"Manda said Jake may have to take a second job."

"It's not my fault those children died," said Francis.

"So what movie are we going to see?" asked Polly, not wanting to talk about the depressing Franks anymore.

"How's about . . . *Alien Rampage?*" said her father, taking his hands off the wheel long enough to wave this morning's newspaper under her nose. "I thought we'd see that, then stop by the arcade at the mall and blow up some stuff. What do you think?"

"Sounds great."

"So, should I swing into town and pick up Bethany?" he asked.

Polly eyed her father suspiciously. "What for?"

"I just thought you might like to have a little friend along," replied her father.

"Why? Is it not working out with your secretary?" she asked sarcastically.

"Hey, Peanut, before I forget, take down this number for me," said her father in annoyance. "Got a pen?"

Polly rummaged through her backpack until she found one. "Yes, sir."

"And a piece of paper?"

"Yes, sir."

"Good. Write this down: 1-800-555-7874." Polly dutifully transcribed it and waited for some explanation as to why she was doing so. Her father, however, was silent.

"Dad, what's this for?" she asked.

"It's the number of a warehouse in Ohio that makes forceps big enough for you to pull your head out of your ass."

Polly rolled her eyes and punched Bethany's phone number into her father's cell phone. Her friend said she would be thrilled to see *Alien Rampage* and to spend the night afterward.

"You know, every once in a while I do things just because I think they'll make you happy," said Francis when his daughter hung up the phone. "It's what dads do."

"It's not because you're terrified of being alone with me?" asked Polly archly. "Three's company, two's a nightmare?"

"I'm alone with you right now, aren't I?" said Francis. "We can have a normal conversation. How's school? How's the love life?"

He couldn't have possibly known how intertwined the two were for her, but Polly's heart skipped a beat nonetheless. "There's this one guy," she said, testing out the word "guy"—not "man," but not "boy," either—feeling like she was getting away with a delicious half-truth.

"Well, watch yourself," said her father. "Boys are after only one thing, and I should know. I don't want you making the same mistake your mother and I did."

It was endlessly frustrating to Polly, the casualness with which he said things like that. It seemed that long ago he had done some convenient refiguring in his head in which she was not this "mistake" he had made, this child that had ruined his life, but just this nice kid he sometimes hung out with. She had a hard time imagining a father like Bethany's, who was around every day, bothering her friend with his overinvolvement in her homework and personal life. She doubted if her dad could even name Mr. March, or any of her teachers. Polly looked down at the CDs in her lap. Willie Nelson, Waylon Jennings, Garth Brooks. "You've got nothing but crap in this truck," she said sourly.

"Goes to show what you know," he answered. "What do you listen to?"

"Nothing. Mom gave away my MP3 player."

"The one I bought you for Christmas?" he asked, and Polly nodded. "What the hell is wrong with her?"

"Dad, it's only gotten worse," said Polly. "She's one step away from buying a gun and taking up arms against the government."

"Don't exaggerate, Peanut," said her father. "I talked to her today. I've offered to milk the cows while you're gone."

"Then you know."

"She's under a lot of stress," said Francis. "You should go easy on her."

"She'd be a lot more relaxed if you paid her the money you owe her," said Polly boldly. If he wanted to speak to her as an adult, she would answer as one. Her father shot her a disgusted look, as if to say, *Not you, too?*

"What neither of you seems to understand," said Francis seriously, "is that a new business takes time to get started. I'm building something from scratch. Do you know how hard that is?"

"Maybe you should have thought about that before you left," challenged Polly. She expected her father to get mad, but he surprised her.

"You know I had to go, Peanut," he said philosophically. "I could have spent the rest of my life going round in circles on that farm— planting and milking and mowing, and starting all over again the next year and the next. But that's not me. I needed a change. You'll understand one day. You'll need one too."

They had arrived at the Frasers' driveway, where Dr. Fraser was letting himself into his steel blue Mercedes. "Quack, my friend!" called her father. "Keeping up the malpractice insurance?"

"I thought you were in jail," said Dr. Fraser, playing along in that way all of her dad's friends did. "They haven't got you for tax evasion yet?"

"No sir, and they never will." Francis laughed.

"Bye, Dad. Hey, Mr. Marvel," called Bethany, running out with her overnight bag. She was dressed for the weather in a short skirt with knee-high leather boots. She wore a hot pink turtleneck, Hello Kitty earmuffs, and mittens on a string around her neck.

"Hey, Bethany," said Francis. "You look like a baby streetwalker."

"Oh, Mr. Marvel." Bethany laughed.

Polly and Bethany climbed over the truck's gate and nestled between the wheel wells, up against the cabin glass. The truck peeled away, sending the girls crashing into one another, making them squeal with laughter and fright as they fought the wind for an old Hudson Bay blanket, anchoring it with their feet and clutching it around their chins. They put their heads together and screamed into the wind.

"Your dad is so much fun," yelled Bethany, pulling the mothball-sharp blanket up around her nose.

"He's not so bad," said Polly, her voice jumping with each bump they hit.

"So I've been dying to ask you," Bethany shouted. "What are you getting Mr. March for Christmas?"

"What do you mean?"

"Polly, you say you love this man," said Bethany in exasperation. "What's he going to think if you don't get him a Christmas present?"

Polly looked at her friend in alarm, but Bethany quickly reassured her. "We have all weekend to come up with something," she said. "Just leave it to me."

The roar of the pickup made it difficult to talk, so the girls fell silent, watching Three Chimneys unreel behind them, savoring the rush of retreating trees and pinprick buildings, safe in the tunnel of air carved by the speeding truck. Polly snuggled down under the blanket and rested her head gratefully on her friend's shoulder. One day she would need a change, her father had said. And deep down, didn't she already know that? She already thought of herself as a *New York Times* correspondent, on assignment in Afghanistan or Islamabad, taking long weekends to meet Mr. March in Berlin, where they would frequent beer gardens and revisit all the romantic haunts of his youth. Her father crested a hill and Polly had a view back, of red clay chilblains peeking out from white snow, of frosted farms and other people's cattle looking up to watch the truck speed past. She was already on her way, she realized, and suddenly she was overcome with nostalgia for this place and these people, even for her mother back on the farm, rooted like a bare-limbed tree, waiting patiently by the empty mailbox for a postcard from Germany.

"Hey, Peanut, check this out!" Francis slid open the glass window that separated Bethany and her from the cabin, and the twang of bluegrass, sharp and warm as moonshine, blasted through. "I know you can't call *this* crap."

"*Wish that I was on ol' Rocky Top, Down in the Tennessee hills,*" her father sang off-key. It was the first song he'd ever taught her, when she was no older than three, the one they danced around the barn to, banging the milk pails and frightening the cows. It was the song he played when he wanted her to know he loved her but couldn't find the words.

> *Ain't no smoggy smoke on Rocky Top*
> *Ain't no telephone bills . . .*

Polly turned around to watch her father drive, her hair whipping her face, her eyes tearing with cold. Her handsome, maddening father was yowling with abandon, grinning back over his shoulder to make sure she was with him, that no matter what happened, they would still have their song, and when it played, everything would be just fine. And everything *was* fine, thought Polly. It was glorious to be young, and free, and by the grace of God, headed out of town. It was glorious to be on the road with a hopeful heart and a loud stereo and for that brief, priceless moment to be able to throw off the heavy yoke of Father and Daughter and to be instead just two united, carefree souls determined to savor one of Life's carefully rationed moments of bliss.

> *Rocky Top, you'll always be*
> *Home sweet home to me . . .*
> *Good ol' Rocky Top*
> *Rocky Top, Tennessee*
> *Rocky Top, Tennessee . . .*

While Francis was driving Polly and Bethany to T.G.I. Friday's after *Alien Rampage*, Margaret was dragging her old clubfooted step stool

out to the barn to care for the Mammoth Cheese. If it had been a
wounded patriot supine on the battlefield, Margaret could not have
nursed it more tenderly. Balanced on her ladder, she stripped away
its gummy bandages and worked handfuls of salt into its raw, naked flesh. She rubbed to desiccate her charge and to toughen its
hide, she rubbed slowly and firmly, as she had once washed her dying
father's pale back, as she had once scrubbed Sultana her milker
when, after a difficult labor, she had fallen into her own bloody
show. She rubbed this half-sentient, watchful creature she had
called into being, aging it and preserving it, insinuating and extract-
ing at once. She took her time, peeling back layer after layer of
cheesecloth, marveling at the innate properties of milk that allowed
it to move from fluid to solid, from something that might spoil in a
matter of hours to something that would keep for years.

You used to be fun, Francis had hurled at her. What happened
to you?

It was getting dark, and here she was, alone with her cheeses on
a Saturday night. She couldn't feel sorry for herself—it was her own
choice to remain at home. Margaret was still an attractive woman,
and she was certain if she ventured out into Charlottesville or Richmond, someone would buy her a drink. But she could no longer hide
her irritation with the rest of society, and knew that because of this,
she would make a thoroughly disagreeable barfly. Men looking to pick
up women did not want to engage in a complex discussion of how
Corporate America was sucking the lifeblood out of the small farmer,
since most of them had themselves just slithered out of their claustrophobic corporate cubicles and were now swapping their maintenance doses of chemical-infused corporate coffee for corporate alcohol
lite. Nor could she accompany them to the movies and sit through
two hours of product placement and random violence, nor choke
down another platter of late-night potato skins laced with God only
knew what Jalapeño Cheddar dust. No, she had no stomach for port-
folios or golf handicaps or grown men playing X-Boxes. Fun to these
men was irresponsible, uninformed, numbed, and bought. Fun meant
shrugging your shoulders when asked to take a stance on genetic

engineering of the food supply and saying something idiotic like People gotta eat, you know what I mean?

Margaret hoisted the cheese back to its resting place in the rafters and walked the rows, bidding her cows good night. Like baked brown loaves they lay, their legs tucked beneath them, their steaming breath rising and falling to Sinatra's romantic anthem of abandonment, "Softly, As I Leave You." Margaret lingered over the twin calves, now nearly two months old, stroking their twitching ears and letting them lick her fingers. It was easy for Francis to talk of letting go—he didn't care whom he disappointed or what he left behind. Family, responsibility, heritage be damned. It was easy to walk away when you were unburdened with the weight of two hundred years and a dozen generations, when you didn't have to keep a daughter safe and provide her a fighting chance against a perilous future. Francis might have left, and her father might have left, and even August might have left, but she was not about to walk away from Polly. No matter what difficult decisions lay ahead, Margaret would not bequeath her daughter the inheritance of anxiety and dread that had been left to her—she would do whatever it took to spare Polly that particular disillusionment.

The sky was white with indecisive snow clouds as she walked alone back to the house. She entered through the front door, an entrance rarely used anymore, since it was inconvenient to the barn, stepped out of her shoes, and let her feet caress the silky, oiled wide-plank floors, let her hand trace the banister newel, worn as soft as a baby's fleece. She lit a hurricane lamp she kept on a table by the door and walked down the paneled hallway to the dark kitchen, scattering shadows before her. She heard the skitter of some of the countless field mice that plagued the house, and smelled the prickly rosemary perfume of a hair pomade she had concocted that morning, steeping on the kitchen counter. Margaret didn't turn on any lights as she kindled a fire in the hearth and warmed her hands over it. It was funny how quickly she had forgotten her anniversary, a holiday she had kept for the past thirteen years. She and Francis had not known the etiquette of divorce in the early days, and the first

Christmas after they separated, he had bought her a coat, an expensive, fur-collared one like you would give to a mistress.

She took a long toasting fork out of the drawer and speared herself a slice of homemade bread for dinner. She crisped it on both sides before the fire, warmed up this morning's coffee, pulled a quilt around her shoulders, and settled in at the old farm table. It was scarred and grease-stained from years of sausage making, dusted white from ells of pie pastry rolled out upon its surface. She remembered an old parlor trick her aunt Louisa used to show her at this very table, when she was no older than Polly, her aunt who would spend hours on the upstairs toilet reading romance novels and eating Russell Stover chocolates, who had been married once for two weeks back in the 1950s, but whose husband was never spoken of by name, at least never that Margaret could remember. On the cold winter Saturday nights of Margaret's girlhood, when her parents stole away to a restaurant or to a show in town, her aunt would open a box of wooden matches and place two upright, their sulfur tips just touching. She would name one Margaret and tell Margaret to name the other after a boy she liked, and then would strike a third match and set the pair on fire. As the wooden matches burned, their tips clung together as if in a passionate kiss, one match peeling off the table like a lady coyly lifting her stockinged leg.

In the chill of the house, in the quiet solitude of the darkened kitchen, Margaret set up two wooden matches. She rested her head on the table, lit a third match, and watched the pair burn, the stronger lifting, the weaker curling herself against the stronger, slowly letting go, slowly fusing herself to her mate. For the life of her, Margaret couldn't think of a man's name that wouldn't be ridiculous, but nonetheless, after her lovers had burned down to a single ash, Margaret lined up another pair and watched herself surrender all over again.

CHAPTER SEVENTEEN

Polly came home nursing her usual hangover after a weekend at her dad's. She and Bethany had played video games until their eyes felt like sandpaper, drinking gallons of soda, challenging themselves to new depths of chemical preservatives and artificial coloring. But this week Polly thought she might have finally hit her limit, when between them they had eaten ten bags of Circus Peanuts, those banana-flavored blobs of orange spongy sugar that were neither peanuts nor, as far as she could tell, had anything to do with the circus.

The light was on in the cheese house when Francis dropped her off, but Polly was in no hurry to see Margaret. She was not in the mood to be grilled on what toxic depravities her father had exposed her to, nor to listen to yet another speech on the brain-corrosive properties of the major motion picture industry. It didn't help that she was starving, and craving something wholesome, for such an admission would give her mother ammunition for a month. She grazed the refrigerator, taking shavings of this and that—a scoop of cold mashed potatoes that she smoothed over with a spoon, five green beans peeled from under their lid of yellow congealed fat—nothing that would be noticed and commented upon; and in this way, she ate her miscellaneous fill. Polly looked for the toaster to warm a windowpane of sourdough bread for her sliver of roast beef, but search as she might, she could find it nowhere. Every time she came home from a weekend away, her mother had thrown out something else. It began with appliances that broke and simply went unreplaced—the answering machine, for example; then the electric can opener, then finally a perfectly good washer and dryer. Polly didn't know where it would end. She envisioned a house stripped down to its bare walls, where she and her mother, huddled in pelts, seared a deer haunch over an open fire.

Polly took her untoasted sandwich out to the barn to check on her calves, who were still young enough to be kept inside away from the rest of the herd. The other day, she had experienced her first twinge of maternal nostalgia when the twins had graduated from their clownish red-nippled milk bottles to drinking straight from a pail. Already she missed their excited tug-of-war, sucking so hard they nearly pulled her over, one hungry twin always waiting, butting up against her impatiently. Now when she poured their milk, they both calmly dunked their muzzles before moving onto their teacup troughs of grain. She hid her hand in their feed and shivered as their long tongues searched between her fingers and lapped her open palm.

The calves had been separated from Sultana when they were three days old, as was customary, and from that time on, Polly had taken responsibility for them. She forked their bedding and mucked their stall, not wanting to give her mother any excuse to complain of extra work. Over the weeks, the calves had stopped searching out Sultana, who for such a champion milker had the maternal instinct of a barn cat, and turned their large fawn eyes on Polly. And Polly couldn't have been a more indulgent mother, leading them, as she did now that they were done eating, to the old chimney, where she turned them free to buck in the waning sunshine, watching fondly as they raced to the edge of the woods, then like children who delighted in scaring themselves, turned tail and ran back to her, kicking their hind legs and leaping high in the air. Everything was funny about calves, thought Polly, their gawkiness, their liquid eyes, their whoopee cushion snorts. They were still young enough that she could gather them up in her arms and rub her face in their soft, clean neck hair.

She turned them loose and they were gone again, leaving her alone and wistful by the old chimney. When she was home, she wished she were with Francis, but when she was with Francis, Polly found herself missing her calves and the quiet routine of the farm, missing even the morning milking she was allowed to skip on nights she slept over at her father's. Nothing her parents told her could have prepared her for this divide. Polly remembered the night, not quite a year ago, they called her into the kitchen for a family conference. It was during her Beatles phase, the group being one of the few on her mother's approved list, and a documentary about the band was coming on PBS. She had been looking forward to it all week, hoarding the minutes she was allowed to watch television so that she could use them up in one luxurious two-hour debauch. But five minutes after eight o'clock, just as a black-and-white eye panned the row houses of Liverpool, her parents, looking very grim and subdued, had turned down the volume and ordered her to join them at the kitchen table. The whole time they explained that *it was not her fault, she had to believe them, and no matter what, they would always love her,* she'd sat stony-faced, watching Paul's silently bobbing mop top over her mother's shoulder. An hour and a half later, during which eternity she'd seen her father cry for the first and last time, and listened to her mother plead with her to ask them questions, to let it out, for God's sake, don't just sit there like that, Polly had finally asked if she could be excused. They let her go, but it was too late. John had already been assassinated and George was dead of cancer.

This feeling of being split in two would be with her forever, she realized. No matter who she was with, she would be wishing for the other, and once there, she would be worried about the one left behind. Polly couldn't wait for the day when she could get away from them both and be rid of this guilt. Then she and Mr. March could begin their new life, and when he asked her to marry him, she would say she was very sorry, the institution held no charm for her.

It had taken them all weekend, but she and Bethany had finally come up with a Christmas present for Mr. March. At first they were hung up on articles of clothing—a cashmere sweater Bethany had seen in a catalog, a hand-knit scarf, underwear (quickly vetoed). Music seemed a safer bet, but Polly didn't trust herself to know what the older generation liked. Finally, they decided on a gift certificate. Bethany thought a romantic dinner for two was a perfect choice, but confusion might arise if he didn't pick up on the hint that he should invite Polly. Nothing would be more humiliating than giving Mr. March a gift certificate to a restaurant and having him choose to dine with someone else. How and where she gave him the present would make all the difference.

Polly looked around for her calves and spotted them playing down near the barn, their instinct leading them back toward their own sweet scent in the straw. From her vantage up by the old chimney, she could see the rest of the herd spread out over the pasture, nosing for the dregs of autumn's grass among the patches of melting snow. Off in the distance, that boy Glenn, the one who'd replaced August, was walking toward two cows in the field. One was mounting the other, she saw, the bottom cow standing still and receptive, desperate for it, even from another female. It disgusted Polly the way her mother and August and now Glenn watched the cows for signs of heat, marking their rears with chalk that would be rubbed off by the mounting, prying up their tails at milking time to look for mucus and blood. Now Glenn was approaching the pair and shoving the top cow off, leading the bottom away from the herd. It was Sultana, Polly saw, the calves' mother, ready to breed again indecently soon, this time to the stud her mother had on loan from Mr. Franklin a few farms over. Her twins were about to be supplanted in the never-ending cycle of offspring around here, the obscene reality of dairy farming that couldn't be divorced from milk if they were to have any.

Polly looked straight ahead as Glenn led Sultana past where she sat, her back against the chimney. He passed by much closer than he needed to, so close that Sultana's muddy hooves nearly came down on Polly's foot. He was handsome in the way of Bethany's rock star posters, skinny and swarthy, with tight angry biceps and his dark hair combed forward over his forehead, and as he passed by, she couldn't be mistaken—no—he winked at her. How dare he? thought Polly swiftly. A boy who worked for her mother. He thought she was nothing more than an easily shocked child, but he had no idea what was in her heart. He thought he was so grown up, only four years older than she with that pathetic little mustache smudging his upper lip, but she was in love with an older man. And she was not afraid of what went on in the bull pen.

She wasn't sure what possessed her to stand up and follow them—maybe it was the implicit challenge in his wink, or maybe she too was caught up in the testosterone lure of the pen behind the barn, its scant acre exercise lot, heavily fenced and wrapped with barbed wire, electrified with unpredictability bred from confinement and boredom. As opposed to the lotus-eater asylum of the cows' quarters, the bull's lot was a place that held the mystique of a maximum security prison. A chute on the side of the pen allowed entry for the cow in service, while his feed was replenished from the outside, like bread and water pushed in under a solid iron door.

When she was younger, her grandfather kept a herd sire, Jolly Sultan, a proven bull with a hangdog head and yellow, malarial eyes. Approaching Jolly Sultan's pen was the only whippable offense of her childhood, for there was no such thing as a "safe" bull, her mother always said, no matter how placid and dim one might seem. But Jolly Sultan had been sold just after her grandfather died, and now her mother had the use of Mr. Franklin's wide-shouldered bull, Hairy Ape. Hairy Ape paced his pen, a stranger here, yet excited like a trucker in a new bar, knowing what he could expect and straining to get at it.

Polly stopped on the other side of the heavily reinforced pen, pressed her eye to the chink between the slats, and jumped to see Hairy Ape's own bloodshot, furious eye staring back at her. His sledge-hammer head smashed into the fence, and Polly knew he would break through; she could already feel the slap of his muscle, the crack of his skull against hers. But as she lurched back from the blow, Glenn heyed Sultana into the service shoot, and Hairy Ape realized his mistake. He raced over to the receptive cow and thrust his muzzle beneath her tail. High-strung, dainty Sultana, whom Polly would have expected to run away and hide herself like a child bride, stood silent and still, her long, reproductive memory blissfully nonspecific, so that all she remembered was the delicious secret itch of her heat, and not the violence that swiftly followed. Hairy Ape scrambled upon her back, ramming away at her pinbones with his angry, extended pizzle until he found his mark and thrust into her, jerking in that universal way that spelled "fucking" in any species, and that inevitably made Polly feel weirdly languorous and paralyzed. The entire episode lasted an eternal ten seconds, and all the while, Sultana stared into space, neither enjoying it nor fighting it, her body little more than a butter churn in which one life-giving milk was dashed into another. When Hairy Ape climbed off to rest himself (he would mount Sultana all through the long night, until her heat was over), Polly looked across the pen to see Glenn Mullins watching her, his own brown eyes dull and dangerous as the bull's.

I could walk to him and it would be over right now, thought Polly suddenly. And wouldn't it be a relief to lay down this burden. To stop wondering when and how and with whom and to have it all be done, right here, behind the barn, in this weird Bermuda Triangle of sex, where clean, empty cows disappear, only to emerge filled, maternal, useful. Whenever Polly imagined the act, it took place on a bald mountaintop where she lay down beneath the stars like an unwanted child exposed by its parents, and He, whoever He was, came to her like a moonbeam. In her mind, as it was happening (His silvery particles tickling her, or was His light a wave, gently lapping?), she would look up at the vertiginous trees above her and say, Goodbye, pine, this is the last time I'll see you as Polly the Virgin, she would look over at the creek rising in its bank and say, Good-bye, creek, this is the last time I'll see you as Polly the Virgin, she would peer over His pulsing shoulder and say, Good-bye, farm and home and childhood bed, when I return I will be some new being, something evolved and tempered, but I will never be what you knew before. I will never be this child again.

He must have read the invitation in her eyes, for Glenn Mullins, as silent and somber as she, took two steps toward her. *No*, thought Polly, with a terror that surprised her, considering what she had just been imagining. She turned and ran from the pen, glancing over her shoulder to make sure he didn't follow and tackle her, having read her thoughts as her word, a promise that she now had no intention of keeping. She ran back to the chimney, touching it as if it were home base in a game of tag, before realizing in confusion, no, she did not want to be there, she wanted to be back in the barn, with her calves, back home in her mother's lap, where she could put off the inevitable a little while longer. She walked back to the barn in a nebula of girlish dreams and womanly anxiety, moving through that liminal space where the desire to give herself away warred ferociously with the equally strong desire to retain her own discrete boundaries, to remain untouchable and untouched, a virgin in all her martial splendor, and perhaps because her heart was so very full, it took her a long minute to realize that while she had lingered at the bull pen a truck had pulled into the driveway, a truck she instantly recognized from when male calves were born on the farm, and one that filled her with horror.

"Mom!" Polly screamed, racing into the barn. "Mom, where are you?"

She ran directly to the calf pens, where she found her mother with Mr. Williams, the owner of the truck, drawing a rope harness around the calves' necks. The twins were so used to Polly's gentle handling that they did not fight the ropes, but stood as calm and resigned as Sultana in the bull pen.

"What are you doing?" Polly shouted, and Mr. Williams, a kindly avuncular merchant, backed up to give mother and daughter some privacy. "You broke your promise."

"I didn't hear you come home," said Margaret, weakly.

"Were you going to get rid of them while I was away?" yelled Polly. "What kind of monster are you?"

Margaret reached out for her daughter, half consolingly and half in embarrassment before Mr. Williams.

"They can't contribute to the farm," she said sadly. "I thought it would be easier if you didn't have to see."

"Are you going to give me away too when you can't afford me anymore?" Polly shouted, hating her mother for caring more about money than what they, together, had brought into the world.

"Polly, I'm sorry," said Margaret, struggling to stay firm. "But we have to let them go. I need you to be mature about this."

"You need," cried Polly, and this time tears threatened to choke her. "I need *you* to keep your word. Haven't I lost enough already?"

Polly raced from the barn before her stricken mother could move to comfort her, and ran back to the house. She threw herself onto her bed and sobbed for her poor useless calves, with their throats already cut, carved up in the slaughterhouse for veal. She sobbed for all the helpless, useless things who had no say in their own destinies, whose feelings were never consulted, who simply had to take it. She sobbed because her stomach hurt from all the junk food she hadn't really wanted to eat, and she sobbed because Mr. March had loved Amanda Frank. She cried as she never had over her parents' divorce, which had happened to someone else, but was now happening to her, and she cried until she fell asleep in all her clothes on top of her unmade bed, and that was where her mother found her, an hour later, after having signed the paperwork and apologized to poor, confused Mr. Williams.

Margaret gently removed Polly's muddy shoes and drew a quilt over the exhausted girl. Nothing had ever been so difficult as leading those two calves onto the veal truck, knowing what they meant to Polly. But Francis was right—she had to think of the future, and if the farm was to survive, she couldn't afford to be sentimental. She knelt beside Polly's bed and brushed the girl's sweaty hair from her forehead. "I'm sorry," she whispered, and Polly mutely opened her swollen eyes, still full of suffering tears. Margaret suddenly remembered a day when Polly was barely a month old, and nursing in her arms. She had looked down to see her tiny daughter staring off into space, her eyes full of tears, though she had not been crying a moment before, and she was struck with the idea that her baby was saying good-bye to her previous life, one she would have to forget in order to become this new person she was meant to be. It had made Margaret unbearably sad, and now she saw that same good-bye in her daughter's tears again, and knew she was the cause of it, and in that moment, Margaret laid her head next to Polly's and she cried too, for everything that she had lost, and everything she was still bound to lose.

CHAPTER EIGHTEEN

The last day of school was set aside for final exams, and Mr. March spent it behind his large oak desk, watching his students work. He could have taken refuge in the teachers' lounge, but on exam day the cluttered closet that doubled as an audiovisual storage room was crammed with teachers smoking off the same tedium he was experiencing. Mrs. Miller would be there, the sixty-five-year-old chemistry teacher, sitting deep in conversation with wide-eyed Jan (he hadn't bothered to learn her last name), a young substitute taking a year off between college and graduate school. *"When I first started,"* Mrs. Miller would be saying, *"I kept a hockey puck in my top drawer, and when they wouldn't shut up, I'd throw it, like this . . ."* and Jan would nod appreciatively, wishing she had a hockey puck, and a stick, for that matter, to use against her seventh-graders. No, he would rather sit right here, watching his students chew their lips as they vainly combed their fact-crammed brains for the name of John Adams's secretary of state.

While his students worked, Harvey stared idly out the window at the Old Marvel Chimney across the road, and thought, as he often did, how much he'd like to buy a sledgehammer and knock it over. The people around here acted as if in the whole history of mankind a house had never burned down or a family been displaced, as if there was something sanctified and totemic about their personal Southern misfortune that exalted it above the common American sort. He turned back to the classroom of bowed heads and scratching pencils, the heirs to that misfortune dutifully inking their disapproving essays on the Founding Fathers' failure to include abolition in the Declaration of Independence, never for a moment applying that failure to themselves or their rabid, stars-and-bars-flag-waving school

mascot, or to the Confederate relic across the street. Twenty bowed
heads, and in the corner sat his Polly, whom he knew to be in some
way connected to that chimney over her shoulder, just another
reason—for her sake—to tear it down. Marvelous Polly Marvel, the
only one in class who mattered. He'd had her intense, curious face
in mind when he made up the final exam, each question a cryptic
poem to his favorite student if she chose to read it so. *Explain what
Jefferson meant by* "The tree of liberty must be refreshed from time
to time with the blood of patriots and tyrants." Or another: *Identify
the quote,* "We are not to expect to be translated from despotism to
liberty in a feather bed." Was she self-aware enough to realize that
history rose and fell not for some dead men in Philadelphia or a pile
of old stones across the street, but for her? For Polly the marvel? The
entire semester had been his way of showing her and challenging her,
setting a Saturn's ring of events and names and dates to spin around
her as their axis.

Yet, something was different about her today, he realized; something had happened. He saw it in the unusual way she wore her hair—
loose and falling over her face—and again in the provocative beatnik
tightness of the black turtleneck sweater that set off her pale face like
a petal. Something had darkened and deepened in his protégé. As
his eyes rested upon her, she looked up in pain, the number of votes
in the 1800 electoral college momentarily escaping her, and for an
instant their eyes locked. Help me find my way, she seemed to say,
and he willed her the answer telepathically, feeling like a cheater passing notes across the aisle. But whatever she saw in his face seemed to
spur a memory, and she smiled at him, a knowing, adult sort of smile,
before plunging back into her blue book, scribbling with a frenzy of
clarity, as if what she had to say about an event two hundred–plus
years old could be the cure for cancer or a prescription for global unity.
The correct answer held that much importance to a girl her age,
Harvey instinctively knew, and it made him sad to contemplate the
day when school would be over for her, and she learned that all the
right answers in the world wouldn't guarantee her a meaningful
education.

"Polly," he said, causing her to jump. "I'm making you proctor while I leave the room. Make sure everyone keeps his eyes on his own paper."

He needed a smoke, but he didn't want to face the other teachers. Harvey walked out of the classroom and down the stairs without knowing where he wanted to go. The cold air was a shock to his system after the overheated classroom inside, and he breathed deeply, warming his hands on a Marlboro. Without deciding to, Harvey found himself walking across the front lawn of the school, then looking both ways before crossing the road to the pasture on the other side. School Street took a blind curve a few hundred feet up ahead, and the road here was dotted with makeshift memorials for inattentive people run down or trapped when they'd lost control and flipped their cars. Harvey had been teaching one day when a terrible squeal brought his class to the window to see a deer split open like a ripe melon and a pickup nose-down in the ditch. He hopped the split rail fence and kept walking.

The chimney rose white as a rib against the deadpan blue sky. It was remarkably preserved for being nearly a hundred and fifty years old, and every few months or so an elderly, black hired man came and applied a fresh coat of whitewash, straining with his pole-taped paintbrush to reach the highest capstone and crevice. Harvey had lived here ten years, but he still didn't understand how that man calmly came and tidied up the symbol of his oppression. If it had been him, he would have blasted it, or stealthily removed one brick at a time until the thing came crashing down under its own weight. But then again, Harvey was forever marveling at what people didn't do. When he read the newspaper in the morning, he was always most surprised at what *hadn't* blown up, or who had *not* been murdered, that peace actually reigned anywhere in the world. If he himself had the constant itch to destroy, then how did others with less impulse control and in far more desperate straits keep themselves from anarchy and chaos? Why was everything not in ruins?

Underneath the whitewash, Harvey saw that humanity had not completely failed him; he was pleased to read the faint emanations of rebellion in the blood-dark lines of a peace sign, and a little above that, *Class of '89 Rocks*. He was happy students snuck across the street at night and defaced what they were forced to stare at all day from their classroom windows, and he only wished that the old black man would stop coming by with his bucket of paint and instead allow the graffiti to march across this moldy old structure like Sherman through Georgia.

Harvey had too much time to think today, and his thoughts were unpleasant. His bad mood had begun when he was awakened by the phone at 5:45, fifteen minutes before his alarm was due to go off. It was his long-held belief that unexpected news was always bad news; and ten years of living with his phone number one digit off from the veterinarian's (he was perpetually amazed by how many livestock emergencies occurred between midnight and 6 A.M.) had only confirmed his theory. So when he picked up the phone to hear his stepmother's breathy Canadian voice on the other end, he was fully prepared. His father, a man he had not seen in nearly thirty years, was not dead, but surely dying, and had asked to see his son.

Across the road, Harvey watched the school buses pull into the parking lot and idle in a cloud of blue exhaust. Leave it to his narcissistic father to die at the most inconvenient time of year, he thought. He was already picturing the hordes of holiday travelers he would have to fight, parents with their airsick children and their stuffed shopping bags shifting overhead in the luggage compartment. Did he really want to get patted down, or forced to wait for hours while the old lady in front of him had her shoes checked for bombs? Was it worth it to take his part in a deathbed reconciliation he neither expected nor desired? Thirty years, it had been. Only the chance to see how cancer had bent and hollowed the old man made him even consider going.

From far away, Harvey heard the bell dismissing his last class. He flicked his cigarette onto the wet grass, checked his watch, then trotted back to school. Walking against the tide of students eager to go home, he shouldered his way through the front doors and down the hall, suddenly worried he would get upstairs to find her gone. It would be three weeks before he saw Polly again, and in that time, his father would have died, and he would have sat shivah, and who knew what would have happened to her? Maybe she would have forgotten everything he taught her. He roughly shoved aside a hapless freshman lingering in the stairwell and strode to his classroom. The desks stood in their tidy rows. A stack of blue books sat on his desk. She had not waited for him. The classroom was empty.

Harvey fought his irrational disappointment as he reached behind his chair for his briefcase. Forget it, he told himself, automatically ticking off what he still needed to do today. Call the airline and get an obscenely expensive ticket to Canada. Pack his dark blue suit. Suspend his newspaper subscription. Miss Polly Marvel.

He swept his students' final exams into his open briefcase, and that's when he saw the single white card printed with his name. He loved that she eschewed cursive for print, as he did. Cursive, more than anything, betrayed a person's age. Harvey ripped open the envelope and read the card inside.

Meet me at the newspaper office. I have a present for you.

"Say there, sport, having car trouble?"

Harvey turned to see Coach Emery, the instructor (he could not bring himself to say "teacher") he liked the very least at school, unlocking the car door beside him. This enormous Angus-necked man drove a tiny white compact and had to fold himself in half to get inside.

"I can't find my keys," replied Harvey. Only minutes earlier he had mentally cursed his favorite student for her trespassing. Ever since he'd found her in his car, he had begun locking his doors. Harvey had already retraced his steps to the classroom and even over to the old chimney, thinking he might have lost them hopping the fence, but they were nowhere to be found. He glanced again at his watch. How long would she wait for him?

"Where you headed?" asked Coach Emery bluffly. "Need a lift?"

It was after four o'clock, and Harvey saw no other alternative. "You could drop me off in town," he said. "I've got a few things to pick up."

"Climb on in."

Coach Emery sped through the parking lot, only to be stopped short at the turn onto School Street. Between the bus stops and the faculty exodus, the road was backed up all the way into town. Harvey tapped his foot impatiently.

"Doing a little Christmas shopping?" asked Coach Emery.

"My tribe doesn't celebrate Christmas," Harvey explained, just as he'd had to explain to everyone over the years, that he belonged to neither the Episcopal nor the Baptist church. And no, he wasn't Methodist, either.

"That must suck."

They lapsed into silence as the traffic inched forward. Christmas was the hardest of all seasons on an exile like Harvey March. He had been raised in a thoroughly secular Jewish household where the Easter Bunny hopped behind the Paschal Lamb and Santa Claus delivered Hanukkah presents, but he had never gotten used to the two-month-long red and green holiday pageant celebrated in Three Chimneys. Mom and Sis were still wrapping the Thanksgiving leftovers in foil when Dad and Junior hauled the ladder from the garage to hang lights from the eaves; meanwhile, seemingly overnight, municipal elves transformed School Street from a common thoroughfare into a plastic wonderland of icicles, ribbons, and candy canes. The Episcopal church even sponsored its own living nativity, populated with donated livestock, robed townspeople, and a local infant standing in for the Babe, and every night the town filed past to marvel at their neighbors' adoring poses, each one so still he appeared to have stopped his very heartbeats in honor of the Christ child.

After what felt like an hour to Harvey, they reached the edge of town. The citizens of Three Chimneys were out in force the week before Christmas, ordering their turkeys from Tinton's Grocery, the only store he'd ever known that still allowed one to buy on account, and buying their trees from the lot by the War Memorial. Most of the real holiday shopping would be pursued on weekend excursions to the malls of Charlottesville and Richmond, but for its box-of-eight ornaments, its *"Joyeux Noël"* welcome mats, and the like, Three Chimneys shopped amongst its own. As they inched along the length of the School Street incorporated business district, Harvey noticed that the Frank Eleven fund drive flyers that had once found their way into the corner of every shop window in town had been replaced by "We proudly sponsor the Mammoth Cheese" peel-off stickers that Leland Vaughn had run off at St. Barnabas's expense. Not only had every business in town donated relief, Harvey saw, but townspeople could sponsor a child to walk beside the cheese on its trip to Washington and thus raise more money. The cheese mania was not confined to the town limits alone, either, for once every week or so, when world tragedy admitted airtime, the local news ran an update on Three Chimneys and its famous cheese. Patrick Lewis and his cohorts had great fun in the newsroom superimposing a Santa hat and beard on their stock shot of the giant foodstuff, just as they had decorated it with turkey feathers for Thanksgiving.

There aren't enough people in town to cause this much traffic, thought Harvey irritably, and before he could stop himself, he reached over and pressed Coach Emery's horn. The football coach looked at Harvey as if in the final seconds of the Big Game he had dropped his pants and taken a crap in the end zone.

"Sorry, sport," he said. "We don't do things like that here."

"You know what?" said Harvey, unable to stand the claustrophobic car another instant. "I'll get out here. Thanks for the lift."

"Any time," said the coach. "Have a merry—"

"You, too." Harvey sighed, as traffic cleared and the coach pulled away. He walked the extra block to the *Three Chimneys Register* office, which Foster Lewis's secretary had decorated with a blizzard of construction paper snowflakes. Through the door, he heard two girls talking over one another as girls that age do, neither really listening in their rush to finish the other's sentences. He realized he had ex-

pected Polly to be alone, and the sound of Bethany Fraser's voice
profoundly annoyed him. He turned the knob and walked in.

"Ladies," said he, by way of announcing himself. "I was
summoned?"

"Oh, hi, Mr. March," Bethany nearly shrieked, and he saw her
shoot the other girl a meaningful look. "We're almost done."

"Done with what?" he asked

"We're running off the program for the Nativity Pageant," she
said, and behind her he noticed the cathode glow of the Xerox.

Polly had not looked up from her work and seemed even more
ill at ease than usual. Yes, there was something different about her,
but he couldn't quite put his finger on it.

"Miss Marvel, are you wearing makeup?" he asked suddenly.

"Doesn't she look great?" Bethany answered for her, and
Mr. March realized who he had to thank for the despoilage of his
protégé.

"What would your mother say?" he asked, mockingly aghast.

"She doesn't own me," answered Polly, self-consciously licking
the gloss from her lips. It tasted like root beer but had the consistency
of bacon grease.

"It's not very becoming."

"Oh, Mr. March." Bethany laughed. "You don't know anything
about what boys like!"

This girl was a quick one, he saw, never having ever given much
thought to Bethany Fraser. But it disturbed him to see her at work
on innocent, viable Miss Marvel, so he scowled at her.

"Oh my gosh, look at the time!" Bethany gasped, winking at
Polly. "I've got to get home. Do you think you can finish this alone?"

"No, Bethany—," Polly frantically tried to stop her friend, even
though the entire time she had sat in the girls bathroom sink letting
Bethany slather her with makeup, they had talked about nothing but
this eventuality. Now that the moment was here, Polly was terrified
and desperately wanted to keep her friend near.

Bethany decisively shook her off and scooped up her backpack.
"Merry Christmas, Mr. March. See you next year!"

She left the two alone in the dim, dusty newspaper office that smelled of what Foster Lewis had earlier eaten for lunch: tuna fish with sweet relish, french fries, catsup. Mr. March leaned against the old, ripped Naugahyde sofa and studied his student carefully. Something had definitely changed in her. She was wearing that Audrey Hepburn black turtleneck sweater and faded blue jeans ripped at the knee, which, left naked to the wind, had chapped to a tender pink. She was leaning against the Xerox like a cartoon version of a bad girl, with her legs straight before her, crossed at the ankles, and her arms defiantly folded across her flat chest. Her thin blonde hair was hanging loose and tucked casually behind her ears, which were among the only unpierced lobes in the entire school, and behind her glasses, her normally invisible eyelashes had been darkened with mascara. Then there was the lip gloss, which only accentuated how painfully thin her lips were. Her nails, he noticed, were painted a deep grass green.

"So, Miss Marvel, why have you lured me here?"

"I thought you called me Polly now," she said. "You established a precedent."

"So I did."

"You know I have my own key to this office," she said. "I stole it and made a copy while my mother had her headquarters here."

"Your criminal record compounds!" said Mr. March, delighted. "Now we're in felony territory."

"I've got nothing to lose," said Polly.

"Miss Marvel—Polly—are you well?" asked Harvey March, for there was a strange glittering breathlessness about his pupil. "Maybe you should step away from the Xerox."

"I'm fine," said she. "I had a very unusual conversation with a friend this weekend. Maybe you know her—Amanda Frank?"

"The woman who had all the children?" He smiled. "Don't tell me you are yearning after motherhood at your age."

"God, no!" said Polly, waving her hand dismissively. "I'm never having children. I have too many plans. Like working in Berlin, for instance."

"It's a lovely city," responded Harvey March noncommittally.

"So I've heard. I'm reading *Berlin Stories* right now. By Christopher Isherwood. Perhaps you know his work?"

"Perhaps." Mr. March smiled.

"He was bisexual."

"Scandalous!"

He wished he could swallow his last sarcasm, for he saw she had become embarrassed by her own enthusiasm, just when he was beginning to enjoy her clumsy flirting. He fought the temptation to put his arms around her and tell her that he too had read Isherwood when he was thirteen, and thought him the most brilliant writer in the world, next to Jack Kerouac, of course. Instead he took her hand and ran his warm thumb over her nails.

"Fräulein Sally Bowles?" he asked, more kindly.

"Green is a provocative color, don't you think?" she said, as if speaking a part in a play. "The color of money. Or jealousy."

"Are you jealous of anyone?" he asked, delighted.

"You taught Manda, I think," she said.

"Did I?" he asked, dropping her hand.

"She doesn't like you much. She says you failed her."

"I've failed a good many people."

"There seemed to be more to it than that."

He wasn't sure where Polly was headed with this line of conversation, for of course he remembered Amanda Frank. He had thought of her often during the media frenzy and had felt sorry for her, doomed to perpetual victimhood, just as she had been back then.

"Manda always struck me as a very pedestrian sort of person," said Polly airily, collecting the first pages of the nativity program and stacking them neatly. "She's doomed to stay here, I think, raising babies until the day she dies. She doesn't have a larger plan."

"Like working in Berlin, for instance?" Harvey played along.

"Exactly. Or experimenting with life."

"How does one 'experiment with life'?" Polly's teacher asked. "You only have one. What would you use as your control group?"

"You know what I mean." Polly cut her eyes at him. "I plan on seeing the world and having tons of adventures."

"Adventures?" he asked. "What sort of adventures?"

"Oh, I don't know. . . . Traveling, reporting from war zones." Polly licked her suddenly dry lips. "I expect I'll have many lovers."

"*Now* who is being scandalous?" said Mr. March.

"Do I surprise you?"

"Are you trying to?"

"What was it you said about the Earth belonging to the living?" she asked, seeking, he could tell, to impress him with her memory. "I have a lot to do before I die."

"'*The Earth belongs in usufruct to the living,*'" Harvey quoted. He had been teaching them that lesson the day he found her in his car. "And I didn't say it, Jefferson did."

"Usufruct." Polly laughed. "That sounds like a dirty word."

"Polly, you seem quite altered today," said Mr. March seriously. "Has something happened?"

Polly shook her head, and he saw she was fighting back sudden tears. "I lost something I loved this weekend. And it made me realize that you can't put your faith in anyone."

"I'm sorry to hear that," said Mr. March, and then without knowing why, he confessed, "My father is dying."

Polly was silent, not knowing what to do with such a sudden and personal revelation. She tried to conjure Stanley March's face from the Internet, but all she could picture was a grainy set of handcuffs. "I'm sorry," she said. "And your mother . . ."

"I'll be an orphan," he replied. "Free at last."

This was not the way either of them had expected the interview to go, for Harvey March was rapidly turning inward, and he could tell Polly found herself growing sad. To salvage the moment, she reached into her pocket and withdrew a gaily wrapped gift box.

"I have something for you," she said.

"You know, I don't celebrate Christmas," he said. "I'm Jewish."

She looked at him as if he'd admitted to not breathing oxygen, for she'd never heard of anything so strange. "Is it against your religion to accept this?" she asked.

"I'll spend years in Limbo," he joked, knowing it was over her head, and took the present from her. "Thank you."

Polly watched as he unwrapped his gift, then looked up at her quizzically. She couldn't explain why she had taken them, and why she had decided they would be the perfect gift. She hadn't discussed it with Bethany, or thought beyond the deed. The gift certificate was in her backpack, tied with ribbon and sealed with a bow, but when she was about to put it on his desk, she'd noticed them, casually tossed onto a stack of exams, gleaming with invitation—to what, she couldn't say in words. To freedom? To a way out? It would be a bond between them, a pact, for by her age, hadn't he said he'd stolen his first car?

"My keys?" he asked.

"You said we weren't rebellious enough. That we had no fire," said Polly, feeling more alive and afraid than she ever had in her young life. "You're wrong."

"You stole my car keys?" he asked again, incredulously.

Polly was silent, worried for the first time that he wouldn't be pleased with her bravado. "I thought you'd be happy," she whispered.

"You asked me to meet you and you stole my car keys?" he asked angrily. "How did you think I was going to get here without my car?"

Polly looked abashed, as if the obstacle had never even crossed her mind. And of course it hadn't. She was only interested in pleasing him, no matter how inconvenienced he was by her efforts.

"But you came, didn't you?" she asked at last. "You found a way."

And she was right, thought Harvey. He had found a way. He had found his way to this dingy newspaper room to claim whatever gift she would offer, and now he was angry that she had offered exactly what he had asked of her. He took a step toward her, and for a second, she thought he was going to hit her.

"Take off your glasses," he said.

In confusion, she did as she was told. Behind her the copier spat out its last page, and the room was suddenly silent.

"Come stand here," he commanded, and she took a few hesitant steps until she was just under his chin. He turned her face up to his and studied her critically. Her eye makeup was thickly and inexpertly applied, giving her the appearance of a ravished silent film star. She has no idea what she's doing, he thought, staring down into her hopeful, yearning face. She is like everyone else in this town, putting her trust blindly in all the wrong places, assuming nothing bad will ever happen to her. He could hear her accelerated breathing and could see that she was too afraid to move for fear of breaking the spell she believed herself to have cast, her success ensured by devotion, determination, and a dab of cheap drugstore lip gloss. Harvey reached into his back pocket and took out his clean linen handkerchief. With the utmost tenderness, he applied it to Polly's eyes, removing what she had so thoughtlessly put there, taking down all the tacky billboards that might spoil his view. He wiped her mouth clean and then he touched it with his own two lips, like Lewis and Clark setting oars into water. Polly Marvel, his river, his breadbasket. She tasted of bending grasslands and bubbling streams pink with salmon, of friendly Indian tribes and the footfall of buffalo. Like the young of any species, she was full of promise, an untapped potential, an intimation of fruitful harvests and resources abundant, with everything to offer and everything to waste. And as he sprung her mouth with his tongue, he could feel her opening under him, every county and province and territory of her surrendering, manifestly his to claim and fully convinced of her own limitless destiny.

When he took his lips away, he saw that her eyes still held his, wide and steady, as if the kiss had been a mere prelude and she was ready to accept whatever befell her next without surprise or protest. She was so young she didn't have any idea what this first kiss would mean to her later when she talked it over with her college boyfriend or explained it to her shrink. She was so young that a kiss was still something inevitable and unquestioned, like homework, a thing assigned and completed and handed back. She continued to search his face as if anticipating some further declaration from him, and that trusting, unthinking presumption, that inability to recognize that something bad had finally happened to her, made him for a moment hate her as he hated everything and everyone else in this ludicrous town.

"Mr. March?"

Polly stood before him helplessly, still savoring the tingle of where his rough cheek had chafed her own. She didn't know what she had done wrong, but Mr. March was clearly disappointed in her. She stood helplessly as he walked to the Xerox and collected the copies of her program, tucked them in her bag, and handed her her coat. The clock on the wall said it was twenty after five and she was already an hour and a half late getting home, but she couldn't seem to move. She stood with her hand on the doorknob, hoping he might kiss her again or say he would call her, ask when he might see her again, say anything to break the unbearable silence. But he was staring at the car keys in his hand, waiting for her to go. Maybe she should say something, Polly thought, but she wasn't sure if women spoke at times like this.

"Mr. March?"

"Don't tell anyone about this," he said.

CHAPTER NINETEEN

Quiet, polite, well-groomed Glenn Mullins had been given detention on this the last day before winter break, for threatening another student with a knife. Another boy had trash-talked his girlfriend and Glenn had merely written on a piece of spiral notebook paper, I'M GOING TO CUT YOU, MOTHERFUCKER, and that was enough to get him detention. "I wasn't really going to do it," Glenn explained to Margaret when he called to inform her he would not be making it to work that afternoon. He was very sorry to leave her shorthanded, but he would be back to work tomorrow, she shouldn't worry. But of course Margaret did worry. How could she continue to trust a juvenile delinquent with the keys to her barn and access to her daughter? When was August coming back to work?

Margaret went about her afternoon chores in a foul mood, for there was a great deal to do today—two of the girls were about to freshen and would need to be dried off, requiring Margaret to measure out special feed; a Christmas order of Wilderness Cheddar needed to be packaged and shipped to a chef in Roanoke, and on top of that, Patrick Lewis was scheduled to come by with his crew later than evening. Margaret did what she could alone—mixing the oats and cob meal, measuring and pouring the feed. She raked fresh hay down from the hayrick and sluiced the floor, waiting for Polly to get home. Three-thirty came and went without a sign of her daughter. Of all days for her to be late, Margaret thought. A few months ago, she would have been worried sick if Polly weren't home, but after the episode with the calves, she was certain Polly was staying away simply to punish her.

When the winter sun finally dipped in the sky and Venus revealed herself, Margaret phoned the school to see if Polly was still there. No, said the secretary, it was the last day of the semester and there were no after-school activities. Meanwhile, the cows, of their own accord, had wandered in from the pasture and were milling about the holding pen, their finely calibrated milk clocks having sounded the four o'clock alarm. Long ago, in some secret bovine caucus, they had established their herd order, and now Tiberia's Queen, their leader, raised her chalky muzzle to voice the herd's collective disapproval at the disruption of their schedule. Her udder ached, she complained, and she was ravenously hungry. The other cows loudly reiterated that if they were not milked immediately, they, too, would surely perish.

At four-thirty, when her daughter had still not shown up, a fuming Margaret had little choice but to let the beasts in and try to milk them all herself. What fresh hell was this? bellowed the cows, backing away from their obviously upset mistress. Margaret had no patience with their timidity today, and cursed them, shouting "Come on" and "Hurry up" and all sorts of hateful things that only made them more upset. When at last Tiberia's Queen inched inside the open gate, the girls behind her panicked and raced in all at once, tripping over one another and skidding on the concrete floor. Forgotten was their normal decorous single file; now up was down and down was up, with high-strung Sultana galloping before her elders and thrusting herself into the wrong stall, with the other cows stumbling about in horror over the breach of etiquette, with Margaret slapping their rumps and ordering the bulking creatures to take their stalls, damn it. She was trapped between moving walls of cow flesh, one eight-hundred-pound animal crushing her into the next, nearly knocking her to the ground. Margaret shoved at Jolly Anna, who sidestepped into Anna's Surprise Avis, who dropped her rear right hoof down hard upon Margaret's foot. The cheesemaker let out an angry cry of pain that only sent the cows more furiously crashing around the barn.

Half an hour she spent trying to restore order, but at last she was forced to concede defeat and limp to the telephone. It deeply wounded her pride to make the call, but she had no choice if she was going to get the cows milked, pack up the cheddars, turn the cheese, and all before the television crew showed up. She punched in the number and waited.

"August, it's me," she said when the phone picked up. "All hell has broken lose here and Glenn got detention and God only knows where Polly is. Normally I wouldn't interrupt your vacation, but I think I've broken my foot—"

He agreed to come right over and Margaret went back to the barn to drag the recalcitrant Sultana from her stanchion. That was where he found her, ten minutes later, sweating and on the verge of frustrated tears. Sultana had lain down and Margaret stood above her, covering the cow's nostrils with her hands so that in a desperate attempt to get her breath, the cow would rise.

"Here, let me," August said, moving the injured Margaret aside. "Sultana, stand up."

The cow hesitated, but upon seeing who'd called her name, finally lurched to all fours. August covered her eyes and led her to her proper stall, redirecting the others, who, repentant, now craved parental guidance. The cows humbly submitted their necks to the halter, and he quickly filled their feed buckets so that they might remain pacified. Margaret watched gratefully, and not a little resentfully. They so obviously preferred him to her.

"Thanks, August," she said, after he had helped her limp to her milking stool and taken one for himself. They were once more pulling in tandem, the warm milk steaming in the buckets, the cows audibly sighing with relief. "I really didn't want to bother you."

"It's no bother," he said.

"It's just that I was in such a bind."

"Things happen," he said, leaning his head into the cow's flank. He hadn't milked a cow in nearly a month and he had developed a whole new set of blisters from swinging an ax and pushing a wheelbarrow. Still, the udders fit his fingers and the muscles of his palms responded. It felt natural and good and he realized he'd missed it.

"So how are you enjoying your vacation?" Margaret asked at last.

"I've been pretty busy," he answered.

"Really?" she asked. Margaret hadn't given much thought to what August might be doing when he wasn't here with her. "Have you given many programs?"

"No, not really," he said. "I've been clearing land."

"Clearing land? For whom?"

"For myself," he said, not looking at her. "I'm building a house."

Margaret let that news sink in. She led Tiberia's Queen to her sleeping stall, brought Queen Anna around to be milked. She had assumed August would live with his parents until they all succumbed and then he would haunt the basement, terrifying whichever Vaughn relative had the misfortune to inherit it.

"Whereabouts is this house?" she asked.

"Down by the river. Near the old Indian burial mound."

"Toward Charlottesville?" she asked, and he nodded. "How do your parents feel about it?"

"I expect they're thrilled to finally get rid of me. Now they can enjoy their twilight hours in peace."

Margaret looked at him quizzically. He put Lazy Anna's Sunday down for the night and brought around Sunday in Tiberia, brushing her udder, trimming where the hair had grown shaggy, whispering softly into her fruitbat ear.

"What made you suddenly up and decide to build a house?" she asked. "Haven't you learned your lesson hanging around this place?"

"Maybe that's what did it," he said, watching the milk hit its pail as if he'd never seen a thing so interesting. "Watching you and Polly on the farm. I guess I just wanted something of my own to care for."

"Well, you know, we could have saved you some money." Margaret smiled, trying to sound lighthearted. "You're like family. This place feels as much yours as mine."

"But I'm *not* family," August said simply, and for a long while after neither of them spoke.

Margaret limped over to the instigator Sultana, who swayed beside her as if she had not been the architect of Margaret's misery. "Orders have been up all month since the cheese was on the news," she said, just to say something.

"That's great."

"I can't wait to see the look on the president's face when it arrives."

"I imagine it will be something to see."

"We've got a much shorter trip than the original," she said weakly, for not even the cheese was sparking his enthusiasm. "At least it won't rot."

"It's not likely," he answered, keeping his eye on his milker. Margaret relapsed into silence, wishing she hadn't called him. Any illusion was better than this uncomfortable truth.

By the time they had milked and fed and bedded the cows, it was nearly seven o'clock, and August turned to bid her good night. There was a time when she would have had to drop several unsubtle hints to get him to go home, but now that he was rushing out, she wished he would stay. This was silly, she thought, two mature adults acting like bashful schoolkids. She was determined to speak and put that night behind them.

"Would you mind helping me with one last thing?" she called. "I need to turn the cheese before Patrick shows up. Polly usually helps me, but . . ."

When he turned back, his face was politely impassive, but she could see it took some effort for him to stay. He walked to the pulley system he had spent days rigging, gently lowered the cheese to chest height, and tied it off.

"Where *is* Polly, anyway?" he asked, getting under the cheese and preparing to carefully upend it. Margaret waited on the other side to slow its descent with the other guard rope.

"I had to sell her calves," Margaret answered. "She's mad at me."

"I guess it had to be done," he said. "Sometimes we have to do unpleasant—"

"Listen, August, about the other night—," Margaret started, but was immediately interrupted.

"Margaret, I'm not coming back to work."

August had not known he was planning to quit until the words came out of his mouth. He had been thinking about it for weeks, turning the idea over in his mind, as he plowed under the brier patch on his new property and swung his hatchet against the invading sap-lings, but some recalcitrant sense of loyalty had forbidden him from simply saying the words "I quit" and severing his life from hers entirely. Tonight, when she'd called on him for help, something had leapt in him, and to his dismay, he'd discovered it was that old hope, that craven need for her to desire him. He had absented himself for a month, but nothing had changed. The moment he saw her again, the moment he heard her voice, his Head and Heart, which like companionate brothers had been pulling together for the past thirty days, sweating side by side, of one purpose and one will, split apart and resumed their quarrel. Alone, he was a man in harmony; with her, he was a man divided. He could not come back to work.

"August, please, you don't mean that," Margaret was saying. "Listen, I know we had a little misunderstanding a while back, but we need you around here—"

"It's not that," August said, and now that he had spoken the words out loud, he felt emboldened to say everything. "I love you, and I always have. But I can't work for you anymore. For as long as I can remember, I've been leading other people's lives. Now I need to live my own."

"You're not being fair!" Margaret cried in exasperation. "I didn't know how you felt, and you're punishing me for not feeling the same way."

"I'm not punishing you. I'm making this easier on both of us."

"You're running away," Margaret said.

"I'm sorry you feel that way," August said, stung. "Glenn will stay on, and he's a good worker—"

"Glenn is a knife-wielding maniac. I need *you* if I'm going to pull off this cheese," she said, hating the sound of entreaty in her voice. "I need you to help me take it to Washington."

"Margaret, you don't need me and you never have," he said simply. "You don't need anyone for anything."

Margaret didn't know what came over her then, looking at her erstwhile friend across the moonscape of the giant wheel. A wordless fury took possession of her, a thwarted rage she hadn't felt since her earliest childhood, and without thinking, as a child would shove over a castle of blocks, she reared back and shoved the twelve-hundred-pound wheel of cheese hard into August's chest, sending him sprawling to the ground. The cheese swung back on its ropes and would have taken Margaret out as well if she hadn't quickly dodged it. August lay stunned in the straw, trying to catch his breath.

"Hey, what's going on?" Polly stood in the doorway of the barn. "Mom, what are you doing?"

"Where the hell have you been?" Margaret turned on her daughter, all her frustration swinging around on Polly. "You were supposed to come right home after school. I had to call August when you didn't show up."

"Where's Glenn?"

"In jail, for all I know," Margaret said angrily. "He didn't come today. I was all alone."

"I'm sorry," said Polly, looking from her mother to August on the ground. "I missed the bus and had to walk."

"It took you three hours to walk home?" Margaret shouted. "Why didn't you call me to pick you up?"

"I figured you'd be busy," Polly lied.

"The news crew is coming tonight; they'll be here any minute. You left me to milk the cows alone. To turn the cheese alone."

"I said I'm sorry," Polly shot back.

"'Sorry' is not good enough," said Margaret. "Now put your things down and help me with this. August needs to go home."

August had found his feet, though he felt like he'd been rammed by a small car. "I'll help you turn it," he said weakly. "Let Polly go inside."

"No," said Margaret grimly. "Polly, put down your backpack, take off your coat, and help me turn this cheese."

"No," said Polly, without moving an inch.

"What did you say?" asked her incredulous mother.

"No. I won't be tyrannized by you anymore." Polly held her mother's eyes defiantly. She had spent the last two hours walking the dark road home, shivering in her light jacket, replaying Mr. March's kiss a hundred, two hundred times. Too much had happened to her today to be bullied by her mother, and she was not about to be treated like a child. Not tonight. "I'm not going to help make a cheese for that liar in Washington," she said.

"I have had about enough from you," retorted Margaret angrily. "I'm your mother and I expect some respect."

"What a hypocrite you are!" Polly cried. "August, do you know what the president did?"

"Polly, you shut up," warned Margaret.

"He used our family motto in his debate and claimed it was his own. He stole from us, and Mom's been covering it up. What do you think happened to the sign over the cheese house door? She hid it so the television cameras wouldn't see it. How pathetic is that?"

August looked at Margaret in surprise.

"How dare you criticize me," said Margaret.

"Margaret. Polly." August rose to separate mother and daughter, who were now so angry he feared they might come to blows.

"You stay out of this, August," Margaret snapped. "You don't even work here anymore."

"Oh sure, why don't you take it out on August now," said Polly. "Everything is always someone else's fault."

Days filled with milking and labor, entire nights spent baking and preserving, the minute scrutiny of everything that entered her daughter's mind or body: all to keep Polly safe and protected. And this was how she was repaid—with treachery and spite and venom.

"Polly, you might not always understand me," Margaret said, trying to calm down, "or agree with what I do, but whether you realize it or not, everything I do comes out of one little four-letter word—"

"Mom," said Polly, as cold and haughtily as possible, "I think 'guilt' is spelled with five letters."

Before she could stop herself, Margaret reared back and slapped her daughter across the mouth.

"Margaret!" August shouted, grabbing her around the waist. Polly stood for a moment in stunned silence, then turned and raced from the barn, jumped on her bike, and pedaled off into the frigid night. Margaret's hand had gone numb after connecting with Polly's face, and she shook the blood back into her fingers angrily, as if rallying a reluctant battalion.

"Margaret—," August began as she shook him off too and stalked back to her position by the guide rope and pulley. "What's gotten into you?"

"Are you going to help me or not?" she asked, her voice breaking. "I've still got to turn this cheese."

Polly rode her bike blindly, not caring where she ended up, not caring if a truck barreled out of the darkness and struck her dead. "*I hate you,*" she screamed into the wind, breaking her mother's cardinal commandment, *Thou Shalt Not Utter the Word "Hate" to Thy Parents*, a rule, like everything else, supposedly for Polly's protection, for how would she feel if her mother or father were hit by a bus, and the last words she'd spoken to them had been ones of hatred? Her mother's entire life was dedicated to saving Polly from herself. "*Well, screw you!*" yelled Polly. "*I hate you for it.*"

She rode by the rough feel of the pavement alone, for not a single streetlight illuminated the back roads near her house, nor was the occluded moon any good for navigation. Her cheeks were numb and her eyes stung; she couldn't feel her chapped hands around her handlebars. She hadn't even registered the cold on her long walk home, a dreamy perambulation given over to the replaying of that life-altering moment, prolonging the time she could have it completely to herself before life set back in and interposed its inevitable banality. On the dark walk home, the kiss broke upon her like waves, it pulled her up short and made her stop for whole minutes at a time, to bring her own surrogate fingers to her lips, pressing as if to stanch a wound. Her body remembered his hands' exact placement upon it, how he threaded his thumbs below her chin and clasped her skull like a jewel cask. More than once, a car passed her, flashing its high beams in concern until she waved it off, telling the driver more than she knew with her beatific, secret smile. Who had not, at some point, been a young person in love, out walking in his or her own greedy solitude, and who would want to strip that moment from another, even in the interest of getting her home safe and warm?

She rode blindly for what felt like hours, and when she pulled her bike up in front of his house, she didn't even know how she'd gotten there. Her legs trembled from their frantic pedaling, her head ached from the cold wind in her ears. He had to let her spend the night, it was the least he could do, and maybe while she was here she would call the police and have her mother arrested for child abuse. She rang the bell and listened for movement inside.

"Peanut!" said her father, answering the door in his bathrobe. "What in the hell are you doing here?"

"Can I come in?" she asked.

"Well, sure, darling," he said, allowing her to push past him.

It was almost painful to step into his overheated living room, having sensation rush back to her extremities all at once. An open box of pizza sat on his coffee table beside a six-pack of empty beer cans. It was her father's particular tic to fit his empties back into their plastic rings as if they'd never been touched.

"To what do I owe this pleasure?" he asked.

Polly pulled a slice of pizza from her father's pie and ravenously ate it. "Do you have anything to drink?"

"Coke's in the fridge. Or would you care for a beer?"

"Coke is fine," said Polly, walking into the tiny kitchen. She was surprised to see he'd taken the time to decorate his spare bachelor apartment for Christmas—more for her sake, she imagined, than his own. He'd put up a balding white pine, bristling with whatever leftover ornaments her mother was willing to give up—none of the nice glass icicles, all of the scuffed plastic Snoopy's in reindeer antlers. He'd strung blinking colored lights around his kitchen doorway, which, because of the surroundings, evoked the ennui of a New Orleans beer joint more than the Christmas cheer he'd intended, and had completed the seedy impression with a sprig of half-melted plastic mistletoe hung from the lintel.

"Who are you planning on kissing?" Polly asked.

"I've got prospects," he answered. He was about to elaborate when the telephone rang.

"Don't answer that," she said.

Francis let the machine get it while Polly poured herself a soda.

"Francis, pick up. Are you home? Is Polly there with you? We had a fight and she's run away from home. Francis, if you're there pick up."

Polly shook her head, and Francis, in no rush to speak to Margaret, let her continue talking.

"If she comes by," said Margaret, "tell her I'm sorry and she should come home before I call the police. Francis, are you sure you're not home? Pick up."

"Peanut, what in the hell are you doing running away from home?" her father asked when at last Margaret gave up.

"I can't live there anymore. Mom hit me."

"What did you do to deserve it?" her father asked.

"Dad!"

Francis grinned at his daughter and patted the sofa beside him. "Come on and tell your old pa all about it."

Polly eyed the dirty clothes cluttering the spot next to him and perched herself instead on the arm of the couch. "Dad, you need to clean this place up," she said, wrinkling her nose. "It stinks in here."

"It's the smell of poverty, Peanut," said her dad mournfully. "It's the gamy scent of the wolf at the door."

"It's the smell of someone too drunk to wash his clothes," Polly said.

"Don't try to change the subject," countered Francis. "Tell me what happened with your mother."

"She's a maniac. First she knocked August down with the cheese, then for no reason she slapped me across the face. I'm not going back there."

"Well, Peanut, you know you're always welcome here," said Francis, walking unsteadily to the refrigerator to inaugurate a fresh six-pack, "but I can't have your mother pissed off at me right now. Business is bad, real bad." He popped the top on another Bud Light and wove his way back to the couch. "I was born unlucky and I'll die unlucky. I've never caught a break my entire life."

"Dad, what are you talking about?" asked Polly, frustrated that he had found a way of turning her problem back around to himself.

"Chimney Eleven Contracting is no more," he said, scattering a stack of business cards that lay on the table. "That house was supposed to be my new beginning. I was all over TV. But now everyone thinks of me as the man who built the Dead Baby House. My heart's just not in it anymore, Peanut. It's too damn sad."

"What does that have to do with me moving in here?" asked Polly.

"You know perfectly well I owe your mother a little piece of money," said Francis regretfully. "And I just worry, sweetheart, that if you come here and live with me right now, she'll involve the authorities, and that's no good for anyone, with business being so bad."

Polly set down her Coke and scowled at her father. He didn't want her either. Nobody wanted her.

"Will you at least give me some gloves?"

"Sure, Peanut," said her father, waving her toward the closet. "You know anything that's mine is yours."

She rummaged in his cluttered closet for a set of huge leather gloves and a scarf, which she wound five times around her neck.

"Now, you ride on home like a good girl. I'm sure your mother is worried sick," he said as Polly walked stiffly to the front door. She glanced back at her father who was shaking his head over his damn lousy luck.

"Fucking business cards," he said. "They make you buy a whole damn boxful."

She rode her bike down School Street past the St. Barnabas Episcopal Church's living nativity, where her friend Bethany was kneeling as the Virgin Mary. Space heaters, their extension cords trailing back to the rectory, kept the adorants warm, and the sight of Bethany's rosy, glowing face bent over the Christ child made her feel even more left out, for once again everyone in the world had somewhere they belonged, except her. For a moment, she thought about creeping into the manger and putting her mouth to Bethany's ear, spilling her secret, and causing the Blessed Virgin to shriek in excitement; but the thought of sharing her moment with Mr. March seemed to defile it somehow, and Polly knew she would keep it to herself, even if he hadn't warned her against telling anyone.

It was Christmastime and she was alone in the world. Baby Jesus slept in his crib of hay, dreaming of peace on earth, goodwill to men, never suspecting he would one day be denied and tortured and crucified. It must be nice to be a baby and not know anything, Polly thought, pedaling past the nativity mournfully. It must be wonderful to be the center of attention, innocent, taken care of, loved, and protected. Not forced to ride around in the cold because St. Mary is a freak and St. Joseph is a drunk and you are too afraid to ride your donkey to the one person who might take you in, for fear of being too forward and ruining everything. Polly pedaled out of town, and stopped before the white paper box and red reflector of Mr. March's driveway. She wanted so badly to go to him, to fling herself into his arms and beg him to take her in. I have no where to go, she thought, feeling the truth of it for the first time in her young life; I am alone in the world. She paused for a long while, but the heat of his kiss had been replaced by the look on his face when she left him, the look of a man who had drunk down to the bottom of his coffee cup, only to find a bug there, the sight of which had ruined every sip that came before it. She was afraid he, too, would turn her out, and she knew that that, of all things, she couldn't bear tonight.

Cold and defeated, Polly pedaled back home. From the road she could see that the yard was crosshatched with the headlights of cars, neighbors who had congregated, no doubt, to come out and look for her. She would ride up with her head lowered and take her punishment, she would make her shaky peace with her mother and pretend things were back to normal, though she knew, as sure as she was born, that nothing could ever be the same between them. But before she faced her mother, there was someone else she wanted to see. Polly rode past her own driveway and down the gravel path that led to her neighbors' house. The enormous house loomed before her in the dark, all that extra room and unused space, doomed to remain half-built, for Polly knew her father would never return to finish a house for children who would never come home. She saw that strangers were still leaving things by the unfinished front steps and on the ground near the garage doors: bouquets of frozen flowers, frosted teddy bears, Christmas stockings full of cracked rattles and icy pacifiers. But also steaming bags of dog shit. And placards that said *Murderer*. Manda and Jake didn't even bother to bring the things inside anymore, but the sympathy cards and the hate mail and the hand-copied novenas kept coming like waves breaking upon the shore. Polly had seen the gifts the day she helped baby-sit and knew most of them were left unsigned, from people whose emotions, kind or ugly, overwhelmed their ability to communicate. Polly felt that way now, walking her bike up the driveway, trying to formulate the question she most needed to ask. *You said he failed you. How did he fail you, Manda? How did he fail?*

As Polly walked up the center of the driveway, the electric door to the garage roared to life. She stopped, and from where she stood, she saw three figures emerge into the naked light: Jake's mother, hovering on the top step to the utility room; Jake, with his arm around Manda's shoulder; and Manda, bent over a tiny being who no longer felt the warmth of the rough plaid wool blanket in which she was wrapped. Polly watched the mother and father carry their limp baby to the car and stoically climb in, their faces numb, their eyes fixed straight ahead. Polly pulled back behind a tree as they passed her, and suddenly the whole world seemed too big for her to bear: the hulking house with its unused rooms, the breathing woods around her, the cheese that swung from its chains back home, the enormity of all the secrets she was expected to keep.

III

THE JOURNEY

"I am myself persuaded that the good sense of the people will always be found to be the best army. They may be led astray for a moment, but will soon correct themselves."

—Thomas Jefferson

CHAPTER TWENTY

A week after Christmas, Margaret received the answer to a letter she wrote informing the president-elect of her town's project. It was the only bright spot in a mailbox full of bills, and she tore into the official envelope without waiting to get inside, only to discover a Xeroxed form letter informing her that any presidential gift of an edible or potable nature was subject to destruction. Destruction. Margaret carried the letter around for days, mortified that she might be suspected of wishing harm to the president and furious at herself for not checking into the legality of the gift before she'd set out to make it. But humiliation is a great motivator, and rather than stand embarrassed before the whole town, she fired off another letter. *What does it say about a country, Mr. President,* she wrote, *when its leaders no longer trust its people? Let our troubled times be no excuse. I beg you to follow the example of your great predecessor Mr. Jefferson, who lived through even more tumultuous times, and accept our humble cheese, which we offer in the spirit of the patriots who came before us.* She signed it "Margaret Prickett," and then wrote below that with a trembling hand: *Omnis pecuniae pecus fundamentum.* Two weeks later a letter arrived from the president's press secretary. *Dear Margaret Prickett,* it said. *What does it say about a politician who cannot bend the rules to accommodate those who have worked so diligently on his behalf? Barring no national emergency, President Brooke would be honored to receive a cheese from the good people of Three Chimneys for his birthday. Please let my office know if we can be of any assistance. Yours truly, Sandy Jameson.*

Margaret read the reply with guilty satisfaction.

Winter passed and the cheese slowly ripened. Margaret was kept busy with the increase in orders generated by the Mammoth Cheese's publicity, to the extent that she found herself in need of another hand. She had heard nothing from August since before Christmas, though Leland kept her informed on the progress of the house he was building: when the foundation was poured, his troubles with the framing, the two-day marathon roofing job. Some days when she was downstairs in the cheese cellar, nestling her contraband raw-milk cheeses in their straw-filled crates, she would pause, convinced she'd heard his voice overhead. She would creep halfway up the stairs and listen, straining to hear him again. *Here, girls,* he would say, or sometimes just, *Margaret.* After several minutes, he would speak again, but always to her infinite disappointment. The voice would inevitably belong to Glenn's friend Andy, the boy she hired to help out when swamped, who, in fact, sounded nothing at all like August Vaughn.

The third week of February found Margaret and Pastor Vaughn seated at her long kitchen table, hammering out the many logistical considerations of the journey. It was a bitterly cold night, and Margaret had kindled a fire in the old stone hearth. Polly sat with her back to it, at the end of the table, silently working on her history homework. Winter forced her into closer proximity to her mother than she wished, for her unheated bedroom was too cold for anything but sleeping. At the other end of the table, Leland had spread a blown-up map of northern Virginia, and studied it like a general refining his battle plan.

"So the route will begin here at Leland-Madison Park to honor the original Mammoth Priest," he stated, inking a star onto the map, "head down Route 20, Constitution Highway, and then onto Route 3 as far as Fredericksburg." He snaked his Hi-Liter across the page. "I've filed the parade permits. Did you file for the rally at the park?"

Margaret nodded. "It's taken care of."

"It's not very far," Leland said, studying his yellow line. "Thirty miles at most, but I figured we can't go much above ten miles an hour, so it will take a few hours."

"And Alan Franklin is giving us the use of his hay trailer?" Margaret asked.

"It's all set," answered Leland. "Evelyn's Sunday school class is decorating it for us."

Margaret paused. "'Decorating'?"

"It will be great," said the minister. "Leave it to me. Now, I was speaking to Bob Crenshaw the other day, and he pointed out something very interesting. The route"—Leland gestured to his map—"goes right past the battlefields of Wildnerness and Chancellorsville."

Margaret eyed the priest skeptically. "Why do we care about Wilderness and Chancellorsville?" she asked. "Those were battles from the Civil War."

"Well, Margaret, you know Bob's great-great-grandfather was wounded at Chancellorsville fighting for the Gordonsville Grays. He's been so helpful with your foreclosure extension, I thought it might be nice to honor his family by paying a brief visit there."

"I think we're getting off message," said Margaret. "This was a cheese for Jefferson."

"But it was also a cheese for the people—you said so yourself," countered Leland. "It seems wrong to pass hallowed ground and not pay our respects. And he's been such a help to you."

"But bringing in the Civil War confuses everything."

"If you're going to be that strict about it, Mom," said Polly, looking up from her homework, "you shouldn't have made the cheese in the first place. It belongs to Massachusetts."

Margaret glanced at her daughter, and Leland quickly interceded. "We don't have to decide now. It's just something to think about."

He turned back to his map. "Anyway, once we're through Fredericksburg, we get into Washington traffic, and that's a real problem. I doubt we'll be given permission to drive a twelve-hundred-pound cheese ten miles an hour up I-95. But I think I have a solution." He trailed his Hi-Liter east of Fredericksburg, past the interstate, and into the pale blue Potomac. From there the current caught his pen and drew it directly into Washington, D.C.

"Float the cheese?" asked Margaret incredulously.

"We have a perfectly good river running to the capital. Why not use it?"

"The Unsinkable Mammoth Cheese." Polly said, laughing. "What if it hits an iceberg?"

"Hear me out," said Leland. "I have a friend down in Nanjemoy Creek who owns a tug and an old car barge. He's offered to pull the cheese as far as Columbia Island, directly across from the Jefferson Memorial. I asked August about the original and he said they floated it down the Hudson River. Why couldn't we do the same?"

"What if it capsizes?" asked Margaret worriedly.

"We'll make sure it doesn't. My friend suggested we put in at Fairview Yacht Club, which is a straight shot east of Frederickburg. It's a small town and it has no connotations of anything."

"We'll never get it to Washington in one day, going ten miles an hour, then floating it," said Margaret.

"Ah, but there are campgrounds at Fairview," said Leland. "We can spend the night there, float it up to Washington the next day, camp out at Columbia Island, and the next morning present it to Adams Brooke on the steps of the Jefferson Memorial. After all, if we wanted to get it there fast, we'd just ship it UPS."

Margaret hesitated. Washington traffic had been her greatest concern all along, and reason, more than once, for her to consider abandoning the project. "Let me think about it," she said at last.

"There's just one more thing," said the priest with a winning look that assured Margaret she would not like what he had to say. "Farwood Purdy wants his name on the cheese."

"What?" she asked.

"Farwood called me the other night," Leland explained, "after he'd seen the cheese on the news again. He thought you were getting a lot of publicity, and since he donated a good portion of the milk . . ."

"I didn't ask him for it, he offered."

"I know," Leland reassured her. "But since he's been so helpful, we might recognize him. And if Farwood gets his name mentioned, it doesn't seem right not to recognize Sam Abbott, and the others."

"This is not NASCAR, Leland," said Margaret hotly. "I'm not plastering my cheese with sponsors."

"If you want to be historically accurate, Mom," said Polly behind her, "the original cheese said *Rebellion to Tyrants Is Obedience to God.*"

"'Rebellion to tyrants'?" asked Margaret incredulously. "We're not a militia, for Christ's sake." She laid her head on the table. "I wish August were here."

Over her schoolbook, Polly cast her mother a look that said she knew very well why August had not come tonight.

"He's been very busy with his move," offered Pastor Vaughn.

"I hope he's settled in by the time we're ready to go," said Margaret somberly. "Without Jefferson, this cheese makes no sense."

The meeting adjourned, a weary Leland Vaughn drove back to the rectory, where Evelyn had left dinner next to his bottle of blood pressure medication. She was downstairs, she wrote in an accompanying note, helping August pack up. There was vanilla ice milk in the freezer. And strawberries in the refrigerator. And Mrs. Burton Greene had phoned to ask if Leland might speak to her son Larry, who had been arrested for driving while under the influence for a second time and was on a sure downward course. If he didn't care for ice milk (here Leland flipped over the closely written note, which continued on the back) there were some no-fat SnackWell's in the pantry, but, she added, "Please save some for August, who is having a rough day (Ask me about this later)." Evelyn signed her name with a few xxx's and ooo's behind it, and all this, thought her husband, when she was just downstairs and might be appealed to by his merely opening the basement door. Leland took his depressing plate of poached chicken and steamed carrots to the table, where he read through the day's mail. Then he ate a bowl of ice milk *and* his share of the cookies.

"I didn't hear you come in," said Evelyn, walking up the stairs twenty minutes later. Her white hair was tucked neatly beneath a kerchief and she was pulling off a pair of cloth gardening gloves.

"August is reaping the rewards of never letting me downstairs to clean up. His room is filthy!"

"Is he nearly packed?" asked Leland.

"Only about thirty more boxes of books to go." His wife sighed. "We're calling it a night. Did you take your pill?"

"Yes ma'am."

"And eat your dinner?"

"Yes ma'am."

"And you found the ice milk, I see."

"Yes ma'am."

"You look pale," said Evelyn, instinctively laying her hand upon his forehead.

"It was a difficult meeting."

"Let me fix you a cup of Sleepytime." She switched on the television so that her husband might catch the eleven o'clock headlines, then left to put the teakettle on to boil.

"So, how is Margaret?" she called.

"About the same," Leland called back. "Thinner."

"Must be hard on her without August to run things."

"I imagine."

"It's less than a week now," said Evelyn, and he could hear her in the kitchen, wiping down the counters and emptying the dish rack.

"*What's* less than a week?" he asked.

"Until it's just the two of us."

"I guess we should be grateful," her husband replied. "We had him about twenty years longer than most parents get to keep their kids."

Evelyn leaned in the archway between kitchen and living room. She took off her kerchief and slowly ran her fingers through her thin white hair. "I always assumed another woman would take him away from me."

"There's no competition." Leland smiled.

"He's moving into that house before the phone is even hooked up," she said. "What's the rush?"

"He's made his decision, Evelyn," he answered.

"He told me he's not going to Washington," she said, by way of proving how out of his right mind her son was. God forgive her, but she wanted to provoke a rise from her husband.

"I think he's just overwhelmed with the move right now," said Leland. "I'm sure when things calm down—"

"He said the cheese could find its way to Washington well enough without him."

Leland frowned. "Son!" he called, heaving himself out of his chair. "Son, could you come upstairs for a minute?"

"Ask him if he'd like some Sleepytime," prodded Evelyn.

A rumpled, sniffly August emerged from the chaos of his bedroom, exhausted from going behind his mother and repacking his books. She had been feeding them into boxes without any respect for alphabetization or their Library of Congress number, which would only make more work for him when it came time to reshelve them at the new place. His eyes were red from silverfish-dusty pages and he was happy to blow that sickly sweet old book smell into his clean pocket handkerchief.

"August?" asked his mother. "Cup of tea?"

"Love some, thanks," said August.

"Your mother tells me you're having second thoughts about going to Washington."

"Seems to me you and Margaret have things under control," said August carefully. "And I'm awful busy . . ."

"But you're our expert. We've been counting on Mr. Jefferson to lead us down the road."

"I'm flattered you think I'm important, Dad," said August. "But I'm sure I'm not so integral to the process. This is between Margaret and the president. I don't see why it is necessary for me to go."

"It's not necessary," said Leland, clearing his throat. "It's just that everyone is looking forward to having you. It's not every day you get to meet the president of the United States."

"You can tell me all about it," said August gently. He paused when he saw his mother in the doorway with his steaming cup of tea. Her eyes were uncharacteristically riveted to the television set, and the dismay on her face caused him to turn and look as well. An un-flattering portrait of Amanda Frank floated over the newscaster's shoulder.

"Lawyers for Responsible Parenting are filing a petition on be-half of Ember Cheyenne Frank, who died last Christmas in her par-ents' care," said the buttery-voiced anchorwoman for Channel 12. "The organization seeks to call attention to the risks associated with high-order multiple births by declaring parents who proceed to term as unfit. Of the eleven children born to the Franks last summer, four have died. Doctors advised the couple to decrease the number of fer-tilized eggs early in the pregnancy, but sources close to the couple say they were discouraged by community and church pressure. Law-yers speaking for the couple asked the court to consider the welfare of the seven surviving children and their older sister."

"What is wrong with this country?" asked Evelyn, angrily switch-ing off the television. "How is prosecuting those poor Franks going to help anyone? It's not going to bring a single one of those babies back to life. "

August rested his hand on his father's shoulder.

"They won't do it, Dad," he said. "It's an utterly frivolous case."

"I'd like to see any one of those lawyers put himself in her place," said Evelyn. "It's easy to pass judgment when it's not happening to you."

From a distance, Leland heard his wife and son's attempts to comfort him, but they were as birdcalls in a sandstorm. The Franks' faith in him was so eroded, he realized, no one had even bothered to give him the news. Mechanically, he walked to the kitchen telephone and dialed Manda's number. Jake picked up on the fourth ring.

"Oh, hi, Pastor Vaughn," he said. "No, don't worry, we're still up."

"I just heard about the lawsuit," said Leland gravely. "I'll come round tomorrow and we'll sort this mess out."

"Don't worry, Pastor," Jake reassured him. "The lawyers say nothing will come of it. No court in America will make it illegal to have kids."

"How is Manda holding up? How are you?"

"We're doing right well," answered Jake. "Manda's upstairs with 'em now. I should get back."

"Listen, I'll come around tomorrow anyway. I have some time between calls."

"Actually, Pastor," said Jake uncomfortably, "the lawyers think it's a good idea if we steer clear of the church for a while. They talk about muddy waters and whatnot."

Leland stood quietly in his kitchen. On the counter, Evelyn's cup of tea had steeped to a dark, unnatural red, and he poured it down the sink. "Well," he said slowly. "If there is anything I can do."

"You've been a great help, Pastor," said Jake. "And Mrs. Vaughn. Don't let it worry you none. We're not losing any sleep."

Leland hung up the telephone. His wife and son hovered worriedly in the archway to the living room.

"If you'll excuse me, I'm going to turn in," the priest said, moving past them toward the stairs. Evelyn and August could do nothing but stand at the landing and watch him go.

"This is going to kill your father," Evelyn said when he was out of earshot. She wanted to shake that newscaster for the matter-of-fact way she'd said the words "church pressure," as if she knew anything about it, for Evelyn didn't for a minute believe that "sources close" to Amanda and Jake would have said any such thing. Her eyes fell on August, leaning against the wall, staring up after Leland, and for the first time in her life, Evelyn wanted to shake him, too. *Do something!* she wanted to shout. *Can't you see your father needs you?*

"He'll be fine," said August. "He doesn't take that sort of thing personally."

"You don't know your father at all, do you?" asked Evelyn. "He takes everything personally. And I think you are a very ungrateful son to pick a fight with him at a time like this."

"How have I picked a fight?" asked August, stunned at his mother's vehemence.

"You should go to Washington with him. You should try to make him happy. He might not have much time left."

"I think he could find a better use for his time than taking a cheese to Washington," said August.

"That is not for you to decide," said Evelyn, struggling to keep her voice under control. "He is your father and you should honor him."

"I do honor him."

"Then why are you leaving?" It came out almost a cry, and Evelyn put her hand over her mouth. She hadn't meant her words to sound so accusatory, but the whole world seemed so irresponsible to her today.

"Mom, I'm sorry," said August softly. "You know I don't want to leave you, but it's something I should have done a long time ago. I'm a grown man and I should be out on my own."

"This is not about me," said Evelyn. "Your father is very sick—"

"Dad is going to outlive us all," her son reassured her. "And I am just down the street. We'll probably see more of each other after I'm gone than we do now. I can still come round to supper, can't I?"

Evelyn was too upset to speak. She dug her nails into the waxy banister.

"Why don't you turn in," said August, giving her a stiff hug. "We've had a long day."

"You go on to bed," said Evelyn, slipping out of his arms and walking into the kitchen, though it was after eleven. "If Manda and Jake have to go talk to lawyers, they are going to need something to eat."

CHAPTER TWENTY-ONE

His mother was convinced the very forces of nature were conspiring to have August move out, for an unexpectedly mild and dry winter had allowed him to make swift progress on construction. All through December he had worked—choosing his perk, clearing his land, digging his septic, expecting at any moment to be shut down by snow or freezing rain. But the new year was a model of temperance, and before he knew it, August was laying his foundation and working with a local contractor to raise the walls of his "cottage," as he called it. In fact, his "cottage" was actually a very thoughtfully designed, five-room, cedar-shingled house, shaped like the letter H with two screened porches, one facing the driveway and one facing the river, enclosing the negative space. With its wide-planked pine floors, unadorned wood work, and white walls, it was humble, but deeply agreeable. August had taken a few drafting courses in college and drawn the blueprints himself. He found he loved working in scale; and having his entire house fit on a piece of blue drafting paper, its walls and windows of a size to be pinched between finger and thumb, its doors little more than morse code telegraphed across a room, let him feel anything was possible. The house he was putting up, he was free to infinitely reimagine.

He had not expected to move until early summer, so by the second week of March when the cottage was nearly finished, August was as surprised as anyone. Other than books, he had very few possessions, and a single U-Haul was all it took to convey him from his old life to his new. Evelyn, who had ridden on the springless seat beside him, wept openly when it was clear nothing was left for her to do—his linens were put away and his silverware drawer stocked, the bags of groceries she had insisted on buying him were neatly distributed between the pantry and refrigerator and his list of emergency numbers tacked to the wall by the door. To her great relief, at the last minute the telephone company had arrived, so, at least, August would not be spending his first night in the wilderness marooned. After he drove his mother home, August returned to his quiet, new house. The rooms smelled of saw-dust and fresh paint, and a wall of book boxes awaited unpacking and alphabetizing. On the counter in the kitchen, his shiny new princess phone sat atop his very own phonebook. August lifted the receiver and listened to his very own dial tone. He thought about calling Evelyn to let her know he arrived home safely; but then he thought of someone else he'd been meaning to call. August cleared his throat, dialed infor-mation, and asked for the University of Virginia's library, Rare Book room, please. It was a quarter to five, someone should still be there. When a woman answered, he requested a librarian by the name of Gillian—he was sorry, he didn't know her last name. Oh yes, Gillian, said the woman on the other end. She was on an extended medical leave. Perhaps someone else might be of service? No. No, thank you, said August. He hung up the phone and stared at it for a long moment. He hadn't even learned her last name. He debated calling back and asking for it—but to what purpose? I built myself a house, he imag-ined telling her. Maybe you'd like to come to dinner sometime? How selfish he'd feel asking a woman on "an extended medical leave" to share his excitement over a new table, set with his mother's displaced china. No, he would leave Gillian, Gillian without a last name, for-ever in the doctor's office, while he slowly went about the buisness of unpacking his books.

His first monastic week passed swiftly; there was much to do, and he found himself even more occupied than he had been at the farm. Already, he saw things he could improve upon, and in the evening hours, in lieu of watching television, he would take a cup of coffee out onto the porch and sketch ideas for additions and little custom-built devices to make his life easier. During the day, he turned his attention to clearing the patch of land he intended for his vegetable garden. Monticello had its rare cultivar vineyards and its acres of English peas, but August's desires were far more modest. He wanted only as much as he could eat with maybe a little left over for his mother to can and put up in his pantry. One morning, two weeks after he moved in, he woke to the first hint of summer wafting through his bedroom window. He fixed himself a morning coffee, pulled on his dirt-stiff work gloves, and stepped outside to set about breaking the ground.

All morning August walked the long rows of his garden, his arms shuddering, his ears cottony with the gas tiller's vibrating roar. The soil was rich with centuries of rotted leaves, streaked red with clay like finely marbled beef. Working Margaret's land had never been as satisfying as this, he thought, as the late morning sun warmed his bare arms and his tiller blade swapped the soil and compost manure he'd spread earlier in the season. The whole while he was plowing her acres and milking her cows, he had never known anything to be missing, but to finally have a plot of his own, he now realized, was like raising a child after years of being an uncle. It was a subtle intensifying of emotional investment, a nervously given, all encompassing commitment, and if the soil smiled for him, he felt it would be like the delirium an infant takes on recognizing his own parent. Jefferson had never had this experience, he realized, almost guiltily. He had a legion of slaves working the land for him, and though much fuss was made when he occasionally stepped into the field to pull weeds of an afternoon, August knew he never had the dirty fingernail connection with the land he claimed to love so much.

August had been tilling for over an hour, raising up and felling a subterranean civilization of purple earthworms and shuttered pill bugs, when his blade caught on something soft and, before he could cut the motor, tugged it, too, to the surface. He knew from having dug the foundation of his house that the soil, so close to the floodplain, was acned with gravel and river rock, but this was soft and pliable, more organic than stone, and his first thought was that he'd dug into the belly of an animal, an opossum or a raccoon. He crouched down and dug around it with his hands, and came up with a parcel, thickly wrapped with oilcloth to keep water from seeping in. Someone had built here before him, he'd discovered, someone other than the Manahoac, for the foundation dig had also turned up remnants of an outhouse—smashed porcelain chamber pots, rotten slats from what appeared to be wall lathing, broken window glass, so thick and bubbled it had to have been hand-blown. August imagined that a family had squatted on the land sometime before the Depression, maybe when the nearby railroad was more of a presence. He asked around—his father had a record, it seemed, of every family who had ever passed through—but no one remembered a house here.

Carefully, he loosened the bundle, sealed tight with red clay. Its husk appeared to be an old black tablecloth, or maybe a panel from a raincoat, but in any case, it had done its job, for when he peeled back the sticky folds he discovered, like the hidden stamen of a tulip, a tiny pair of shoes, barely damp after decades in the earth. The shoes were brown leather, of a style popular a hundred years ago, of a size to fit a five- or six-year-old boy. They were worn down to the nail hobs at the heel but only lightly scuffed at the toe, as if they had belonged to a boy prone to pull back, a hellion of a boy, fighting his parents at their every attempt to lead him. What an extravagance on his mother's part, thought August, gently lifting the shoes on two fingers, to bury still perfectly serviceable footwear. A century ago, when these shoes were worn, leather didn't come cheap, and shoes of this quality would have been passed down when outgrown, to a younger sibling or a needy cousin, or when worn transparent, placed in the church poor box. How deeply his mother must have loved her son to bury what was still of use to someone else. Maybe she simply could not stand to see another child walking in her boy's shoes. Or maybe it was even simpler than that, he thought sadly. Maybe this boy was the end of the line, an only child or the youngest of strangers here; gone, with no one left to inherit.

August felt something wedged in the toe of one of the shoes, and fished out a square of old newsprint, folded into a rough packet. He teased open the paper, taking care not to rip the weakened creases, looking for a name or date, some clue to the boy's identity. Inside he found nothing but a reprinted bit of verse and a pale brown feather. No, not a feather, he realized when he looked more closely, but a loose curl, snipped, no doubt, from the same restive head. He read a bit of the long, sentimental poem that surrounded it, called "The Sick Child."

But oh, my heart is sad to-night!
What means this wild unrest?
My mother, come and lay my head
More closely on thy breast;
And place thy soft, familiar hand
Upon my burning brow—
'Twill calm the wildness of my brain,
That beats so madly now!

"What do you have there?" a voice called from across the field, and for an instant, he had the crazy idea that the voice belonged to the boy's mother, indignant with him for spying on her grief. It took him only a second to realize the spectral voice was too familiar, and when he looked up, he saw Margaret, of all people, walking toward him. She strode across his field as if she owned it, and smiled at him like a day, and not three months had passed since they last spoke.

"I was plowing the garden and this turned up," he answered, taking his cue from her casualness. He handed her the shoes and oil-cloth, and as he had, she lifted the shoes on her palm and studied them as if to divine the lineaments of their owner. He watched her read the poem, all twelve stanzas of it, and bring the lock of hair to her nose, seeking out the clean scent of the boy on whose head it had curled. She looked at him then, as if appreciating his sadness that such things grew in his soil.

"I remember when Polly's feet were this small," said Margaret wistfully.

"So do I . . ."

The last time they'd met hung between them, and August found it difficult to reconcile that furious women with the suddenly nostalgic one before him. The three months had aged her. Wiry gray hairs grew at her temples, escaping the ponytail holder and hidden brown hairpins she used to contain them, and she was even thinner, wearing her bony wrists like a pair of manacles. Margaret straightened and handed the parcel back to him, her swagger gone.

"What do you think I should do with them?" he asked. "They've been here so long, it feels wrong to move them."

"Put them back and plant around them," she answered without hesitation. "It will be our little secret why your rows are crooked."

It was the answer August wanted to hear, and he knelt back over the hole where he'd first unearthed the shoes and dug it a little deeper. He wrapped up the hair and the poem and returned them to the boy's shoe, then sowed them back under, placing a stone on top so that he wouldn't accidentally plow them up again.

"So, what brings you out this way?" he asked, when he was finished and Margaret had not spoken.

"I had a few minutes after milking and I thought I'd swing by and check out the place," she said, not even trying to sound convincing. "Your father told me all about it."

"Well, this is it," said he, gesturing to his field and house. "It's modest, but it's my own."

"I like it." Margaret nodded appreciatively. "Will you show me around?"

August wiped his hands on his pants and led her across the field. It took him no time to walk her through his library and living room, the short galley kitchen that formed the center stroke of the H, and into his office and bedroom.

"You designed this yourself?" she asked appreciatively.

"And built most of it," he answered. "I had help, of course."

"I guess you could have called Francis." She smiled ruefully, and he laughed.

"That would have been a delightful partnership."

They ended the tour back in the kitchen, where, not knowing what else to do, August put on a kettle for some tea.

"I'd like to make these cabinets more like pocket doors," he said, seeing Margaret admiring them. "It would be nice if they slipped back into the wall when I wasn't using them. Then I could enlarge this window looking out onto the river and I think make a more appealing view."

"But it's so nice the way it is." Margaret laughed. "You just can't leave a good thing alone."

He felt the barb in the compliment and said nothing.

"This is a really lovely house, August," she said quickly. "You should be proud of yourself."

"It's coming along."

Margaret stood silently in his kitchen, running her fingers over the butcher-block counter that he'd spent a full day sanding and buffing mellow. He still didn't know why she had come or what she wanted from him.

"Glenn is working out better," she said at last. "He broke up with his girlfriend."

"I'm sorry to hear that," he said. "About the girlfriend. I'm glad he's working out."

"And I apologized to Polly. I don't know what got into me that night," Margaret said, staring out the window. Behind her, the kettle trilled like a bird. "I wanted to apologize to you, too."

"No need," he said. "Things happen."

"No, I have to say it." Margaret turned to him. "I was feeling overwhelmed—"

"Margaret, really," said August, embarrassed, "you don't have to."

"I behaved like a spoiled child," she said, despondently. "I lost control of myself and I'm sorry."

"It's forgotten. Don't worry about it."

August lifted the kettle, but she waved him off. He set it back on the stove without pouring himself a cup either. A breeze blew in off the river and behind Margaret the sheer white curtains that had once hung in his mother's kitchen sighed languidly.

"So, it's done," she said at last. "The cheese is done. Patrick and the crew are coming back this afternoon to film the finishing touches."

"That's great," said August.

"Channel 5 is going to follow it all the way to Washington. Patrick has been doing everything in his power to promote it."

"You must be very happy," August offered.

"People are seeing it on TV and coming out to the farm. Business is up in town because of it. I haven't seen everyone so excited since—" She stopped herself, and he knew she wasn't flattered by the comparison between her cheese and the Frank Eleven.

"I thought you might like to come by this afternoon and see how it turned out," she said at last.

"In time to be on television?" asked August. "Do you want me or Thomas Jefferson?"

"Couldn't you both come?" She smiled weakly.

"I've put my costume away," answered August. "Thomas Jefferson would not have liked the man I had become."

"You certainly picked a fine time to realize that!" declared Margaret woefully. "Can't you put it on one last time and come with us to Washington? You've been there since the beginning. If it weren't for you, I never would have known about the cheese."

"I don't want to be part of the Mammoth Commercial."

"I am doing everything in my power to keep it from *becoming* a commercial," said Margaret.

"You can't protect it," he said sadly, shaking his head at her naïveté. "It already has a life of its own. It's out of your hands. "

Margaret stared at him defiantly, unwilling to concede the truth, yet he could see the crack in her confidence, that inkling of fear that he was right.

"I should go," she said after a long pause. "I have a lot of work to do before the crew arrives." She moved to the door, and he followed her.

"We're leaving next Monday when the kids have off for spring break. I know it would mean a lot to your father if you came along," she said. "And it would mean a lot to me."

"If I came, I would have to come as myself," he said.

They had reached the driveway, and Margaret climbed into her car. "Come as whomever you'd like, just come." She turned and retrieved from the passenger seat a package wrapped in tissue paper. "Here," she said, tossing it through the open window. "I made this for you last Christmas. It's probably too warm to wear it now."

August thanked her and watched her speed down the driveway. Walking back to his house, he unwrapped her present. It was a hand-knit scarf, worked in a pattern of red, white, and blue.

*   *   *

It had been Patrick Lewis's idea to set up the Cheese Cam, with its link to his station's Website. Margaret, who did not own a computer, thought it ridiculous to point a camera at immobile foodstuff, but Patrick had assured her that was exactly the point. It appealed to his younger audience's sense of irony, didn't she see, and wasn't it in her best interest to excite a whole new generation about the wonders of cheese? Since the camera didn't take up any room and she didn't have to watch the live feed, Margaret had agreed. Unbeknownst to his employer, Glenn Mullins had taken to stripping off his flannel shirt and giving the ladies out in Internet Land a little extra man flesh for their money.

Margaret returned from August's to find Patrick and the white satellite news van already parked in her front yard. They were half an hour early, leaving her no time to even run a brush through her hair. But there was nothing to be done about it now, she decided, and those idly watching the Cheese Cam from their offices or dorm rooms saw only her large welcoming smile when she ushered the crew into the barn.

"So where is our friend Mr. Jefferson?" asked Patrick while he clipped a Tootsie Roll–sized microphone to his collar. "He's joining us for the interview today, isn't he?"

"I'm afraid he couldn't make it after all." Margaret smiled. "Other important presidential business to attend to."

"That's too bad." Patrick frowned. "I was counting on him."

"I told you I'd try."

"But he'll be there next Monday, right?" asked the weather man, leading her away from the Cheese Cam. "For the launch? He's half the story."

"I'm sure he will be," Margaret lied, trying to forget August's set face.

"Let me ask you a question." Patrick leaned in a little closer. Behind them, the bearded cameraman arranged his hot clieg lights, lending her barn the aura of a football stadium. "Does that poor sap really think he's Jefferson, or is it just an act?"

It wasn't that Margaret hadn't called August a sap a hundred times in her heart, but hearing the words from someone else made her surprisingly protective. "Of course he doesn't really think he's Jefferson," she said hotly. "But he's convinced Jefferson still has something to offer the people of today."

"Fashion tips?" quipped Patrick Lewis.

"Jefferson believed in the unlimited potential of our country," Margaret said. "August tries to remind people of that."

"Well, I like it better when he sticks to the cheese. We'll keep him on message next Monday."

"When you're ready," said the cameraman.

"Since we have no Jefferson, let's just take some background footage," Patrick said. "Margaret, do whatever it was you were going to do, and I'll make up something later. Remind people there's less than a week left before the cheese goes to Washington. Blah, blah, blah."

Margaret tried not to be insulted that this most pivotal moment in the entire process was being reduced to "background footage." She tried to ignore the camera, though the hot lights on her face gave her the unpleasant sensation of standing guilty before Patrick Lewis and all of his viewers, a feeling that only intensified when she drove her specially designed blue steel trier deep into the cheese's heart and removed a plug. Any one of a hundred frailties might be hidden beneath that innocuously smooth, mellow, protective rind—her cheese could be bitter or gassy, slitty or rancid; the curd could be too short and crumbly or weak and pasty—and she would never know. What she feared most in such a large cheese was whey taint, a sharp, utensilly bitterness caused by trapped pockets of unpressed whey left in the flesh. Should she draw out the trier and find a specimen riddled with holes and reeking of ammonia, it would be only what she deserved, Margaret thought grimly. Allowing a news crew access to this reckoning had been sheer hubris on her part.

The yard-long, pencil-thin cylinder of cheese on the trier looked fine at first glance. It left the requisite sheen of fat on the instrument, it displayed a close, firm texture without being corky, and best of all, it was free of stray holes. Margaret brought the specimen to her nose and breathed deeply: a nutty, faintly barny smell, not at all unpleasant or fruity with overferment. She broke off a small piece at the end, noting that it ripped cleanly, and when she pressed it between her fingers, it gave, but not too much. Margaret was ecstatic. Given all her improvisation and all her makeshift equipment, the cheese was turning out better than she could have hoped. She broke off another small bit and placed it on the tip of her tongue: sharp and salty, with a hint of alfalfa, milder than cheddar but with its own unique tang. It was a bit of a mélange (only because she knew her own milk so well could she detect the faint flintiness of Sam Abbott's pasture), but on the whole it tasted very similar to its smaller, better-bred cousins ripening in rows downstairs in her cheese cellar. Margaret tried to hide her undeniable relief and present a calm, assured face to the cameras, but inside she was screaming with joy. Her cheese was delicious. It would not embarrass her.

She pushed the plug back into place and carefully removed the trier, leaving the rind once more intact. Patrick Lewis, she saw, had wandered off and was idly forking hay with one of her pitchforks, tossing it in the air and watching it lazily drift to the ground. The cameraman had his lens trained on her, but he, too, seemed bored, not for a moment appreciating the tension of the moment. She had only herself to blame. She had acted so confident these past few months that no one suspected she might be eating herself alive with worry. Margaret longed to throw herself into someone's arms— Polly's or August's—and sob with relief, to pour out her fears now that they were banished. But she had only an indifferent cameraman and Patrick Lewis, wasting her hay.

"It's ready," she said at last.

"Great," said Patrick, tossing aside her pitchfork. "It looks like we pulled it off."

"What do you mean?" asked Margaret.

Patrick unclipped his microphone and handed it to his cameraman. "No need to thank me," he said, with a wink. The cameraman unplugged and folded up his lights. Together, he and Patrick walked to the van. "Check-out the ten o'clock news," Patrick called as he climbed into the van. "We'll run you tonight on the Great Cheese Countdown."

CHAPTER TWENTY-TWO

In the morning, before she caught the bus to school, Polly stood against the spine of hatch marks in her kitchen doorway, her age and height carved into the wood like that of her mother and grandfather and all the other Pricketts who had sought to graft their growth onto this old house; and though the frame still read sixty inches (two inches shorter than Margaret had been at the same age, but an inch taller than her grandfather), she knew it was wrong. She couldn't prove it—not by the door—but she was smaller. She had to be.

Her friends were no help proving her theory. If anything, she was larger than life to them now that her mother and her farm were constantly on TV, and the other students, boys and girls whose lack of interest in her had previously contributed to her social malnourishment, now crowded around her like a warm layer of fat, causing Polly to take up more space in the hallway, in the lunchroom, in her seat on the bus. Her shadow cast itself like a flagpole as she crossed the schoolyard, but she knew, despite all these outward signs, that she was nothing but a comma, a bean, a mote, for how else could she explain the way his eyes skipped over her every day in class, as if she had permanently shrunk below his line of vision.

Mr. March handed back their exams in seventh period, laying each one facedown on the desk. Polly tried to catch his eye as she did every day, but today was no different from last week or the week before. She had worn her black turtleneck sweater and her jeans that were ripped at the knee. She wore her hair exactly as she had that day in the newspaper room, and kept her face free of the makeup he had removed. She had taken great pains on her test to give the kinds of answers she knew he wanted and she hoped he might read in them the passion that threatened to overwhelm her this long, cold winter of her exile from him. She didn't know what she had done to make him angry, but she must have done something, for when she flipped over her exam, she saw it was given a C like everything else she had turned in this semester. What had been an A or even an A+ last fall had slipped to average or even below in the new year.

True to her word, she had told no one about what happened, not even Bethany, and because she hadn't been able to talk about it, she had become like a hypochondriac with a secret pain, magnifying and worrying the memory until she was consumed with it. As he walked the rows, she closed her eyes and replayed the memory of his kiss for perhaps the thousandth time, shivering at his touch, moaning at how apathetically she had stood by, letting his mouth take its own direction without any input from her. She knew tongues and hands went places beyond the obvious. She knew clothes came off and pledges were demanded and given, but she didn't know in what order or what initiative she should have taken. Her heart sank at how inexperienced she must have seemed to him. If only she could have a second chance. If only he would flip off the classroom's fluorescent lights and press her against the pink, blue, and green window-shade Map of the World, though the chalk tray might be digging into the small of her back she would give back this time, with a passion that would bring him to his knees.

"Miss Marvel, will you be joining us today?" he asked, startling her. Everyone had pulled their desks into a circle while she sat daydreaming.

"Sorry," she mumbled, filling the gap between Bethany and Drew Powell. Drew sniggered as he opened his notebook.

"Today we'll be discussing the biggest scandal of Jefferson's presidency, and a cloud that still darkens his reputation two hundred years later. Can anyone tell me what happened in the winter of 1802?"

Polly raised her hand, but his eyes skipped lightly over her.

"Miss Fraser," said Mr. March.

Bethany glanced at her friend beside her. Polly lowered her hand. "James Callender broke the story of Sally Hemings," she said.

"Correct. And what was that story?"

"That the president had fathered several children with a slave, the half-sister of his dead wife."

"And who was James Callender?"

Polly raised her hand.

"Miss Fraser?"

"He was an alcoholic newspaperman hired by Mr. Jefferson to smear John Adams during the campaign of 1800," said Bethany. "When Jefferson didn't make Callender postmaster of Richmond, he turned on the president."

Polly sat miserably in her desk. Her friend's bright face followed Mr. March like a sunflower.

"Correct. And he cited as proof a son named Thomas, who bore a remarkable, if 'dusky' resemblance to the president. The actual paternity of the Hemings children has never been conclusively proven, but it hardly matters, does it? Sally Hemings was Jefferson's property. If the president's personality did not make it probable, the evils of slavery certainly made it possible. Sally was his to use as he pleased."

Drew Powell raised his hand. "I saw a movie that said they fell in love in Paris."

"Which brings up an interesting point," said Mr. March, and this time, Polly noticed he glanced fleetingly in her direction. "If we are to believe the Hemings oral tradition, Jefferson and Sally fell in love when he was forty-four and she a mere fourteen, and their relationship continued for thirty-eight years. It invites the question, is love possible for two people of such radically different ages and stations in life?"

For the first time since Christmas, Mr. March seemed to be speaking directly to her. Polly raised her hand and after a brief hesitation, he nodded in her direction.

"While it's not likely," said Polly carefully, "I think it's possible for two extraordinary people to fall in love no matter how uneven the circumstances."

"And what are your arguments in favor?"

"In a democracy, we are taught to judge by individual merits, not by age or social rank. Just because she was young doesn't mean she didn't have something to offer. And being older and more powerful, he had much he could teach her." She held his eyes and hoped he would read in them how deeply she missed him.

Mr. March studied her for a long minute, then slowly turned away. "The answer is no," he said simply, and with a tinge of sadness. "There can be no honest love without equality. No matter what Jefferson told himself, Sally Hemings had no free will. In his *Farm Register*, he refers to his slaves as his children. With no education and no rights, she was no better than a child, and for her to tell her descendants the president saw her as an equal partner would have been self-delusional."

No one in the class spoke. Bethany looked over at her friend with the deepest sympathy.

"Miss Marvel, do you have anything to add?"

"No, s——," she started miserably. "No, sir."

At the end of class, Mr. March passed out another round of paper, and groans went up before the students realized it was no pop quiz, but a mimeographed permission slip.

"When history happens in one's own backyard, a good student owes it to himself to bear witness. This is for you to accompany the New Mammoth Cheese to Washington. Mrs. Andrews and I will be chaperoning two classes, this period and fifth period. Make sure your parents understand it is a three-day trip, and that you'll need to bring money for food."

The bell rang and everyone rose to leave. "Miss Marvel, will you remain a moment, please?" said her teacher.

Polly hesitated in the doorway. Slowly, she walked back to his desk. From beneath the stack of extra permission slips, she caught the silvery gleam of his car keys.

"Miss Marvel, I'm worried about your grades," he said, retrieving his briefcase from his bottom drawer. "They've slipped dramatically since last semester."

"I know," said Polly.

"I always hate to see a good student get lazy, and I have to tell you, I'm very disappointed in your progress."

"I don't think I'm doing anything differently," Polly challenged.

"Your writing has gotten sloppier. You're daydreaming in class. You're making assumptions you have no business making."

"If you mean today—"

"I do," he said, opening his top drawer and transferring a half-eaten sandwich to his briefcase. It looked to be some pale, thin lunch meat on Wonder bread, and the thought crossed Polly's mind that such processed food was bad for him. She bit her lip, however, and said nothing. "I thought you understood the power dynamic at work in our society, but it seems your head is filled with romantic illusions."

Where was the man who gave her a ride home after the humiliating fight with her father? Where was the man who gently tipped his face to hers? He seemed so distant and cold to her now.

"I think you've changed toward me since what happened," she blurted.

He looked at her blankly. "What do you mean?"

Polly felt a strange panic well up inside her at the thought of saying it out loud. "You know," she practically whispered. "In the newspaper room."

Mr. March measured her over the rim of his glasses. "Is that what this is about?" he asked. "Is that why you've been acting so strange the last few months?"

"I haven't been acting strange," said Polly.

"It's nothing to be embarrassed about," said Mr. March, giving her a wry, sympathetic smile. "Young girls get crushes on their teachers all the time, and occasionally they get carried away. I'd forgotten all about it."

Polly stared at him in disbelief. He was making no sense to her. "But it wasn't just me," she stammered. "You—you kissed me."

Mr. March looked at her sternly. "You can't believe I initiated that," he said. "It would be wrong. You're only a girl."

She watched him load his briefcase with papers, a half-eaten speckled plum in a plastic bag, a ballpoint pen. Inside the briefcase, she saw a red and white pack of Malboros, the most colonial of cigarettes.

"If you'll excuse me," he said. Polly stood back and let him pass. She could only remember what it felt like to have his good opinion by measuring how badly it felt to have lost it. It used to be that when she raised her hand, even if he didn't call on her, he would reward her with a secret smile that said, I would much rather hear what you have to say, Miss Marvel, but one must at least pretend equanimity. Before, he never left the classroom without finding her eyes and wishing her a silent Till Tomorrow, but now, he walked out as if she held no more weight in his mind than a nub of chalk or a dusty eraser.

She walked downstairs in a daze and was surprised to see Pastor Vaughn in earnest conversation with Bethany, who rolled her eyes in Polly's direction. He was a somber figure against the wild-eyed, matted-beard Rebel mascot on the wall. Having a priest in school must be bad luck, thought Polly, like having a crow in the house.

"Well, hello," he said, having noticed her as she tried to inch past. She couldn't bear one of his stupid jokes today.

"Hey, Pastor Vaughn," she said.

"I was just telling Bethany how much our neighbor Manda would appreciate a visit from her friends about now."

"I'd love to go," gushed Bethany. "It's just that with school and this trip coming up . . ."

"I hope the Mammoth Cheese is no obstacle to helping your neighbor," said Leland gravely. "It's supposed to unite us as a community."

"Oh, it has!" Bethany assured him. "It's just that—"

"I'll go," interrupted Polly.

"Really?" Pastor Vaugn smiled delightedly. "That's marvelous. I'm just on my way to see your principal about donating the school's Spring Fling proceeds to the Franks' legal defense fund."

"I'll go today," said Polly, ignoring Bethany's huge eyes upon her.

"That's a good girl," he said, and rewarded her with an approving pat on the arm.

Outside on the bus, Bethany turned to her friend and said, "You wouldn't catch me dead out there. That place is cursed. You know they're talking about putting her in jail for killing her babies."

"She didn't kill them," replied Polly. "They died."

"She has a violent history. My cousin said Manda brought a shotgun to school in eighth grade and pulled it on a teacher. And you'll never guess who it was."

"I don't care," said Polly.

"Mr. March," cried Bethany gleefully. "Our very own. He's a man who inspires grand passion."

Outside her window, Polly saw her teacher cross between two buses to the parking lot. She still remembered the weight of his keys in her palm the day she took them, and how the leather key chain smelled of tobacco and motor oil. But having told no one, she had no corroboration, no hearsay witness to turn to. Tell me it happened, she wanted to demand of Bethany. Remind me what it was like.

"You know, I used to wonder what you saw in Mr. March," her friend said, craning her neck to watch their teacher slip into his battered Carmen Ghia. "I mean he's not classically handsome or anything. But he has this magnetism about him. He smolders, you know."

"He's not so great," said Polly tightly.

"Oh, come on," said Bethany. "You have to see it. He's dangerous. I can never tell if he likes me or hates me."

"Of course he likes you," Polly said shortly. "He likes everybody."

"Do you think so?" asked Bethany, with the self-absorbed anxiety only the very pretty can manage. "Because I sometimes get the impression he's waiting for me to say something stupid, so he can pounce, you know. I think he's a cat person more than a dog person. He's secretive that way."

"You're thinking about it way too much," said Polly coldly. "I don't believe he cares about anything we do."

"Did you guys have a fight or something?" asked Bethany, putting her hand on Polly's arm. "Because you sound very down on Mr. March."

"I'm not down on him. I just don't think he's God's answer to Life, that's all."

"Listen, I would never try to come between you two," Bethany said in deep seriousness. "I think he's really sexy and all, but what you had was special. I would never get between that."

"We didn't have anything," Polly shook her off. "He's just a teacher. He's old, for Christ's sake."

"Got your period?" asked Bethany kindly. "Because I've got some Tampax if you need it."

After milking, Polly informed her mother she was going to the Franks'. Margaret gave her two frozen casseroles she had been meaning to deliver, and the business card of her divorce attorney. "She handles custody cases, too," Margaret told her.

Polly had not been back to her neighbors' since the night she ran away from home. Their house is not cursed, she told herself, walking the long, shadowy driveway. But it was hard not to think so. The hulking building was dark except for a light in the kitchen and two glaring floodlights, illuminating the dog pen on one side and a patch of bare dirt on the other. Since Ember Cheyenne's death, the Franks had kept even more to themselves. Rumors circulated about what went on inside the house. At school, Polly heard the last infant to die had choked to death while Manda and Jake were in the bedroom having sex. Ever since Polly could remember, Manda had been a magnet for this sort of talk. Years ago, Bethany's cousin, who was in the same grade as Manda, told the girls the doctors had pumped a gallon of sperm from Manda's stomach, and when they'd had it analyzed, they found it came from five different men. But Polly had seen the woman's grief-hollowed face that night, and she for one did not believe the stories.

Having learned from last time, Polly avoided the front door and entered the house through the garage. It was junkier even than the front yard, packed tight with torn cardboard cartons of donations. It seemed strangers were treating the Franks like victims of a hurricane, in need of an entirely new secondhand life, so they sent chipped plates and pilled sweaters, a waffle iron, and out-of-style shoes, along with baby clothes and toys. Unable to use most of it, and too tired to cart it to the dump, Manda and Jake let it accumulate in their garage, until there was no room for the truck or minivan. Polly inched her way around the boxes and finally reached the steps leading into the house.

"Hello, Manda?" she called, sticking her head inside. The door was unlocked and she let herself into the utility room. "Manda?"

Around the corner, Polly saw a massive, gray-haired black woman seated at the kitchen table. Before her, on the place mat like a chicken dinner, lay one of the Frank children. As Polly watched, the woman poured something thick and white into a raised tube. It took a moment for Polly to realize the tube snaked under the child's shirt and into its stomach, but when she did, she thought she would vomit.

"Who are you?" asked Polly.

"That's Cecile," said Manda, walking into the kitchen with two more of the babies. "The lawyers hired her to help during the day. What are you doing here?"

"I brought you these," said Polly, placing the casseroles in front of Cecile, unsure if she was a nurse or a maid. "I thought I could help out a little."

Manda didn't seem impressed by the offer. She strapped the babies into two food-stained bouncy seats and handed them rattles, which they promptly dropped.

Cecile glanced up from the baby on the table. "Missus Frank," she said in her Deep South accent, "you need to get some more formula."

Manda nodded but made no move to leave the kitchen. "I'm sorry you're getting sued," said Polly. "That must suck."

"Missus Frank!" said Cecile.

"I heard you the first time," snapped Manda. "Let's go outside," she said to Polly. "The formula is in the garage."

Polly followed her out back out into the garage, where she had failed to notice Jake's library of white plastic shelving along the walls. Here, they stored enough diapers and canned milk to last the children a year.

"That woman has a sass mouth," said Manda, as soon as the door was closed behind them. "I know she's spying for them. She listens to every word I say."

"It's good to have help, though," offered Polly.

"Her salary is being added to the lawyers' fees."

The box of formula Manda wanted was on the top shelf, and she pulled two old paint cans around to boost herself. Polly watched her former baby-sitter stretch, and wondered what it was men found in her to desire. Before she was pregnant, Manda was skinny and muscled like a boy, her long black hair the only concession to femininity. She wore flannel shirts and work boots; she raised dogs and shot a gun. Now, still pendulous with pregnancy weight, she at least looked to Polly like a woman. Her hips had swelled and her breasts, loose underneath a ratty sweatshirt, rustled like sneaking animals. But maybe hypersexuality was simply in her gene pool. Everyone knew the Sawyer girls were sluts, just as all the Sawyer boys went to jail, and it had been this way at least for all of Polly's lifetime. Manda's sister Nina had four babies of her own—two of them black—and her other sister, Susan, moved to Raleigh when the father of her three boys repeatedly violated his restraining order. Perhaps there had been a hint of this familial fecundity about Manda even before, when everything on the surface had been flat and angular.

"Is it true you pulled a gun on Mr. March?" Polly asked.

Manda looked at her sharply. "That was a long time ago," she replied.

"Not so long," replied Polly. "Ten years."

"I don't remember."

"You don't remember if you pulled a shotgun on someone?"

"If I did, he deserved it," answered the older woman.

Manda had once let Polly hold her gun. She was ten and had pleaded until Manda finally emptied the chamber of bullets and set her rifle on the girl's shoulder. Polly still remembered how heavy and cold it had been against her collarbone. She had fit her eye to the sight and aimed at one of her mother's cows in the field. BAM, Manda had said, startling her so badly she'd dropped it with a clatter.

"If what he did was so awful, why didn't you tell someone?" Polly asked.

"Nothing ever happens to men like that," replied Manda. "And anyway," she said loudly, as if to someone eavesdropping, "they can't use that against me in a custody hearing. I was a juvenile." Manda threw down an empty box Jake had left when he'd removed the last tin of milk, and dragged out the sagging case beneath it, motioning for Polly to open the door back into the house.

"Mr. March kissed me."

Polly didn't know why she said it, except that she had to tell somebody or she feared she might lose the certainty of it altogether. Manda looked at her pityingly.

"You're lucky it ended there."

CHAPTER TWENTY-THREE

When the town was done, Margaret no longer even recognized her cheese.

Or to be more precise, it was there, her creation, hidden somewhere inside the red, white, and blue bandstand that had been erected around it, and beneath the bunting canopy that crowned it, and like an allegiant wizard, peering out from behind stars and striped curtains, pulled back with gold braided ties. It rested on its hay-strewn dais surrounded by a court of papier-mâché cows, iconographic cows, black and white cows, Holstein cows, grazing a field of names and logos. Proudly sponsored by: Hollywell Farm. Speedy Sheet Metal. First Virginia Savings and Loan. A generator powered an ivy vine of flashing lights that spelled out *God Bless America*, and in each upper corner, like the cardinal winds on an antique map, was suspended an angel, Gabriel-like, touting the cheese's mammoth arrival.

It had taken Pastor Vaughn the better part of an hour to convince Margaret to allow her beloved Cheshire inside the confused church-and-state coach that was to convey it to Washington. The children had worked so hard, he told her; she should consider the permits and the police escorts and the publicity and the president. What would people think if she backed out now? And after all, argued Pastor Vaughn, the trappings were no more important than the route they took to get there.

In the end, she gave up, for what else was she to do? Margaret closed her eyes and allowed the ten strong men Pastor Vaughn had brought along with him to carefully lower the cheese onto a specially fashioned round wooden board, then convey that to the monstrosity of a float hitched to the back of Leland's bus. Somberly, she accompanied it to the park, where it currently rested in state, waiting for the early-morning dedication and send-off.

"So, where's our Jefferson?" asked Patrick Lewis, pushing his way through the crowd to where Margaret sat dejectedly on a picnic table. "It's almost nine o'clock."

The small semicircular pull-off was now overflowing with towns-people and news reporters, sitting on the hoods of cars, eating sweet, melting Krispy Kremes and sipping Cremora-bleached coffee from Styrofoam cups. Between the crisp weather and the brass of the Three Chimneys Junior High School marching band, the morning felt like the evening of a high school football game, with all its anticipatory mingling and laughter. Margaret was learning firsthand how little it mattered what a parade might be for—the parade itself was reason enough for most.

"I don't know," she answered. "I thought he'd be here by now."

"This is quite a turnout," he said. "Happy birthday, Adams Brooke."

After his last visit, Margaret had come to loathe the easy famil-iarity of the features reporter. She still could not tell when he was being cynical or sincere, for the two attitudes had emulsified into some new hybrid emotion—an appreciative contempt, or amused patriot-ism—that he seemed perfectly comfortable adopting. From the eager, greedy look on his face, Margaret knew the crowd that turned out for her cheese meant ratings for him, but at the same time, he seemed to honestly believe a mammoth procession was exactly what this country needed right now, and that the very act of forward move-ment, if it held off nihilism for another day, was worth the effort. She tried to let go and share his ease with the ambiguities of the situa-tion, reminding herself, as she had been for days, that she was no Dr. Frankenstein to recoil in horror at what she had created. It was only a cheese, for Christ's sake. It was only a cheese.

"Oh, wait a minute." Patrick Lewis stood up on the seat of the picnic table. "I think I see our Mr. Jefferson now."

Margaret leapt to her feet beside the reporter, surprised at her own sense of relief. She scanned the tops of heads but couldn't make him out, until the reporter pointed to a figure walking up the road, dressed in an auburn wig and breeches and wearing a deep-cuffed jacket. Even from far away, however, Margaret could see that this was not her Jefferson. The man approaching was shorter and squatter, with a belly like a Franklin stove.

"It's not him," she said.

"Who cares," replied Patrick Lewis. "It's *a* Jefferson. That's good enough." He gestured for his cameraman to follow and set off to interview the newcomer, leaving Margaret to sink back down, more depressed than ever.

In the end, Patrick Lewis had no shortage of Jeffersons to interview, for over the next half hour, ten more appeared, none of them August: members of "Living History Associates" who rented themselves out for congressional functions, or laypersons who made the rounds of Revolutionary War reenactments. There were tall Jeffersons and short Jeffersons, a black Jefferson, and even a female Jefferson in the spirit of Pope Joan, her chest tightly wrapped and tucked under her double-breasted jacket. Margaret had never fit August into the larger canvas of historical re-creationists, and was surprised to learn there was a flourishing cottage industry in the resurrection of great men, and women for that matter, for Martha Washington, too, appeared at Leland-Madison Park, along with a Dolly Madison in voluminous petticoats. Wherever they walked, the crowd, intrigued by these little bubblings up from the great historical magma that flowed just beneath the surface of American culture, congregated around them, anxious to play along and quiz the great about the greatness of their day. A lead Jefferson eventually emerged, a man who looked even more uncannily like the original than August did, and who could boast of having once played the Republican National Convention. Margaret saw him giving a lengthy interview to Patrick Lewis and felt jealous on August's behalf, until she remembered he didn't do this sort of thing anymore.

Margaret drifted through the crowd, glancing over the shoulders of Girl Scout Troop 419, who had just finished painting a banner in large red letters—*Three Chimneys Proudly Presents the New*

Mammoth Cheese—though Margaret didn't see where they would fit it on the already congested float. Pastor Vaughn stood beside her creation, posing for photographers. When he saw her, he beckoned her to join him, but Margaret waved him off. She drifted over to Polly, whom she found with her friend Bethany and the other students chosen to man the milking stools before the papier-mâché Holsteins. They were huddled around a palm-sized television screen, watching the live feed of the Mammoth Cheese. Seeing her mother, Polly shot her a warning look. Earlier this morning, she had made it clear she was traveling with the school group, and, as such, expected to be left alone. Margaret was not so old as to have forgotten the deregulatory joys of a middle school field trip, and so, with some sadness, she had provided pocket money and a pledge to distance herself.

At 9:45, Leland tapped the microphone of St. Barnabas's portable PA system and called the milling crowd to attention. He stood beside a bronze marker erected by the Jaycees bearing a bust of the Elder John Leland.

"Friends and neighbors, presidents and first ladies," began Pastor Vaughn jovially once, after several promptings, they quieted. The pastor himself looked happier and more purposeful than he had in months, thought Margaret. He was as invigorated by the crowd as she was drained by it.

"In 1801," said Leland, "our brothers in Cheshire, Massachusetts, created a twelve-hundred-pound cheese to honor Thomas Jefferson for his defense of religious liberty. That cheese was conceived by the Elder John Leland, a great cleric, and a good friend of my family, who thirteen years previously sat here in this very spot and convinced James Madison of the necessity of the First Amendment. It is my great honor to stand in place of that intrepid preacher today and inaugurate the new Mammoth Cheese for a new president. In the spirit of the great Jefferson, our newly elected Adams Brooke has vowed to defy the tyranny of special interests and corporate greed to give America back to her citizens, the individual farmers and small entrepreneurs that made this country great. It is with gratitude equaling that of our Northern brothers that we re-create their historic cheese and, as a community, escort it to the nation's capital, where it might attain the stature of the original."

Leland paused, then cried out like a prophet for a new crusade, "Now, my good friends and fellow citizens—Cheese-ho, and on to Washington!"

Amidst the cheers, Margaret cast a final look over the crowd, and reluctantly took her place beside Leland inside the bus. Just outside the park, on Route 20, an Orange County sheriff stopped traffic, while two state motorcycle troopers hit their sirens to begin the procession. Leland turned the key in the ignition.

"We're off!" he cried.

As the cheese pulled out, the stream of supporters returned to the corridor of cars parked along Route 20 and waited their turn to fold into the line. Margaret looked back at her neighbors, still cheering, waving miniature American flags. Her imagination had always taken her as far as the cheese's generation, and if she was feeling ambitious, to the moment it was unveiled before the president—but the middle path, how she would get there, she realized, had, in her mind, been consigned to someone else. No, she now admitted, not just to anyone, but to August. August was by her side, helping her navigate the media and crowds, and leading her safely into Washington. But August hadn't come. She dropped into her seat. If she had reacted differently that night in the barn, would he be here beside her right now? When she rejected him, could she have foreseen how greatly she would miss him?

Margaret sank back in her seat as the car horns honked and her neighbors sped her on her way. She was so lost in misery, she barely even noticed that Leland had stopped the VW not half a mile beyond the park, to the annoyance of the police escort and the dismay of those still waiting to join in behind.

"Do we have room for one more?" he turned and asked Margaret, who upon recognizing the reason for the delay sat up straight and, for the first time all day, felt the faintest stirring of pleasure. There was a God after all, thought she, glancing guiltily at the minister, when his son, dressed as no one more exalted than himself, opened the passenger-side door and somberly climbed in behind her.

"Badger."

By eleven o'clock, the sun had risen high enough that Polly could peel off her woolen gloves and pretend to milk the stiff paper udders before her bare-handed. For the past hour, she had flung candy at the boys and girls, the parents, the grandfathers on their turgid tractors who lined the route to watch, some in dull wonderment, some thrilled to be caught on camera by the newscopter that had flown over the parade for the ten o'clock send-off. Some waved signs that said *We Love You, Patrick!* while others shielded their eyes against the bright April sun, rooted like scarecrows, and about as interested, waiting for the mile-long procession to pass so that they might cross the road to the work waiting for them on the other side.

For her part, as much as she hated playing handmaid to a cheese, Polly couldn't help but get caught up in the excitement of the day. She felt very important perched high above the crowd, raining candy down upon them like milk caramel hail. She was amazed that she lived in a country where traffic could be held up and red lights run, simply because her mother had filled out a permit wishing it so. Before today, she had believed the movement of cars in their courses to be as eternal and uninterruptible as the changing of the tides, having only once before seen the busy world give way in a manner approaching the likes of this, and that was for her grandfather's funeral, where only one lone pickup truck had dared jump the procession— "a motherfucker," her father had called him, "with no respect for the dead."

Beside her, Bethany pointed to the side of the road. "Raccoon!" she cried.

Polly wondered how she could have ever liked Bethany Fraser, who now sat at the next cow over, tossing candy with the self-conscious largesse of a homecoming queen in training. She had monopolized Mr. March all morning, offering to help him take his head count, fetching him coffee. Polly herself had avoided him, taking care he should see her not seeing him. Now he rode behind them in the bright yellow school bus with the other chaperon and students. She wondered what he was doing to pass the time.

Slowly, so slowly, the miles ticked by. The procession rolled past ranch houses and farms and cows grazing in the alley pastures of power line rights-of-way. Beside the float, sallow children pedaled their bikes, their hands outstretched for candy—*Gimme some! Gimme some!* they shouted, weaving into one another and laughing before veering off down dirt driveways, their winter-grimy parkas flapping behind them. Just past Locust Grove Elementary School, skid marks like a black rainbow careened out of the driveway and into the ditch. They had been traveling for nearly two hours and had gone only fifteen miles.

"Skunk!" Drew Powell yelled, and then everyone smelled it at once, the gasoline perfume of roadkill, almost pleasant in its olfactory fuck-you. "Dead but not forgotten" was the message of the skunk.

At the intersection of Route 3, where the procession would have to turn right to continue on to Fredericksburg, the motorcycle cops in front stopped and dismounted. The cheese, still traveling by its own momentum, pushed the light, tin-can VW bus forward another few feet before coming to a standstill. They stopped and sat for thirty eternal minutes to give traffic behind them a chance to drive around. A few of the drivers were angry at having been held up so long, but many more found the improbable spectacle delightful—and honked their support as they drove past. Two scrawny boys in camouflage hunting vests sped past in their jacked-up pickup. "Hey, y'all," they shouted, "who cut the cheese?" *Who cut the cheese?* Polly and the other kids on the float had never heard a joke so funny. A few cars later, another teenage boy with a bristling flattop yelled the same thing, and about five minutes later, they were treated to the same witticism again. *Who cut the cheese? Who cut the cheese?* The twentieth time they'd heard the joke, even Drew Powell, unrelenting propagator of the classic "A monkey says *what?*" had to admit its charm had considerably faded.

*   *   *

With the fervor of one following the Stations of the Cross, Leland slowed to read each historical marker they passed. Just think about Constitution Highway, he said. It begins all the way back at Monticello and connects Jefferson with his bosom friend Madison's home at Montpelier. It doglegs through Orange, then sweeps past Leland-Madison Park, but there a marvelous transformation takes place—it changes from road to time line. Just a few miles from where we began, my children, said Leland, our Colonial heritage sputters out. And then, mile by mile and field by field, we pass through four long years of bloody Civil War.

And the silver historical markers planted like wildflowers along the side of the road proved his point. Within miles, they ceased referring to the glories of ratified amendments and personal liberties and turned their attention instead to the minutiae of battle movements, to flanking and fires and midnight retreats. At ten miles an hour, half the speed of a victorious cavalry, but twice that of an exhausted, gangrenous foot soldier, the Mammoth Cheese rolled its way deep into the heart of Confederate Virginia. Here, a terse Greek Revival house still flying its Rebel flag gave way to a tender young strawberry farm, gave way to the dusty road leading off to Mine Run and New Hope Church, gave way to a giant white billboard shouting, *America, Get Out of the United Nations*. Route 20, Constitution Highway, was taking them into the country known as the Wilderness, a name earned back in the 1700s, when old growth was stripped away for ironwork furnaces, leaving nothing behind but stunted oaks and gnarled pines, secondary growth and thick tangles of underbrush. *Here was one of the bloodiest battles of the war*, said Leland. *My granddaddy told me that in the woods at night in early May, you can still hear the screams of the wounded, roasting in the numerous brushfires that ignited combustible Wilderness.* August and Margaret said nothing, for each was momentarily taken back to childhood, when after hearing the same story, they had lain awake long, sleepless May nights listening for the footfall of ghostly soldiers.

Twenty miles and three hours after they left Leland-Madison Park, the cheese made a lefthand turn into the split-rail-fenced battlegrounds at Chancellorsville, the site of Lee's greatest victory, Stonewall Jackson's mortal wounding, and the hallowed spot chosen for the procession's lunch break. In the end, Leland had won Margaret over with practicalities: The battlefield at Chancellorsville had a parking lot big enough to accommodate everyone who had come along with the cheese, as well as bathroom facilities and picnic tables.

"What the hell are those?" asked Margaret as they pulled up to the Visitors' Center. Dressed in various shades of gray, several dozen dirty, bearded men stood at attention for the cheese's approach.

"From the looks of it, I'd say it was the infantry," replied August behind her.

A gold Lexus pulled in next to the bus, and Bob Crenshaw bounded out. One soldier in his mid-sixties, less bedraggled than the rest, stepped forward to meet him. He carried over his arm a blue cotton umbrella and wore upon his head a tall, mangy beaver hat.

"General Extra Billy," Crenshaw barked out, saluting. "It is indeed a great honor."

Margaret leapt from the bus. "Bob, what is going on?"

"I'd like to introduce you to Brigadier General William 'Extra Billy' Smith, who led the Gordonsville Grays, among others regiments, during the Battle of Chancellorsville. He was already elected governor of Virginia when a few months later he led his troops on to Gettysburg, isn't that right, General?"

"It is, sir," drawled the older man. "It was my honor to serve the Confederacy as both a soldier and a politician."

"Bob, what does this have to do with our cheese?" asked Margaret.

"Mister Jefferson belongs to us all, ma'am," replied Extra Billy. "'I support the State governments in all their rights, as the most competent administrations for our domestic concerns and the surest bulwarks against antirepublican tendencies.' First inaugural."

It took only moments for Patrick Lewis and the Fox News van to descend on the Civil War reenactors and their colorful general. Billy called his men to order and made them run through a series of drills for the camera, while Margaret watched in mounting dismay. Patrick Lewis turned his microphone back to the cheesemaker.

"By bringing the cheese to Chancellorsville, are you trying to send the president a message on states' rights?" he asked. "Is this a neo-Confederate cheese?"

"Patrick, turn the camera off," Margaret ordered, before stalking back to the bus. "Leland," she asked. "Did you know about this?"

"Margaret, dear, I don't see the harm," answered the priest. "Extra Billy was quite a character, you know. My great-great-granduncle served in Congress with him."

"This is becoming a circus," said Margaret grimly. "If you don't do something, I'm going home and you can deliver this cheese yourself."

"Let me see what I can do," said August, climbing out of the back of the bus. "When he's not leading the troops, Extra Billy is really Parker Seward, a circuit court judge from Albemarle. I've met him a few times."

Margaret watched August assume the mantle of interpreter and intermediary, arguing her case to Judge Seward in the men's shared historic language. After a few minutes, he turned and walked back.

"In honor of Mr. Jefferson," said August, "they'd like to see the cheese safely to the Potomac." Margaret's face fell, but he continued, "From there, I convinced them to entrust it to us—we'd take it the rest of the way to Washington."

"So, they're only coming as far as the beach?" asked Margaret.

"It helps that the judge gets seasick."

"Well, I think it's a shame they're not coming the entire way," said Leland, climbing out to greet the soldiers. "They add a fine martial flair to the parade."

"Does your father have any more surprises for me?" Margaret asked once Leland was gone and she saw him click his heels and bow deeply before General Extra Billy.

"He didn't mean any harm," said August. "He doesn't like people to feel excluded."

"I'm realizing that."

All around them, neighbors and friends were streaming in with their picnic baskets like the spectators who brought their carriages to the early battles of the war. August leaned into the back of the bus, reaching over the clutter of tent poles and paint cans and empty doughnut boxes, for the cooler Evelyn had packed. He opened the lid. "Looks like Mom made deviled eggs. I love those."

"August, thank you," said Margaret abruptly. He looked up, confused.

"For what?"

"For speaking to them. For everything."

Margaret willed him to meet her eyes, but he seemed enormously interested in the fried chicken his mother had packed. By the Visitors' Center, a young black woman leading a battlefield tour of middle-aged white couples stopped to watch the Confederate drill. When it was over, everyone applauded.

"Shall we find a shady spot?" August asked, moving toward the picnic grounds.

Margaret followed doggedly behind, and when she turned back to check her cheese, she saw that Extra Billy's brigade had taken up their positions around it.

Waffle House. Ramada Inn. Econo Lodge. Hollywood Video. Aunt Sarah's. Carlos O'Reilly's Mexican Café. Only a scant mile before, the Gordonsville Grays had stopped the procession outside of Old Salem Church, where everyone on the float was treated to a long, boring story of how sharpshooters had picked off Union soldiers from the galleries. Then, perversely, they stopped to salute the monument erected to the 15th New Jersey Division, their Northern counterparts who had fought and died there. The historical markers had by now given way to the bold pica signage of suburban Fredericksburg and the highway had widened to six lanes, keeping the police escort busy at the stoplights. The cheese, with its attendant angels and cows, rolled left into Old Fredericksburg, down William Street, and past the graceful brick buildings of Mary Washington College, where equally graceful girls with winter tans cheered the procession along. The students upon the float had squandered their candy miles ago, and now had nothing to offer but tired waves. They'd been on the float almost five hours.

The float rolled across the old stone bridge that spanned the Rappahannock River, but when, several miles later, General Extra Billy ordered a salute at Chatham Manor (one of only three homes in America to have been visited by both George Washington and Abraham Lincoln alike, he said), Polly's patience was at an end. There were still another ten miles to go, and if she had to spend it here on this stool, she thought, she'd go insane. Abruptly, she stood.

"Where are you going?" asked Bethany, looking up from her palm-held television.

"I'm going to take a walk."

"I'll come with you," she said.

"No, if too many of us get down, we'll get in trouble."

"I don't care, I've got to get off this thing."

So while the float was stopped outside of Chatham Manor, Polly slunk around the huge orange cheese and her extremely bored classmates playing bloody knuckles, past the non–August Jefferson mimetically reading a book about himself, and off the end of the float. With Bethany on her heels, she walked against the stopped traffic, past the antique cars that somehow show up in every parade no matter how automotively irrelevant, past four convertibles festooned with bunting and flags, and in which sat the various Jeffersons. Up ahead, the frustrated police escort was making the cheese move along, and the cars began inching forward.

"I know where you're going," said Bethany, jogging beside her to keep up.

"I'm not going anywhere."

"I know who you're looking for."

"I'm not looking for anybody."

"He's on the school bus. I talked to him at lunch."

Polly walked faster, hoping to leave Bethany behind. She had watched her shamelessly throw herself at Mr. March during the break, daring to eat the potato chips from his boxed lunch, packed along with everyone else's by the PTA mothers. It was disgusting the way she laughed at everything he said and even slapped his hand playfully.

Bethany was running to keep up with Polly. "Listen, I know what this is about. There is nothing going on between us. We're just friends."

"Oh, shut up, Bethany."

She had reached the big yellow bus driven by Mrs. Warmos, a prematurely old woman whose husband poured kerosene on their front yard so that he wouldn't have to mow the grass. The bus was creeping forward, but Polly jumped on the step outside and knocked loudly on the glass. To avoid running her over, the bus driver reluctantly opened the door. Polly climbed on board, with Bethany still close behind her.

She saw him immediately, halfway down the right aisle with his feet propped on the wheel well, engrossed in a book. *What is he reading?* she wondered, as if his choice would provide the key to understanding his distance. She realized she'd put no thought into what would happen once she got here; what could she say to him, after all, with a bunch of middle school kids watching them and teachers weird in their weekend clothes? Polly suddenly felt supremely conspicuous standing in the doorway, swaying past muttering Mrs. Warmos to the unsteady rhythm of the lurching bus. As she moved forward, the bus stopped short, sending her stumbling into the nearest seat. Mr. March lifted his head at the sudden movement up front, for as one of the chaperons, he had to be concerned with kidnappings and hijacks, didn't he? His eyes landed on her, appraisingly, but lightly, impersonally, like a man at a department store rack skipping a shirt the wrong color. To her dismay, they came to rest just over her shoulder, on the treacherous, traitorous Bethany, whom Polly could feel simpering, just by the subtle greasy shift in the air.

But she had not climbed aboard this bus to see him, she told herself angrily; she had come for a change of scenery, nothing more. She lifted her chin and made her way down the aisle, past classmates dozing or playing five-card stud, the tinny music from their head-

phones leaking out around their ears. She did not deign to glance at
him when she walked past, but kept her eyes fixed ahead and took a
seat near the back of the bus. She wanted the last row, to be as far
away from him as possible, to show how little she cared, but it was
crowded with junior varsity cheerleaders, practically in one another's
laps, whispering through their routines.

Rock. Rock Steady. 'Cause your team ain't even ready . . .

Polly stared out the dusty window as the parade wound down-
hill into seven miles of woods. The road narrowed and curved toward
the river; she could smell the faint aroma of salt and fish. Red clay
trails disappeared into the pine forest, and from time to time houses
appeared in the clearings, beachy cedar houses gabled like chalets.
The parade passed the charred remains of a building at the mouth of
a lane of shanty cottages, where six or seven black children stopped
climbing through the ruins to watch the cheese drive by. They stood
by solemnly as car after car honked, its inhabitants waving and cheering, hoping to stir some enthusiasm in the children and thus in themselves after seven hours of driving. But the children did not return
the waves and cheers, they merely watched the enormous cheese pass,
mystified, then turned back to clamber over the broken roof beams
and around the lone standing firebrick chimney.

Polly listened to the echoing honking all around her, and the
hollow sound made her feel trapped inside a bell. She would never
emerge from these woods, she now understood; she would live, grow
old, and die where she sat, staring out of this window, listening to
the soft girlish voices behind her chanting Rock. Rock Steady.

Up ahead, trolling lazily over the cheese, two black buzzards rode
the currents down from the mountains.

CHAPTER TWENTY-FOUR

"Do you smell something?" Margaret asked. It was nearly sunset, and they had finally reached the outskirts of Fairview Beach, a tiny ladder of a town with two parallel roads and eleven cross-street rungs. They had rolled past its main attractions—the volunteer fire department, a local grocery, a bait shop—and had just reached the entrance to the campgrounds when Margaret smelled smoke. She turned to look behind them, and at the exact moment she saw the cloud, the temperature gauge in front of Leland soared to HOT. Leland slammed on the brakes and the Channel 5 news van, following too closely, swerved, just in time to avoid hitting them, sending a ripple along the entire procession. Leland jumped out of the bus and stared in dismay at the black-lung ruin of his engine.

"But I checked the belts," said Leland weakly. "Twice before we left."

August and Margaret scrambled out to join the distraught priest. "Oh, Dad," said his son.

"Watch out," said Margaret, pulling Leland away. "It's still burning."

The police escort that had ridden ahead, now circled back to ascertain the trouble. Patrick Lewis, his cameramen, the Gordonsville Grays, and those closest in the procession all crowded around, staring dumbly, as if to read the engine's dying wishes in its acrid smoke signals. One of the police officers radioed back to Fredericksburg for a tow truck.

"A minor setback," said Leland bravely. "I'll find a place to repair it tonight and we'll be back before you know it."

"Dad, maybe it's time to retire the bus," said August gently.

The priest shook his head. "We'll be back before you know it."

Margaret glanced over her shoulder at the stalled procession behind them. All the way down the line, tired and hungry travelers climbed out of their cars to see what was wrong. The float was blocking the entrance to the campground and, more important, the restaurant on the pier.

"Maybe the news van could pull it the last few blocks?" she suggested to Patrick, who looked on archly. "The Yacht Club is just down the road."

"Insurance," said Patrick, shaking his head. "It's a bitch."

"We ordered the trailer hook especially for the Volkswagen," Pastor Vaughn said. "I don't know if it will even fit another car."

The long journey had cast a heavy inertia over the group, and for a few minutes no one moved. Maybe this is a sign, thought Margaret; maybe we should turn around and go home.

"It's flat from here," said August, taking charge. "Margaret, you steer the trailer and we'll push it." Short of calling another tow, she didn't have a better idea, and so it was decided. The kids jumped down and August unhitched the float.

"Where do you want me?" asked Leland, prepared to man either end.

"Right here, waiting for the tow truck," replied his son. "We have plenty of people."

With a great heave, August and the infantrymen pushed the float past the entrance to the campground, and like an unclogged drain, the caravan behind funneled itself around Leland's stalled bus and into the parking lot. They pushed it down Fairview's narrow streets of single-story tidewater cottages, whose screened porches, like spindly daddy longlegs, stretched out for the river breeze. Off-season residents stepped onto their lawns to wonder at the sight. *Watch the pothole*, they called helpfully. *Careful of that turn*. Margaret struggled to maneuver the heavy trailer, and when it came time to turn onto Eleventh Street, August had to run around to help her. Shoulder to shoulder, they tugged the hitch the opposite direction from how they wanted the float to go, and the Gordonsville Grays shoved hard to get it over the rough pavement. August piloted the twelve-hundred-pound cheese with the same calm assurance he did everything else, thought Margaret. He flashed her an exasperated smile, his first intimacy of the day, and as she smiled back, she felt the absurdity of their predicament begin to melt away a bit of the day's tension. No, nothing had gone smoothly, but they were almost at the Yacht Club, and August was here beside her, and the soldiers she dreaded having along had proven to be generous and helpful men. For a moment all the day's trouble was forgotten.

Fairview Yacht Club, when they pulled in, was nothing more exclusive than a few dry-docked powerboats, several tethered fishing trawlers, a front-end loader, and a crane. Tufts of pampas grass straggled along the edge of driveway down to the narrow beach, where pale green crabgrass took over colonizing the sand. The crowning glory of the beachhead was a wooden bar shaped like a longboat. It was rented out for parties by the marina's owner, who lived and entertained in the white, modular two-story clubhouse built on pylons over the boat wash. In a gesture Leland the joker would have appreciated, he had written on the building's two narrow bathroom doors: *Outboards* and *Inboards*.

They pushed the cheese into a gravelly clearing next to the launch ramp, where it was to spend the night. To her surprise, Margaret saw a few middle-aged women already waiting for them, and when they voluntarily kissed the sweaty, hardtack infantry, she realized they were the Gordonsville wives, come to retrieve their husbands after a long day's march.

"Well, ma'am," said General Extra Billy, "if that is all, we'll be off."

"Thank you for your help," said Margaret graciously. "And for your successful bivouac of the cheese."

"It was our pleasure. Anything in memory of Virginia's favorite son."

She watched the soldiers link arms with their wives and head back to their sensible sedans, the odd bachelor or two finding his place in the backseat like a coddled older brother. The wives were as down-to-earth as their cars, outfitted in jeans and pastel sweatshirts, their hair cut short because they didn't have time to fuss with it. They handed the keys to their husbands, and together, they headed home.

"You've rescued me twice today," said Margaret almost shyly when the last car pulled away and she and August found themselves alone. They were still standing on either side of the hitch, looking out over the river so as not to have to look at each other. One by one, across the water, the channel buoys blinked on, warning night travelers away from the underwater deadfall of fishnets and stakes. Behind them, weathered hulls knocked like wooden shoes against the pier.

He glanced over, embarrassed. "You should find some rocks to brake the wheels. You don't want it rolling into the water."

Margaret nodded, but made no move. Silently, they watched a Leviticus-bearded man in a Budweiser cap row his dory in to dock and haul in his dripping, wire crab pots.

"So what made you change your mind?" she asked at last.

"What do you mean?"

"What made you decide to come after all?"

"Dad is sick," said August. "It might be the last trip we take together."

"Oh," Margaret said.

"Mom would never have forgiven me if I stayed at home."

"I'd better brake those wheels," she said. With a sigh, she moved away, toward the rubble jetty by the pier. Seeing her go, August roused himself.

"The tow truck should be here by now," he said. "I'd better get back to Dad."

Though he was only feet away, it felt to Margaret as if August were already beside his father, on his way out of town. As if the laws of physics commanded her to move in opposition, she walked even farther down the jetty, so that he might not see she cared. He watched her stoop and shoulder several rough hunks of bluestone.

"Well, good night," he called. She was silhouetted against the last ember of sun and when she turned, her face was lost in shadow.

Margaret carried the heavy stones back to the float and placed them before the wheels. The float's pasture was littered with candy wrappers and Coke cans from the students who'd ridden upon it, and she swept them up with an old push broom she found leaning against the marina's clubhouse. She swept up the trash and smeared the dirty footprints, righted the listing papier-mâché cow that had come loose from her plywood base. She climbed onto the cheese's dais and slowly worked her way around her creation with a dry rag, trying to remove as much of the road dust as she could. She had wanted to cover the cheese for the ride, but Pastor Vaughn had insisted they leave it naked to the world, that all might marvel at it. No one would eat the rind, anyway, he reminded her, so where was the harm?

August was gone, Polly was having dinner with her school friends, and Margaret was once again alone. She spread a canvas drop cloth over her cheese to keep off the night's dew, and drew the star-spangled curtains around it. From the crab house down the beach, she heard laughter rise with the gravitational pull of Patrick Lewis's jokes. Her neighbors would be there beside him, sharing beer and buttering hush puppies, and a sudden and powerful hunger rose up inside her. Enough feeling sorry for yourself, Margaret commanded. She had the rest of her life to be alone. Tonight she would enjoy some company.

Margaret slipped off her shoes and walked barefoot down the cold, pebbly beach toward the restaurant. On their rare summer vacation days, her parents used to drive her to the Potomac, and while they played the slot machines legal on the piers, she swam and scoured the beach for the prehistoric sharks' teeth that famously washed ashore here. She'd brought Polly to the same beaches when she was younger, and together they spent whole afternoons picking up and mostly discarding any vaguely triangular rock or ocean-worn shell. Even with their losing a tooth a week, as she'd read somewhere prehistoric sharks did, Margaret had to marvel at the never-ending reserve for curious children, and wondered now if perhaps a few in her own collection were as suspect as those she'd always found for Polly at the end of the day, as the car was packed and idling, just when all hope seemed lost.

Because the pier extended over the water, Tim's Crab House II was technically in Maryland, providing a source of great excitement

to the children. Now we are in Maryland, they laughed, leaping onto
the pier. Now we are in Virginia. Now we are in Maryland. Margaret
walked past them and into the large, brightly lit restaurant. Every table
was filled with a neighbor or a friend, sunburned and windblown from
the drive. The Jeffersons had spread themselves through the crowd,
so that half the tables were headed by a head of state. In the back,
she spotted Polly at a long table of her schoolmates, watched over by
a chaperon at each end. While the other kids laughed and joked,
reaching across the table for one anothers' fries and being smacked
away, Polly sat quietly, pushing her food around her plate. She was
speaking to no one, not even her friend Bethany, who sat at the other
end of the table. For a swift moment, Margaret considered pulling
up a chair beside her daughter to shield her from her exuberant, sloppy
classmates, but Polly's certain mortification stayed her. She turned
instead when she heard her name called, and reluctantly joined the
large, crowded center table anchored by Patrick Lewis, presiding over
a bushel of steaming crabs.

"Day one of the grand cheesy procession," said the reporter,
sloshing beer into a plastic cup and handing it to Margaret. "We've
had the infantry and our first casualty. Are they back with the bus
yet?"

"Not yet," she answered.

"They'll never find a mechanic at this time of night," Patrick
predicted. That it was far, far too late seemed to be the consensus,
judging by the bobbing heads around the table. Starstruck Bob
Crenshaw and several of Margaret's neighbors had insinuated themselves into Patrick Lewis's entourage and hung on his every word.

"You know, we're not the first to set sail from here," Patrick
informed her. "The owner of the Yacht Club told me that in 1988
three Italian gondolas poled from Fairview Beach to Washington to
celebrate the two hundredth anniversary of the Constitution."

"Why should Italians care about our Constitution?"asked
Margaret.

"Why should we care about their Renaissance?" he retorted.
"Their history is ours, ours is theirs. We're all One Big Family, right?"

Patrick Lewis was drunk. He couldn't have been here more than an hour, but she noticed two empty Bloody Mary glasses beside him and a nearly drained pitcher of beer. His cameramen sat hunched over their crabs, conditioned to his bluster, but her neighbors strained to hear his every word, and nodded appreciatively. Margaret downed the beer Patrick had poured her and ordered a better one.

"Nineteen eighty-eight was their fortieth anniversary," continued Patrick, and Margaret, not understanding, asked him to repeat himself. "Of their Italian Constitution. Nineteen forty-eight—that's the year I was born. It's hard to think of yourself being the same age as a constitution."

"Old and moldy," said a cameraman, reaching for another crab.

Patrick chose not to hear him. "My sources in the newsroom say our ratings today were great. Tomorrow, live satellite feed up the Potomac."

"I hope it helps the president," said Margaret.

Patrick leaned in, and his beery breath reminded her of Francis.

"Now that it's just the two of us," said Patrick over the din of the restaurant, "why are you really doing this? What's in it for you?"

"Why do you keep looking for an ulterior motive?" asked Margaret.

"Because no one does anything without an ulterior motive," said Patrick. "I'll tell you a little secret . . ." The reporter drained the last of the beer into his own glass, then stopped a waitress and generously ordered another round. "My sources in the newsroom say the House is scheduled to vote on the Family Matters Act the day we arrive."

"That's great," said Margaret.

"Yes, it's convenient, isn't it?" Patrick said, smiling. "For Brooke to inoculate himself the very day he sells you out."

"What are you talking about?" asked Margaret.

"My sources say the farm lobby is poised to file a discrimination suit if the amnesty goes through. If your debt gets forgiven, why shouldn't Archer Daniels Midland's? It's unfair to penalize them for being too large."

"They don't need the amnesty," retorted Margaret. "They get ninety percent of all the subsidies."

"A level playing field." Patrick smiled. "That's all they want. I guarantee, the amnesty will be the first thing to go."

"Patrick, your sources are wrong," said Margaret coldly. "The president is committed. He ran on it."

"He might be committed, but his bill is like this crab," said Patrick, lifting a steaming creature from the bright red pile. "First the House will gut it." He peeled back the crab's apron, and divested her of her feathery lungs. "Then the Senate will rip off its legs." He broke the crab in half and twisted off her claws. "And when they are done, he'll be left with a few meager bits of meat that most people will find not worth the trouble."

He popped the juicy white flesh into his mouth and licked his fingers clean of Old Bay seasoning. "You know, Foster's and my grand-daddy was a waterman down in Tappahannock. He would turn the crabs over and show us their bellies. If the apron was long and pointed like the Washington Monument, it was a male; if it was domed like the Capitol Building, it was a female. But why we should be looking for Washington in the sex of a scavaging crab, he never did say."

Margaret stared down at the spread of soggy newspaper used to line the table. On top was an issue from a few weeks ago when the president first introduced the Family Matters Act. *Uphill Battle in the House,* announced the headline. The accompanying photo was of Adams Brooke standing alone in a field of genetically modified wheat that stretched into the horizon and out of the frame.

"I'm tired," said Margaret, pushing back from the table. "I'm going to turn in."

"The evening's just started," said Patrick. "Come on, have another beer. The station's buying."

Margaret shook her head and took her leave of Patrick and his crew. Bob Crenshaw quickly slid into her spot, claiming his turn with the reporter. Everyone said he had a great speaking voice, she heard him confide. Did Patrick have any pointers on how he might get on TV?

Her appetite gone, Margaret walked back to the dark beach. Behind the restaurant, heavy metal throbbed from a Quonset hut dance hall that had long ago been surrendered to the local motor-cycle gang. Margaret took a seat nearby on the cigarette butt–littered sand and stared up at the sky. She used to know her constellations by heart, but now she only remembered a few. Calliope, the Great Bear, was fleeing the hunting dogs unleashed by her son Boötes, who failed to recognize his own mother. Enormous Hydra slithered all the way from Libra to Canis Major. As placed in the constellation, Hydra of the Hundred Heads had but one; and Margaret wondered if a single regenerative head wasn't all the treachery any monster needed. As she watched, a star fell through Ursa Major, but no, she realized, it was moving too steadily to be a star. A satellite, most likely, vacu-uming up images on one side of the earth to beam them down on her, thousands of miles away. She sometimes felt she could extend her arm when a satellite flew past and catch a war halfway across the world in the palm of her hand.

"Mom, is that you?" Polly nearly tripped over her mother as she lay prone on the beach. "What are you doing out here?"

"Looking at the stars," Margaret answered. "Why aren't you with your friends?"

Polly shrugged in the darkness.

"Sit with me a minute," her mother said.

"I'll get sand in my clothes."

"Just for a minute."

Polly reluctantly took a seat next to her mother, pulling her legs up to her chest against the cold night air. Margaret lay still, and nei-ther spoke for a long time.

"Was it fun on the float?" she asked at last.

"It was okay."

"Are you looking forward to tomorrow?"

"I guess."

"It was a surprise to see August, wasn't it?" she asked, not know-ing why she mentioned him to Polly. She hadn't even realized she was thinking about him.

"August was a better Jefferson than any of these guys," said Polly.

"I think so too."

Margaret was silent. Another satellite rounded the horizon. "Do you remember your dad used to tell you Sputnik was watching to make sure you did your homework?"

"I remember. Then I found out Sputnik crashed in 1958."

They fell silent again. Margaret sat up and ran her hands along the sand, letting the grains sift through her fingers. When viewed from the vantage of Hydra, her life and Polly's were indistinguishable, no more important than countless billion others. Out on the river, the red navigation lights of a few late pleasure boaters were moving at the same steady rate as the satellites above.

Margaret sifted another handful of sand and discovered a smooth black triangle left in her palm. "Look," she said hopefully, showing her daughter. "A shark's tooth."

"Mom," replied Polly. "That's just a shell."

By the time Leland's bus was repaired and he and his son were back on the road, it was after ten o'clock. It was twelve miles from Fredricksburg to Fairview Beach, and with no traffic it would take them not even twenty minutes to get there, but they could not deny it felt singularly anticlimactic to be going back over the same ground that they had so triumphantly trodden earlier today.

"I don't think the mechanic believed I checked the belt," said Leland, who insisted on driving. His night vision was not what it once was, and he slowed every time another car approached them on the two-lane road. August found himself clutching the dashboard every few minutes.

"I'm sure he believed you, Dad."

"It looked fine to me. I even flushed the radiator."

"These things happen. Can I turn down the heat?" August asked. "It's burning my feet."

He felt out of sorts, but he couldn't really blame it on his father's driving or the stifling bus. All day, ever since he'd first climbed into this bus at the park, August had felt dissociated, like he was watching himself from a great distance. It was the feeling he'd had the one and only time he flew to meet Letta where she lived outside of Boston, for their disastrous weekend of halting conversation and desperate sightseeing. Maybe it had just been nerves, but sitting on the plane, he had been unable to summon his own parents' familiar faces, or to convincingly describe Letta's hazy features. In transit, he had released family and not yet grasped love, and so he hung unmoored, afraid that if God chose that moment to pluck him out of the sky, he would die without a self, having left it in the care of others. It was a liberating yet melancholy feeling, and one he experienced again today on the road with his father and Margaret and the cheese.

"If you can't believe a priest, who can you believe?" asked his father.

Their past several hours of conversation had gone along this line, first while waiting in the office of the only open mechanic in town, breathing in the queasy bouquet of brake fluid and air freshener, then later at the country-cooking restaurant, where, over dinner, Leland described, in lengthy detail, his pretrip maintenance routine. August was unsure if he should be worried about his father's fixation; indeed, he spent most of their time together these days scanning him for signs of trouble. Another car approached, and Leland slowed.

"Well, I think the trip is off to a great start, if I do say so myself," declared the priest.

August looked at his father in disbelief. "How can you say that? We were accused of being Rebel sympathizers, the bus broke down, Margaret is miserable—"

"What do you mean Margaret is miserable?" asked his father. "Her cheese is a huge success."

"You've been a priest half your life," said August. "How can you not see when someone is suffering?"

"Son, I think you are misreading the situation," said Leland. "The whole town is here to support her. Three Chimneys is presenting the most remarkable gift Washington has seen for two hundred years. Margaret is getting just what she wanted."

"But that's exactly it. You've taken over and made it about the town," explained August. "You've been so busy tending your flock, you've forgotten the individual sheep."

A set of blinding high beams rounded the corner ahead of them, slicing through the dark cabin of the bus. Without thinking, Leland slammed on the brakes, sending August crashing into the dashboard.

"What are you doing?" August asked angrily.

"That truck," said Leland. "It was in our lane."

"No it wasn't. You had plenty of room."

"I didn't," said his father. "You didn't see it from my angle."

"Dad, pull over," demanded August.

"Why?"

"Pull over."

Leland did as he was ordered, and August swung open his door. Outside the temperature had dropped nearly to freezing, and he shivered in his light sweater. He walked behind the bus and its tail of a trailer hook, and over to his father's door. Leland stared straight ahead.

"Come on, Dad," said August. "Open the door." Leland didn't move.

The woods were impenetrably black around him, but the bus's headlights reflected off the small green road sign on the shoulder. *Passapatanzy*. What kind of name was that? Once a meteor fell near Three Chimneys and August had gone with some boys to look for it. As they approached the woods where they had seen it land, something green and glowing emerged from the darkness. August shot at it with his pellet gun, but the ping and ricochet showed them it was nothing more than a road sign, just like this one.

"Come on, Dad," he said, more kindly this time. "It's too dark here. Let me take over."

Reluctantly, Leland opened the door and switched places with his son. August adjusted the seat and mirror to his taller frame, and pulled back onto the road. They drove several miles in silence.

Who were those boys out prowling for aliens? August wondered. He couldn't remember their names or faces, only the unfamiliarity of them. How many fluorescently lit church basement rec rooms had he played in, keeping company with other preachers' children, most as shy as or shier than himself, while upstairs their parents talked of the oil crisis and the steeply climbing divorce rate? While their parents outlined strategies for universal healing, the children had been left to play Truth or Dare or to sneak out in search of Other Life.

"I had no idea there were so many Jeffersons in the world," said Leland when August had not spoken for some time. "I imagine our lot today only scratches the surface."

"Does it make you feel better to know other men dress up as their heroes?" asked August, only half-kidding. "That it wasn't just me?"

"The dressing up never bothered me, son," replied his father quietly. "I guess I just always wished you'd found a hero closer to home. There are some honorable men in your own family. Even if they never became famous."

August looked at his father. "It's not about being famous, Dad," he said. "Jefferson was extraordinary."

"Who can compete with that?" Leland laughed uncomfortably.

"No one expects you to."

"Still. A father wants to make his son proud," said Leland. "You'll understand someday when you have children of your own."

August looked over at his father in exasperation. "You're always talking about children I'm never going to have. When are you going to face reality, Dad?"

Leland fell silent. "I don't know how to talk to you tonight," he said. "I only meant I haven't lost faith in you, if children are what you want."

"Maybe I don't want children. Does everyone in the world have to want what you want?" August asked more vehemently than he meant. He wasn't sure why he was so angry, but if it weren't for Leland, Margaret would never have made a cheese, and if she hadn't made a cheese, the bus wouldn't have broken down, and if the bus hadn't broken down, he wouldn't be alone with his father, discussing all the things he would never have.

"I must have been a pretty awful dad for you not to want to be one."

August glanced over sharply to see Leland staring out the passenger window into the fathomless woods, and was startled to recognize the same expression of misery he'd worn for years over Margaret. Surely he had never meant to punish his father by not having a son of his own, and yet why else had he spent years loving an unattainable woman, pushing aside all others in his pursuit of unhappiness, except to shirk the burden of continuing the line so dear to Leland?

"I'm no one special," said Leland softly. "I understand why you chose Jefferson over me."

"It's silly to be jealous of a man dead two hundred years," chided August.

"About as silly as being jealous of children never born."

At the truth in his father's words, August looked over. To his surprise, he saw that his father had tears in his eyes.

"I worry, son, that I counseled Amanda Frank to have all those babies because I wished them for you. Or for myself. And now this cheese. I worry I've done everything to make myself important for you."

They drove silently then, in the dark cradle of trees, each afraid to say *I love you, I forgive you, father, son,* and confuse things all over again.

CHAPTER TWENTY-FIVE

Jake left for his rounds at five-thirty in the morning, came home at noon, closed the bedroom door, and slept until four, when he left for the Philip Morris plant in Richmond, where he worked the night shift because it paid time and a half. The lawyers' fees were killing them, he told Manda, so his friend Asa got him a job sweeping up tobacco shavings from the half a billion cigarettes rolled there every day. Each night, he came home red-eyed and smelling like a packet of chaw, but more rested than his wife, simply for having been elsewhere. Do you think I like working two jobs? he'd yelled, shutting her out of the bedroom so he could sleep. We need the money. But it was so convenient, thought Manda, and so easy, pushing his broom to the beat of his headphones. Scoring free packs of cigarettes. Driving alone through the night armed with the perfect excuse: We need the money. She tried not to hate him for being able to leave.

So Jake was at work when Rose got bit. He had a cell phone, but he told her it didn't work inside the plant. Cecile had left, and Manda and her mother were giving the babies their evening bath when they heard her scream. They swiftly wrapped the dripping babies in towels and laid them shrieking in their cribs, then raced into the backyard, where the floodlights on the side of the house revealed Rose cornered in the forbidden dog pen, clutching her arm and kicking at Bix, the one male of the pack that despite Manda's late, militaristic training had continued to lunge. Manda grabbed the dog by the collar and flung him halfway across the kennel before scooping up her sobbing daughter, whose mauled arm now hung limply by her side. She rushed her inside and furiously scrubbed the wound with soap and water, pulling back a flap of loose skin to flush the raw meaty muscle. Rose screamed the whole time, while over the monitor, the wet, abandoned babies screamed upstairs. Mrs. Sawyer sternly handed Manda alcohol and gauze, made Rose wiggle her fingers to make sure nothing was damaged, then poured the little girl a shot glass of bourbon mixed with honey. *Drink this, sugar,* she said, and soon the girl's screams quieted to whimpers.

"You should take that child for a rabies shot," said Mrs. Sawyer.

Manda sat on the couch with Rose on her lap. She knew her mother was right, but what would the doctor say? The doctor would call the lawyers and the lawyers would take Rose as they wanted to take the other babies. They would put her in jail for letting her girl get bit by a dog.

Upstairs, the babies were still crying. Her mother was waiting for her to see to them, but Manda couldn't let go of Rose. She worried if she so much as relaxed her grip, a lawyer would suddenly appear in the doorway and whisk her off into the night. Her mother stood and waited, until at last she could take the screaming no more and marched angrily upstairs. Manda rested her cheek on Rose's thin brown hair and closed her eyes.

"You feed them. I'm done," Manda's mother announced once she had dried the babies and seen them into their pajamas. "I've been through five of my own. Enough is enough."

Manda nodded dully. She didn't blame her. If she herself could walk away, she was certain, she would. With Rose on her hip, she followed her mother to the front door, where she watched the older woman light a cigarette, then climb into her car. She watched the red sparks of the car's taillights disappear down Snakehill Road. She stood with Rose and watched until the road settled back into darkness. In her arms, Rose buried her head and began sucking her thumb, a habit she had broken years ago.

Upstairs, the babies were waiting for their bottles. Manda hesitated at the bottom of the steps, listening as the seven children's rhythmic cries gradually resolved into that of a single child, her enormous, demanding other child. Put her down, it insisted. Pick me up. Comfort me, Mama. Comfort *me.* She should go to it, she knew, but Rose was clinging to her, and she couldn't seem to move her feet.

Outside, the dogs were barking, stirred up by the appearance of a drought-driven deer that had come to stare at their drinking water. She leaned against the banister, feeling the dogs' yelps add themselves to the other baby's insistent voice. All the cries were now one extended cry, huge and echoing in her head. Comfort me, Mama, it begged.

Manda carried heavy Rose up the stairs to her bedroom. She laid her in bed, but Rose clung to her shirt, so Manda climbed in beside her.

"That was a bad dog," said Rose dreamily.

"I'll take care of it," answered Manda.

"I just wanted to pet him," said Rose.

"I'll take care of it," echoed her mother.

Manda held Rose until the bourbon eased her to sleep. By the hall light, she was able to trace the faint reminder of stitches on Rose's forehead from a dive off the monkey bars last month at school, the lump from a nearly shattered kneecap after wrecking her bike, the nicks and scabs and purple blossoms up and down her arms and legs from furious daily play. She gently stroked the bandage on Rose's arm. Could she hide it from Cecile tomorrow? What would the lawyers say?

She lay with Rose for a long time, listening through the wall to the other baby crying, hiccoughing now in anger. She was spending too much time with Rose, it sobbed. *What about me?* She lay and listened until Rose was finally asleep, then she slid out of bed and tucked the blanket tightly around her daughter. She walked down the hall, past the other baby's bedrooms, and downstairs to the front door. Across the dark yard, she walked past the dog pen and let herself into her old house. The electricity had been shut off months ago, but she felt her way to the hall closet, fumbling inside until she touched the cold barrel of the .22 she'd first used to hunt as a girl. On the shelf above, she found her box of shells.

Manda made her way through the darkness to the kennel and hesitated for a long time at the gate, staring at the creatures in pity. It wasn't their fault, was it, that she was such a bad mother? They

couldn't help their instinct for chaos. But half-trained, she now realized, was more dangerous than not trained at all, because it gave
the illusion of harmony, of understanding between man and beast,
where none rightly existed. Manda unlatched the gate. The frantic
litter rushed her, all but Bix, who limped in circles in the corner of
the pen from when she had inadvertently broken his right front leg
throwing him off Rose. The black and tan beagles leapt in the air,
waiting for a signal to calm themselves, to sit, waiting for an order
that never came, because Manda realized that it was simply too late
for them. She stepped away from the open gate and they cowered
before her, bellying the ground, looking up with their rolling eyes.
She cocked her gun and they whined in confusion. Their instincts
told them to run, but their training paralyzed them. And so they
groveled at her feet, pleading with her and hating her until she lifted
her gun, pointed, and fired a single shot into the air.

The crack echoed in the leafless woods. For a long second, the
dogs hesitated, and then, as if the signal had been given for their first
spring chase, they bounded into the forest, tonguing their freedom.
Manda didn't feel guilty for turning them loose. It was getting warmer
and they would find food—wild rabbits and other people's cats. Maybe
they would form a pack or maybe they would splinter and join the
established packs she heard running through her woods at night. The
more timid of them might show up in a yard miles away and get herself taken in as a pet, but that family should watch closely, thought
Manda, for their pet was ruined and unreliable, she had seen to it.
One night, as the new owner reached down to stroke her, the dog
would turn and snap, and even if she never did it again, the memory
of that once would be poison enough.

Inside the kennel only guilty Bix remained. He sat quietly now,
weakened from the pain of his broken leg. As Manda approached,
he watched her steadily. *It wasn't your fault*, Manda told him. *I'm a
bad mother*. Then she reloaded her gun, took aim, and shot him between the eyes.

* * *

Before she left, Manda scrambled two eggs for Rose's breakfast. She mixed them with milk and a few parings of cheese the way her daughter liked them, then fried up two strips of bacon and placed them on a plate. She poured Rose a glass of orange juice and set the meal on the table before her booster chair. She wrote a simple note to her daughter saying that she loved her and hoped she would grow up to do well at school. Then, she carried the crying babies out to the van and fitted them into their car seats. It was two o'clock in the morning.

She set off on the route she and Jake had driven them so many times before. Steadily, she drove down Snakehill Road and past the deserted shops of School Street. She hadn't realized it the first few times they set out, but the route Jake chose was a map of their old life together, before the babies came. Once on School Street, it wound past Three Chimneys Junior High, where they'd met as quietly failing students in the same math class. On nights when they couldn't get their children to sleep, he would turn down the dirt road near the creek where he had first kissed her when they were fifteen. It had been their first hunt together, though she was a five-year veteran, having received her first gun at age ten. She was running Turbo and he had a bloodhound whose name she did not recall, but she did remember they had trouble picking up a scent, for it had been an especially dry summer. While her uncle and Jake's two cousins stopped to smoke a joint, she and Jake plunged deeper into the brier after the dogs. Turbo flushed a lanky swamper right at this creek, but it was precisely then, just as she was raising her gun, that Jake had stopped and kissed her. His kiss took her by such surprise that her finger squeezed the trigger anyway, firing off a bullet that struck nothing, but came to rest, she imagined, in a bed of leaves, as harmless as an acorn.

Now, as the babies shrieked behind her, she drove by the many coordinates of their lovemaking: fields and abandoned houses and the cemetery where Jake's people were buried. They did it outside, almost exclusively, for someone was always home at their houses, watching television night and day. They did it anywhere, in any season, even once in knee-deep snow, in their boots, standing against a tree. They were going to get married and they shared everything. She told him the truth about her history teacher and the time she brought her gun to school. Straddling her over his great-grandfather's tombstone, Jake had sworn revenge, but Manda had told him to forget it. It was over. They had each other now.

Usually by this point in the drive, the rhythm of the car had begun to ease the babies toward sleep. But not tonight. She glanced in her rearview mirror and saw them ball their fists, open their deep red mouths, and scream for comfort. *August had a touch of colic*, Mrs. Vaughn had said one of the days she came to help. *After I'd done all I could, I would stand in the shower and run the water full blast so I couldn't hear him.* But Manda had tried that and when she stepped out, they were still crying. They would never stop crying and they would never go to sleep because they had been very poorly trained. She saw that now. She finally understood the danger of a ruined pack.

As Manda drove, from the corner of her eye she thought she saw a flash of tan outside her window, like that of a dog running alongside the van, keeping pace with her in the woods. Pastor Vaughn hit a dog, he told her. It wasn't one of hers, but she thought about it for weeks after. She used to worry that it would limp out of the woods, mangled and dying. Would she have the guts to finish it? None of her neighbors would. They would shut their eyes and turn away and wish they had never seen such a sad sight. They wouldn't have the courage to put a suffering beast out of its misery. She kept her eyes on the road, but the memory of that dog, like that of Bix on the floor of the kennel, rose up and kept time beside her. Without meaning to, she found herself driving faster and faster, taking the soft dirt turns too sharply. The children in the back cried harder for being tossed side to side.

Manda left the dirt road she was on for an even rougher path through the woods. Branches snapped as her van plowed through, the muffler protesting potholes. She was driving uphill, to the bluff where she and Jake came often as teenagers. At the end of the trail, she reached a meadow, and there, in the glare of her headlights, three twenty-foot crosses, like those that crowned Golgotha, appeared out of the night.

Back when she and Jake first started coming here, the center cross was painted gold and the flanking two pale blue, but wind and rain had peeled them back to their raw Douglas fir. At some point she learned theirs was not the only such stand of crosses, they were the brainchild of a Baptist preacher from West Virginia whose plan, before he died, was to erect them every fifty miles of interstate the width and breadth of America. Here, she and Jake had come after her junior prom with a six-pack of warm beer stolen from Tinton's, where Jake bagged groceries, and here they had stripped off their clothes in the shadow of these crosses, feeling holy and profane at once. Her skin remembered the itch of the wool blanket he laid down for her, and how she shivered as the spring night slid between her naked flesh and Jake's above her. It was solemn and exalted prom-sex they had that night, and Rose was born nine months later. After the Pergonal and the HCG shots, when their doctor sent them home to do it, Jake suggested they come back here. It was their lucky spot, he said.

Manda cut the engine and looked at the shotgun on the seat beside her. All she remembered about their last time here was the dull throb in her right thigh from the weeks of injections, and Jake shouting, *Lord if you love me, send me a son.* It had none of the rapture their old unconsecrated sex had, for they had spent too much money on all that medicine, even buying it cheap off the Internet from other people's leftover stock. She couldn't relax under the crosses, but thought darkly, *God forgives the young and reckless, but once you're a parent, he watches you jealously.* We should be having sex in bed, she whispered to Jake, but he was too far gone to hear.

Give me a sign, O Lord, thought Manda, leaning her head against the steering wheel. *What is Thy will?* Death, as she imagined it, was a peaceful white nursery where she might sit in a rocking chair and watch her children sleep. They would doze for hours, each in his or her own crib, snoring softly, dreaming, and after she fed them, they would fall asleep again. Her only regret was over Rose, absent from her lap. But she would do this for Rose and for Jake. She would send the children on before her and then join them in that large, sunny room. Manda cocked her gun and rested her chin heavily on the barrel. *Give me a sign, O Lord,* she begged again. *What is Thy will?* She closed her eyes and waited, but God was mute. He spoke no word of comfort, gave no stern advice. Everyone had abandoned her, thought Manda, even her Creator. She turned her ear to Him and He answered her with silence.

Silence.

It was so unfamiliar she almost didn't trust it. Manda turned and stared into the backseat. There sat six children asleep in their car seats. Their tiny hands rested in their laps. Their tiny mouths hung open. Their lids fluttered like moth wings over their tiny, milk-fed dreams. All were fast asleep, except for her seventh, little Infinity Amanda, who gazed out the window, noticing for the first time the depths of the nighttime sky. Manda's hand began to shake on the gun. And then the shudder spread up her arms, and over her chest, until her whole body began to tremble as from an ague. She had the sudden memory of her fertility doctor explaining the strange truth about women's bodies. A girl child only five months in the womb, he said, already has seven million eggs in her two tiny ovaries. Seven million in ovaries no bigger than two grains of sand. But that is the crest. After five months in the womb, the eggs begin to die off. No one knows why—why a woman needs so many in the first place, why nature would swell only to retreat like a tide. But by the time that same baby girl is born, she will have only two million eggs, five million already dead. And by the time she hits puberty, she will be left with only half a million, of which she might release four hundred over the course of her whole lifetime. Manda sat behind the steering wheel with the gun against her heart. If she was very, very still she could almost hear them dying. All those chances. All those eggs. From seven million to four hundred. And from four hundred to eleven. And now but seven remained. She thought of her missing four, and how they were like shells that rolled out of the great riptide of life and death only to be pulled back into the sea. She had lost so much, she thought with a sob, and now she was ready to lose the rest. She was about to become what they had accused her of being. Manda slowly lowered the gun and returned the safety to the trigger. When she glanced back into the rearview mirror, little Infinity Amanda, the smallest of the small, named for her mother and her father's favorite car, little Infinity Amanda, her precious, her beloved, oh God, her child, was fast asleep.

She had Pastor Vaughn's number in her wallet, in case of emergency, and she dialed it on the car phone. The phone rang and Manda shut off the headlights, sitting in the bosom of the comforting, silent dark.

"I need some help," she said when Mrs. Vaughn answered the phone. "May I come by?" And though it was three-thirty in the morning, Mrs. Vaughn sounded wide awake. *Come right away, dear*, the priest's wife replied, not needing to ask a single question. *I'm not going anywhere.*

CHAPTER TWENTY-SIX

Leland slept so poorly, he couldn't be certain he slept at all. He spent the night in semiconsciousness, tossing in the confines of his sleeping bag, unsure of who or where he was. Sometimes it seemed to him he was lying beside his son in a tent on the beach, but at other times he had the sensation of motion, as if he were being borne along helplessly in a great, slow procession. At the head of the caravan, he saw a man his own age wearing a cleric's collar, but something about the wildness of his hair and eyes told Leland this man was no Episcopalian. They traveled relentlessly all night long, up and down mountains, across fallow fields, fording streams, until at last they reached their final destination—a fossil white sepulchre, standing alone upon a hill. To his surprise, he found, of all people, Manda Frank inside, dressed in her hospital gown. All these miles and many toilsome roadblocks had led back to her, the one he'd wronged. *Forgive me my trespasses*, he whispered. With eyes full of compassion, she leaned over his bier. *I do, my son*, she replied. Then, as tears of gratitude coursed down his cheeks, she plunged a knife into his side, and calmly spread him on a cracker. Leland awoke with a start to find August snoring beside him in the weak dawn light. Rolling over, he realized his knife wound was nothing but a rock he'd neglected to clear when they pitched their tent.

Giving up on sleep, Pastor Vaughn climbed over his son and out across the gray threshold of morning. Even on his feet, he could not be certain he was awake. A brackish fog, smelling of crab shells and dogwood, snaked through the campsite, hiding one neighbor's tent from another and erasing the river, only yards away. The whispery drizzle that settled upon his face and hair lent the air a volume, which made him feel as if he were still slogging in dream time. Most

mornings at the beach began with the promise of rain, Leland reminded himself of his many Nags Head vacations. It was his early-
riser's burden. By mid-morning, when everyone else awoke, the sun
had always broken through, burning off his lonely fears of a ruined
day.

Leland drifted up the misty beachhead to the grocery and bait
shop, where a sign on the door read: *I Got Crabs, Worms, and Gas at
Avery's Market*. A bell over the screened door announced him to a
middle-aged woman, whose back was turned to him as she started the
morning coffee. It was a cozy local grocery with wide-planked wooden
floors and shelves filled with familiar dry goods: sugar, flour, motor
oil. On racks behind the counter, the proprietors sold GMCO maps
and fishing licenses and Rebel flag paperweights that read *Save Your
Confederate Money, Boys—The South's Gonna Rise Again*. Leland saw
a white Styrofoam cooler of night crawlers labeled "25 for $1" next
to a stack of fruit pies.

"Be right with you," the woman announced, not turning around.
"You'll get the first cup."

"Take your time," said Leland.

He caught a glimpse of his unshaved face in the mirror over
the counter. Under his coat, he was wearing the rumpled red flannel shirt and khakis he'd slept in, and without his collar, he might
have passed for any early-morning local fisherman. Like his father,
Leland had always been old-fashioned in his dress, fixing the white
neck band in place, pulling on his dark pants and jacket before he
left the house every day, but this morning, he was grateful for the
incognito. The collar meant he was open for business, and this
morning he didn't feel confident in his ability to dispense wisdom
or advice.

"You here with the cheese?" the woman asked when the pot
began to drip.

"Yes, ma'am, I am," replied Leland.

"Can't say I follow politics, but I do love a good parade," she
replied.

"What's one without the other?" said Leland, smiling.

The woman seemed kindly, with large square dentures and hair dyed the color of fresh beef. She wore an old-fashioned housedress over slacks and a sweatshirt. He made her out to be about his age.

"It's a shame more towns don't do like you," she replied, straightening the fishing licenses. "It's not like the old days. Back then, we all pulled together."

"Yes, ma'am," said Leland sadly.

"People today," she snorted, for her husband had come home late last night and left before dawn this morning, so she had spoken to no one in nearly twenty-four hours. "They don't know the first thing about responsibility. The government does everything now. In our day, you weren't forced to wear a helmet to ride your bike down the street. You didn't sue someone if your coffee was too hot."

"No, ma'am."

"We didn't have all these violent video games and cable TV. We had friends. And we looked after each other. That'll be fifty cents," she said, handing him a steaming paper cup of coffee. He emptied into it three packets of sugar and four Cremoras. Over her shoulder, something caught his eye.

"What are those?" he asked, pointing to a display of refrigerator magnets.

"Declaration of Independence," she replied. "Barely bigger than a postage stamp, but with a magnifying glass you can read every word."

"I'll take one," said Leland, passing her a dollar fifty for the coffee and magnet. Behind him, the bell over the door jingled, and two young black men in fishing gear walked in. The woman behind the counter cut Leland a look, then casually began wiping down the Confederate paperweights. "Yes, things were different back then. What can I do for you gentlemen?" she asked brightly.

Pastor Vaughn left the grocery sadder than he'd entered. He sipped his coffee and burned his tongue as he walked across the rough-paved parking lot. By the edge of the road stood an old-fashioned telephone booth scratched with initials like an overwashed cup. Leland stepped inside and pulled the folding door behind him. He fished in his pocket for the change he'd just received, then punched in the eleven familiar digits. To his surprise, his wife answered on the other end.

"Evelyn?" he asked.

"Leland, is that you?"

He had not expected his wife's piping soprano so early in the morning, not at Manda Frank's house. "Is everything okay?" he asked. "How did you get over there?"

"I rode with Manda," said Evelyn, "She had a rough night, but she's fine now."

"Rough how?" he asked. "Are the children well?"

"Everyone is fine. We can talk about it when you get back."

He could hear Evelyn moving on the other end, working while she spoke. He heard the crank of a dial and a slamming door, then the rush of water running. Laundry.

"Tell Margaret I saw Francis in town," Evelyn continued. "He said they have the girls under control. Everything is good on the farm."

"She'll be happy to hear it."

An old, begrimed phone book in a metal cover sat on the shelf under the receiver. Leland pulled it out and opened it at random. Brewster, Amalia; McMaster, B.; Perez, Raoul and Sheila. Kids had drawn peace signs and penises in the margins, and a few names, he saw, had been circled, tagged with "For a Good Time Call." The print in the phone book was very small, and Leland squinted. Shifflet, Brandy.

"Leland?"

"I'm here."

"Have you taken your medicine this morning?"

"Yes, ma'am," he lied. But he would, as soon as his coffee cooled enough to allow him to swallow a pill. The two young black men in fishing gear stepped out of the store with a bag of night crawlers and a six-pack of beer for their cooler. *She was a might nice lady*, one of them said.

"How's August?" Evelyn asked. "Is he enjoying himself."

The men climbed inside their pickup and backed it toward the phone booth. Leland could see inside the rear window. The younger of the two was staring down into the bag of night crawlers as if crooning to them.

"I think he is," replied Leland.

"I might stay over with Manda until you-all get home," said Evelyn. "I'm not doing anything around the house."

"That's a good idea."

"Leland?" asked Evelyn, concerned. Leland glanced again at the phone book, flipping to the Fs. Frank, Franklin. Frank, Frank. Why would a parent do that to a child?

"Will you tell Manda I'm sorry?" he asked suddenly. "Will you let her know, no matter what happens, I will never forsake her."

There was a long silence on the other end. "She knows," said Evelyn at last. "That's why she came to me last night."

Leland stood with the receiver to his ear, listening to his wife's measured breathing. In the background, music played, something twinkling and childlike, and from far away he heard Rose meowing like a cat.

"Would you like to speak with her?" Evelyn asked. "She's giving the children their first solid food today. Applesauce. We made it this morning."

"No," said Leland, rousing himself. "Just tell her I'm thinking of her."

"I will," replied his wife. "You give our love to everyone. And get home safe."

Leland bid his wife good-bye and replaced the dog-eared phone book. The two young men in their pickup were gone and the parking lot was empty. Outside, the mist was already lifting, and far off in the distance he could make out the squat silhouette of a tugboat chugging its way around the bend from Nanjemoy Creek. Leland took the long gravel driveway to the marina. When he reached the cheese, he realized he was not alone. Margaret had awoken even earlier than he and made her way down to the rock jetty. She had forgotten her gloves, and stood blowing on her cold, red hands.

"If I'd known you were awake, I'd have brought another coffee," said Leland, coming up beside her. She turned and smiled at him.

"Thanks, I'll get some later."

"No, take mine. I should be cutting back anyway."

Margaret gratefully accepted the warm coffee and sipped it while watching the tug. "It's hypnotic," she said. "I've been watching for nearly an hour, and it doesn't seem to have moved any closer."

"It'll be here before you know it."

She nodded, and together they stared across the water.

"When I woke up, I thought it was going to rain," she said. "But it's clearing off."

"It should be a fine day," agreed Leland.

"Is August awake?" Margaret asked.

"I left him sound asleep."

"I went to see him the other day," she said. "He's built himself a fine house."

"About broke Evelyn's heart," said the priest. "But he needed to be moving on."

She nodded and sipped half of the coffee before speaking again. "Does he ever talk about the farm?"

Leland glanced over, reading the pattern of her questions. "I expect he misses you and Polly a good deal. You were like a family to him."

Margaret laughed sadly. "Families are easy enough to trade in these days."

"Not for everyone," he replied. Far down the river, the tug wheezed at a fishing boat crossing its path. Leland felt the sound rattle deep in his lungs. "Margaret," he said after a moment. "Did you want to make this cheese?"

"Why would you ask such a thing?" she chided. "Of course I did."

"When I suggested it, I worry I didn't have your best interest at heart," he confessed. "That I did it to aggrandize Three Chimneys and myself."

"If that was your sin, Leland, it was mine, too," said Margaret. "I did it to save the farm."

"It seems nearly impossible to do anything selflessly these days," mused Leland.

The two fell silent. In a few hours they would be under way. By tonight they would be in Washington, and by tomorrow they would have met the president. And then? Leland pushed the melancholy coda aside. He didn't want to dwell on the long ride home, pulling behind him an empty, rattling trailer.

Polly stood at the rear railing, watching the campground dwindle to no more than a few rusty freckles on shore. Their barge had arrived at nine o'clock, and it was another hour before the float was secured and they got moving. By then, the river was crowded with boaters ready to accompany the cheese to Washington. The tug pulled the barge out of the shallows and into the center channel. There, they turned north at a messy osprey nest woven over the seasons with twigs and shiny potato chip bags, and what looked to be the red yarn scalp of a Raggedy Ann doll. Polly's classmates ducked and screamed as the mother osprey buzzed the barge, but Polly stood fast and felt the draft of the bird's heavy brown wings. Soon, she too was reduced to nothing but a fussy dot as they left her behind.

Polly was not unhappy to leave Fairview Beach. Last night, after she quit her mother, she had climbed into her sleeping bag in the tent she was sharing with Bethany and waited for her friend to return. Every ten minutes, Polly consulted the ghostly face of her glow-in-the-dark travel clock, growing more and more despondent with each passing hour, until, finally, just before midnight, she heard the tent flap move. *You should have been with us*, Bethany whispered, crawling inside. *Some of us went down to the river with Mr. March and sat on the rocks. Did you know Pocahontas was kidnapped just upstream from here? One of her father's allies sold her to the British for a copper pot.* Polly lay still and pretended to be asleep. She hated the idea of Bethany's sitting in the dark beside Mr. March. He was the chaperon, she thought furiously. He was supposed to be protecting her, and for all he knew, she could be floating past, facedown in the river, while he gave Bethany a lesson on the treachery of alliances. *I think I was*

Pocahontas in a previous life, Bethany whispered. *I had a really intense feeling sitting there.*

Now Polly stood at the rear railing with the other students while August pointed out the sights. *There's the entrance to Aquia Creek,* he said. *They used sandstone from the quarry there to build the White House and the Capitol Building.* Polly glanced over at the creek's wide mouth, but saw nothing beyond obstruction stakes rising through dense hydrilla. In the center of one loose pad, a small motorboat of fishermen cast their lines for bass. They shielded their eyes and tipped their hats to the float as it passed by.

Under other circumstances, Polly would have loved the ride up the Potomac. She'd been on a boat only once before in her life, when Bethany's parents took them waterskiing at Lake Anna. She'd loved the tooth-jarring rhythmic crash as they sped over the choppy water, flying over larger boats' wakes and belly flopping back down again. She'd failed at waterskiing and Mr. Fraser eventually lost patience, circling back again and again to pick her up when she dropped the rope, but she enjoyed riding better anyway, even the dull no-wake taxiing in and out of the dock. Under different circumstances, she could have appreciated the budding sycamores along the shore and the drunken zigzag of mallard hatchlings learning to swim near Wade's Bay. Like her classmates, she might have held up a quickly scrawled sign asking a neighboring yacht to "honk if they liked cheese," and then laughed herself stupid when it released a low foghorn fart of approval.

But today, Polly barely registered the sights. She had come to a decision last night in the tent while Bethany fell asleep dreaming of Indian feathers. She needed to find Mr. March, and yet, she was terrified of finding him, for if he rejected her offer of today, she had nothing left to give.

On the Virginia side of the ship, Patrick Lewis was reading the five-day forecast, live from the Mammoth Cheese. He was clean and well shaven, and none the worse for all the alcohol he had consumed the night before; only a faint puffiness under the eyes gave him away. *I can read the weather stone-cold drunk,* she heard him tell one of the

Jeffersons, who waited to be interviewed. *And if you think I'm bad, you should see the anchors.* She walked past them and around the other side of the cheese's dais, upon which it rode pharaonically, ferried in state up the Nile. There, she found him, standing with Bethany and a group of students, watching the tug up ahead. The towline between the workboat and the barge was submerged and so long that the two vessels seemed to be moving upriver independently of one another. But they were connected, Polly knew, and if an unwary boater crossed between them, his hull might be sliced in two.

As opposed to Patrick Lewis, Mr. March was not weathering the trip well. His thinning hair bristled on his head as if he'd forgotten to bring a comb and had run his fingers through it wet. Even though the day promised to be warm, he wore a dark navy pea coat over a turtle-neck sweater and jeans, an outfit that made him look, Polly thought, even more like a spy than usual. Bethany leaned against the railing beside him, stretching her arms languorously over her head so that her flat white stomach peeked out from beneath her sweater. It was in that stretch and in her willingness to go to the rocks that Polly knew what she must do. It was why Mr. March chose her over Polly, as he had chosen Manda Frank, with her rustling breasts, before her. Compared with them, Polly was a pale, icy virgin, a trembling child. He spoke of Jefferson and Sally Hemings and said true love could never exist be-tween a master and a slave. But her bondage was within her power. He had taught her that. Polly knew how childhood came to an end.

"Children, look!" Pastor Vaughn called from the starboard side of the barge. "It's the ghost fleet of Mallow's Bay."

Automatically, she followed where he pointed off to the Mary-land shore, but saw nothing more than a few meager islands, sprout-ing saplings and moss. As her classmates dutifully gathered round Pastor Vaughn, Polly saw her chance to speak to Mr. March alone.

"During World War I, the army had the great idea of building cheap, wooden steamships faster than the Germans could sink them," said Mr. March, mildly surprised at her appearance. "They commis-sioned a thousand boats, but red tape held them up, and by the time the Germans surrendered in 1918, not one of the ships built had crossed the Atlantic. In the twenties, the diesel engine made them obsolete, and eventually there was nothing to do but sink them. They burned over two hundred ships around Mallow's Bay. It's the largest shipwrecked fleet in the Western Hemisphere."

"That seems wasteful," she said.

"As always, Miss Marvel, the mistress of understatement," replied Mr. March. He stared off toward the bobbing stand of trees and scrub. "Over time, the ships decomposed into their own ecosystems. Each vessel became its own little island."

She saw the spectral outline of boats now in the marshy archipelago. A blue heron preening on what would have housed a gun turret. A rotting hull like a submerged snapping turtle just below the surface. She glanced from its landscape to that of her teacher's face. His unshaven jaw was rough and splintery too, and the eyes behind his glasses bloodshot. This is what he would look like in prison, she thought.

"Mr. March," she said seriously. "I need your help with something very important."

He raised an eyebrow, inviting her to go on, but she couldn't speak for a long minute. "It's something I've given a great deal of thought," she said.

"Yes?"

"These past few months, I've acted very immaturely," she confessed. "Stealing car keys. Avoiding you."

"You're only thirteen. It's not so unreasonable," said Harvey.

"But age is no excuse. You said yourself the concept of childhood is manufactured. What I'm trying to say is—" Polly took a deep breath and spoke very quickly. "I am ready to become a woman, and I want you to—help me."

He looked at her quizzically, as if she had just spoken Korean or demanded a kidney. He couldn't misunderstand, could he? she thought woefully, but then he pulled her away from the nearby crowd of students.

"Polly, this is a completely inappropriate conversation," he admonished. "What if someone heard you?"

"I don't want to get drunk in college and waste myself on some stupid fraternity boy," she insisted. "You are the best teacher I've ever had. I want it to be you."

Mr. March shook his head angrily. "You're in love with me and you're saying what you think I want to hear. But I don't want that."

"You're wrong," she said defiantly "I'm not in love with you. I'm doing this for me. For my own liberation. Are you not attracted to me?"

"It's not about attraction," he answered swiftly. "It's about what's right. And might I add—what's legal."

"What's legal?" said Polly, turning away in deep disappointment. "Then you're not the revolutionary I thought you were."

From the front of the boat, an excited cry arose. The tug driver, unfamiliar with the upper Potomac, had overshot the channel by several feet, bringing the barge perilously near to one of the ship-wrecked islands. This close, Polly saw, the sapling's roots grew in a topsoil of splinters and rusted rivets, so shallow she might thrust out her arm and send the entire tree backward, crashing lazily into the water. With the back of her hand, she brushed away tears of shame and frustration.

"Look at me," said Mr. March under his breath. She turned, and for an instant saw in his eyes the same danger she'd read in Glenn Mullins's. "You swear you want this solely for you?" he asked slowly. "You believe you would be a better person for it?"

"I swear," she said gravely. "If it's not you, it will be someone else. I am through being a child."

Almost imperceptibly, her teacher's face softened. "Polly, my patriot." He sighed.

At the Hallowing Point on Mason's Neck, the river turned nearly ninety degrees west, and the channel, which had skirted around Cranny Island on the Maryland side, now meandered back toward Virginia. A dense planting of trees hid the restricted zone at Fort Belvoir, but the boys of Three Chimneys Junior High craned their necks in the hopes of seeing a fighter jet, as they had glimpsed a row of Blackhawks downstream at Quantico. After the excitement of Mallow's Bay, the trip had settled into a dull river voyage, given over to picnicking and games of cards, and every now and then enlivened by an improbable rumor, such as the one spread when the barge passed Mount Vernon. Someone had it on authority that the rose garden at George Washington's home grew several inches higher each year due to the extraordinary number of cremated bodies scattered there. By the time the rumor reached Pastor Vaughn, guards were patting down visitors for urns, but then they were past Mount Vernon, and the idle conversation trailed off, attaching itself to other points of interest.

Because the barge was forced to stick to the deeper switchback channel, it had taken the procession nearly six hours to travel from Fairview Beach to the Wilson Bridge. Now, as they approached the I-95 overpass, everyone on board felt as if they had, at last, reached the final phase of their journey. The tug disappeared; the shadow of the bridge fell across the barge; speeding cars hummed overhead like a swarm of bees inside a hollow tree; and then, as if coming out the other side of a magic wardrobe, the barge emerged into a brightly colored regatta of sailboats and kayaks. Hundreds of boaters had put in near Old Town Alexandria to satisfy their curiosity about the floating cheese, and many planned to follow along the last few miles to Washington. One group had chartered the yacht *Potomac Belle* and thrown a Mammoth Cheese party. They waved fondue forks from the deck and raised cocktails in honor of the passing foodstuff. Everyone on the barge was on his feet now, pressed eagerly into the railings as if their straining weight would get them into harbor faster.

Margaret stood at the front of the barge as the cheese passed beneath the Fourteenth Street Bridge. She had been to D.C. several times in her life, always by car and blinded by panic at the one-way streets and incomprehensible highway exchanges. Now, emerging from beneath the arched stone bridge, she was greeted by postcard Washington—lanky Lincoln contemplating a wonderland of cherry blossoms, and, soaring up to her right, the great white umbrella of the Jefferson Memorial. Inside his pantheon, the nineteen-foot bronze president stood gazing toward the White House, so that from this direction, she felt a bit like they were sneaking up behind him. She glanced over at August, who, in profile, could have sat for his likeness. He stood with his hand on his father's shoulder, awed into silence by the majesty of the monuments. Feeling her eyes upon him, he turned to her, grinning gleefully, the excitement of magnitude and arrival momentarily erasing any trace of self-consciousness.

Directly across from the Tidal Basin, the river opened up into the Pentagon Lagoon. The tug and barge followed the small stomach-shaped waterway underneath another low bridge and past the massive five-sided Department of Defense, until they rounded the bend to Columbia Island Marina, where they would put in for the night. It took some maneuvering, but the tug backed the barge into the double-wide boat launch, the gangplank was reattached, and within the hour, Leland had driven his bus up the ramp and straight into a perfectly framed view of the Washington Monument. The priest climbed out and turned three hundred and sixty degrees. To the north lay Arlington National Cemetery; to the west, the Pentagon; to the east, and across the water, the Lincoln and Jefferson Memorials; and beyond, the Capitol and the White House. Leland breathed deeply and thanked the Lord for a safe passage. Overhead, a jet, taking off from Reagan National, grazed the treetops with the full-throated cry of an eagle.

"I went to seminary just over the hill in Alexandria," said Leland, "but I don't remember it being so loud."

"I do," said August. "There was always traffic."

It was nearing midnight, and a cold wind blew in off the lagoon. Leland, August, and Margaret sat huddled in white plastic chairs filched from the nearby marina café. They sat guarding the cheese, watching the sailboat masts rock wildly in the slip like the needles of a Geiger counter. Across the water, office lights glowed in the white straightedge of the Pentagon; a line of red brake lights stretched as far as they could see down the Beltway and into Virginia. The makeshift campsites on either side of the marina's launch ramp were quiet, but even this late, cars sped by on George Wash-ington Highway behind them.

"I forgot you lived here when you were young," Margaret said to August. "It's strange to think of you being anywhere else."

After a shared dinner of pizza and coffee, they had pulled their chairs around to face the lagoon, and August's had ended up very close to hers. Around his neck, he wore the muffler she'd knit him for Christmas.

"He was born in Three Chimneys," Leland reminded her. "That's what counts."

"My first distinct memory of you"—Margaret smiled—"was in the seventh grade. You brought a bug to science class—I'd never seen anything like it. It was enormous, with red eyes and long orange legs. It had sharp wings and in my memory it had antlers, but I guess that is sort of unlikely . . ."

"I remember that bug," said August. "It turned out to be a—"

"—A seventeen-year cicada," Margaret finished. "None of us were old enough to have seen one before. I remember Mr. Barrett told us they lived underground for seventeen years sucking the blood out of trees, waiting to be born. I had nightmares for weeks."

"I can't believe you remember that," August said, laughing.

"How could I forget?" she asked. "Three weeks later, they were everywhere. Plagues of them. I remember Daddy had just planted some peach trees and we ran around covering them with cheesecloth, but it was too late. They were ruined with eggs. Leland, if you want to talk about noise, those cicadas were much worse. You couldn't talk on the phone, you couldn't watch TV, you couldn't hear yourself think for the noise."

"It was right before school let out," said August. "I used to lie in bed with pillows over my head, they were so loud. I felt responsible, somehow. As if bringing the bug to school had made them hatch."

"That's funny," said Leland. "I don't remember that at all."

"You don't remember Mom sweeping husks off the sidewalk day and night?"

Leland shook his head. "Bugs. Traffic. I guess a person can get used to anything."

"I guess she can," Margaret echoed softly.

All around them, the camp was settling in for the night. Battery lanterns in tents clicked off, laughter from the woods died down. But Margaret was not in the least sleepy. Tomorrow this would all be over and they would return to their old routine. She and August might never again have an opportunity to sit like comrades-in-arms, snuggled down in their coats so that their shoulders pressed together in the dark. When she glanced over at her friend, she caught his eyes upon her, tracing her face as if in search of that seventh-grade girl who was afraid of bugs. Before he'd walked out, August had been more of a concept, like "loyalty," or "diligence," than a physical presence in the world. But now, his long, relaxed body radiated heat beside her, and she imagined what it would feel like to press herself against it.

"I'm going for a walk before bed," she said. "There's a great view from the park across the road."

She rose and paused a moment, looking up at the sky. Though there were as many stars out as the night before, the lights of the city obscured them, and she had trouble identifying even a single constellation. She stood for a minute, but when neither man stirred, she stooped and kissed Leland on the cheek.

"Good night," she said.

They bid her good night, and watched her slowly walk across the parking lot, until she finally disappeared from view. Pastor Vaughn cleared his throat.

"That was an invitation if ever I saw one," he said.

"What do you mean?" replied August.

"Seemed to me she hated to go alone."

"Dad, if Margaret wanted one of us to go with her, she would have said so."

"You can refuse to see from both directions, son. Before you wouldn't admit she didn't love you, and now you won't admit she does."

"A person doesn't change overnight like that."

"No, but they do sometimes come to their senses," said Leland.

August didn't answer. He had been trying to remember what Margaret looked like back when he first met her. She was not the most beautiful girl in class, but she had always been one of the strongest. He closed his eyes and saw her clearly, tall and thin in a light cotton dress. She walked to his desk, where he sat with his discovery, and put her head against his, staring with wonder and apprehension into the grass-filled jar.

"It's funny you remember the noise the first summer we moved home," mused his father. "All I remember is the quiet."

"You know, maybe I will take a little walk," said August, casually rising. "Are you sure you'll be all right here, alone?"

"I doubt the cheese is a prime terrorist target." Leland smiled.

Leland watched his son set out in the direction Margaret had taken some minutes ago, then slid his chair to be closer to the Mammoth Cheese. As on the eve of a battle, the air seemed charged tonight, and it would not have surprised him to find the woods of Columbia Island dotted with bonfires or sentries calling out, "*Who goes there?*" He wondered if the original Mammoth Priest had sat watch over his cheese the night before they entered the capital. It would have been much quieter, he imagined. And darker. With no brightly lit monuments and only a half-finished White House across the way, Washington would have been indistinguishable from the plot of land upon which he now sat. Something in that equivalent darkness struck Pastor Vaughn as especially democratic.

The closer he'd gotten to Washington, the more he'd found his thoughts turning to his counterpart. The Elder John Leland was a rustic preacher, known for his love of freedom and for casting out spirits—"groaners," he called them. When he delivered the Sunday sermon before Congress the day after he delivered the cheese, many laughed at his rough speech and passionate delivery. Even Thomas Jefferson seemed embarrassed. Pastor Vaughn looked around the woods to those who had pitched their tents alongside him. Most who'd joined the procession had been attracted by the absurdity of the offering, he knew. And yet, maybe in the end, the joke would be on them. For the purity of a gesture had a way of shining through all attempts to disparage it. Pastor Vaughn leaned his head against his white plastic chair and gazed up at the Washington Monument, soaring over the trees. It looked like a blade against the night sky, beckoning him and warning him away. Washington was rattling its sword.

Leland didn't realize he was dozing until a noise startled him awake. By the orange light of the parking lot, he saw a female figure approaching, but he could not recognize the face.

"Who's there?" he called groggily.

"It's just me, Pastor Vaughn." Polly Marvel stepped out of the shadows. "I'm looking for my mom. Have you seen her?"

"She said she was going for a walk," answered the priest, pulling himself upright in his chair. "It's late, though. Shouldn't you be in bed?"

Polly made no answer, but walked around to his side of the float and stared up at the cheese, sleeping beneath its canvas blanket. "I'll be happy when this is all over," she said.

"You're not excited to meet the president?" asked Leland. "To see Washington?"

"We went to the Smithsonian once with Dad," Polly said. "There are a bunch of restaurants across the bridge. Mom told me not to take so many shrimp from the buffet, I'd never eat them all."

"I love a good buffet," said the priest appreciatively.

"So, Mom's not around?" she asked again. "I was hoping to talk to her about something."

"I think she and August walked across to the river," he answered. "Is something on your mind?" he asked when she had not spoken for several minutes.

"I was just wondering," she began, not meeting his eye, but continuing to stare at the cheese, as if expecting it to rise up like a flying saucer, or to burst from its cocoon and fly away. "You and Mrs. Vaughn have been married a long time, haven't you?"

"Almost forty-five years."

"You never thought about getting divorced?"

"I can honestly say we never did," answered Leland. "We had our rough times like everyone else, but we worked through them."

"I think it's wrong to go back on your word, once you've given it," said Polly. "I'm not like Mom and Dad."

"I think people are often too quick to walk away when things get difficult," responded Leland carefully. "Relationships are about compromise. I often let Mrs. Vaughn think she's right even when I know she's wrong. It's what people in love do for each other."

"So if you love someone, you should give them what they want?" asked Polly.

Leland, thinking of his son and Margaret, slowly feeling their way toward one another after so many false starts, replied, "Once you're sure, you usually want the same things."

Polly seemed to mull that over for a long while. "Thank you, Pastor Vaughn," she said. "You've been a great help."

"Any time," he said, smiling. "Now, you should go to bed. We have a busy day tomorrow."

"I need to talk to someone first," Polly told him, taking her leave. She buried her hands deep in her pockets. "You should bundle up. It's cold tonight."

"That reminds me," he called to her. "Did you happen to catch the Mexican weather report?" Polly turned back dutifully, but just then a plane flew overhead and swallowed the stupid punch line forever.

Good-bye river. Good-bye trees. She walked through the thickly wooded park, following the strobe of headlights through the guard-rail of the George Washington Highway. Earlier in the evening, some kids had built a fire in the low chimneys here and roasted marshmallows. They were long gone, but the smell of charcoal and burnt sugar still hung in the air.

Good-bye cars and commuter buses and monuments she would never visit. She might stand in line one day to read the sentiments carved on all those white marble walls, but she would be someone else by then, no longer the self she took into the woods tonight.

This was what she wanted. What she'd asked for. And yet she couldn't shake the feeling it had been his plan all along. She saw him up ahead, standing alone in a grove of pines. His arms were folded across his chest and the headlights of the oncoming traffic flared off his glasses, hiding his eyes. He was waiting for her. She was his prize pupil.

The scene was not as she'd imagined it. There was no mountaintop or moonbeam. His hand, when it grasped hers, was cold and firm, and not much bigger than her own. Overhead, white clouds scudded across the sky like the moon's vaporous breath.

Good-bye night. Good-bye clouds. Good-bye girlhood.

"It's better this way," he whispered, and she felt his hot, liberating breath against her neck. "We both know it's wrong to love a child."

CHAPTER TWENTY-SEVEN

Across the highway, in Lady Bird Johnson Park, Margaret sat on a cold park bench overlooking the water. When she was filing the special permits to camp at Columbia Island, no one had told her their site lay in the flight path of Reagan National Airport. She would never get to sleep tonight. Each time she heard an engine straining against the atmosphere, she flinched, waiting for it to fall out of the sky. But then she remembered the summers spent at her aunts' house by the railroad tracks and the F&P freight train that barreled through at precisely 1:54 A.M. every night, passing so close it shook the windows loose in their wooden sashes. After a week, she learned to sleep through it, and after two, when it missed a trip, she woke at its absence. Leland was right, she thought, a person could get used to anything.

"I suppose a Mammoth Cheese would just about satisfy a nineteen-foot Jefferson."

Margaret started at the sound of August's voice in the dark. He slid onto the park bench and joined her in gazing across the water. On the opposite shore, the familiar monuments glowed white like aspects of the moon—the Doric temple where Lincoln sat enthroned as Olympian Zeus; the unadorned Egyptian obelisk to honor our country's father; the pantheon of Jefferson, with its Augustan cupola.

"Are we being presumptuous with this gift?" she asked. "Adams Brooke is no Jefferson."

"The ancient Greeks would have been scandalized to see how we've elevated our leaders, no matter how beloved. Jefferson was a mere mortal, after all, and towering stature was reserved only for the gods."

"I never thought I'd hear you refer to Jefferson as a mere mortal."

"I never thought so either."

They fell silent, watching the rippling reflection of the monuments in the river. The backlit cherry blossoms fluttered like a million luna moths above the branches.

"Patrick Lewis made a joke last night about being the same age as the Italian Constitution," she said at last, to have something to say. "How do they expect a document no older than a weatherman to attain any sense of sacredness?"

August laughed. "I used to be appalled at how easily other countries ripped up their constitutions, until I realized how young we must seem to them. Democracy is just another experiment for most. One that might or might not last. In the grand scheme, maybe a single document is not so important."

"How can you say that?" asked Margaret in surprise. "The Constitution is the greatest inheritance in the history of the world."

August shook his head and gestured across the water. "What incentive do we have to think great thoughts for ourselves when we have the thoughts of great men to hide behind? Maybe Jefferson was right and we should shake it up every so often. It's dangerous to raise up anything or anyone too high. It invites abuse."

Margaret made no reply.

"I've always been scared of you," said August simply.

She turned to him in dismay. "What?"

"All of our lives you've seemed to know exactly who you were and what you wanted. You've always been in complete control."

"In control?" Margaret laughed ruefully. "Last night Patrick told me the Family Matters vote was purposely scheduled for the day we'd arrive. That the president wanted the country to see how the small farmer supported him, even as he sold us out."

"Do you believe him?"

"Adams Brooke stole my family's motto," she admitted for the first time aloud. "And instead of speaking up, I blackmailed him with it in a letter. I told myself I was letting Patrick bring the cameras to put pressure on Congress, but that wasn't it. I was worried about the president."

"A family motto," said August. "It's no big deal in the scheme of things."

"But aren't the small lies the worst?" asked Margaret. "They are like a million drops of acid rain on one of those statues."

She looked across at the low domes and sudden spikes that formed Washington's cardiogram skyline. "I feel like the faith that brought me here is gone," she said. "Every four years we go through the same cycle of hope and disillusionment. I honestly thought this time would be different."

"Tomorrow you have a once in a lifetime opportunity to speak to power," said August with feeling. "It doesn't matter how you got here. Say what you came to say."

"I don't even know what that is anymore."

"Maybe disillusionment is the key to growing up," August said softly. "Sometimes I think the only power we have is the ability to say no. No to the marketplace. No to those who use us to benefit themselves. And when those more powerful than ourselves go astray, the only way to call them back is with a resounding No. You taught me that."

"And yet," sighed Margaret, "I am dying to say Yes."

It was dark where they sat, in between the yellow pools of two streetlamps. She could see August only by the reflected light of Washington, and it gave him an unearthly bluish tinge, like an apparition. She had invested so much time and energy in Adams Brooke and his amnesty, when the last honorable man, if not in America, at least of her acquaintance, was sitting right here beside her.

"August, I am so sorry I've taken you for granted," she said. He sat silently so long she feared he hadn't heard her.

"And I'm sorry I didn't kiss you when we were both sixteen," he replied at last.

When August leaned in, Margaret kept her eyes open. She had no memory of the day they had walked to the old chimney and she had eaten cheese from the tip of his knife, the day that haunted him. If he had tried then, she would have let him, as she would have let anyone unobjectionable, accepting their thirsty lips as no more than proof purchase of her desirability. It was easy to crave a soft, spoiled girl, whose own self-love was infectious, but now she was old, and sharp as baling wire, and she wanted to see what a man looked like who was willing to kiss an electric fence. She half-expected August to pull back in confusion, rubbing his mouth against the shock, but to her surprise, he pressed his lips gently to hers, as if sensing her defense and loving even the barricade. She had seen this mouth curled around a stalk of alfalfa, chewing the sweet grass as he went about his chores. She had seen it whisper in the ear of a nervous cow, seen it smile at her daughter's capering, and frown over some imperceptible catch in a tractor engine. She realized she'd seen it in a hundred incarnations, and yet every one was but a prelude to its true shape, which was that of a mouth interlocked with her own, unburdening itself of decades of love. Margaret closed her eyes and understood, in that moment, the true meaning of amnesty, which was not, she now knew, a forgiveness of debt, but a forgiveness of self, of one's own selfishnesses and cruelties, one's myriad small disappointments and epic failures. August's kiss bestowed that pardon upon her, and in returning it, she forgave him, too—for having spent years in a relationship to which he had failed to invite her, preferring to love his own deified marble, rather than the flesh and blood she was. Yes, thought Margaret, as she allowed herself the exquisite surrender, a person could get used to anything.

Another plane followed the glassy strip of Potomac in for a landing. The two old friends sat back and watched its descent from their park bench, neither speaking nor touching, merely savoring the alien majesty of their capital city, content to have found one another at last, here on the opposite shore.

When August left her, it was nearly one o'clock. For so late at night, traffic was constant enough that he still had to wait several minutes to cross the highway. He looked over his shoulder to where she remained on the park bench, the scarf she had knit for him now wrapped around her neck, her hands swimming in his bulky wool gloves. His own hands were still warm from being buried in her hair, but the rest of him trembled with emotion, something uncomfortably close to panic. He had loved Margaret and then hated her, and now, she was his and he didn't know how to feel. He was unused to success.

The oncoming headlights swept the marina-side woods, felling the long shadows of trees like a clear-cut. At the next break, he jogged across the highway and stepped over the fence that separated the road from the picnic grounds. He turned down the pine needle path toward his tent, and tried not to notice the two shadowy figures moving against a nearby tree, for having just left an assignation, he was loath to disturb someone else's. If he had found the courage he had tonight all those years ago, he wondered, would he have grown up to be the sort of boy who snuck away to meet girls in the woods? Suddenly, he felt greedy for experience, and found himself irrationally thinking of Gillian, the woman he met in the doctor's office, and what it would have been like to kiss her, too.

August averted his eyes, but just barely, for he was guiltily aroused by the proxy groping. In the end, he had pulled back from Margaret on the bench, reluctant to commit himself too far before he knew his own mind, but now, he wished it were her naked back against the rough bark of the tree and his mouth hungrily upon hers. He hurried past, but something about this pair nagged at him. There was a mismatch in the size of the two bodies, and a furtive awkwardness of arms and legs struggling to find purchase. At the risk of seeming voyeuristic, August turned and looked more closely, and even as he did, a low moan escaped the stand of trees, like that of a child in the throes of a nightmare. Then suddenly August was running, for even in its inarticulation, he recognized the voice.

"*Polly!*" he shouted.

Mr. March turned, just as August tackled him, bringing them both to the ground. From beneath, Polly squirmed out and crawled across the cold path, buttoning her shirt as she went. She watched in horror as August drove his fist into her teacher's face again and again, and maybe she screamed, she couldn't be sure, for the blood was pounding in her ears too loudly and a plane roared overhead. She

saw her teacher zip his pants as he pulled away from his attacker, and
then hurl himself at August, shouting—she thought she heard; she
would never be sure—"She came to me. I didn't force her to do anything." But then August had wrestled him to the ground again, and
was sitting on his chest, raining punches, one of which broke Mr.
March's glasses, for she heard him cry out, unmistakably this time,
"You motherfucker, I can't see."

Polly threw herself upon August, scratching and biting to get
him off her teacher. August barely felt her attack, but it gave Mr.
March a chance to kick free and right himself. By the headlights, Polly
could see he was bleeding from a cut to his forehead and another to
his mouth.

"If I ever see you again, I'll kill you," said August.

Polly waited for Mr. March to come at August again; she was
still clinging to his coat and her teacher would have a free shot to
the stomach. But after the furious struggle, he merely knelt, trying to
catch his breath. The plane overhead had broken for the clouds, leaving only a faint whine behind. Harvey March wiped the blood from
his mouth.

"Keep fighting, Polly," he said. Then he turned and walked away.

"Where are you going?" cried Polly.

August folded her in his arms. "Are you all right? Do you need
to see a doctor?"

"*Mr. March, where are you going?*" she screamed after her teacher's
retreating figure. "Get off of me, August," she shouted, struggling to
break free. "I'm not a child. I wanted him to. I wanted him to."

But August would not let go. Polly fought wildly, pummeling
him with her fists, ripping at his hair, leaving long scratch marks down
the side of his face. At last, when he thought the danger had passed,
he released her, and Polly whirled away from him. "I hate you, August
Vaughn," she screamed. "You've ruined everything."

"Polly, we need to find your mother," said August sternly. "We
need to call the police."

His mention of the police brought her up short. She would never
let Mr. March go to jail. With great effort, Polly calmed herself.

"We don't need the police," she said. "Nothing happened."

"Then Margaret—"

"August, I'm fine," she interrupted. "Nothing happened. I don't want to upset Mom. Let's just get through tomorrow and I'll tell her when we get home."

August hesitated. He remembered what it felt like to be thirteen and to have no say in your own life. He examined her closely and saw she did not seem to be hurt.

"That man is your teacher," he said at last. "He is supposed to protect you."

"Mr. March was there for me," she said. "Which is more than I can say for any one of you."

August, absent these last three months, had no reply. "Let me walk you back to camp," he said at last.

Polly lay miserably in the dark, a prisoner in her tent. He said he was going to bed, but she knew August was out there, making sure she didn't sneak out. She heard him stifle a cough. She heard him shift his weight from one foot to the other. He didn't trust her, either. She closed her eyes and imagined Mr. March creeping up to strangle him from behind, then stealing her away like Pocahontas. But even as she imagined their getaway in the stolen yellow school bus, she knew it was too late. Mr. March was gone.

She knew it on the humiliating, empty walk back. She felt his absence in the distant hum of traffic and the weak halo around the cobra-head lamps of the parking lot. It was in her neighbors' snores and ghostly white sailboats in dock, and in everything going about the business of being, when she had been changed forever. Or rather, not changed. She lay in the dark, remembering his hands on her, so sure and unfamiliar. *Say it*, he whispered in her ear. I want you to, she answered. His hands were inside her shirt and they were cold like her father's hands when he came in from the barn and stuck them on her belly to make her squeal. *Say it again*. Once, she and Francis had gone sledding at the edge of their property where the land was especially steep. Her dad's long legs dangled off the back of the Flexible Flyer, she had climbed on top of his back and clung to his neck, and together they had flown down the hill, until she felt herself slipping. Then she was rolling, over and over, pulling him and the sled with her; they rolled until they just missed a lone poplar tree by inches. Polly lay panting, staring into the bright blue sky. Her mittens were matted with snow and she had ice in the cuffs of her parka, but she was on fire inside, and her cheeks ached from laughing. Polly heard her teacher's zipper lower and then her hands were being eased inside his jeans. I want you to, she said.

It's all your fault, she wanted to shout at August, who was still out there. She smelled him, she felt his heavy, obvious silence, like that of a parent lurking in the next room to eavesdrop on a telephone conversation. No one gave her credit for knowing her own mind. Only Mr. March. And why should he ever come back? Why would he come back for a little girl?

In the sleeping bag beside her, Bethany slept with her mouth open, a reservoir of drool staining the tattered Hello Kitty pillow she'd slept with since she was three years old. The close tent stank of stale alcohol from where Bethany and some of the other girls had snuck off with a group of local boys who offered them Zima from paper bags. She felt a lifetime older than Bethany now, and couldn't imagine ever again sitting in her rock-star-papered bedroom, dreaming of wedding dresses. She knew too much about injustice now, and oppression, and if she had been foiled in becoming a woman, she was certainly no longer a child. No matter how long August stayed, she could outlast him. A people determined to be free could never be enslaved.

It was four o'clock before August finally gave up and crept off to sleep. Polly waited half an hour more, then climbed over her drunken tentmate to let herself out. She shivered outside of their warm, girlish terrarium. The traffic on the highway had slowed to an occasional truck rushing past. Everyone was asleep. She had no idea where Mr. March was or how to reach him, but she knew she had to make him understand he had taught her well. *Mr. March, I love you*, thought Polly. Rebellion to Tyrants Is Obedience to God.

In his white plastic chair, Pastor Vaughn was dreaming. He was standing at the pulpit of St. Barnabas delivering his Sunday morning sermon, but the pews were empty. *Give us this day our daily bread*, he intoned. Just out of his line of vision, he saw a figure move. It jumped from row to row, always just out of sight, and though he moved quickly, he was never able to catch it. *And forgive us our trespasses as we forgive those who trespass against us*. He glanced down at his prayer book, and when he looked up again, he saw a young girl race from the back of the church, leaving the doors open behind her. Outside, the sky glowed molten red, and a sirocco wind blew, lifting the hair on his forehead. It was only then that he realized—of course—he must be at the center of the earth.

CHAPTER TWENTY-EIGHT

Margaret Prickett awoke in a new country. It was a hopeful terrain, rich with contentment and vast provinces of possibility. Banished were the lingering doubts of yesterday, for in this new dominion, love fed love of country and patriotism seemed possible again. She left her tent, having slept better than she had in months, and walked to the bench where she and August had, at long last, declared themselves. Across the water, at the base of the Jefferson Memorial, workmen set up rows of chairs like dominoes, suited men securing the perimeter. Margaret unfolded the speech she had drafted last night, and read over it aloud. Before her stood the president of the United States; beside her, her daughter and true love. And in between was the gift of a lifetime: a cheese for the people.

"Behold what America still has to offer, Mr. President," read Margaret to the pigeons who pecked along the river walk before her. "We are not wholly corrupt. We can still summon from the land works of majestic power and beauty. In this cheese, we give you the history of a place—millennia of our mountains eroded into loam and red clay Pamunkey soil; eons of grass grown upon its back; centuries of our forefathers' cultivation of this plot; decades of a bovine's growth and pasturage. Every footprint that drove a seed that sprouted a blossom that fed a beast is in this cheese, Mr. President. Every generation's sustaining toil, every aspiration for its children, every buried parent created this specific run of earth from which sprang this particular creation, which we now present to you as a token of our thanks for its continuance. Cherish this individuality, which others yearn to destroy, Mr. President. Don't sell it out to the long chrome corridors of the efficient factory, with its hairnet, plastic-gloved, pasteurized and homogenized future. When you feed the corporation, it swallows not only our future, but the past that brought us here."

Would she have the courage to make her speech? Her hands trembled just holding the folded notebook paper, and she felt a rumble of stage fright deep in her stomach. But then she remembered August's words of last night. It was her one opportunity to speak to power, and if she did not speak strongly, she would regret it forever.

Margaret returned to a marina bustling with excitement. No matter what a jaded American might think about the political process, the president—Democrat or Republican—retained a certain star power, and as such, meeting him provided great cause for excitement. As they brushed their teeth and shook the wrinkles out of their carefully packed Sunday clothes, the citizens of Three Chimneys experienced that heightened awareness of living a day already in the past tense. April 6, a square on a calendar, had lost all objective meaning once it dawned as The Day I Met the President. The sun, which on any pedestrian day would have shone unnoticed, broke through especially dark clouds The Day I Met the President. The wind that had been blowing cold from the northeast last night suddenly reversed itself The Day I Met the President, bringing with it a warm—one might even say, hopeful—breeze. For Bob Crenshaw, threading his collar with a necktie, every detail of the day added to the narrative he was rehearsing for his wife's mother back home, who for years had been dining out on the anecdote of once having stayed in the same hotel room as Franklin Delano Roosevelt, a mere day after he'd quit it. Bob knew, as well as any, that an occasion of this magnitude had only the slightest personal import; it was more a gift to those not present, so that decades from now, when that quaintly framed portrait of Great-grandfather shaking hands with President Adams Brooke was placed upon the mantel, one's heirs could recite the president's many accomplishments and failures as if Great-grandfather had been a witness to them all. And who knew what inspiration might arise from even that briefest encounter? After all, a young boy from Hope, Arkansas, had vowed to become president after a handshake from JFK.

Margaret looked for August in the crowd, and was disappointed not to see him; August oversleeping on such an important day seemed out of character. She spotted Polly in the throng, standing with her friends near the doughnut table set up by the local chapter of the DAR. Polly looked tired, but even roughed by sleeplessness, Margaret was struck by how beautiful her daughter was growing up to be. She had her father's classic Roman nose and the deep wheaten hair of Margaret's girlhood before it had darkened to brown. The goofy, smart-alecky nine- and ten-year-old was giving way to a more serious and thoughtful young woman, who took in the world as if testing it for weakness. Whatever my sins, thought Margaret, I gave birth to a remarkable girl. Love was making Margaret charitable even to the obscenely pink-uddered Holsteins and the ruddy-cheeked angels that festooned the float. What had been an embarrassment of tackiness only yesterday now, upon second consideration, struck her more as inspired folk art and a fittingly artisanal pasture for her unique cheese.

"Are you Margaret Prickett?" A young bald man in black plastic-framed glasses held out his hand. "Sandy Jameson."

"Of course, Mr. Jameson," she replied, shaking his hand. She instantly recognized his voice as the man from Campaign Headquarters who'd interviewed her before the election.

"It's gonna be incredibly tight," he said, consulting a leather portfolio bristling with printed E-mail pages. "The president is coptering in from Richmond, then leaves for Camp David to meet with the Saudis at noon. We have exactly half an hour for cheese and speeches."

"It sounds like we're an imposition," said Margaret dryly.

"No, no, he's gonna love it," said Sandy. "He's been talking about nothing else all week."

Margaret eyed him skeptically, but the press secretary was already moving away, directing the police escort and briefing his staff. As she watched, Leland approached excitedly.

"Have you ever felt your entire life was leading up to one moment?" asked the priest. "This is Three Chimneys' finest hour."

"Have you seen August?" asked Margaret, barely listening. His father looked around quizzically.

"Now that you mention it, no."

Margaret walked away from the noisy crowd, determined to find the one person she most wanted to see. She walked behind the café, where his olive green tent was the only one still standing.

"Knock, knock," she said. Through the lightweight fabric, she saw a shadowy body stir inside.

"What happened to you?" Margaret exclaimed when he stuck his head through the unzipped flap. August touched his hand to his swollen, raked cheek. He couldn't tell if his stomach ached from the punches or from being startled awake after only three and a half hours of sleep.

"I tripped in the dark walking home last night," he said.

"You should watch where you're going," said Margaret. "That face is too handsome to ruin."

He smiled weakly, conscious of how he would have once cherished those words. When he looked at Margaret now, all he saw was her thirteen-year-old daughter's hastily misbuttoned blouse.

"It's after eight o'clock," she said. "You're going to miss the big event."

"I'll get dressed and be out in a minute," he said.

Margaret hesitated, not having anticipated this cool reception after last night. August intently studied the ground by her left foot.

"All right then," she said, too brightly. "I'll see you."

He nodded and ducked back inside the tent. Margaret walked miserably back to the launch ramp, fighting her nagging anxiety. She was sometimes short with Polly first thing in the morning. It didn't necessarily mean anything.

"Leland, let's get the bus warming up," said Sandy Jameson, directing traffic. "Margaret, make whatever last-minute adjustments you need to. We're ready to roll."

Leland took his seat behind the steering wheel and turned the engine. Dutifully, Margaret boarded the float, where her creation slumbered behind its canvas cloth. The stage fright of earlier this

morning returned and she wished August were here beside her. Or
Polly, who seemed to be watching her from the crowd of students with
bright intensity.

"Margaret," said the *Three Chimneys Register* photographer, "let's
get one last shot of you and the Big Boy."

Over his shoulder, she saw August walking through the forest,
making his way to join them. Everything was going to be all right, she
told herself. She would get through this morning. She would say her
piece. She would go home. Margaret drew the red, white, and blue
curtains and tied them back with their spangled braid. But as she lifted
away the drop cloth, the fabric came away stickily, like skin from a scab.
The underside of the cloth was stained red, as if with blood.

"What is it? What's wrong?" Sandy Jameson asked, seeing her
face. "Holy fuck!" he shouted. In giant red, dripping letters slashed
across the rind, he read the words: "Rebellion to Tyrants Is Obedience to God."

"What's going on?" asked Leland, cutting the engine and climbing out of the bus.

Margaret stared in disbelief. She turned to him. "Leland?"

Pastor Vaughn stared at the vandalized cheese, dumbfounded.
"I was here all night," he stammered. "I never left my chair."

"Did you fall asleep?"

"I don't—I don't think so," he said. "But. There was a can of
red paint in the bus. The kids used it to paint the banner."

Margaret turned back to the cheese as if expecting the rind, like
a skinned knee, to have magically healed itself. Rebellion. Tyrant.
She remembered the phrase, but with the haziness of a childhood song
lyric, or the poetry of her marriage vows. She had the memory of sitting at the kitchen table, watching her daughter rock back in her
chair, tilting toward the fire.

"Margaret, I don't know what to say," said Pastor Vaughn.

But Margaret wasn't listening. She was watching her daughter in
the crowd of horror-struck students. Some of the girls clung to one
another, as undone by the criminal defacement of the cheese as they
had been by the death of Chase Andrew Frank. Some of the boys, not

daring to snigger in the presence of men with guns, reacted as they thought the Secret Service would wish, vowing to "beat the living shit" out of whatever psycho was responsible. For their own part, the agents assigned to accompany the cheese moved rapidly to confirm that the words were not some helter-skelter threat against the president. Everyone seemed to be in motion—gesturing wildly, offering advice. *We can wash it off*, she heard Leland say from a distance. *It's just the rind. We can wash it off.*

Polly alone did not move. She stood in the midst of confusion, pale and defiant, staring back at her mother. Margaret leapt from the float and stormed over to her daughter.

"Did you think about anyone besides yourself?" shouted Margaret, grabbing Polly by the arm. "Did you think of Pastor Vaughn, or any of your neighbors? Did you think about how this would make the president look?"

"I'm not sorry," said Polly defiantly. "Adams Brooke is a liar and a hypocrite. And so are you."

"Have you lost your mind?" cried Margaret.

"I declare myself free of you. And of Dad. And of this small-minded country," swore Polly.

"I knew you were mad at me," said Margaret, "but I never thought you would stoop to something so selfishly childish. You are a spoiled-rotten little girl. You are—"

"Don't," August interrupted, able to stand by no longer. Last night, he had worried only about her teacher returning; he had never thought to guard Polly from herself. In the end he, too, had underestimated her. "This is *our* fault," he hurled at Margaret. "Your own daughter was being molested and we didn't even notice."

"August, you shut up!" screeched Polly.

"*What?*" demanded Margaret. "Polly, what is he saying?"

"Last night I stopped Polly's teacher from raping her."

Polly paled before the shocked faces of Bethany and her classmates. Margaret stepped forward, but Polly threw her off.

"I love Mr. March," Polly raged. "He is the only person who cared about me. He's the only one who put me first."

"Polly, why didn't you come to me?" asked Margaret.

"Maybe you haven't noticed, Mom, but you've been a little busy lately," retorted Polly.

Margaret looked helplessly to August, who turned away. He knew this morning and he didn't tell her. Last night, while they— Suddenly, his distant behavior made sense. It wasn't about her. Or rather, it was all about her—her blindness, her failure. She made one last feeble attempt to explain herself.

"Polly, I was working so hard to save the farm," she said. "To protect your future."

"What makes you think I want the farm?" asked Polly. "Did you ever ask me? What if I want to become a journalist or join the Peace Corps? What if I want a life separate from you?"

Margaret stood helplessly before her daughter. Before Polly was born, Margaret wouldn't have cared if the earth had opened and swallowed everything in her life. Good-bye dairy, with your straw-filled stalls. Good-bye fields and stream and house and chimney. Good-bye memories and friends, mother and father. And husband. She loved Francis but she could live without him. She loved her life, but death didn't scare her. Then Polly was born, and overnight, she understood the meaning of fear. On the morning of her birth, after she had labored all night long, she had taken her new daughter to the window just as the gray dawn was spreading over the mountains, striking each tree like the tip of a match. She was so greedy for her baby, she wished she could be pregnant with Polly and hold her in her arms at the same time, she wished they could remain as they stood in the picture window, never to be interrupted from their gazing across the mountain, or separated, or disturbed. Their life together would never be purer than at this moment, Margaret had realized. Polly's cells were her cells, the energy that ignited her was her mitochondria, the food in her belly was Margaret's milk. Nothing unfiltered by Margaret had gone into this unadulterated vessel of baby.

But each new sensation, each new experience would erode the mother in this child, make her less of Margaret and more of herself.

She'd spent the next thirteen years trying to protect her from a hostile world, but in the end, she had lost her all the same.

"Margaret, the president will be arriving any minute," said Sandy Jameson nervously. "We've got to go. Just pretend it's supposed to be there."

Beyond him, the blue lights of their motorcade spun hypnotically. All around, men in suits spoke furiously into hidden headsets, news crews and neighbors milled about in confusion. August stood behind Polly, staring at the ground, but Polly held Margaret's eyes with the same expression she'd worn as that little baby. Everything else might have altered—her limbs had lengthened, her mind sharpened—but her probing-finger gaze was still exactly the same, testing to see where her mother was strong, and where she would give. Slowly, Margaret turned and walked to the driver's side of Leland's bus.

That's it then, thought Polly, her chin trembling despite all efforts to control it. I am free. Through the bug-spattered windshield, she watched her grim-faced mother turn the engine. Polly was not so far gone a revolutionary that she did not hold out some desperate hope of reconciliation with her motherland, but seeing Margaret put the bus in gear and step on the gas ended any illusions she might have had. Mr. March was gone. Her mother was leaving. Polly knew she should feel triumphant to have earned her emancipation at last, but instead she felt more abandoned than she ever had in her life.

The police escorts hit their sirens and the presidential press secretary ran to his black sedan. Margaret gunned the engine, but instead of following the others across the parking lot and over the bridge, Leland's bus lurched backward. The crowd watched in shock as Margaret threw the vehicle into reverse and sped the float down the steep incline of the launch ramp, hitting the brakes at the last possible instant.

"Mom!" cried Polly. "What are you doing?"

For a long second after it sailed off the trailer, the float skimmed the surface of the lagoon, weightless as a water bug. The generator that powered the lights still ran; the hollow cows, like their real-life counterparts in a flood, perched upon an island rooftop. On its dais, the graffitied Mammoth Cheese remained perfectly dry, and those on shore stood motionless, as if the slightest movement would tip the scale. Quickly enough, however, the river pushed through the cracks in the cheap plywood base. Margaret climbed out of the bus and turned to her daughter.

"The only power we have is the ability to say no," she said. "Nothing is worth losing you."

In an instant, the Secret Service agents were on top of Margaret, afraid of what she would do next, pushing her face into the bus and pinning her arms behind her back. Polly stared in amazement as they handcuffed her mother like a public menace and shoved her toward the police car. Margaret called out for her as they shouldered her past, but Polly couldn't hear what her mother said, for at just that moment, a helicopter came in low over the river, which even she recognized as the familiar olive drab of *Marine One*.

The chaos of the blades was deafening, but inside his insulated cabin, Adams Brooke would be sitting in a padded white captain's chair, an open file on his lap. Was his wife with him? Their black standard poodle curled at his feet? As they banked over the Pentagon, he would be pushing aside the blue pleated curtain, and perhaps looking down on the chaos, asking an aide beside him, *What's going on down there? Beats me,* the aide would answer with a shrug. His tousled white hair, his loosened tie, his long toes inside navy blue socks, wriggling contentedly out of their loafers: Polly could imagine him so clearly. What are you thinking up there, demanded Polly, while we struggle below? Do you even know who we are? Is my mother's offering anything to you? Her friends and neighbors stood gazing up into the belly of the giant aircraft, struck with awe and the realization this was as close to the president as they would probably ever come. A shadow. A gust of wind. And it was all her fault. Polly took one last long look. Then she was running down the launch ramp and up the stairs to the long wooden pier tethered with sailboats. Peeling off her jacket as she ran, she dove into the icy water of the early-spring Potomac.

"*Polly, stop!*" screamed Margaret.

But Polly stroked furiously, her heart pounding against the frigid water. Behind her, she heard the splash of others jumping into the river after her. If she could just reach the cheese, she could keep it afloat. She could push it back to shore and they could dry it and clean it and give it to the president another day. Polly's arms and legs cramped from the cold and exertion, she swallowed a mouthful of water tasting of diesel fuel, but she reached out a hand and felt the rough face of the rind just as it tilted into the water. *Hold on!* she heard someone cry. *I didn't mean it,* she sobbed. *Help me save it.* She felt a hand reach out for her and fingers tangle in her own, as she kicked to maneuver herself beneath it, pitting her ninety-five pounds against its twelve hundred. *We have to save it.* But it was too late. Like a mammoth coin dropped in the cosmic wishing well, the cheese promptly sank, taking Polly Marvel with it.

Pastor Vaughn alone was not surprised to see his bus roll backward, and the float, discharging its angels and Holsteins, go crashing into the water. As the generator took in water and the lights shorted in a shower of sparks, he found himself thinking of Sodom and Gomorrah, or those who danced before the Golden Calf, or perhaps more appropriately, of the many unwary towns going about their business the first drizzly morning of the forty days and forty nights. This was what God's displeasure looked like, he thought. This was the sickening lurch of recognition they must have felt, conscious of their own hubris even as it was too late to escape their punishment. From the time he counseled Manda to have her eleven children to this moment, he had been on a collision course with the Creator. No, he would not compound his sin by believing Three Chimneys' pride on a par with the Tower of Babel or even the nostalgia of Lot's wife; it was simply that of any not-too-remarkable American town, so busy looking out that it had consistently failed to look in.

"*Polly, stop!*" he heard Margaret shout, even as her daughter raced past him. In an instant she was at the end of the pier, and then she was arcing into the river like a girl who had been diving all of her life, instead of someone who only occasionally cannonballed into her mother's cow pond. He didn't even know he was running after her until he heard his son shout his name. When he looked over his shoulder, he saw two more police officers tackle August, who'd tried to leap in after him, while others, swearing and shouting for backup, jumped into the water in their heavy dark clothes.

He felt the plunge like a punch. And then he was under, the water stopping his ears, plugging his nose, of such an intensity as to unravel any conscious thought. He gasped for breath and made himself move his arms. The Elder John Leland's wife had been turned out of her home at age four by a brutal stepfather, he thought randomly. She wandered in the snow until her feet were frostbitten and lost to exposure. Later, she developed a canker in her throat that left her speech so ravaged, only her husband ever understood her. When he would go baptizing in the hills of Orange County, the Elder Leland sang this hymn:

> *Christians, if your hearts are warm.*
> *Ice and snow can do no harm . . .*
> *Children, prove your love to Him*
> *never fear the frozen stream.*

Polly reached the float, which now lurched at a crazy angle, the Angel Gabriel tipping his trumpet into the water like a drinking straw. She had lost her glasses, and her unfocused green eyes darted frantically.

"Hold on," he called. "Don't let go."

"I didn't mean it," she sobbed. "Help me save it."

"I'm coming," said Pastor Vaughn. "Just hold on."

Leland took another furious stroke and caught her by the hand. *No,* cried Polly, trying to throw him off. *We have to save it.*

Then the world shifted and down, down into the occluded emerald river it towed them. Leland clung to Polly's hand, though like a lovesick mermaid she was dragging him down with her. Underwater, the priest opened his eyes and saw her terrified face, as she struggled to push the anvil of cheese up and off of her.

With all his stone fonts and holy oils, Pastor Vaughn had never understood the lure of a good old-fashioned revival baptism. The hungry river, the dripping clothes. His faith, oiled upon the forehead, was a cerebral faith, living in intellect and memory. But now he wondered if the Baptists weren't on to something. There was a soul-shaking honesty to the icy plunge. As the water took him, he found himself praying like a Baptist. *Give us this day our daily bread, And forgive us our debts as we forgive our debtors.* There was no Anglican trespassing for the Dissenters. And in that, too, they were more humane. For a trespass implied violation, whereas a debt, at least, might be repaid.

They were inches from the bottom, and Pastor Vaughn kicked backward, wrenching Polly's arm so fiercely, he feared he'd pulled it from the socket. He could feel her body scrape the surface of the rind, her knees plowing into the rocks on the river bottom, but then his own feet found purchase, and he was pushing off from the bottom, gripping her to him, shooting them to the surface like a champagne cork. They met the angels going down.

> *Fire is good to warm the soul;*
> *Water purifies the foul;*
> *Fire and water both agree;*
> *Winter soldiers never flee.*

Taking aim, he thrust her into the corona of sky and sunlight, blinded by the beauty of the cerulean April morning. Upon the death of Chase Andrew Frank, he had preached a sermon on what a parent owed a child. Life, he'd declared, nothing more. Now Polly was safe, and Leland realized the time for repayment was at hand. No one, not even him, could escape the debt of being born. And what a sad, beautiful, comical obligation it was.

Leland was falling.

Was it possible to pass and still be present? he wondered, almost idly. Just look at the Old Man in his front yard, surviving centuries of weather and neglect. The tavern had been consumed, but the hearth remained, transformed from utilitarian appendage to centerpiece.

August.

Yes, he thought. It was possible. Behold, I show you a mystery: We shall not all sleep, but we shall all be changed, in a moment, in the twinkling of an eye, at the last trump; for the trumpet shall sound, and the dead shall be raised incorruptible, and we shall be changed.

Evelyn.

Pastor Vaughn looked up at the blue sky far above him, fractured by a veil of bubbles. Inch by inch and cell by cell, he felt his body hardening. Ossifying. Tempering. He was becoming a man of stone, funneling up from the water, reaching for Heaven. He looked down and saw them all below—his weeping son and his mystified neighbors; his wife, reaching into Manda Frank's dryer for a load of wash; and Manda herself, aiming a spoon of applesauce into a tiny mouth. From high above, he saw Polly sputtering, clinging to an upturned, bobbing cow, reaching out for the hand of an officer she had never met, but would never forget. My family, thought the man of stone. Strong, and resolute, he would watch over them all like the Old Man in his front yard, their sentinel and eternal guardian.

For a glorious, eternal second, Pastor Vaughn soared above them all. Then the cold Potomac insinuated itself into his mortar, and his stones, one by one, floated free.

CHAPTER TWENTY-NINE

The funeral took place on a fine spring day when the dogwoods were in bloom. Disease had wiped out many of the trees in neighboring counties, but Three Chimneys had escaped the catastrophe, and the arbor behind St. Barnabas flared pink and white. The docent had thrown the windows open, letting in the scent of Easter hyacinth and jonquils like clean laundry drying on a line. She remembered that Pastor Vaughn had often noted how many people died in the spring. They held on through a long, cold winter, he said, only to relax when the weather broke. Spring was his busiest time of year.

Once again strangers filled the pews of St. Barnabas. Because of the sensationalism of the pastor's end, newsmen and film crews returned one final time to record the town's observation of grief. Few congregants spoke to them now, however, for the loss of their beloved pastor had quieted them, as a serious playground accident will bring even the rowdiest children to heel. There was the sense that with Leland's passing, a piece of their common history was gone forever. His death was as if one of the School Street oaks was cut down, or the War Memorial demolished; it was the melancholy of not only a friend, but an irreplaceable artifact lost, and how were they to speak to strangers of that?

The person with whom the press most wanted to converse remained stonily silent. Polly sat at the end of the first pew, but she felt as though she were sitting in the center of the church, with a brilliant spotlight shining upon her. Every face turned to watch her as she walked in, every camera panned, every reporter whispered into his microphone, *There goes the young woman for whom the pastor, Leland Vaughn, gave his life*. As much as her mother and Mrs. Vaughn assured her that the pastor had died of a stroke, one that might have stolen him at any moment, Polly knew she was to blame. She remembered little of the actual event: the swift descent beneath the millstone of the cheese and the sandy implosion as she hit bottom; the wrenching tug on her arm and the feeling of flying as they shot back up to the surface. But at the last moment, just as Pastor Vaughn had thrust her to safety, she had opened her eyes and seen his face. He, too, had broken free of the water. She alone knew his face was not slack with stroke, as they told her, but rapturous and abandoned, like that of a convert surrendering to a higher power. Then he was sinking again, this time without her. Now, whenever she closed her eyes, it was his face she saw, and she was once more in the icy, green bosom of the river, where all the blankets her mother piled on her and all the steaming cups of milk did nothing to warm her.

To acknowledge the tragedy, Adams Brooke sent the vice president, who sat with his wife in the first row, nodding along with the ceremony. The vice president was a pious man who had himself considered divinity school before choosing law, and now Polly saw him unconsciously mouthing along with the officiant the *Domine, Refugium:* "Lord, thou hast been our refuge, from one generation to another." It was a habit that annoyed his wife, for she thought it presumptuous, in the manner of singing along at a concert others wanted to enjoy. She gently pressed her husband's knee and he guiltily broke off before automatically joining in again at "For we consume away at thy displeasure, and are afraid at thy wrathful indignation."

Between Polly and the vice president sat her mother, August, and Mrs. Vaughn. Though Mrs. Vaughn had been asked to deliver the eulogy, she immediately deferred to her son, declaring herself altogether too shy to speak before a crowd. Everyone said how well Mrs. Vaughn was holding up; she had received the news of her husband's death with the external grace befitting a clergyman's wife. But inside, she felt as if the convicts down by the riverbank had stolen into her house and cleaned her out. She walked the empty rooms, touching familiar objects suddenly impermanent. She couldn't even think of it as her house anymore, for the rectory belonged to the parish, and once Leland's replacement was found, she would need to leave. Surprisingly, the thought distressed her little, for without her husband or son, it could hardly be called home any longer.

The night August delivered the news, he'd slept downstairs on the couch. She went alone up to bed, and removed her makeup as always, tucked her hair under its net, and slid beneath the cold, clean sheets. The yellow circle of light from the bedside lamp fell upon her untouched biography of Rosalynn Carter on the night table. Evelyn's eyes were too swollen with crying to read, but she was hours from sleep. Though she had never shared this feeling with Leland, for fear of a lecture, she had always held the pagan belief that if one of them should die without the opportunity to say good-bye, he or she would find a way to contact the other from the Other Side. So tonight, she closed her eyes and waited for a sign. She lay for a long time, listening for any message in the creaks of her old settling house, for a word in the wind at the window, for a dimming of the lights. She even listened to the pounding of her old, weary heart, deciding that if it skipped a beat, that was Leland's farewell. But there was nothing. The room was as quiet and chilly as ever, the pictures remained straight, nothing moved on her dressing table. At long last, she climbed out of bed, pulled on her white terry robe, and crept downstairs.

August lay asleep on the sofa, under a thick down comforter, and she didn't have the heart to wake him. She walked instead to their old television set, a machine she had barely touched over the years, always content to let Leland or August turn it on for her. Now, she settled herself in Leland's chair and, with the television muted, randomly switched channels in the dark. Several years ago, August had requested they get cable, which none of them ever watched, but it comforted Evelyn tonight to have so many choices pass by. She watched snippets of movie reruns and Infomercials. She learned she could have a tighter abdomen in just ten days or she would receive her money back. She understood now why men found this so addictive, for the world's passing by, summoned and dismissed with the push of a button, acted like a tranquilizer on her, and after a little while, she found herself growing sleepy. Evelyn rose to turn off the television, which had come to rest on one of the all-night news channels. But as she did so, the image on the screen held her transfixed. Sicily's Mount Etna was erupting again, read the newscaster, and as the grieving widow watched, fireworks of orange lava exploded high above the mountain and fell to earth in a shower of sparks.

"Behold, I show you a mystery," intoned the priest at the altar, reading the lesson from First Corinthians. "We shall not all sleep, but we shall all be changed, in a moment, in the twinkling of an eye, at the last trump; for the trumpet shall sound, and the dead shall be raised incorruptible, and we shall be changed."

The officiant, an old friend of Leland's, and a bachelor who often spent his holidays with the Vaughn family, delivered the ceremony with great feeling, but everyone in the congregation felt him to be inferior in every way to their pastor. His voice was reedy; he looked down too much. It was difficult to put one's faith in a man who obviously used hair spray. He finished the lesson, and motioned for August to rise and deliver the eulogy. Polly saw her mother's hand reach out to squeeze his. Dressed in his black wool suit, he looked more like his father than Polly had ever noticed before. She had sometimes wondered why he never became a priest like Leland and everyone else in his family, preferring to work the land than to read Scripture or think about the universe. If one didn't have to declare allegiance to God, Polly thought, she might like to be up there, commanding devotion and offering comfort. Over August's shoulder she saw the bronze plaque inscribed with the names of all those who had served St. Barnabas over the years. Pastor Vaughn's name hung suspended at the end, with this year's date as yet uncarved. There had never been a woman priest at St. Barnabas, noticed Polly, which now struck her as wrong. Who better than a woman, with her secret store of suffering, to understand the mysteries of the human condition?

As August took the lectern, he looked out to Margaret. They had spent every evening together since they got home, and though no one spoke of it, Polly knew they had reached an understanding. At the kitchen table they went over property settlements and the minister's will. She saw her mother shake her head and heard her say, *Let it go. I almost lost something far more important.* She knew they were talking about the farm and her, and she knew her mother had agreed to file Chapter 11 and take her chances. For Polly, it was comforting to have August back in their house, for it had taken her little time to realize that August, no less than his father, had saved her life.

When she thought of Mr. March now, and the night in the woods, it was with the same cold and suffocating sensation as the river induced in her. She had been terrified her first day back at school, wondering what she would say to him, but her fears had been dispelled by a substitute in the form of the vice principal, a middle-aged woman who informed them that their previous instructor had been terminated for conduct unbecoming an educator. Polly stared straight ahead as the vice principal encouraged them to seek counseling to make sense of this troubling matter. She never looked at Polly directly, but Polly knew everyone was wondering what they had overlooked in their classmate that might be responsible for the destruction of two lives. After school, she rode her bike to his house. The driveway was empty when she arrived. The blinds were raised, as they never had been while he was in occupancy, giving the house a look of wide-eyed surprise, as if it too were caught off guard by all the unwanted attention. Polly parked her bike against the side of the house and peered through the pane of the front door. The living room was empty and swept clean; she saw the broom and dustpan propped in the far corner. She realized she'd never seen inside to know now what was missing. Did he have a sofa? A television?

She walked the perimeter of the house, looking for any note or sign he might have left her, but there was nothing, not even a slip of paper in the trash can out back. Mr. March was gone forever, and she had no way of ever finding him again. She imagined him driving out of town, past the trees of School Street, which now wore dark purple ribbons on behalf of Pastor Vaughn, past the rectory, where friends and neighbors had heaped flowers on the Vaughns' doorstep. He would be driving west, into the interior of the country, where he would disappear like a lost tribe of one. If only she might have a last chance to tell him that, despite everything, he was still the best teacher she ever had. She had wanted a lesson and he made her live it. History was not something found in books, she now understood. It was alive and dangerous. And as much at work in the world as either God or the Devil.

She took her mother's hand as August started to speak.

"When the hospital gave us back my father's effects," said August, clearing his throat, "they said they found this in his jacket pocket." He reached into his own blazer and removed a small square, which he placed upon the lectern. The congregation leaned forward and the camera lenses zoomed.

"I don't know where he got it," said August. "I don't remember it ever being on the refrigerator at home. The writing is so small it's almost impossible to read, but the handwriting is so familiar, and the color of the parchment, and the signatures at the bottom—even if you couldn't read a single word, it would be instantly recognizable. 'When in the course of human events,'" he recited. "My father had in his possession, at the time of his death, a miniature facsimile of the Declaration of Independence."

When the nurse had handed it to him, August had held the document in his palm a very long time. As jealous as his father had been of Jefferson, he had chosen to carry around that man's finest hour, his hope for a new nation. August had walked downstairs to the hospital gift shop and bought a magnifying glass. Jefferson had pulled lines and ideas from other writers, but from old and tested ideas, he had combined them into something radical and new.

"In the same way we may not stop to read every word of this document, or think about the freedoms we live under, " August continued, "so may we often fail to appreciate those who matter most to us. But like this document, which even in so reduced a form is instantly recognizable to every American, so should be the other self-evident truths in our lives. A child's smile. A father's sacrifice. The loving support of a community. Unlike Jefferson, my father was never a famous man, but I can think of no one who in his everyday life better exemplified the sort of citizen Jefferson wished every American might be. Jefferson believed our country to be infinitely perfectible. If it is not in our power to change our country, it is certainly possible to recognize the potential in ourselves. I know that's what my father would have wanted for us. I know it's what he struggled toward in his own life."

August fell silent, and turned to the simple black coffin beside him. His father lay inside, rouged and coiffed back to a semblance of life, but August wanted to remember him fresh from the water, having given his life for Polly's. He slowly returned to the pew and took his seat between his mother and Margaret.

"Thank you, August," said the priest. "Before we commend our brother Leland to the ground, let us each take a moment of silent prayer."

Polly dutifully bowed her head along with everyone else, and closed her eyes. She feared that here in church, as at home, with the darkness would come the chill of the river. But now, as she sat in quiet meditation, her mind turned to thoughts of all the young girls who had sat in her place over the years and of all those who would come after. Hundreds of girls, maybe thousands of girls, all with bowed heads and clasped hands, just like her own, yet each with her own personal history. Together they stood with their feet in the river, looking down through the cloudy water to their distant white toes. Looking down the length of shore, Polly saw this was not the river of her recent tragedy, but rather the warm, summer water of afternoons with Margaret spent looking for sharks' teeth. For a swift, vertiginous instant, she had the sense of being caught in the grand current of all those who had come before and all those who would come after. She was but a palmful in the shining river, rushing past and feeding into something even larger. For God was like History and History like God. Each might be small and large, individual and corporate at once.

Behind her, the intrusive crinkle of plastic, magnified tenfold in the silence, interrupted her prayer. She tried to keep Pastor Vaughn's face before her, and the majesty of the river, but the sound continued, like someone unwrapping piece after piece of candy, until finally she shifted in her seat and peered beneath half-closed lids to determine the source of the disturbance. In the back row by the door sat the Franks—Jake and Manda, Rose, and the seven babies—

dressed in their Sunday best: the boys in white jackets and pants, the girls in lacy white dresses with bows in their hair. It was the first time they had been out as a family, and the contrite community had greeted them like long-lost relations, for Pastor Vaughn's sake renewing their offers of help and food, and even the opportunity of a job closer to home for Jake. The babies smiled at all the attention, curious about the world outside of their several nurseries, and the women of St. Barnabas lifted them up and kissed them, humbled and grateful for a second chance. Once the service began, the children sat quietly in their car seats, intently watching the proceedings as if understanding every word. But it was nearing lunchtime and their older sister Rose was fidgeting. To keep her quiet, Manda peeled back the film on slice after slice of American cheese, and passed the singles over to her daughter. Polly had always marveled, along with Margaret, that her country would name such a processed and unnatural product after itself, yet hungry Rose, with a smile as if remembering the funniest of jokes, gleefully ate every individually wrapped, plastic little one of them.

ACKNOWLEDGMENTS

I would like to begin by thanking my dear friend, Kate Fleming, whose off-handed comment about Thomas Jefferson's cheese was the inspiration for this novel.

Great thanks to Fenton Nolan of Airwell Farm who took a morning to teach this poor novelist how to milk a cow. Thanks also to his neighbors Debbie and Garnett Smith of Edgewood for opening their stables to me. Thanks to the Reverend Jack Sutor who gave me a glimpse into the life of the Episcopalian clergy, to Rikki Carroll for her amazing cheesemaking course, and to Bob and Mary Merriam for being such generous and gracious hosts the same weekend. Thanks to Tim Etheredge of the Virginia Cooperative Extension, and to Chuck Bowie of Fairview Beach Yacht Club. I would also like to thank my fabulous in-laws, John and Donna Redmond, for helping out with medical questions, and the staff of the University of Virginia NICU for allowing me to visit and take notes.

As always, a million thanks to my friend and agent Molly Friedrich (thanks especially for giving us your bathtub!), and to everyone at the Aaron Priest Agency. My family at Grove has been beyond supportive through the writing of the book—thanks Lauren and Dara and Deb and Judy and Eric and Charles and everyone else. Thanks Morgan for your unfailing support and creativity, and Elisabeth—I don't know what I would have done without you. Your suggestions were invaluable, as were your patience and generosity. I promise never to do it to you again! I would like to thank my many friends who endured talk of butterfat content and Jeffersonian arcana. Thanks especially to Dan Smetanka who has believed in me always, and my great friend David Conrad who suffered my early drafts.

Any book about family could not be possible without cannibalizing from one's own, and I need to thank my hysterically funny and always frank father, Gene Holman, for letting me use his classic forceps joke in this book. I would also like to thank my sister, Shannon, the unwitting victim of that joke, for being such a good sport through my many years as a thoroughly rotten older sister. Thanks to my aunt, Marilyn Malone, who made the long car journeys with my mother and me, eating candy and offering help. But it was my mother, Gerri Workman, who so tirelessly drove and redrove me along the cheese route, who phoned local dairies for me, who took videos of marinas, and sat with me under the bellies of aircraft from Reagan National Airport. Mom, there are never enough words to thank you.

And Sean? Where to even start? I look forward to spending the rest of my life and raising our increasingly mammoth family with you.